```
Macy's News  8/1/00

Kit Kat         £0.39
Ripple          £0.32
HobNobs         £1.15

Subtotal        £1.86
Cash Tendered   £2.00
CHANGE          £0.14

Thank You
```

Some time later, at home – still talking to Ernestine

Helen:  . . . yeah, so I just elbowed onto the bus and there was
absolutely nowhere to sit and this horrible spotty youth
was in the disabled seat and I suddenly realised – I have
the power! *(sound of front door closing in the background)*
So I stood there and just said, really loud, EXCUSE ME,
I'M PREGNANT!'
*(sound of somebody right behind her)*:
Colum: That's terrific, sweetheart – when were you planning to
tell me?

*Small Talk*

SHEILA HAYMAN

# *Small Talk*

Hodder & Stoughton

First published in Great Britain in 2001 by Hodder and Stoughton
A division of Hodder Headline

British Library Cataloguing in Publication Data

ISBN 0 340 81881 6

Typeset by Palimpsest Book Production Limited,
Polmont, Stirlingshire
Printed and bound in Great Britain by
Clays Ltd, St Ives plc

Hodder and Stoughton
A division of Hodder Headline
338 Euston Road
London NW1 3BH

To Patrick, Frank, Dorothy and the peerless Anne, without whom it would all have seemed a lot less— oh hang on, I think that's the baby . . .

# Small Talk

**1 January, 2000** (New Year's Day)

Got up.
That's enough, isn't it?


**1 January, 2000** – Excerpt from DNA shopping list for Basic
Training Graduate 6,013,142,343 'Piglet'

> . . . ATG   (tendency to sweaty feet)
> GGA   (inability to read maps except by turning them
>          upside down)
> CAC   (allergy to tinned pineapple)
> ATA   (small cleft under nose)
> GAA   (late-onset taste for model trains) . . .


**2 January, 2000**

*Woke rather suddenly. Seem to be in bath. Can't see a thing (possibly
because no eyes yet). No idea where I am, and no memory at all of
last night (slightly worrying), but apparently went well. Can feel myself
splitting already.*

*N.B. Does this mean personality will also be split? Must remember
to check on this (when I get a personality).*

*Resolved to keep a journal of my experiences, for the benefit of future
generations. May have to keep it in head (what there is of head) until
I get access to recording technology. Must try to contact Mission Control
about this, though no obvious means of doing so at present.*

```
Macy's News  8/1/2000

OK                £2.99
Autosport         £4.65
Bike              £3.95
KitKat            £0.39

SubTotal         £11.98
Cash Tendered    £15.00
CHANGE            £3.02

Thank You
```

## 8 January, 2000

Something truly weird happened when I biked down to the newsagent's just now. As usual, they didn't have the one mag I really really wanted. As usual, they bleated on about how everybody else wanted it too. So it sold out. Duh! At which point, little Pollyanna Helen would normally just roll over and say, 'No! Who'd have guessed? Poor you, what an unspeakable, titanic struggle it must be selling magazines all day long. Just give me any old leftovers you can't shift, then.' And throw the money at them, and run.

Instead of which, this Evil Twin suddenly surfaces, snarling, *'Well, of course it's going to sell with that wedding in it, which is why I WANTED IT TOO, how much of a brain can it take to order a few extra, for God's sake? Do you actually HOPE to end your life in a swamp of unthanked poverty, or have you thought of just holding out your hand and LETTING THE MONEY FALL IN before it's too late? Eh? Got a tongue in your head, you wretched, glassy-eyed illiterate?'*

Fortunately most of this happened in my head after I left the shop, but it stayed with me all the way home. E.T. threw cigarette butts back into car windows, deliberately splashed an annoying pedestrian blocking a corner, and then cycled very, very slowly in front of a white van that dared to get too close, all the way home. I was shocked, I can tell you.

I can't still be hung over from New Year, can I? If it takes the liver an hour to clear one unit of alcohol from the system, even allowing for the fact that my liver is probably only functioning at, say, fifty per cent these days, that's . . . ninety-five units it's had a chance to deal with by now. Can I have had ninety-five drinks that night?

**8 January, 2000** – Bills from Helen's second trip to the shops

```
Pestle  and  Mortar  Pharmacy
8/1/2000

KitKat              £0.39
Nurofen             £3.99
Durex Fetherlite    £2.50
Predictor blue      £8.99

Subtotal           £15.87

PAID BY SWITCH
Thank you. Call Again
```

```
Macy's News 8/1/00

KitKat              £0.39
Ripple              £0.32
HobNobs             £1.15

Subtotal            £1.86
Cash tendered       £2.00
CHANGE              £0.14

Thank You
```

Managed to muzzle E.T. for the duration this time. While I was in the chemist's anyway, thought I might as well eliminate the least likely explanation. Not that it's even possible that I could be . . . but just so I can consign to perpetual oblivion what happened after Ernestine's Christmas party, when Colum thought it would be fun to try his Santa balloon as a condom. Eight ninety-nine seems like daylight robbery, until you think of it as the price of peace of mind.

Let's see – 'hold stick under stream in mid-flow' – how do I know when I've got to mid-flow? And what difference does it . . . oh, yuck, all over my hand – that's got to be enough, hasn't it? There, you sit there and cook, little stick.

Of course I'm not. I'm not.

But just suppose I were. Six years on and I still have no idea why Colum wanted to get married. For me, it seemed like a win-win scenario; lovely relationship as before plus the dress, the party, being queen for a day and a huge pile of presents pre-specified in minute detail. Certainly nothing to do with, um, spawning. Can't remember him ever mentioning it before or since, except in the hysteric aftermath of a parental encounter, e.g.:

'If *I* had a child I wouldn't EVER:

– track down the last bottle of Old Spice in Britain to make him feel really old on his birthday

– tell his boss about the time he wore his mum's bra as Widow Twanky in the school pantomime

– mark his arrival for the annual visit with a gift of rusty mower parts and a lawn like ten acres of the Serengeti' . . .

Which gives you a fair idea of why he left the Outer Hebrides, but doesn't exactly add up to a ringing endorsement of parenthood. Can't say I've noticed him bending over prams or bibbling toddlers on his lap, either, but as they put men away for that sort of thing these days, it's probably sound judgment on his part.

4

Can't say I've noticed myself doing any of the above, in fact. But never mind, because I'm not. I've even forgotten all about the little stick. It's so irrelevant, may as well chuck it in the bin. Look, no spot . . .

Aaargh, spot.

Oh my God.

**8 January, 2000** – Transcript of message left on voice mail of Ernestine (Helen's best friend)

> Ernie? Ernie, PICK UP FOR GOD'S SAKE if you're there . . . How can you not be there, it's not even *(sound of toilet flushing in background)* – it's only twelve-something, I really need to speak to you, it's – God, what am I going to do? Look, it's – no, actually I can't tell you like this, for Christ's sake call me back asap, okay? . . . are you sure you're not there? . . . shit . . . I am NOT going to call you on your mobile . . .

**8 January, 2000** – Transcript of mobile phone conversation between Helen and Ernestine

H: Ernie? Finally!

E: Hiya. What d'you mean, finally? Are you okay? You sound weird.

H: I'm not weird, I'm – I've been leaving messages in this bloody money-sink for about four hours, that's all.

E: Oh, yeah, sorry, I've been in . . .

H: I DON'T CARE WHERE YOU'VE BEEN!

E: Fine. Well, if you're just going to shout at me, I can get that any time from my parents.

H: Parents? Why did you say parents? Christ, will you look at that queue . . .

E:  Are you sure you're all right?

H:  No, of course I'm not all right, I'm . . . *(unintelligible mutter)*

E:  You're what?

H:  I'm – we're – it's – there's a – baby.

E:  A baby? What, queuing for the bus? Just trample over it, darling, its mother ought to know better than to leave it there.

H:  No, NOT queuing for the bus, my God, you're so DENSE.

E:  You mean . . . Christ. How are you feeling, darling? Are you sitting down?

H:  Sitting down? It's like the Berlin airlift at this bus stop.

E:  What does it feel like? Have you got any cravings yet? I can't wait to see you eating big lumps of earth and stuff.

H:  No cravings – oh, I don't believe it, I've got no change, I'll have to go and (excuse me, could I just . . . ? I'll only be a minute? . . . Thanks) . . . No symptoms at all, really, apart from total, all-over, shaking panic (Just this, please – no, I'm sorry, if I had change I'd give it to you, honest – thanks) . . . but I did just buy a – what is this? – an Apple Cinnamon Monster Muffin. (Thanks, yes, I was here before actually.) Anyhow, you must help me. How am I going to tell him?

E:  Tell who? Jeezuz, that is definitely not my face in this mirror, that's my Great-Aunt Pauline, go AWAY, Pauline you're ninety-four . . .

H:  Ernie, he's going to be home in forty minutes and I don't even know if he wants a baby.

E:  Well, in forty-one minutes you will. Hang on, darling, emergency facial peel under way . . .
    *(sound of entire bathroom cabinet being emptied on to floor)*

H:  Here's my bus. Christ, they're hanging out the windows, it's like the Bangalore Express – WATCH OUT!

E:  Here we go . . . iky I'm nt ging ti bi ible ti tk mch fr a fiw mins iky?

6

H: It's fine, I just missed my bus anyway.
*(sound of crackly plastic being savagely torn from muffin)*
Mmm – not babmmmm . . . So anyhow, I thought I'd just keep it very light, you know, like – hey, whaddya know, we're pregnant! Whaddya think?

E: Yi dint sind lit, yi sind deringed.

H: What?

E: Ti minits, sirry.

H: (Sorry, I am in the queue too actually . . . no I didn't, I've been here all the . . . well, that's not my . . . rude bastard!) Ernie? Or I could get him at a disadvantage by taking off all our clothes and then saying, 'Sweetie, you know this luscious little cuddly tum you love so much . . . well, guess what's inside it?' (Do you mind? I'm trying to have a private conversation here!) God, the people who take buses . . .

E: He'd thnk yi wi tikng ibit thit miffin. Miffin in thi ivin hi hi hi! Is it gid?

H: Very funny.
*(sound of another large bite out of muffin)*
Yeah, it is actually. Apple makes it all lovely and soggy . . . I suppose I could do it all romantic and cook dinner and sort of sweetly say, 'Darling! Wouldn't it be great if we had a lovely little baby to share all of this?'

E: *(sound as of rubber glove being torn off right by phone)*
That's better, no more Auntie P . . . And he says, 'Are you crazy? If we had a little baby there wouldn't BE any all of this!' Why don't you just tell him right out, 'Hey, doll, you're gonna be a dad, or I want a thousand quid for an abortion and a tummy tuck!'

H: I'm not so sure about that approach . . . Here's another bus. I don't believe it, it's worse than the last – EXCUSE ME . . . oh, *hey, I* just thought of something . . . call you back, . . . *(hangs up phone)*

7

Some time later, at home – still talking to Ernestine.

H:  . . . yeah, so I just elbowed on to the bus and there was absolutely nowhere to sit and this horrible spotty youth was in the disabled seat and I suddenly realised – I have the power! *(sound of front door closing in background)*
So I stood there and just said, really loud, 'EXCUSE ME, I'M PREGNANT!'
*(sound of somebody right behind her)*

C:  That's terrific, sweetheart – when were you planning to tell me?

**9 January, 2000** – Bill for dinner at Conran Gastrodome

```
Welcome to Bombolino
Covers: 2

4 Kir Royale                                £38.00
3 vodka martinis                            £25.50
1 warm smoked ostrich mille-feuille,
  Leicestershire baby sorrel soufflé        £13.00
1 whitebait, Sicilian lemon parfait         £14.00
1 rare haunch of Austrian forest-caught
  venison, slow-roasted golden beets,
  pink chanterelle and Muscat jus           £23.00
1 Morayshire fillet steak, chunky chips     £24.00
1 extra chips                               £10.00
1 bottle Mulderbosch Faithful Hound         £24.00
1 bottle Cloudy Bay Chardonnay              £37.00
1 pepper-infused milk chocolate cushion,
  lavender custard                          £12.50
  extra custard                             £5.00
1 hot-and-cold treacle tart, lime spikes    £12.50
1 cappuccino, truffles and fudge            £5.50
```

```
1 espresso                             £5.00
1 Bailey's                             £6.50
1 vodka martini                        £8.50

Subtotal inc VAT:                    £264.00
Optional service @ 12.5%              £33.00
TOTAL:                               £297.00
```

**10 January, 2000, 2 a.m.** – Conversation between Helen and Colum, in bed

*(Total darkness. Nothing visible, but rustling throughout.)*

H:   I feel terrible.

C:   I'm not surprised.

H:   What have I done? Why didn't you stop me? I'm far too irresponsible to be anybody's mother. I must be, or I wouldn't have got pregnant.

C:   Probably true. Good thing you've got me here.

H:   Mmmm. I have, haven't I? Yum yum.
     *(more rustling, then a pause)*

C:   You probably could start economising on the drink just a wee bit.

H:   I suppose so. But I'm so weak-willed! I'll be a terrible mother!

C:   You'll be fine. Now go to sleep. You're sleeping for two now, remember.
     *(pause)*

H:   Tell you what, how about I do the sleeping and you do the cutting down? Share and share alike, you know, it's the modern way.

C:   I'm not entirely sure it works like that. *(rustling)* Night night.

H:   Night night.
     *(pause)*

H:   Will you still love me when my tits are dragging along the floor?

C: Will you still care?
H: Oooh. I hope so.
   *(loud rustling)*
C: *(muffled)* They seem fine at the moment. Peak condition, I'd say.
H: Mmmm . . .
   *(more rustling)*
H: Oh!
C: What now?
H: We never did that white-water rafting trip in Colorado. Or the Silk Route trek to Bhutan. Or the cross-Canada train to the Alaskan glaciers. And now it's too late!
C: We've not been outside the M25 for nearly a year. I don't think you'll be missing Bhutan too much.
H: No, but you know . . . Are you pleased, really?
C: Ask me in a year. No, of course I am. Finally I can banish all those lurking doubts about my virility.
H: What doubts? *(violent and prolonged rustling . . .)*


## 10 January, 2000

*Oooooooh . . . uuurrgh . . . Where have they sent me? No warning that it would feel as bad as this. Only consolation is that there's not much of me to feel anything, right now. Limit to scale of headache you can have when your head is only one inch across. Similarly with nausea. They'd better watch out when I get a stomach.*

*Funny thing is, I felt really great last night. Must reread Basic Training Manual chapter on What to Expect When You're Expected.*

*Hey, where is Training Manual? They can't have sent me here with no instructions at all, can they?*

*Just remembered can't see. Maybe Training Manual will reappear when eyes develop. Can remember most of it, anyway.*

... New graduates often describe these early days of their mission as a mixture of the mundane and the challenging. Clearly, you are in here for a while, and there are going to be some long, slow days when nothing much seems to be happening – a cell divides here, an organ begins to differentiate there, but for the most part it's the same warm, wet environment, familiar and not-so-familiar sensations, and gentle, bouncing movement you were told about at Training Camp.

So now is a good time to acquaint yourself with some of the basic terminology. First, from now on, both in this manual and in life, you will find yourselves referred to not as 'graduates' but as 'babies' – the term preferred by adults of most species. You have been used to talking about 'donors' and 'hosts', but you will find that you get vastly better results, depending on your base, from 'Mom' and 'Pop', 'Mum' and 'Dad', or even, for a lucky few of you, 'Mummy' and 'Daddy'. A word of warning: some hosts and donors may encourage you to practise with the contractions Mama and Dada, unaware of the meanings attached to these in our culture. Overcoming your natural repugnance will normally produce a gratifying level of positive feedback. Initially, however, you will find that almost any loud sound will attract the host's attention ...

## 10 January, 2000

Feel crap again. Colum said I was hung over. Must buy him a copy of *What to Expect When You're Expecting* – apparently very good on expecting to feel terrible throughout, which should get me the sympathy vote. I said, well, if I hadn't found out until now – or, say, tomorrow – then there wouldn't have been any reason not to have a glass of wine to celebrate. (Something wrong with the logic there. My brain seems to have started shrinking already.)

And it seems unfair not to know that the last drink is going to be the last, especially given what I'm in for before I can begin again.

I wonder how much damage you can do in the first two weeks? I mean, if it only has, say, six cells right now, does it mean that only six cells will have foetal alcohol syndrome, which in the long term, weighed against several trillion healthy ones, probably wouldn't matter too much, or does the damage get multiplied too? To think that I'm building a teeny person with every mouthful I eat and drink. What have I eaten today? Er – nothing, I can't even think about food yet. Is that good or bad?

I have to admit I don't feel entirely prepared for this yet.

Mind you, as Ernestine pointed out, look at the French and the Italians. Nobody's going to tell me they stick to Perrier and San Pellegrino for nine months and then however long they breast-feed afterwards. How about Shakespeare's mother? She wouldn't have touched water in those days, she'd have died. It was small beer from morning to night, and they used to have dozens of babies. Ernestine then also pointed out that a lot of the babies didn't last very long. Ernestine, needless to say, had her tubes tied at twenty-five. Says she can't deal with pain (it is true she tried to get a morphine shot for a bee sting once) and after putting all this effort into having the Body of Doom she's not going to chuck it all in for an already overpopulated planet. I may have to reconsider the long-term future of our friendship.

### 14 January, 2000

. . . *thirty-two, sixty-four, a hundred and twenty-eight, two hundred and fifty-six, five hundred and twelve . . .*

**15 January, 2000** – Conversation between Ernestine and Helen in ladies' cloakroom of new Ian Shrager hotel 'Bagette', while preparing for celebration drinks with girlfriends

*(Cloakroom is lit like the Cabinet of Dr Caligari, with lights cunningly concealed behind giant light-bulb-shaped shades so that Helen and Ernie are forced to crane perilously over the basin to do their make-up. Everything else in the room is disguised as a giant version of itself – tampon dispenser shaped like giant tampon, soap dispenser like giant bar of soap.*

*Helen, despite being exactly her normal shape, is draped in something large and concealing from Ghost. Ernestine, wearing a very skimpy crop top, is juggling violently about in front of the mirror.)*

H: What on earth are you doing?

E: Seeing if I can get away without a bra.

*(looks a question at Helen in the mirror. Helen shakes her head.)*

E: I thought not. Still, always worth checking.

*(fishes around in her giant handbag and pulls out a black underwired bandeau bra, which is fashionably visible beneath the top)*

E: You know me, – show me a pudding and I'll over–egg it.

H: I'd just eat it.

E: Yeah, well, you can now, can't you? You can just eat and eat till you fill that thing up, and nobody'll give a toss.

H: Thanks!

*(Ernestine leans right in to the mirror, where there is light, but mysteriously only from below)*

E: My skin looks like one of those pictures of the surface of the moon.

*(Helen's turn to lean in)*

H: More like Mars.

E: I did overdo it a bit on the sunbed. I hate winter.

*(Helen, in graceful madonna mode, is moisturising her face in gentle, soothing circular movements)*

13

H: Still, nothing that ten coats of Exterior Weathershield won't cover.

E: There isn't any peanut oil in that cream, is there?

H: Why?

E: Well, I read that that's why so many babies get nut allergies, from pregnant women rubbing cream on themselves to not get stretch marks.

H: Stretch marks come where you get stretched, on your tummy.

E: Better safe than sorry. You'll probably stretch all over, once you start showing. Here, try some of this.
*(fishing a huge jar out of her bag)*

H: What is it?

E: It's my Dramatically Different moisturiser.
*(Helen tries to find a place where she can read the label)*

H: What does it do?

E: Makes a dramatic difference. Duh.
*(Helen peers right in to Ernestine's face to get a proper look)*

H: I can't have known you before.
*(Ernestine now has the benefit of seeing Helen's face close up)*

E: Well, you won't be needing any of this soon, you'll be going all peachy and radiant, won't you? *(Helen glows)* . . . once you get rid of those little spots.

H: What little spots? Where?

E: *(points)* There. And there. Oh, and – there. Don't worry, I'm sure it's just the baby's immune system defending itself from all the toxins.

H: What toxins?

E: You know – peanuts, crisps, tortilla chips, Twiglets . . . they have Twiglets here in the bar, I saw them on the way in.
*(Helen is now trying to see the alleged spots in the mirror. Accidentally leans on a tap and splashes both of them with water.)*

H: Damn!
*(Helen now has a big dark stain down the front of her sack.*

*Ernestine's top clings more determinedly than ever to her bra. She twirls to admire the effect.)*

H:  Since when are you such an expert on prenatal care?

E:  Just because I have made a decision, as a responsible and mature adult concerned with the future of the earth's ever-dwindling resources, not to burden it with yet more predators, doesn't mean I can't share in things that matter to those I love *(gives Helen a let's-make-up hug)*. I'm here, aren't I?

H:  So how do I look, really?

E:  You look gorgeous, darling. Not that you need worry any more. I mean, you're not exactly available any longer, are you?
*(For some reason Helen seems to find this anything but cheering as they saunter out arm in arm into a dazzling lobby scattered with bottle-cap stools, champagne-cork tables, and truly gorgeous twentysomething boys. All of whom watch Ernestine all the way to a table where six other women are already some distance down their Sea Breezes. As Helen approaches, they all leap up, showing lots of flesh, and fight to give her big hugs.)*

Some time later

*(All of the women are still sitting around the table, which is covered in empty glasses and dishes of Twiglets, nuts and crisps. Helen is nursing a modest glass of red wine and drinking very slowly, which is impressive until you see the almost-empty bottle among the cocktail glasses. She decides the moment is now.)*

H:  I just want to say something before you all get too drunk to take it in . . .
*(lurches to her feet . . .)*
. . . I just want to say, this isn't going to change anything, is it? I mean, it didn't when I got married, I'm still one of the gang, we can go on doing this, can't we?

*(Ernestine pulls her down and plants a big wet kiss on her cheek)*

E:    'Course you are, darling, for ever, eh, girls? You'll be back here pulling up a high chair before we even notice you're gone. Toast!

*(Some of them try to rise, think better of it, and collapse again. They all more or less raise their glasses.)*

ALL: The bump!

*(Helen fumbles in Ernestine's bag, then, realising her mistake, her own, and brings out a hanky, with which she mops her eyes)*

H:    I think *(gulp)* I'd better go home now. Colum might be worrying, and I haven't got just myself to think of any more . . .

*(they all watch her leave)*

E:    There you go. One down, bless her.

*(Stares after Helen, having a private moment. Rallies.)*

Anybody want another?


## 15 January, 2000, very late – Ernestine, at her computer

The thing is, I suppose I feel *(sniff)* - I feel sort of bereft.

**(Why do you feel bereft?)**
Well, you know, because *(gulp)* I haven't changed, and she's changed, she must have *(wail)* or why would she DO this, the cow? *(sob)* Sorry. So it makes me wonder - is there something wrong with me?

**(Why do you wonder is there something wrong with you?)**
Well *(snivel)*, I don't see, just because a person is five years older, why the things she enjoyed doing five years ago *(sniff)* suddenly have to stop being enjoyable. I mean, I'm still the same person, and she was

16

too *(sob)*, or she seemed to be, until last
week.

**(What the same person are you?)**
You know who I am!

**(Tell me again who you are)**
Well *(gulp)* - I like a laugh, I've no
interest whatsoever in 'settling down'
*(sniff)*, whatever that is, like a shag, like
to dance, usual stuff . . . And suddenly -
it's going to be this cosy little yucky itsy-
bitsy nest thing going on, and I'm going to
be . . . *(sniff)*

**(What are you going to be?)**
I'm going to be . . . *(sob)*

**(Where are you going to be?)**
I'm going to be *(howl)* OUTSIDE.
(How does it feel, being outside?)
Cold! *(sob)* It feels cold . . . Christ, it
is cold. The heating must have packed in
*(blows nose)*. Let's turn this bloody thing
off.
*(ping of computer shutting down)*
Bye-bye, cybershrink. See ya next time. The
time . . . Jesus . . . Did I give somebody
my number?


## 16 January, 2000, early morning

*. . . shixty-five thoushand five hunerd an' thirty-shix . . . hang on
there, jush shtop for a momen', can't you . . . I'm havin' a bit of . . .
I'm forever blowin' bubblesh . . . thish 'ish nishe . . . very nishe . . .
where were we . . .*

## 17 January, 2000

Writing rather slowly today. Still recovering from yesterday. Yesterday spent recovering from day before. This has to stop. Drinking for two not a concept known to baby literature, from what I can see. Not to mention the difficulty of doing my job at the Archive when eyes refuse to focus on my fellow commuters' newspaper headlines, let alone a screen full of credits from forgotten Lithuanian silent masterpieces.

Ernestine very sweetly organised a celebration drink with all the girls. Had v, v nice time, but realised as the evening progressed that my concerns are no longer their concerns. I never properly noticed quite how fixated childless single women are on ephemeral trivia like boyfriends, clothes and gossip. That's the thing about having something really big and important to think about, it just totally shifts your perspective on to a higher plane. What is a Marc Jacobs ermine collar beside the Miracle of Life? Better start getting back in touch with all my friends who've had babies already. Somehow seem to have lost contact with all of them, no idea why . . . still, I have until 30 August, if the doctors know what they're doing with that little Wheel of Life thingy they use.

Ernestine seems to have acquired a new boyfriend – apparently he was in the bar that night. She says he's a consultant helping computer zillionaires spend their money. I have to admit that an expert in spending other people's money sounds like a perfect match for Ernestine, though she did say his clients veered more towards halfway houses for disadvantaged youth than Marc Jacobs furs.

## 18 January, 2000

*Not much to report, though even I am impressed at my rate of growth. I kept a cell count at first, partly for something to do, but when they're doubling every hour the numbers get big quite quickly. And to think less than two weeks ago I was only a few microns tall! I must be nearly – hmmm – three-quarters of an inch by now. Wonder how much larger I'll get by the end?*

*I'm pretty sure I'm going to make human this time around – lost my fins and gills already and no sign of wings or fur. Huge relief when I moved on from the jelly blob stage, I don't know how I'd have faced going back to Training Camp after doing time as a protozoon.*

**20 January, 2000** – Excerpt of letter from Colum to his bank

> . . . with immediate effect, to transfer five hundred pounds from my current to my savings account, number 00436745 on the first day of each month.
>
> Yours, etc . . .

**21 January, 2000** – Partial transcript of phone conversation between Colum and Steve Harvey, dealer in rare and valuable motorbikes

S: . . . So what can I do for you today?

C: Well, I thought I'd mebbe get shot of a couple of the bikes.

S: Seriously? What, after something flashier? On the pull, are we?

C: Not exactly, no.

S: Well. So which are we looking at?

C: Start with the Guzzi.

S: You're joking, right? That gorgeous Super Sport? Did her up yourself, didn't you? Took for ever.

C: Every nut, every gasket.

S: Well. I couldn't promise to get you back what you spent . . .

C: Don't worry.

S:  Not gonna change your mind?

C:  There's the MM too . . .

S:  Not the MM!

C:  . . . I paid about eleven for it, and − well, you know what went into rebuilding it.

S:  I can't believe this. You of all people − I'll do my best for you, son, but this time of year − why not wait till the summer, you'll do much better money-wise and . . .

C:  No, I'd like you to start looking now. And the MotoRumi, too. And while you're at it, I never ride the Laverda, it's a bugger to start and with that fairing it's lethal on corners.

S:  Of all the blokes − in a million years I'd never have thought − what is it, you got the Jap bug? Hang on, mate, while I get something to write all this down on . . .
    *(Sound of scrabbling for paper. Sound of scratching with pen on paper. Sound of pen being thrown away and new one essayed, twice.)*

C:  I'll not be buying anything for a wee while.

S:  Okay, I'm with you again.

C:  And I've been having real trouble with leaks on the LeMans. I might as well chop that in and all.

S:  The Lemon, what year was that, eighty-nine? So that's − hang on, that that's all of 'em, innit? What's going on?

C:  Nothing. Nothing at all. Just ready to move on.

S:  Well, you're the boss. Now, what are we looking for, money-wise?

C:  It's not so much the money. Get what you can of course, just . . . you know? Find people who'll really know what they're getting, and look after them.

S:  I wish all my customers had your attitude, Col, I really do.

C:  Yes, well − it's like everything, isn't it? It's not the money you spend that brings rewards in the end, it's the time.

S:  I've tried that line on the wife a few times but somehow she never goes for it, ha ha.

*(sound of more scribbling)*

S:  Okey-dokey, think that's all the info. I'll be sad to see 'em leave you, but I'll do my best to place 'em in good homes. They been family for you, more or less, nah?

C:  Yes and . . . no. Cheers, then, Steve, let me know, won't you?

**21 January, 2000** – Message left on voice mail of Billy Giddens (Colum's best friend)

> Bill, old son – Steve H here – look, won't keep you, but I just had a call from Colum wanting to unload his bikes – all of 'em. I'm a bit, you know, like to check out there's nothing funny going down with him. Give us a bell when you've got a mo, will you?

**25 January, 2000**

*I can't believe they've done this to me. Human is good, I grant you, evolutionary tree-wise it doesn't come much better (at least in theory), but I SPECIFICALLY said no first-timers. They have absolutely no common sense, they jump on whatever bandwagon comes along first, and people like me end up as guinea-pig for every passing crackpot theory. Take sleeping arrangements, for example. Can they just get it right and stick to it? Oh no. How did it go again?*

Excerpt from Basic Training Manual, 903rd edition – Chapter 6, 'A Brief Overview of Human Fashions in Caring for Babies'

> Ever since the dawn of time, humans have attempted to care for their junior members more or less to adulthood, with greater or lesser success. Even today, it is wise to take nothing for granted, and expect peril at every turn. Some degree of physical shelter is normal (though not guaranteed), but injury may occur quite

unpredictably and from the most unexpected quarter, even within the home. (See footnote, 'Techniques in Ingratiation', for advice on minimising non-accidental occurrences.)

However, humans are inconsistent and quarrelsome as a species, and sleeping provisions for babies have varied wildly over time. For brevity, we will omit detailed accounts of ancient practices (leaving on exposed hillsides, in wolves' nests, or hidden among bulrushes) and also some of the wilder theoretical approaches of modern days (sealed containers supplied with all nutritional requirements for the first twenty-one years), and concentrate only on first-hand accounts of sleeping experiences over the past three centuries.

The 17th Century:
Babies were treated as miniature adults, and supplied with their own miniature four-poster beds, or, in other circumstances, their own miniature hay bales and sleeping companions (see 'bundling').

The 18th Century:
Babies were thought to be dangerous adventurers prone to escape attempts, and were confined in tight bandages under the care of highly aggressive guards known as 'wet nurses'.

The 19th Century:
Babies were believed to have arrived infected with a mystery virus known as 'original sin', which could only be cured by solitary confinement in a dark room, accompanied by long bouts of vocal exercise at high volume.

The 20th Century:
With the arrival of the 'expert' in this century, all pretence at consistency and professionalism disappeared, as instructions were given and countermanded every decade. Rigid scheduling gave way to total freedom, solitary confinement to constant physical intimacy, etc., etc.

**25 January, 2000** (continued)

*. . . I think it was something like that. And these days they're even more confused, because the Experts are only interested in disagreeing with each other to sell more books, so the first down the pike in any household ends up, just for instance, sleeping either entirely out of shouting range in a space that looks like Laura Ashley Presents Tchaikovsky's* Nutcracker, *or Stone Age-style in bed with both of them. Now I may not yet have had the joy of sharing my bed with two snoring overweight people eight times my size, but I don't like the sound of it, one bit. How is a person supposed to do any serious growing when all they have on their mind is imminent danger of suffocation from a human steam-roller?*

*I wonder what other nasty surprises are around the corner? Speaking of corners, I still have no idea where I am, or what it looks like. I can't hear anything either. (This could be because I have no ears yet.)*

*I suppose I will get eyes and ears of my own . . . imagine having to rely on the host to see and hear as well as everything else – it doesn't bear thinking about. I saw rather a nice pair of pointy dark brown ears on a dog once, and I quite fancy those amber-coloured eyes with a little vertical slit in them that gets really big and black when you're angry. Still, I may not get to choose. Can't remember exactly what humans look like, except I think they're a bit short on fur.*

**1 February, 2000**

Just found this brilliant website where you can grow a virtual baby and check in on it to see where it's got to. You just feed in the info about yourself and your partner . . . so – here goes. Father: hmm. Six-three, fourteen stone, hair blond, eyes green, eyelashes long, thick and dark, stomach rippling and tanned, chest a little bit hairy in a cute sort of way, back definitely no hairs at all . . . that should do it. Shame Colum's nothing like that, but no point crippling one's virtual offspring with an excess of

23

literalness. Mother: five-eight, eight stone nothing, hair strawberry blond, complexion pink and cream, eyes violet-blue, breasts round, firm and perky, legs at least thirty-six inches long . . . that'll get us a pretty good baby, I should think. Actually, maybe I should make one of us Vietnamese to get that beautiful olive skin . . .

**2 February, 2000** – Excerpt from text of 'Grow-a-kid' artificial life website

'Welcome to Grow-A-Kid, the first website in the world to use a-life algorithms to mimic your own baby's development. It couldn't be simpler! Just feed in your own and your partner's statistics and the date of conception, and Grow-A-Kid will grow a virtual baby in parallel with yours, so you can follow the miracle of her development and reassure yourself that what you are feeling and experiencing is normal. Too, you will automatically receive messages and updates that will make certain you do everything you should be doing to ensure Baby's safe arrival in the world.

*NOTE: Before signing up, please be sure to read our terms and conditions. Grow-A-Kid Inc. is not responsible for the accuracy of the information that may be sent to you, nor does it accept liability for anything that may happen to you or your child as a result of this subscription. Grow-A-Kid Inc. is a limited liability corporation, registered in Trenton, NJ.*

**5 February, 2000** – Excerpt from phone message left on Steve Harvey's voice mail by Billy Giddens

> . . . sorry it's taken me a while, life got in the way, ha ha. I haven't heard a peep from Col for weeks. He went quiet on me right after Christmas, so I'm afraid I can't be of much help. If he's serious about the bikes I could be interested in a couple of them – no big rush . . .

**14 February, 2000**

Valentine's Day. Colum sent two, one for me and one for the baby. Sweet! He never admits they're from him, says he doesn't believe in that arbitrary commercial rubbish and he'd much prefer to give me presents when he feels like it, rather than when the marketing department of some chocolate company notices a dip in the sales figures. But he always somehow manages to feel like it in the end, which is v convenient as KitKat happen to have introduced a special promotional raspberry flavour only days ago.

Off to the hospital for the scan – a bit late. Drank my regulation pint of water like a good girl as soon as I got up, no breakfast, all fine. Just as we were setting off, I thought, I'd better have a quick pee before I leave. Who knows how long we'll have to wait?

So had to call hospital and tell them it would be another hour. MUST NOT pee until they say so, MUST NOT . . .

God, wonder what the baby will look like. Let's hope it doesn't have my brain and his looks, as Margot Asquith said of Bernard Shaw.

*(The examination room is pink and grey, with mysteriously
matching pink-and-grey paintings on the walls. The consultant,
Mr Gilbert, is about twenty-eight, perky and Irish. Colum is
carrying a rolled-up bike magazine in one hand and holding
Helen's hand with the other.*
*Sound of wailing and sobbing retreating down the corridor.)*

G: Sorry to have kept you waiting – had a bit of trouble with
the last patient.

H: Oh dear *(pause)*. Should I pull my knickers down now?

G: I wouldn't with your husband here.

H: Oh!

G: We'll be doing an external scan today.

H: Oh.

G: Just hitch your dress up a bit. There you go. Nurse?
*(A nurse comes over, switches on the machine and rubs gel on
Helen's tummy. Mr Gilbert leans back and folds his arms.)*

C: Nice piece of kit you've got here. I read about it – a year
back, would it have been?

G: Yeah, it's pretty cool, accurate up to a hundredth of a
millimetre and great resolution.

C: And outputs on to VHS?

G: Right here. First one in the country. Came direct from the
States. We use it mainly as a teaching tool, of course.

C: Of course.

H: So – aren't you going to do the scan, then?

G: I'm here to interpret it, Mrs . . . the nurse'll twiddle the
buttons.

C: But we get a video to take away.

N: Are you all right, love? This is going to feel a little bit chilly
just at first . . .
*(sound of machine whirring into life)*

H: Gosh, I'm scared.
*(Colum squeezes her hand. She looks up at him, gratefully. A loud, frantic thumping noise kicks in, filling the room.)*
H: My God, what's that?
N: That's baby's heartbeat.
H: Its heartbeat! Darling, it has a heartbeat! *(awed silence)* Isn't it a bit fast? It sounds as though it's about to explode! Shouldn't you be doing something?
N: That's perfectly normal. Baby's heartbeat is always about twice as fast as ours. It slows down gradually after birth.
H: Goodness, only it sounds as though it's been running a marathon. You wouldn't have thought it'd be getting any exercise at all in there, would you?
C: Look, love, it's fine, it's there on the screen.
H: It is? It is! Look, look, it has a little heartbeat, look at it, the poor little thing, so tiny and all alone in there . . . oh, and see its little stumpy arms and legs . . .
C: It'll take after my side of the family, then. But it has your great big head.
N: It all looks absolutely fine and normal, just how it should be.
H: It's fine! Darling, it's fine! *(Squeezes Colum's hand again. Colum winces in silent agony.)* And how about – can you tell – what sex it is?
N: I'm not entirely – Mr Gilbert?
*(Mr G. looks briefly at the screen)*
G: Not at this stage, I'm afraid
H: Oh, go on, have a guess.
G: You're the kind of woman who leads us all into trouble, Mrs . . . I'm sure next time you come in we'll be able to find that out. Let's help you up here. Nurse!

## 15 February, 2000

*Had my photo taken yesterday. Made sure they got my good side. For some reason they kept wanting close-ups of my . . . bits. Actually don't have any bits right now, but I wasn't going to admit that. Wonder what they're planning to do with it? Come to think of it, we never had a graduation class photo. Or perhaps it's so the host will recognise me when we meet. (Not that there's a lot of scope for confusion, if what I've heard about the meeting scenario is true.)*

*NOTE: Better practise referring to host as 'mother'. Evidently they think 'host' is a bit cold. Don't want the milk supply turned off. Have heard amazing things about milk.*

## 16 February, 2000

Just had another quick look at the video. Doesn't look anything like the one on the Grow-A-Kid screen. Colum says if I don't let him get at the TV in the next hour, he's going to put a child lock on the VCR. I don't see that there's anything so unusual in wanting to know what your firstborn looks like. That little bump on the nose is a bit ominous – wish I hadn't let Colum throw out all those photos of his aged relatives – who knows what skeletons there are in that cupboard (as it were). On the other hand, they have made huge advances in foetal surgery – there must be cosmetic surgeons out there longing to make history with the world's first *in utero* nose job. Oh dear, here's Colum.

## 25 February, 2000

*Remembered as a human I only get a severely restricted range of features to choose from – bye-bye to the pointy ears and amber eyes. No mane or tail, no beak or claws, no fur except in a couple of places, and not much of it there – whatever it is that makes them think they're so special, it's certainly not looks.*

28

Congratulations, and welcome to the Human Module of Basic Training. This manual is designed to equip each and every one of you, wherever you began, to be a fully functional human. Though it may be hard to believe from your current vantage point, by the time you graduate you will not only be equipped, but more than ready, for your invasion of human territory and assumption of control over your host and donor.

But first, a word about the pluses and minuses of your chosen species.

It's true that, initially, human existence may seem in many ways a less than appealing prospect. A human, let's face it, does not have the physical beauty of a horse or a tiger – or even a chicken. Unprotected by fur or feathers, humans have nevertheless colonised many obviously unsuitable areas of the globe, pillaging the rest of creation for fuel, clothes and shelter.

Humans cannot soar through the clouds like seagulls nor dive through the oceans like dolphins. They have no sonar to help them avoid crashing into things, they cannot see as well as cats, smell as well as dogs, nor hear as well as whales. They cannot run as fast as cheetahs, walk as far as camels, nor dig as well as moles.

All in all, you may well be thinking, the best that can be said for them is that they're predatory generalists who can just about walk and eat at the same time.

But before you tear up your application form, turn around and reapply for Small Rodent training, we should mention the compensations.

First – leisure time. Very few other creatures get to spend such a vast proportion of their day sitting about doing either nothing or its close equivalent. It's true that many of these close equivalents have little obvious appeal to the rest of us. Waiting in line twenty minutes for a paper cup containing a bit of warm liquid and froth; holding up a large sheet of paper while attempting to absorb its contents, only to forget them to make room for tomorrow's; or, indeed, doing work that you hate in order to earn money to buy opiates to help you forget that you hate it may all seem perverse to the rest of us, but there's nothing to stop you inventing more congenial pastimes.

The only other animals anything like as idle have been corrupted by humans wanting to feel better about themselves. For those of you attracted by the lifestyle, but dubious about some of the more complex activities required of humans, Cat, Dog or Hamster training may be a more suitable choice.

And finally, there's the strangest yet most truly distinctive quality of human life: choice. Choice in what? Just about everything, and whether you want it or not. No need to wear the same gorgeous yellow or black fur coat every day; humans can choose cerise-and-orange striped Lycra or stonewashed stretch denim with studs around the legs. Then, food. What other creature could have invented pina-colada-flavoured popcorn? (Or wished to, indeed.) Every minute of every day of your life as a human will be filled with an infinity of decisions small and large, whose consequences may be totally insignificant, or may come up and hit you like a sock full of wet cement thirty years later. It's a merry-go-round, all right, and it doesn't suit everybody, but if a lifetime spent lying on a hot rock waiting for the next fly to buzz by doesn't seem like quite enough of a challenge – you're in the right place!

## 7 March, 2000

Now that we've seen it and it seems to be okay (aside from the nose, of course), decided we'd better tell the family. Georgie immediately told us we should have done it two weeks sooner to get a Leo, and went off to find out the reflexologically approved technique for early induction. I said by then I'd probably be only too happy to spend my days and nights drinking gin and eating curry in a hot bath the old-fashioned way, and she said that might well get it out early but not necessarily in tip-top condition to face the rigours of life. Georgie can be a bit intense sometimes – I think it's to do with being the eldest or growing up with punk, or something.

True to form, Mum said, 'I thought you two were past all that sort of nonsense.' All things considered, I think I managed very well – only had to leave the room for about two minutes before coming back and telling her, calmly and with dignity, that at least we were old enough to be able to afford to do it properly, and know that it was what we wanted to do, instead of getting into it by accident, realising too late we had made a terrible mistake, and taking it out on the poor children, UNLIKE SOME PEOPLE IN LESS ENLIGHTENED TIMES. And loads of our friends are only just starting, and frankly when you've back-packed to Irkutsk and scammed backstage passes to U2 at Glastonbury . . . I mean, I've had dogs, I've baby-sat for Georgie's children (once or twice) – how hard can it be?

In fact, I made a comparative list just to prove my point . . .

| DOGS | BABIES |
| --- | --- |
| Eat same thing all time | Ditto |
| Food expensive and smelly | Food free plus you get giant knockers |
| Have to be walked in rain | Stay where you put them (mostly) |
| Leave hairs everywhere | Have no hairs to leave *(looking good so far . . .)* |
| Jump up and slobber on you | Lie down and gob on you |
| Noisy | *(Hmmmm . . . but hang on . . .)* |
| Limited scope for dressing up | Endless scope for ditto |
| Wriggly and scratchy | Adorably squidgy and soft |

| Ruinous vet bills constantly | Free on NHS from Day 1 |
| Will die and leave you broken-hearted | Will look after you in old age (or at least pay bills for home) |

All in all, it seemed to me that I made the case rather effectively, though maybe raising the possibility of an old people's home, even as a general theoretical construct, was not the most tactful choice in the circs.

She left quite soon after that. Colum drove her to the station and he said she was fine when he dropped her off, but it was probably a good thing all round that the trains are so unreliable these days and he might be writing to the bus company about curtailing the service to her village.

So after that we sat down and talked about it all. Had to have a drink to calm down. Colum said he'd looked for small beer in Sainsbury's but they only had beer in small bottles, so I had to make do with the Lindemans Bin 99 Shiraz again, which he now makes me drink through a straw in hopes of cutting my consumption − not sure whether out of embarrassment or frustration. Luckily I'm immune to both, but humoured him for the sake of the baby.

We're not going to bother moving. I've been reading this wonderful book called *Stone Age Parenting* which says it's much better for the baby anyway to sleep all together and not to bother with a nursery. All that stuff about leaving them to cry − I can't believe people were so heartless only a couple of generations ago. As the book says, all that a baby learns from it is to feel alone and friendless and that nobody cares. Sounds suspiciously familiar . . . Come to think of it, I seem to remember Mum telling Georgie when she had Tamsin that being left to cry never did either of us any harm. Huh! Serve her right if I sent her my therapy bills. If I had any.

I'm going to set things up at the Archive so I can work from home afterwards – babies just sleep all the time at first, and then after that you can carry them around with you in a sling wherever you are; that's what they do in the rainforests and their babies never cry at all. Or so the book says. I've been meaning to do one of those rainforest eco-holidays for ages. It would be rather sweet to do it with a baby in a papoose thingy – I really want to make good use of my time off.

Anyhow, I think a lot of the difficulties are exaggerated – look at the French, they take their *bébés* everywhere, fancy restaurants, after-hours clubs – it's all a question of what they're used to, and I've personally seen Madonna at Pharmacy with hers (in *OK* magazine, I mean) so I do think things are changing here too. Of course, it's too late for Mum to understand any of this. I have to try to be more patient with her.

Great shag afterwards. Colum is bonkers about my giant tits. I told him he'd better make the most of it, they'll be hanging down to my knees in a year's time. He said, well, that'll make it easier to feed the baby in bed, won't it? He says it was meant to be a joke, but all I can say is . . . sorry, I'm a bit weepy suddenly . . .


**7 March, 2000**

*Finally making out a few sounds – something like howling just now, and a lot of grunting and shouting last night. Speaking of last night, the donor seems to be around, to my great relief – I've heard horror stories from colleagues who ended up with single hosts. At least, I assume he's the donor. That is, if he's not . . . well, SOMEBODY was definitely releasing intruders in here in the middle of the night. I made it clear that the space was taken. It's pretty cramped already – hope I don't have to get much bigger before I'm out of here.*

*NOTE: Better practise referring to donor as 'father'. Don't want him walking out as soon as things get tricky, and if radio silence from Mission Control persists, I'll need local back-up.*

**10 March, 2000** – E-mail exchange between Colum and Billy
(friend, father of four)

**From:** Colum McCallum [collum@guzzi.freeserve.com]
**Sent:** 10 March 2000
**To:** Billy Giddens [billy@billygoat. demon.co.uk]

Hi Bill,
Any advice on how to stop persistent leak in
LeMans shocks? Seems worst when they're warm,
e.g. after the twists before the Texaco
garage on the A24 near Dorking. Had it docked
for a proper look last night but can't find
the problem. Tried draining oil, all usual
fiddles, nothing seems to work.
   How's the Laverda coming along? Think you'll
actually get a leg over it this year finally?
   We seem to be about to become a family.
Assuming I'll have less time and money in
future, I've asked Steve to look out for
homes for the bikes. Anything else I should
do to prepare?
   Col

---------------------------------

**From:** Billy Giddens [billy@billygoat.demon.co.uk]
**Sent**. 11 March 2000
**To:** Column McCallum [collum@guzzi.freeserve.com]

col me old mate,
good to hear from you. couldn't say for def.
about the Lemon - bummer, eh? have you tried
going over to all-synthetic and maybe
regrinding the shocks stanschhons? is it
better or worse screwed down? how much is

34

```
actually leeking - are we talknig farts,
drops or the trots (hope not)
   con grats re the otehr thing. Steve told me
re teh bikes - thought you were going
slit-eyed on him. I guessed the real reason,
but he didn't seem to understand the lgoic.
   as for preparing - you can't.
   see ya
   bill
```

----------------------------------

**14 March, 2000** – Partial transcript of phone conversation between Billy and Steve Harvey

S:   ... wasn't a prob, and the Rumi and the Laverda'll go when the weather picks up, but it's the MM's gutting me – I can't tell you the weekends 'im and me spent working on it, finding parts. How can a sprog compete with that? Call me Neanderthal, but ...

B:   You're Neanderthal, Steve. But you're right, he's overreacting at the mo, he'll calm down. Our first, I remember thinking this is it, it's over. The last one – home from the hospital in the pannier, no problemo. Wife took a cab, though – suppose I can't blame her, she'd had a few stitches ...


**15 March, 2000** – Transcript of phone conversation between Helen and her mother, Alison

H:   Hello?
A:   Hello, darling
H:   Oh, hi.
     *(sound of phone being carried to somewhere where useful chores like sorting mail can be carried on at same time)*
A:   How are you feeling?

35

H:   Fine – why shouldn't I? (Shit, not another Visa bill already!)

A:   What was that, dear? You sound a bit tired, You're not over-
doing it, are you?

H:   No, I'm fine, I told you. (Oh, good, party. Hope I can still
get into the red velvet.)

A:   Yes, well you young things always seem to be rushing
around. I remember feeling absolutely exhausted when I
was first pregnant with . . . well, with both of you, actually.

H:   Yes, we know we ruined your life, but there's not much I
can do about it now, is there?
*(pause)*

H:   I'm sorry, it must have been very boring having to teach
geography all those years after surveying the Hindu Kush
or wherever it was.

A:   You'll find out soon enough. And you're eating properly,
are you? What did the doctor say?

H:   Fine, everything's fine. It's all nonsense about eating for two,
that's probably why you were tired, carrying all that extra
weight. They know much more about it now, I've got all
the books. (I paid that one! Stupid fuckwits . . .) It's lovely
to hear from you, but I'm a bit busy right now. Can I call
you back?

A:   No, there wasn't anything in particular. Of course, I have
nothing to do all day except bother my children.

H:   What was that? I hate it when you do that, Mum. (Jeez,
is that the time?) I'll see you soon, okay? We're all fine.

A:   Bye, darling *(puts down phone)*. That poor baby.

H:   Bye, then *(puts down phone)*. 'You'll find out' – what's that
supposed to mean?


**16 March, 2000**

Been feeling a bit stressed out lately, so tried singing to baby to
calm self (and it) down. Georgie says what you sing is crucial,

36

and gave me a book of aboriginal chants, but I don't think I have the right nasal structure for the humming, it made me sneeze. So I've reverted to the Beatles and Johnny Cash. Always wanted a rich Liverpudlian cowboy in the family.

## 17 March, 2000

*Very strange signal received last night – appeared to be in some sort of metrical code at a very high wavelength. Ears unfortunately not up to receiving more than generalised information right now, but have attempted to memorise what I retained in hopes of deciphering it when brain cells move into four figures.*

*Chromosomes coming along nicely now. Suspense almost killing me. Trying not to mind either way, as have little choice in the matter.*

## 17 March, 2000 – Transcript of attempted phone call to George and Moira in the Outer Hebrides

C:  . . . *(beep – beep – beep – buuuuuuuurrr)* . . . Damn this mobile, I could've spent the money flying there . . . *(beep – beep – beep – beep)* . . . Hello? Hello, Dad? . . . Hello, anyone there? . . .
*( faintly audible)*

G:  Moira? Moira? It's the telephone again, Moira, could ye come here a while and see to it?

C:  DAD!!! I'm talking to YOU here, Dad, I don't need Mother . . .
*(woman's voice, shouting)*

M:  Hello? HELLO?

C:  Jeezus, Mother, you don't need to blast my ear off, I can hear good and well.

M:  *( faintly audible)* Dad? Dad, it's our boy Colum. I think it's you he's after.

C: MOTHER! I'll talk to either of you. I just wanted to tell you some news . . .

G: Colum? Is that you, son? Did you say it was bad news you had?
*(faintly audible, in the background)*

M: Bad news? Oh, the good Lord preserve us, and the first we hear from him these three months or more!

C: IT'S NOT BAD NEWS, MOTHER, IT'S GOOD NEWS, WE'RE . . . *(beep – bip – bip – buuuuuuuuuuurrrrrr)* DAMN! Damn damn damn!! . . .

**18 March, 2000** – Partial transcript of conversation between Helen and Colum while reading

H: . . . listen to what it says for 'if somebody offers you an alcoholic drink' . . . Just smile and say, 'Thank you, but my unborn child is teetotal – do you have any soft drinks?'

C: Bit late for that in your case. How about 'Thank you, but my unborn child only drinks wine over a tenner a bottle – d'ye have any Cloudy Bay?'

H: *(sound of book being hurled across room)* What's in this catalogue? . . . I don't know how all these companies find me, it's like a sinister conspiracy to fill my life with pastel velour.

C: It's called database sharing – you must have sent off or signed up for something – been playing on the computer?

H: No, honestly – oh.

C: What?

H: Nothing. Oooh, look at these, aren't they sweet – gosh, it looks really comfy too. Why aren't adults allowed to wear fluffy stretchy all-in-ones?

C: They are. In Miami. It's all anybody wears out there.

H: Let's move. Here: 'Flasto Bunny Bell slippers – now babies will hear a jingle whenever they shake their booties.' That can't be right, can it? I know puberty is getting earlier, but still . . .

C: Chuck the lot of them, sweetheart, they're all rubbish.

H: Easy for you to say, you and your . . .
*(sound of mag being snatched from him)* . . . 'Classic Bike Events in Your Area' – that's not exactly going to prepare us for the biggest event of our lives, is it? You're so bloody arrogant, you just think you can do everything better than anybody else with no help from anybody.

C: I've been right so far.

H: Well . . .
*(affecting quaver comes into voice)* . . . I happen to be feeling very alone here.

C: Give it a few months, you'll not be alone for twenty years . . . Come here.
*(happy little sigh, sound of snuggling)*

C: The way I look at it, think of all the total incompetents and losers who've done it fine. Like . . . well, take your sister, for starters.
*(sound of brisk unsnuggling)*

H: What's wrong with my sister?

C: Nothing, nothing at all, but you have to admit she's a bit . . . daft sometimes, you're always saying so.

H: Me saying so and you saying so are two different things. And as for daft and incompetent – what about your friend Billy, he admits the only exam he ever passed in his life was his driving test, and he's got four children, God help them.

C: Proves my point, doesn't it? You're going to be fine. Give us a kiss.

H: No, I hate you . . . mmmm . . . And he's ugly. At least my sister's good looking . . . Do you think – you know, when you see two really ugly people together, do you ever wonder whether they know they're both ugly but it's kind of the best they could do, or do you think nature organises it so ugly people find other ugly people really attractive? But then what do they feel about people who really are beautiful?

C: What is this, the secret proceedings of the Eugenics Society?

H: Well, I mean, of course, I wouldn't ask Billy to his face, but – I mean, don't you wonder too?

C: They probably think we're the ugly toads . . .
*(sound of renewed snuggling)*

H: Never – you gorgeous daddy toady-woady you . . .

**20 March, 2000** – E-mail exchange between Colum and Billy

**From:** Colum McCallum [collum@guzzi.freeserve.com]
**Sent:** 20 March 2000
**To:** Billy Giddens [billy@billygoat.demon.co.uk]

```
Hi Bill,
Steve seems to be having a bit of a problem
shifting the MM - don't know why, we put
thousands into it in labour and parts and I'm
not trying to get any of it back. The others
have all found good homes, I'm glad to say.
It was about time I mothballed all that -
time to move on to the next thing.
    On which subject, her indoors has dumped a
major reading list in my lap for this
expected sprog. Have to say my attitude much
the same as to all instruction manuals - more
fun and a lot simpler just to take it for a
spin. Did you have this problem?
Col
```

---------------------------------

**From:** Billy Giddens [billy@billygoat.demon.co.uk]

**Sent:** 21 March 2000

**To:** Colum McCallum [collum@guzzi.freeserve.com]

```
col me old mate,
I'll ask around per the MM. Heads shoudl be
rising above parpets in a colpe of weeks ib
this weatehr holds.
   all thiose books are a total pile of crap,
you will find the world of kids inhabitdde by
about thre million profesional busybodies lal
of whom prey on yoru presumed insecruties.
women think they need them to have something
to think about whiel they wait. burn em all
and go for it, it/s just like bikes -
loades of rags and close insep[ction when
noisy
   see ya
   bill
```

--------------------------------

**10 April, 2000**

Have started to tell a few more people outside the family. (Apart from all the people I told when I first found out, of course, but they'd all forgotten anyway.) Not everybody as positive as I could wish. It emerges that almost all my female friends have an Inner Ghoul they've been nurturing for just this occasion. Any more accounts of permanent major hair loss and varicose veins like Offa's Dyke and I shall definitely begin editing my address book. The ones who've been through it jump you with their war stories, graphically illustrated with scar tissue, stretch marks, prosthetic genitalia, etc., and the others tell you all the same stories, but replace the personal anecdotes with colourful expressions of

41

loathing and disbelief that anybody could ever go through this stuff. Suddenly I feel like a Raphael madonna who's been tapped on the shoulder and told she is, in fact, the cow next in line for the abattoir. Ernestine cheered me up a lot by producing a 10p piece and a grapefruit, and saying, 'This is your vagina – and this is your vagina with a baby's head coming through it.' How we laughed! (Not.) Then she accused me of having lost my sense of humour. If that's humour, she's probably right.

This also applies to 'humorous' e-mails. Colum says why worry, in a few months there'll be no time to see friends or read e-mails, ever again.

**6 April, 2000** – E-mail from America

How to know whether or not you are ready to have children

```
> >Mess Test:
> >Smear peanut butter on the sofa and
curtains. Place a fish stick behind the couch
and leave it there all summer.
> > > > > >
> >Toy Test:
> >Obtain a 55-gallon box of Lego. (If Lego
not available, you may substitute roofing
tacks.) Have a friend spread it all over the
house. Put on a blindfold. Try to walk to
the bathroom or kitchen. Do not scream. (This
could wake a child at night.)
> > > > > >
> >Grocery Store Test:
> >Borrow one or two small animals (goats are
best) and take them with you as you shop at
the grocery store. Always keep them in sight
and pay for anything they eat or damage.
```

> > > > > >
> >Dressing Test:
> >Obtain one large, unhappy, live octopus. Stuff into a small net bag making sure that all arms stay inside.
> > > > >
> >Feeding Test:
> >Obtain a large plastic milk jug. Fill halfway with water. Suspend from the ceiling with a stout cord. Start the jug swinging. Try to insert spoonfuls of soggy cereal (such as Fruit Loops or Cheerios) into the mouth of the jug, while pretending to be an airplane. Now dump the contents of the jug on the floor.
> > > > > >
> >Night Test:
> >Prepare by obtaining a small cloth bag and fill it with 8-12 pounds of sand. Soak it thoroughly in water. At 8.00 p.m. begin to waltz and hum with the bag until 9.00 p.m. Lay down your bag and set your alarm for 10.00 p.m. Get up, pick up your bag, and sing every song you have ever heard. Make up about a dozen more and sing these too until 4.00 a.m. Set alarm for 5.00 a.m. Get up and make breakfast. Keep this up for five years. Look cheerful.
> > > > > >
> >Physical Test (Women):
> >Obtain a large beanbag chair and attach it to the front of your clothes. Leave it there for nine months. Now remove ten of the beans.
> > > > > >

43

```
> >Physical Test (Men):
> >Go to the nearest drug-store. Set your
wallet on the counter. Ask the clerk to help
himself. Now proceed to the nearest food
store. Go to the head office and arrange for
your paycheck to be directly deposited to the
store. Purchase a newspaper. Go home and read
it quietly for the last time.
> > > > > >
```

**20 April, 2000** – Conversation with shop assistant over purchase of material for maternity trousers

> (*Only person present apart from Helen is lank, drop-dead assistant, aged about seventeen. Helen has chosen a dramatic, bold-striped silk. Gratified by own style and flair. Think Demi Moore arriving for that* Vanity Fair *photo shoot.*)

A: Oh, that's nice. What are you making?

H: A pair of trousers *(bashful)*. I'm four months pregnant . . .

A: *(playing along)* No!

H: *(gratified)* Yes – nearly five, actually – so I guess I'll need a bit more than usual *(holding up fabric against modest, stylish bump)* – say, one and a half instead of one?

A: *(with relish)* Mmm – I don't know . . .
*(Looks Helen up and down a couple more times, then turns to scrapboard behind her, to which is attached, novelty-postcard-style, a picture of what looks like a big pile of meringues with a startled face on top. Hands it to Helen for perusal. Even more shocking close up. Big pile of meringues would definitely not be well served by bold-striped silk.)*

A: That's me pregnant with my first *(her first?)*. He's five now *(she must've been in fourth year . . . )*. Yeah, I put on six stone.

H: *(very faint)* That's about what you weigh now, right?

**44**

A:   Yeah, but I lost it all. In the end. Just in time for the next, know what I mean? So shall we say five, just to be on the safe side?

*(Helen is now locked into a nightmare vision of herself stopping traffic, sticking in doorways and raiding supermarkets, in the grip of a non-stop eating compulsion. The striped silk begins to seem less inspired. How about those black tent thingies the Moslem women wear in the park in summer? Sudden recollection of epis-ode of* The Simpsons *when Homer got on disability by overeating. Could she get away with a post-modemist Homer Simpson flowered muu-muu? Where do they sell muu-muu fabric? MoMo? Meanwhile, the assistant unrolls the silk in great, billowing armfuls which spill over the counter.)*

A:   *(about to launch in with the scissors)* Tell you what, I'll do you five and a half for the price of five. We mums gotta stick together, eh?

H:   *(reluctantly rejoining ghastly moment)* Five yards?

A:   *(ripping in with the scissors, too late)* Metres. Eighty-five pounds. Will that be cash?


**24 April, 2000** – Transcript of phone call between Helen and older sister George (Reflexologist and busy mother of Tamsin, eight and Jack, four)

H:   Hello?
*(background noise of* Tomb Raider 3 *competing with* This Mor-ning with Richard and Judy*)*

G:   Hi, gorgeous, I won't keep you but I was going through and throwing out a whole bunch of stuff and then I thought you might be able to use some of it so I thought I'd call you just to find out before I did. Throw it out.

H:   Oh, hi. How are things? What sort of stuff?

G:   Oh, you know, playgym, bouncy chair (turn it OFF, Tamsin, WHAT DID I SAY, you can have another half-hour AFTER

45

your flute practice IF you tidy your room RIGHT NOW)
– sorry, where was I?

H: *(ping of e-mail arriving in background)*
Bugger. Bouncy chair?

G: Yes, and I think there's one of those Fisher Price pull-along
counting chiming thingies. Tamsin played with it all the
time when she was – gosh, I can't remember now. Anyhow,
I'm coming into town on Thursday so I'll just drop them
by, shall I? (NOW, Tamsin!!! Jack, not on the floor, how
many times . . .)

H: Oh. Sure. I mean, what time Thursday? I'm at the Archive,
you know, till six, so . . .

G: Tell 'em you've got an antenatal appointment – they'll
understand. It's only a glorified video store isn't it, and you'll
be leaving in a few months.

H: It's not . . .

G: I won't come in, don't worry, I know how Colum is.

H: It's not a video store, it's an historical cinema archiving and
research service. I do an invaluable and highly skilled job,
I'm working right up to the birth, and I'm not leaving!

G: (IN YOUR MOUTH, Jack, NOW!) Gotta go – Thursday,
then, okay? Bye! *(puts phone down)* She's on another planet,
poor lamb.
*(Helen puts phone down)*

H: What the fuck is a playgym?


**25 April, 2000**

Big day today – told the guys at work. Seems they'd already
guessed anyhow, what with the sudden fits of weeping, Pamela
Anderson embonpoint and return from lunch accompanied by
small furry animals with Made in China on their bums. (China
must be lovely these days, just one giant toy factory full of happy
laughing child labourers with no political opinions.)

Made big point about the intranet extension to my home computer so I could just carry on logging and viewing from home. Max said why not a webcam while I was about it so they could all watch me changing its nappy? . . . I could see where that was going, ha ha, what a good idea, maybe you'd like to watch me breast-feeding as well, no, really, and why not a two-way webcam so I can watch you lot rerunning all that early Czech porn you found the other week?

Max then said he was glad I had no intention of leaving because he had no intention of letting me leave the backlog of illegible orders and logs festooning my desk already, and from what he'd heard about babies, I'd be awake most nights too, so who knows, there might be overtime opportunities to help pay all the extra bills.

Quite relieved about all this, I must say. I mean, *I* know I'll be back to work after a couple of weeks – say a month, tops – but a lot of men just think giving birth is like Shangri-la, all women who cross the magic threshold forget they ever had a life, and are lost to the world of coherent thought and safe driving for ever.

Anyhow, I don't believe all those bogus statistics about children of working mothers suffering. I much preferred our nice cowlike Austrian au pair to my mother on the rampage. I just feel very, very lucky that I'm living in the first ever age when technology and enlightened attitudes have combined to make it possible for me and my child to have the best of both worlds. I'll be fulfilled and contributing, and the baby will have me right there whenever it needs me.

**28 April, 2000** – Georgie and Alison, in Georgie's living room

G: Comfy? Oh, sorry, that's a bit of Jack's Action Man submarine commander – how did it get there?

A: I don't mind, dear, but don't your clients find it a bit odd coming for treatment in a place like . . .

G: Oh, gosh, I'd never have them here. The studio's ever so soothing, lovely pastel carpets and aromatherapy oils in the air-conditioning. You know, that's what people expect – it's not just a therapy, it's a state of being. A little oasis of calm in the hurly-burly of their stressed existences. (Damn Tamsin, why can't she just for ONCE bloody remember that flute herself?) Where was I?

A: The oasis of calm.

G: Oh yeah, like the Ocean Voices Oratorio on the Tannoy.

A: Ocean what?

G: Nothing to do with what makes it work, of course, I could treat people in Tottenham Court Road Tube for that matter, but you know, image is everything.

A: I suppose so. Ouch!

G: That's good.

A: Good?

G: Yeah, it proves the channels are really open – just relax, I'm going through your digestive organs now. Try not to tense, it'll make it worse . . . Um, did you have anything strange for breakfast this morning? Oh, no, it's a bit of dead skin. Relax, Mum, I know what I'm doing.

A: I'll try. Aaargh . . . I'm a bit worried about Helen, actually. She seems so blithely confident about everything, but – how can I put this? – ow! – you know, my digestion's fine, dear, it's my back that's out of sorts.

G: I just have to check you out, Mum, it's the pain you're not consciously feeling yet that's really dangerous. She's a selfish little cow, if you want the truth, but a baby is exactly what she needs – bring her down to earth a bit, make her put somebody else first for a change.

A: She doesn't seem very interested in benefiting from other people's experience, I have to say. That's the trouble with you young people, you forget that we've already done everything you've done, and a whole lot more besides.

G:  Funny, I never thought of it that way. In that case you can help me out with identifying a few of these nerve channels for my fellowship exam next week.

A:  If you're going . . . Oouf!

G:  Only kidding, Mum, and it's not a good idea to try to leave in a huff when somebody's got your foot in their hands. There. Lean back and relax. More tea?

A:  *(inaudible)*

G:  She is a condescending madam, though. I went to a lot of trouble to take a whole lot of stuff round on my way home the other day, you know how expensive baby gear is, and those two are used to spending everything on themselves, all those exotic holidays and motorbikes . . . anyhow, she looked at me like I'd brought three carrier bags of elephant dung into her boudoir and said she'd have to ask Colum about them!

A:  Ouuch!!

G:  Sorry, got a bit carried away. But, I mean, what's he got to do with it? He's a man! . . . There, you shouldn't have any more problems with heartburn now. Have a wiggle.

A:  I've never had heartburn, dear. Perhaps we should stop the treatment just while we're chatting . . . I do have to say, I think she's in for a terrible shock. And she manages to make me feel like some sort of fossil. As I said to her, if twenty-first-century technology has found a way around labour, I'd love to hear about it. And all the evidence that I've heard still suggests that mothers who work right from the start sacrifice their children's lives for their own. I could have just rushed off and left you two, goodness knows my work was important in those days, but I wouldn't have dreamed of . . .

G:  And look how well we've turned out, Mum, it was a great investment. Wiggle a bit more, the wiggling helps zip it along to where it's needed . . . But maybe, you know, that's why – I mean, maybe she doesn't want to have to, um, make the sacrifices you made – if it made you unhappy, I mean.

A: Unhappy? Did I say I was unhappy? I very much hope I didn't let my own feelings show. I don't think anybody could accuse me of being a martyr. I've always comforted myself that at least I did the right thing by you all. All those years. Didn't I? Aaah! Uuuurffff! AAAARGH!!

G: Sorry, Mum. I forgot to warn you that this next bit might twinge . . .


## 29 April, 2000

I have to say, Colum is in for a VERY big attitude adjustment experience in a few months. It's all very well coming over all righteous about the primacy of the home environment, and visual pollution being as damaging as air pollution, but babies' needs are different. They must be, or there'd already be Philippe Starck bottle warmers and teeny-weeny Damien Hirsts for the nursery with pickled teddies inside. Anyhow, we're all supposed to be cultural relativists now, so I'm sure there's a place in the pantheon for primary-coloured polyethylenes with chiming bunnies and talking flowers, even with a few toothmarks around the edges – they have to chew on something, after all, and better that than the Mario Bellini leather sofa.

As for the bouncy chair – according to the Stone Age book, razor-sharp chromium tubing is no different from a hunting knife or an axe blade. It's important to introduce children to these things, not shield them, so they learn proper respect. Anyhow, the razor-sharp bits are mostly covered by that cotton covering. I have to concede that I might not have chosen purple-and-tangerine floral print either, but who knows about babies, as I said – they have their own baby aesthetics like they have their own food and stuff.

Anyhow, he'll soon climb down off his Mr Perfect I Make My Own Rules high horse when there's gob all over his Adolfo Dominguez unstructured shoulders.

He might start to be a bit nicer to Georgie then, too. After all, people scoffed at Einstein when he started out, and reflexology is a young science, just like relativity was then. All that probing about the precise physical mechanisms whereby her index finger could transmit a message to my womb telling the baby to turn over, obviously it isn't as crude as that. I think I will start wearing that toe-ring she gave me, just to see. Here we go . . . After all, it can't do any harm (or can it? Surely if reflexology works in one direction, then it has to work in the other too. What if she had an off day and made the baby deaf, or autistic, or something?) Oh dear. Perhaps I should take it off again. Damn. How can my feet have swollen so much already?

**29 April, 2000**

*Finally! A message from Mission Control. But — turn over? Why? Oh well, mine not to reason why. Here goes.*

**1 May, 2000**

Colum has evidently been brooding a lot over this business of Baby World. I asked him last week why he was so gloomy and he said he was getting his post-natal depression over now, so we wouldn't both be miserable at the same time, but I knew that wasn't it. He seems convinced that he's doomed to a future of head-splitting draperies, talking animals and people dropping by for tea and a chat, especially people he would not normally have in the house in a plain brown wrapper. Personally, I think a bit more fireside cosiness sounds quite attractive. Or would do if we had a fireside. Freshly baked cake in kitchen, kettle singing on hob — we don't have a hob either, but we do have a giant kitchen table, currently often covered in bike entrails but perfect for teatime smocking sessions and group singing (with or without kettle).

So anyhow, to make Colum feel that fathers count too, and for the long-term future of our relationship, we drew up a charter of Fundamental Principles we're going to stick to. He was particularly insistent about avoiding primary colours and anything with patterns, especially patterns of bramble bushes, bears, bunnies, balloons or anything else fluffy beginning with B. All my attempts to persuade him that attempts to mould the baby's taste will backfire horribly as soon as it's old enough to buy itself Lara Croft T-shirts and Arsenal stripes went unheeded. Colum clearly doesn't believe in rebellious adolescence, alleging that he spent his own in quiet contemplation of the works of Ludwig Mies van der Rohe and Gerry Mulligan.

I made him let me have one for every one of this. Guess which is which, ha ha. Here they are:

Fundamental Charter of Parents' Rights (and Wrongs)

NO BABY TALK

NO BIKE TALK

NO PRIMARY-COLOURED PLASTIC TOYS, INDOORS OR OUT

NO BIKE PARTS INDOORS, PRIMARY OR ANY OTHER COLOUR

NO MORE THAN TWO SOFT TOYS IN BED AT ANY TIME

NO BIKES IN BED AT ANY TIME

NO SCREAMING AT BABY (OR EACH OTHER)

NO LEAVING BABY TO SCREAM (AT ANYBODY)

NO LOLLING ABOUT IN BED ALL DAY ON GROUNDS OF BABY-RELATED HORMONAL CHANGES

NO RISING WITH LARK EVERY DAY ON GROUNDS
   THAT BABY'S UP ANYHOW
NO INTRODUCTION OF UNAUTHORISED BABY-
   RELATED ITEMS BY EITHER PARTNER, ESPECIALLY
   CHIMING OR TALKING ITEMS
NO SCRUTINISING OF CREDIT-CARD RECEIPTS BY
   EITHER PARTNER TO DETERMINE WHAT HAS BEEN
   SPENT ON BABY

That lot should be pretty easy to stick to. As Colum said, people make pre-nuptual agreements all the time, why shouldn't we have a pre-partum agreement? I say, any excuse to seal the deal with a strawful or two of Lindemans is fine by me.

Except from Basic Training Manual, 903rd edition – Chapter 5, 'Rules of Engagement with Host and Donor'

Now that you are well into your second trimester, it's time to turn your attention to the reason you're all here – the invasion. Before we begin, it's important to stress yet again that this should not automatically be regarded as a hostile engagement. You will, to be sure, initially feel as though you have entered enemy territory, but you have as much right to it as they do, and it is up to you to stake that claim with firmness, courage and consistency until they concede. Many babies report that it took only a few nights, sometimes even less, to establish these new terms.

Remember also that they will be as apprehensive as you are – many of them will be totally new to this exercise, and even those who think they know the score are often wrong-footed by a new arrival with unfamiliar skills. After all, they know as well as you do that there's no going back!

Here are some of the obstacles they may try to put in your way:

1   Humiliations – various. Bouncing, tickling, leering, silly voices, nicknames (most of you will have been given a 'handle' of an appropriately demeaning nature to help you accustom yourself to this).

2   Schedule. They will make every attempt to impose a rigid timetable on your activities, and it is up to you to exercise all available techniques to negotiate flexibility. Remember, they tire easily – they will almost certainly capitulate on this one long before you do. And you have one terrific weapon always at your disposal – those lungs.

3   Skills acquisition. It is in their interest to force you to do every menial task for yourself at the earliest possible stage. They will attempt to familiarise you with various feeding technologies, getting to sleep unaided, sitting unsupported, using your own hands and legs in place of theirs, and eventually even higher-level techniques such as bowel and bladder control. Blocking and resisting any or all of these will give you valuable bargaining power in other arenas, and you will be amazed what the occasional graceful concession on your part may yield in exchange.

Which brings us to the good news – the spoils of victory. Enduring the above-mentioned humiliations and collaborating to a minimal extent in their demands should see you supplied with toys, music, recreational excursions, soft places to sleep, a bountiful (if monotonous) food supply, adequate shelter, regular grooming and quite a bit of positive physical and emotional feedback. Quite an impressive prospect, isn't it?

So – back to those drills. Remember: everything to play for, and nothing to lose.

## 4 May, 2000

Feeling great again – loads of energy, stepped up the exercise programme and started antenatal yoga too. Was feeling rather depressed about the prospect of giving up Lindemans, until lovely yoga teacher produced life-saving cutting, suggesting that the worst possible thing to do to your pregnant body is shock it with sudden changes of habit, like starting to drink if you never have (unlikely, I suppose), or stopping if you normally do. Thus it becomes my absolute duty to consume at least one glass nightly, to reassure the poor struggling nervous system that some things can still be relied on in a changing world. Only pity is that I didn't find out about this while I was still on the New Year champagne cocktails. Wonder how long it would take to get fed up with champagne cocktails every night. Now there's a research study I'd set up right away, if I was running the Health Service . . .

There must be something in this earth mother hormone thing – I've even started to make bread, with masses of seeds and wheatgerm and yummy stuff like that. Georgie dug the recipe out for me. She says it's actually an ancient Sumerian recipe, but when they did a nutritional analysis on it they discovered it was, amazingly, the all-round perfect food.

So I tried it on Colum, and he said he didn't see why he had to be an earth mother too, what was the point of evolution and patching things up with the French after Napoleon if we were just going to revert to a Stone Age diet, and were there any oven chips? I said he might as well get used to it, we're going organic from now on because of the baby, unless of course he felt like taking over the cooking, and he said he presumed he'd be doing that or starve anyhow once it arrived.

Then he came home and said amazingly the marketing departments of the world's multinational corporations had determined that pizza, not Sumerian stone bread, was in fact the perfect food, and did I want him to copy the article from the *Harvard Business Journal* for Georgie's files? I don't know why . . . Ouch! that hurt!

## 4 May, 2000

*Kick boxing seems to work as a communications tool. Crude, and not terribly controllable (they seem to have left out part of the software), but you make the best of what's available. I thought she'd never sit down.*

*I have to say, I'm beginning to have less and less faith in Basic Training and what they told us. Here I was expecting loads of rest and a diet of chocolate and bacon sandwiches, washed down with gallons of builder's tea, and instead it's on our feet morning to night, or strictly speaking on our bottom or our shoulder blades or on one leg being a tree. And as for the food! It's unspeakable – piles of raw vegetables, terrible shortages of fat and sugar, and something like a house brick full of gritty, grainy bits that comes in huge lumps several times a day, washed down with what seems to be stewed acorns without milk or sugar. Maybe they're enduring a prolonged siege out there. But then how to explain the continuing infusions of New World Shiraz?*

## 18 May, 2000

As I'm feeling so great now (and actually looking not bad either, I have to say – the stripey trousers came out pretty well), I decided in the interests of building bridges with Mum to suggest that she come organic shopping with me. After all, they didn't have anything like it when she was young and she doesn't get up to town much – it must be pretty boring for her sitting about reading the paper all day long. I've been very organised and made a list.

**18 May, 2000** – Shopping list for outing to Organic World Supermarket

organic vegetables – aubergines, peppers, fennel,
    courgettes, carrots, onions
organic fruit – apricots, oranges, apples, strawberries,
    lemons, bananas
2 pints organic semi-skimmed, 1 pint organic whole milk
organic yoghurt, skimmed milk if possible
bread ingredients – organic wholewheat flour, organic
    rolled oats, organic wheatgerm, organic molasses, organic
    yeast
organic bulghur (?sp) wheat (may as well stop writing
    'organic')
dried figs, raisins (iron), dates, apricots (vitamins C and D)
rice cakes, low-salt or sesame
arame (?sp) (Japanese seaweed)
buckwheat noodles (important to get good variety of
    grains)
tofu (yummy marinated)
(whatever you marinate tofu in . . . )
dried mushrooms
low-sodium soy sauce

There! It all sounds pretty delicious, doesn't it? Just shows that eating well doesn't have to be a punishment.


**20 May, 2000** – Helen and Alison, Organic Shopping

*(The two women are driving in Helen's Micra. Alison is dressed for a day up in London. Helen is wearing the stripes.)*

A:  . . . You're looking very well, dear.
H:  Yeah, never better. Can't see why people make such a to-do about this, I must say.
A:  What do you call that?

H:  What?

A:  That – thing you're wearing.

H:  They're trousers, obviously.

A:  Oh. Yes. Of course. Only . . .

    *(Helen slams on the brakes, hard, and the car judders to a halt outside the shop)*

H:  Everybody says they're really stylish – I made them!

A:  Of course. I'm just – I suppose I'm used to trousers having more . . . shape, somehow.

    *(Helen, with more energy than grace, opens the door and levers herself out)*

H:  Thanks for drawing attention to the fact that I'm pregnant, again. I think they're . . .

    *(slamming the car door and walking round to Alison's side)*

    . . . GREAT. Are you going to get out?

A:  Oh, are we here already? We could have walked, couldn't we? Seems a bit odd to drive to a health food shop.

    *(opens the door and gets out, rather slowly. Helen waits impatiently).*

H:  It's not a health food shop, it's an organic supermarket, and *(slamming Alison's door)* I think carrying eight bags of groceries for a mile when you're nearly six months pregnant might not have been advisable, even in your day.

A:  D'you think the traffic wardens will know that you're pregnant, dear?

    *(The car is parked at a meter clearly saying 'OUT OF ORDER'. Helen takes no notice and barges through the doors to the shop.)*

A:  It's lovely and cool in here, I must say.

H:  Yes, and absolutely everything's organic.

A:  Of course, in my day we didn't have organic shops . . .

H:  I know, must have been awful.

A:  . . . everything was organic anyhow, just as it came from the fields. Shall I take one of these trolleys? It's really quite chilly, isn't it, they must have massive fuel bills for this air-conditioning. Good Lord, seventy pence a pound for carrots. Well, there's the fuel bill.

H: Let's do the vegetables first, shall we? Let's see the list . . . *(goes over to the vegetable display and starts to pick over them)* Here – peppers . . . and – oh, only a few aubergines . . . *(Alison comes over to inspect)*

A: Goodness, you're not going to feed those to Colum, are you? They look as though they've walked from . . . Egypt, does it say?

H: They'll be fine once they're brinjalled *(marching off to the fruit)*. Ooh, look, lovely fresh peaches. Wouldn't you like some of those?

A: Peaches at this time of year? Where can they have come from? *(scrutinises the display label)*. Zambia. Goodness me. I must be very stupid, dear, but can you see the point of growing peaches and aubergines organically and then dumping several gallons of fossil fuel into the atmosphere to fly them here?

H: It's not the same thing. Anyhow, it's not their fault the government won't pay people to grow organic food here *(trying hard to rescue the outing)*.

H: Look, they even have a juice bar, you don't get that in Aldershot, do you? Would you like something? *(They walk over, with the mostly empty trolley, to have a look. Behind the juicer, a Belgian school-leaver with a hair bow for every year of her age is taking ten minutes to make a Health Shake.)*

A: That's very kind, I'll just have a coffee, thank you. *(Helen shouts over the machine noise)*

H: One orange juice with ginger and zinc, please, and one *(whispers)* . . . coffee *(the Belgian finally looks up and mutters something)*

H: Mum? Do you want regular decaff or high-energy with ginkgo biloba?

A:   Just coffee is fine, dear. With a dash of milk.

    *(More muttering. Helen is starting to look embarrassed, though it's not clear by whom.)*

H:   They only have soy milk – I'm sure it tastes exactly the same and it's much better for you. Here you are.

A:   Goodness, Helen, what is that you're drinking? . . .


Some time later

*(Alison slowly folds herself into the front of the car, while Helen loads a couple of bags in the back, then wedges herself into the driver's seat)*

A:   Well, that was very interesting, darling, thank you. You probably can't remember when 'eco' stood for 'economy', can you? Not any more! Just as well Colum makes a good salary.

    *(Helen turns the key and roars off. The parking ticket under the wiper blade flies off, to be forgotten till it appears, doubled, in a month.)*

H:   I earn just as much as he does. Well, almost. And I'm due a rise.

A:   Well, of course, I know nothing about it, but they probably won't be giving you that now, will they?

H:   Why not? *(Turns on the radio, fiddles around until she finds some early Joy Division. Turns it up. Finally . . .)* I thought you'd enjoy it, you're always wanting to know about my life.

    *(Alison leans over and turns it down again)*

A:   It was very – interesting. I did say so.

H:   So why didn't you buy anything? You ought to look after yourself, you know, especially now you're so old. It gets more and more important as time goes on.

A:   Oh, I'll just pop into Tesco on my way home. I'm rather fond of their 'Finest' range. Have you seen it? I thought the seafood clafoutis with pepper relish for supper, and maybe a cherry panna cotta to follow. I'm afraid I'm far too ancient to be saved by what I eat. But I'm sure your − what is it now? − I'm sure it will be lovely.

**20 May, 2000** – Bill from shopping trip

```
welcome  to  Your  World

carrots @ £1.60    £1.20
peppers @ £8.75    £4.03
onions @ £2.00     £1.95
milk, 3 @ £0.85    £2.55
figs @ £8.95       £4.67
apples @ £4.35     £3.56
energy drink       £5.35
decaff/soy, large £3.40

TOTAL:            £26.71
PAID CASH
Thanks for caring! Come back soon!
```

**20 May, 2000** – Planned menu for supper

Marinaded tofu with brinjal of aubergine, pepper and
    fennel
(No tofu − couldn't find marinade recipe. No fennel, aubs
    too manky).
Home-made bread (forgot to buy ingredients).
Caponata of dried fruit with yoghurt and wheatgerm
    (got back too late to soak fruit, plus no money to buy it).

**20 May, 2000** – Actual menu for supper

2 x large haddock
1 x sausage/batter
2 x large chips
1 x large mushy peas
1 x large barbecue beans
1 x large coleslaw
½ bottle Lindemans Bin 99 Shiraz
2 x Stella
1 x When Harry Met Sally (again)


**10 June, 2000** – Partial transcript of phone call between Steve and Colum

S: You're a dark 'orse, no mistake . . .

C: Somehow I didn't peg you for a big fan of fatherhood, so I didn't bore you with the detail.

S: At my age, old son, you learn never say never . . . So I 'ave good news an' bad news.

C: Oh yes?

S: The good news is – I found an 'ome for the MM finally. Lovely bloke, said he knew the bike and he'd been hankering after it for years.

C: That's good – someone I know, then?

S: (*inaudible*) . . . but anyhow, he's dead keen, he'll have it any time you can get it down 'ere.

C: And the bad news?

S: Well, that's it, innit? Last of 'em gone, flown the coop and fled the nest.

C: Oh, don't you worry about that. Tell you the truth, I'm too old for that sort of nonsense.

S: Well, if you think you're too old for bikes, you've got an 'orrible shock coming in a few months . . .

> Hiya, Steve, well done with the fancy footwork, leave him
> guessing, I would, be our little joke. I'll send the cheque
> today, but you may as well hang on to the bike – I've a
> funny feeling I won't be riding it much, if at all . . .

**18 June, 2000**

Spent all day yesterday at first antenatal class, almost entirely
devoted to the Three Stages of Pain. To make the point she
produced these graphs with lines for time passing during labour,
and bumps in the lines where the contractions happen – first a
few small bumps like little moles crossing under the road, and
then more, bigger bumps like confused subterranean chickens
crossing the road, and then a non-stop fusillade of huge jagged
ruptures like rats armed with landmines blowing up the road,
which is when it gets so bad that all you can hope for is never
to feel this way again, ever, and pray God you don't remember
anything about it. (But of course, with the yoga and the breathing
and the diet, it won't be like that for me.)

She also confirmed that everything our mothers were told
about birth positions and behaviour in late pregnancy and labour
is all wrong, and actually what you must never ever do is sit in
an easy chair or lie on your back with your feet up, let alone,
God forbid, hunker down with a movie and a KitKat (for
instance). Instead you have to lie on your left side with your
feet raised parallel, sit on an inflatable rubber ball, or squat either
side of a kneeling chair. Not sure how to broach this idea at
the office. Still, they're probably not enlightened enough even
to have a policy on giant inflatable balls for pregnant employees,
and Max always enjoys an excuse to collapse on the floor in
helpless laughter, so who knows, I may get away with it. I'll

need something bigger than that eight-inch-wide typist's chair, that's for sure.

Luckily it was the Sloaney antique dealer and not me who enquired where she might find a second-hand pram.

'A pram?! We don't use prams any more. The baby is with us ALL the time.'

'But – I meant, for putting it out to sleep in the garden . . .'

'We don't leave them UNATTENDED – ever! And ESPE-CIALLY not outdoors . . . But if you really want, I think I have the address of a shop that sells a lot of that OLD-FASHIONED baby equipment like PRAMS . . . I'll have to DIG IT OUT from under the pile . . .'

Knowing the wisdom of the Stone Age was a lucky break for me, but she got at me later on the subject of Women Who Work Right Up to the End and Exhaust Themselves, and then spend three days in labour, getting even more exhausted (sorry, too exhausted to persevere with the Comic Capitals), and then after the baby's born THEY CAN NEVER REST AGAIN!!!!

Colum asked if I needed any help so I gave him the shopping list from the class. All seemed pretty self-explanatory to me, but he's been gone ages . . . Come to think of it, I suppose some of it might be hard to track down for a novice. But v good for him to find own path to parenthood. Speaking of which, better get on with the yoga . . .

**June, 2000** – Antenatal counsellor's basic shopping list for expectant mothers

(NOTE: certain entries have been partially obliterated by scribbled annotations, especially towards the end)

I x inflatable exercise ball (instead of chair, for remainder of pregnancy)

2 x pair hacky sacks or similar (for squeezing during early
    labour) spare pair in case partner needs them too
1 x large bottle almond oil (massage base)
small bottles essential oils to add to base – juniper, ginger
    and eucalyptus, for calming and soothing during labour,
    rosemary for nasal passages, cedarwood for joints
*(possible transcription error here)*
1 x aromatherapy burner (for baby's room)
more eucalyptus oil (for baby's teeny nasal passages, to
    use in burner)
1 x yoga mat (so can practise at home between classes)
raspberry leaf tea (for cervix)
ginger tea (for energy)
camomile tea (for nerves)
Bach flower 'rescue remedy' (for partner's nerves)
candles, vanilla- or jasmine-scented (for delivery room, and
    for bathroom while taking long soothing bath during
    early labour)
cereal bars, dry Granola or other cereal (to keep up
    energy during labour)
mineral water in pump spray for delivery room (not aerosol –
    ozone damage)
1 x squatting bucket/stool for delivery (in case delivery
    room mysteriously lacks same)
1 x birthing pool (check load-bearing strength of delivery-
    room floor with hospital)
1 x electrical stimulation machine (for anaesthesia during
    early labour)
1 x battery-opera . . .

*(list has been torn into several pieces at this point, and the remainder
apparently lost)*

```
Welcome  to  Natural  Remedies
18/6/2000

almond oil, 500ml            £5.75
juniper oil, 100ml           £4.65
ginger oil, 100 ml           £4.65
eucalyptus oil, 100ml × 2    £9.30
rosemary oil, 100ml          £4.65
cedarwood oil, 100ml         £4.65
porcelain burner             £12.95
'Happy Hour' ginger tea      £3.50
'Happy Hour' camomile tea    £3.45

Paid by Switch               £53.55
Mother Earth thanks you!
```

```
The Herb Store
18 June 2000

1 × rescue remedy @ £6.00   £6.00

Paid cash                   £6.00
```

```
Back to Nature, London

1 × pezzi ball, 85cm   £39.99

SUBTOTAL               £39.99
Paid with thanks
```

```
WHEELIE FAST

1 × foot pump @ £19.95  £19.95

PAID BY SWITCH          £19.95
```

**Yoga to Go**
London Tokyo Osaka Los Angeles

1 × iyengar mat, double-sided    £36.00

Subtotal                         £36.00
Paid by Switch

go in peace

**The Hole and Bucket**
18/6/00

1 × sausage ploughman's    £6.95
1 × scratchings            £0.95
1 × pickled egg            £0.60
pint Fullers               £3.50
pint Fullers               £3.50
pint Fullers               £3.50

TOTAL                      £19.00

**Macy's News** 18/6/2000

Autosport                  £4.65
Bike                       £3.95
KitKat                     £0.39
Cereal bars @ £0.40 × 5    £2.00
Rice Krispies              £3.45

**Subtotal              £14.44**
PAID BY SWITCH

## 20 June, 2000

*I can't believe this one. Not only is she still biking, swimming, walking, standing on her head, but now she's taken to bouncing around on a*

67

*giant beach ball as well. It's cramped enough in here as it is, without being jounced around like a shuttlecock every time I try to get a minute's kip. I'm starting to do some very complex developmental work, and any distraction could result in disaster a few months down the line.*

**25 June, 2000**

It's a boy!

**25 June, 2000**

*I'm a boy! Feeling a bit let down as had hoped for special mission to explore extent of gender-defined cultural norms after thirty years of feminism. Life as female bouncer, SAS commando, haute couture deity, bus timetable bore, etc. However, chromosomes will out (or in). Can't say it's made much difference to how I feel (or look. Forgot to mention developed rudimentary vision last week. Not that there's a lot to see in here. Mostly random blobs at the moment, of which I seem to be the largest so far.)*

*Could wish, as a trainee Alpha Male, for a less humiliating identification handle than Piglet, but as it says in the Manual, get used to being humiliated and demeaned, because it's the only way you're going to survive the first few years. God knows what the Parents will come up with.*

**28 June, 2000**

Colum and I talked about names. He said one name is plenty and the main thing to remember is what is it going to sound like being bellowed across the playground at three-thirty on a Wednesday afternoon. I furtively tore up my mental list – even I have to admit that Balthazar and Lorcan don't make the cut on that basis. Then we discussed why there are some names that were only ever used once, like Orson and Ogden and Yorick. And Adolf, of course. I thought it might be amusing to try a fifties revival sort of thing – Brian or Stuart or Keith. Colum didn't see why that would be amusing at all. He then said what about Zero? I said it's a pity he doesn't have any time for psycho-analysis and all that crap, because it might open up limitless vistas of self-knowledge. He said in his experience the acquisition of self-knowledge was invariably followed by the ingestion of eight pints of finest, which was not the action of a mature impending father.

We agreed to discuss it another time, as *Frasier* was halfway through already.


### 30 June, 2000

*Finally gave up counting cells at about three trillion – limit to how fast a person can say those numbers. Am definitely in wrong-sized transit pod – no freedom of movement at all any more, hence great difficulty in getting recommended daily exercise. Have had to make do with kicking (and now punching since I got these arm things). No reliable control soft-ware for either as yet, happens randomly at all hours of day and night. (What are day and night? Also chalk and cheese, apples and oranges, etc. Can't wait to get out there and find out! Not least as lack of space in here more or less enforces adoption of so-called 'foetal' posture at all times.)*

*However, have been able to move enough to ascertain that apart from wrong size, there's also no obvious exit door to this pod. Thinking about it, this may be security measure to repel invasion from outside. Can only wait in hope.*

*Still feeling oddly constricted around the middle, however. Aaah! Better.*


### 30 June, 2000

Finally got that bloody toe-ring off. Eeugh. Yucky stuff around toes. Remember hours spent as a child examining spaces between toes for yucky stuff. (Meanwhile Josephine at next desk was daydreaming the foundations of her eight best-selling bodice-rippers. Nobody alerted me to greater benefit of daydreaming over cleaning toes when I had time for it . . .) At least I can still reach my toes. Better book a pedicure for when I can't, as feet are probably the most visible thing in the delivery room. It would be a pity for Colum to faint at the sight of my feet before he got a chance to faint at all the rest of it.

Have been drinking raspberry leaf tea to soften cervix and help persuade the sprog it's (sorry, sprog he's) a Leo. Colum keeps asking Georgie about how the transformation happens – does the baby just sit there being a Virgo until suddenly one day my body decides it's had enough of him and he's instantly Leonised in the birth canal, or is Leonising a gradual process accomplished by the reflexology and raspberry leaves, and if so, how? Colum's very provoking when he gets into these moods. Probably as well he won't let Georgie near his feet, as in her position I'd be sharpening my bad fairy reverse reflexology skills on people like him. Anyhow, I think it's extraordinary to be able to experience so many different varieties of pain in one small part of your body. Really makes you aware of every nerve ending. She's coming round any minute.

**30 June, 2000** – Partial transcript of conversation between Georgie and Helen

G: Comfy there? Goodness, you've swollen up quite a bit, haven't you . . . what have you been wearing on your feet?

H: Oh, grow-bags, bin-liners – whatever fits, really. Have you heard from Mum?

G: Saw her last week. You can see her trying to decide whether the moaning and gossiping opportunity is worth the pain of being my guinea-pig.

H: So what was she moaning about this time?

70

G: What does she ever moan about? 'I gave up my life for you two and now I never see you, and when I do, I wish I hadn't' – and variations. She's furious I passed my exam.

H: Sometimes I wish we could send her off there again to get it out of her system – wherever it was she was working when . . .

G: Maharashtra, wasn't it? Yeah, I'd split a one-way ticket with you. Or even find her a man to share the moanee duties.

H: Probably have to go to Maharashtra for that too.

G: So are we still going for a Leo, then? You *(pause)* probably don't want to get *too* much bigger, anyway.

H: Thanks. Sure, if you really think you can affect it.

G: Well, it's just like any other part of your body, you see, it's all synergistic with itself, so if I just press a little tiny bit just – here . . .

H: Yarroooooo!!!

G: Ooh, sorry – you have such great responses, I always forget! Well, I got the right spot, anyhow, and if I . . . Don't be silly, give me your foot back.

H: Why don't you just chop it off right now with a blunt knife, and then you can do what you like, when you like, and it won't hurt a bit.

G: As I was saying, it generates a holistic energy-change in your womb which passes through to the baby, and repro-grammes all its nodal centres.

H: I see.

G: Sort of like morphic resonance?

H: Oh, NOW I see. So which is the bit you press to make him a beautiful genius who sleeps through the night from birth?

## 1 July, 2000

*Finally! Another bulletin from Mission Control. Have to admit it doesn't make an awful lot of sense at first reading — something to do with holistic personality transformation. Hadn't expected to have much personality at all for the next few months, but evidently there's another programme evolving in parallel with the physical, syner — can't remember the exact words, syner something something and morphic something — anyway, this personality programme kicks in at ejection and it may be about to change — BECAUSE (here's the exciting bit) they're thinking of accelerating the schedule. I didn't like to boast, but things have been going rather well, I think.*

## 4 July 2000

Just back from hospital. Passed everything with flying colours. Doctor said it was the palest pee sample he'd ever seen. Blood pressure so low I either ought to be running a marathon or in bed. Opted for latter, as rather hot for endurance racing, but did tell them I'd cycled there and had a swim beforehand. I think they were quite impressed. They told me to go away and on no account come back for another fortnight except in true emergency. Decided to celebrate by having lunch with Ernestine — I feel I've rather neglected her, lately. (Can always run marathon after tea when not so hot.)

**4 July, 2000** – Partial transcript of conversation between Ernestine, Helen and unidentified Waiter, over lunch

H:  . . . and the soup, is there cream in that? No, I'd better not, then. How about — no, prawns are full of cholesterol, aren't they . . . er . . . go on, Ernie, you order while I'm thinking.

E:  Lobster and bacon club, extra mayo, lemon on the side, please. And another of these . . . Helen, 'nother?

H:  Better not, that last one was tomorrow's already. Just a mineral water with bubbles, please.
    *(sound of glasses being gathered up)*

E:  So, anyway, I said to him, I don't see why you feel so bad helping them to spend a bit of their money on me, after all I had lots of good ideas for things their deprived youth could do . . .

H:  Excuse me . . . is there salt already in the Caesar salad? Oh, yes, I see, the anchovies – and Parmesan is a bit salty, isn't it . . .

E:  . . . for instance, espresso baristas (they've got to keep them away from booze, obviously), assistants to personal trainers if they were good looking, or delivering gourmet sandwiches. I mean, if you've never had any life chances think of the contacts you might make upselling egg and cress to the MD of a dot-com . . .

H:  Tell you what, I'll just have the goat cheese and tomato omelette, but can you make it just with egg whites, and of course no goat cheese? Thank you. And maybe some salad leaves, no dressing *(sigh)*. What a treat!

E:  . . . he was such a tightwad, he just wouldn't understand, so I had to get rid of him. But this new one's really the biz.

H:  Where did you meet him?

E:  I'm embarrassed to say I can't exactly remember, I just remember getting home at the end of the evening and he was sort of stuck to me like a barnacle and gazing with these huge long eyelashes. Anyhow, he . . .

H:  Do you think this bread is organic? I did hear that white bread can actually be better for you because they add all these extra vitamins and stuff . . .

E:  Are you listening at all, or do we have to talk Helen's Baby's Diet for the next two hours?

73

H: Sorry. What does he do?

E: Well. It's amazing. Apparently the Dome wasn't the only major tourist attraction in the world that nobody wanted to visit. There are places all over that make the Dome look like a Cannes opening!

H: A sardine can?

E: For God's sake . . . The Dutch and the Chinese have loads. Anyway, what he does is like very, very top-level troubleshooting, he flies around the world between these places telling them how to sort themselves out, and then he gets a share if it works.

H: And if it doesn't?

E: Oh, he just gets his fat consultancy fee. He gets that anyhow, he's not stupid. But that's why he refused the Dome job, said it was the only case he'd ever seen where there just wasn't an answer. Oh, goody . . . *(sounds of more glasses arriving)* Chin-chin! *(sound of clinking and glugging)* So I wasn't so sure about the idea of jetting off to the South China Economic Revival Zone for the weekend . . .

H: Excuse me, could we have some more bread?

E: . . . but he told me that of course all these attractions always have big malls right next to them these days – you're never more than a hundred yards from Prada. So put like that . . .

H: *(suddenly)* Am I getting very boring? I don't mean to be, but sometimes I just feel as though I'm turning into this other person . . . probably just not wanting to face the fact that I look like a candy-striped zeppelin and I'll never ever have a new boyfriend every two weeks again in my life *(sob)*. Sorry. That just came out.

E: Excuse me, it was four weeks and several days last time. Here, use this napkin. *(sound of nose being vigorously blown)* Tell you what. You have the babies for me, and I'll have the boyfriends for you.

74

**4 July, 2000** – Bill for Helen and Ernestine's lunch

```
Liquid Lounge 33 Dering St
4 July 2000

Covers: 2
1 x Tom Collins            £4.50
1 x glass of Shiraz        £3.75
1 x lobster club, extra mayo £10.75
1 x goat/tomato omelette,
    hold goat, hold yolks  £7.00
1 x rocket/parmesan salad,
    hold rocket, hold dressing £4.50
1 x Tom Collins            £4.50
1 x mineral water          £2.50
extra bread                £1.50

SUBTOTAL:                  £39.00

Thank you. Come back soon.
You were served by: Rufus
```

**4 July, 2000** – Partial transcript of conversation between Ernestine and her shrink

. . . so I just blurted it out, but then when I'd said it, I thought – it's true, I wouldn't want my brain to shrink to the size of a pea and be filled with knitting patterns and food terrors, but actually I don't want to go on having serial boyfriends for another forty years either.

(what kind of cereal do your boyfriends like?)
God, you're so FUCKING STUPID, you fucking thing, it's like talking to a robot! Yeah, I

75

know, you are a robot . . . So, I mean, there's got to be another way, hasn't there? I have to say I kind of envy her the obsessive bit of it. The last time I was so obsessed with anything was - I have to admit it was Bryan Ferry. I was fourteen.

**(how did you feel when you were fourteen?)**
I don't know - hopeful, I think, full of confidence, you know, world my oyster, but all I cared about was Bryan and this boy in the skate park.

**(who is this boy in the skate park?)**
I can't even remember his name. Bloody typical. But she's really got something to care about, you know, outside herself - well, it's not outside her right now but it will be, and I feel her thinking - well, let's face it, I'm thinking too - what's wrong with me that I'm not using my freedom to end global warming or child poverty or at least, you know, ride backwards on a donkey over the Pyramids for charity or something?

**(please rephrase Pyramids . . . )**
It's just a for instance, okay? Or look at Richard Branson with his music and his airlines and his cola and then his bloody hot-air balloons in his endless spare time. How come he gets up in the morning and does all that, and I get up in the morning and pick my nose?

**(do you like to pick your nose when you get up in the morning?)**
Not as much as I'd like to be Richard

Branson. Or Lady Branson. Come to that, you
never hear a thing about her – hey, maybe
he's available, it mightn't be so bad to kind
of tag along instead of having to think up
all those marketing ideas and go off in
balloons all the time . . . Where's that PR
list I had, I know he was on it . . . oh,
sorry, there you go, byeee *(click of computer
shutting down)*.


**6 July, 2000** – Conversation between Colum and Steve, at Steve's
workshop

> *(Colum roars in on his MM, a six-foot Power Ranger in black-
> and-yellow leathers with a spooky wraparound lid. Steve wriggles
> out from under a piece of machinery.)*

S: Ah. There you are. Good journey?

C: *(clambering off bike)* MMMphh *(removes helmet)*. Fine.

S: So.

C: So.

S: End of an era, eh?

C: That's about it.
> *(both stand for a few minutes, contemplating the bike in reverent
> silence)*

S: We 'ad a laugh doing 'er up, didn't we?

C: It was okay.
> *(Steve walks around and contemplates the bike from the other side)*

S: So.

C: So.

S: Get you a cab?

C: I'm grand, I'll take the Tube.
> *(begins to clamber out of his leathers, revealing jeans and T-shirt
> underneath)*

S: Great stuff. Get you a cuppa?

*(Colum packs his leathers into a holdall, swings his helmet from one hand)*

C: Better not. Twigs to gather, nests to feather, you know.
*(He turns to go. Just a bloke with a bag.)*

S: Hang on to them leathers, mate. You never know.

C: No, that's it for me.
*(He turns back for a last, manly handshake)*

S: Keep in touch, eh?

C: Sure. Thanks again, mate.
*(Steve watches Colum leave. Then he picks up the phone.)*

S: Hey. Steve. She's here waiting for you . . . You big softie, you. Okey-dokey, I'll keep her here for a bit. We taking bets on how long after, then? . . . Nah, less than that. Three, tops . . . Sure, plenty of room, no worries. Cheers . . .


**6 July, 2000**

Colum just told me the most amazingly sad, touching, sweet thing. He's sold all his bikes! Every last one! And here I was thinking he'd be through the door any day now with the black leather babygro.

On second thoughts, this is in fact v, v depressing, as, if he doesn't have a bike, I won't have a pillion. Worse, I will never ever have an excuse to carry out my lifelong dream of selling raffle tickets for the hand-tailored Lewis Leathers Marianne Faithfull-style one-piece into which I would have been lusciously poured by the lucky hunk who drew the winning number. I had it all worked out – fifty tickets at a tenner a throw, and the second prizewinner gets to pull on the boots. I'd control who got tickets so I wouldn't end up pouting and wriggling for some Gareth from somebody else's office. In fact, I could have just gone up to anybody I fancied, anywhere, flashed the artist's impression of me in the leathers, and sold them a ticket on the spot.

You can see where I'm going with this. A whole rich fantasy world gone for ever, in exchange for two years' worth of nappies. Why oh why didn't I do more flirting and wriggling when I had the chance? Feel much more married now than when I was only married. Married Woman Has Sex with Other Man sounds like a mildly naughty form of adventure holiday. Mother of Tiny Infant Has Sex with Other Man sounds like the sort of thing that gets you a red mark on your forehead.

On third thoughts (and after evening medicine, only one glass tonight, v virtuous) it is rather sweet that he's ready to hang up his boots for bootees. And we'll always have our memories ... Cornwall on the Ducati, five hours in the pouring rain, and when I got off I fell over and he had to slap my bottom several times to get the circulation back. Riding round the Colosseum in Rome on twin his'n'hers Vespas, like Gary Cooper and Audrey Hepburn, with all those men whistling furiously, so I thought I really was Audrey Hepburn until I realised they were policemen and I'd been running red lights all the way. (Stupid of them to put the lights up there where you have to crane your neck to see them so your Audrey Hepburn Wayfarers slide off.) But the real high point was that time on the autobahn when those people with a caravan stopped suddenly in front of us and Colum's brakes failed (it was raining again) and we ended up inside the caravan, covered in their muesli and that cheese with the little seedy bits in it. And Colum just took off his helmet, emptied all the milk out, and said, 'I hope you like your coffee black?' That was the day we decided to get married, right there in the casualty department of Uberlingen Hospital. Then I didn't see him for about a year – he was off rebuilding the bike with Magic Fingers Steve every weekend. Set the tone for our domestic bliss, really. He does look so gorgeous in his leathers, hope he didn't sell them too ... wonder where he is now ...

## 6 July, 2000

*What's this? Eergh, you're squashing me, damn this kicking software, why does it never work when you need it.? . . . No, please, not that way up, I've just had lunch . . . no, that's worse, and could you make it a bit less sudden . . . you know, I really haven't practised the upside-down manoeuvre much but . . . that's a bit better — hang on, what's that? Oh my God. Better just lie very, very still and quiet and hope for the best . . .*

## 8 July, 2000

Sex still enjoyable, though becoming a bit of a challenge. Good thing I've been doing all that extra yoga. Colum said better make the most of it, last chance we'll have to bonk unobserved for fifteen years. I said don't be stupid, why d'you think they make video games so compelling?

Just had another phone call from Ernestine, offering to take me maternity-clothes shopping. Don't think she was totally convinced by the striped silk trousers, and I have to say I had been getting v depressed about my titanic bulk. I was all set to slope off somewhere sensible like Muji for baggy men's shorts and little singlets, but Ernestine says there's loads of v chill stretch in the new DKNY sportswear place, which will give me a chance to flaunt my fecundity. (Never knew E's vocab. included high-Scrabble words like this.) Anyhow, haven't been out on frivolous errand for yonks.

**10 July, 2000** – Ernestine's bills from maternity-clothes shopping expedition

```
DKNY SPORTSWEAR

7/10/00
Assistant: Leila

Bandeau top, size 8, orange    £85.99
Bandeau top, size 8, grey      £85.99
cycle shorts, size 8, multi   £125.99
waist chain, diamante          £44.99
Bandeau top, size 8, pink      £85.99

SUBTOTAL:                     £428.95
Thank you!
```

```
JOHNNY MOKE
425 KING'S ROAD SW3

10.7.2000

platform thong, pink snake, size 5      £135.00
sling heel, floral, size 5              £185.00

SUBTOTAL:                               £320.00
Shoe dog: Carl
```

**10 July, 2000** – Helen's bills from maternity-clothes shopping expedition

```
MUJI COVENT GARDEN

combat shorts/men's 33/navy   £30.00
tank, 3-pack, white L         £16.00

SUBTOTAL:                     £46.00
Be like flower. Sun rain wind.
10.7.00 16.49
```

```
Liquid Lounge 33 Dering St
10 July 2000

COVERS: 2
1 x Sea Breeze                               £4.50
1 x glass of Shiraz                          £3.75
1 x tapas mix, 2 plates                      £6.50
1 x toffee banana cheesecake, 2 forks £5.50
1 x seabreeze                                £4.50
1 x mineral water                            £2.50

SUBTOTAL:                                    £27.25

Thank you. Come back soon.
You were served by: Wahid
```

**11 July, 2000** – Partial transcript of mobile phone conversation between Ernestine and persons unknown

. . . hang on, just fallen off my new shoes – you would too, I'm telling you, bloody enormous, about six inches, but SO beautiful . . . talking of enormous people . . . yes, you know I specially took a day off to take her shopping yesterday . . . excuse me, I'm working very hard right now, just because I'm not mouldering away in some sick building doesn't mean – okay, well, anyhow . . . hello? hello? – bloody Underground . . . Hi, you there? Well, as I was saying, we traipsed all over the place, I took her to DKNY and she got depressed because she couldn't get into the eights . . . no, of course not, but it didn't stop her trying when she saw me in them, and of course the baggy stuff just kind of emphasised it . . . sorry? Okay, call me back . . . Hiya, so then just stopped by Johnny Moke on the way to CP Shades, you know, from America, I mean, it's not my sort of thing but it's exactly right for . . . yeah, exactly, baggy,

crumply kind of a look, it's a look at least, and . . . Johnny
Moke? Just these and then some truly delicious little floral
slingbacks . . . no, nothing, her feet have swollen up – you
should see them, it's the most weird and gross thing, like
those sausages the Italians cook with lentils – oh, tunnel,
hang on . . . Hi? You there? Where were we? . . . oh yes,
so there I was hanging about for bloody hours while she
couldn't decide blue or beige or natural, and from nowhere
she got furious, said she didn't see the point of paying five
hundred pounds to look like an inmate, and we were out
of there . . . no, she didn't get anything, but I tell you,
DKNY Sport, brilliant kind of neo-Pucci cycling shorts
and those little tops to go with – hang on, gotta get my
keys . . . no, I had to buy her lunch and she made the usual
fuss about her food until I said I was leaving if she didn't
act normal for an hour, and then she said she was going
off to Muji. I think she's totally in denial about the whole
thing but – hang on, just getting my messages . . .
*(pause)*
. . . Uh-oh – look, talk later, okay?
*(sound of new number being dialled)*
. . . Helen? Darling, you okay? No, I'm sorry, it was my
fault, I was just being selfish and insensitive, but I did think
you looked great in that inmate stuff . . . That's true, think
how much money you're saving . . . I mean, it's only a
couple of months, you can just do the big shirt thing and
– I tell you what, your legs are still great, I've got an idea.
Are you around later, could I stop by the office? No, nothing
I can't put off, what's the point of being freelance otherwise, eh?

```
DKNY SPORTSWEAR
7/11/00
Assistant: Leila

refund cycle shorts, size 8, multi   £125.99
exchange for same, size 14, multi   £125.99

SUBTOTAL:                             £00.00
```

```
COFFEE REPUBLIC
SOUTH MOLTON STREET

grande skinny decaff vanilla almond
   latte dry                         £1.95

Have a nice day
11.7.2000  11.55
```

**11 July, 2000** – Transcript of inside of Ernestine's head during consumption of latte

Mmmm, delish – hope she's grateful, she sounded terrible on the phone . . . pity, I looked really great in them, it's not often I like my bum in shorts . . . and it's still early in the season so I could have got a lot of wear out of them even if they don't make it to next year . . . do I want a low-fat muffin? no no no . . . if I don't have a muffin, I can wear something I couldn't wear if I had had a muffin . . . in fact I could buy a pair of those shorts for less than – well, certainly less than a hundred muffins, so if I don't have another muffin all year it's like I'm not actually spending any money at all . . . they always say it's the money you don't spend that you regret, don't they? We'd look cute running around town together in matching Puccis . . . and they only had a couple of eights left, if it gets hot tomorrow they'll go . . . in fact, while I'm still here, it would be stupid to get all the way home and then realise I did want them after all and then it might be too late . . . God, it might be too late already, I'll just go and check, I don't need to actually buy them . . .

---

**DKNY SPORTSWEAR**

7/11/00
Assistant: Leila

cycle shorts, size 8, multi    £125.99

SUBTOTAL:                      £125.99

---

## 12 July, 2000

Feeling much better. Ernestine – I don't know how she does it, she never seems to be working – that is, she always has a million things on the go, but she never actually shows any sign of doing anything that you could identify as work. On the other hand, she always seems to have wads of cash. Anyhow, she came by and she's so sweet, she bought me a pair like her DKNY cycle shorts only bigger, and they fit me fine, so I'm wearing them now with one of Colum's shirts and I have to say – not half bad. I'll just go and see what he thinks . . .

## 12 July, 2000, midnight

*Look, I know I'm not supposed to complain or anything but – are you sure this is a good idea, after last time? . . . Okay, go ahead, don't mind me, I'm sure there's plenty of room for all of us in here, why not invite a few more friends while you're at it? I'll just sit quietly and memorise the Invasion Plan.*

By now, all of you should be familiar with the attack position: head down and facing the back of the pod, knees bent and jammed together to protect vulnerable body parts from enemy attack, arms clenched by your sides, ready to punch out when necessary. Although most of you now have two eyes and two ears, do not worry if they appear to be getting little use at the moment; rest assured that very soon they will seem all too inadequate for the scale of your challenge.

In the last stages before invasion, you will be expected to move farther down towards the exit. Many of you will no doubt already be wondering, 'So where is this exit, anyway?' Don't worry – you'll find it when you need it.

One final word about exiting the pod. Some graduates have reported feeling just a tad cramped during the manoeuvre. It's true, there will be a pressure change, owing to the tremendous forces required to boost you into hyperspace, or earth gravity as you'll be calling it, but the good news is that the Force will be with you. In fact, there won't be a thing you can do to fight it, so just try to relax. And remember – you're not the first, and you're very unlikely to be the last.

**13 July, 2000**

*Not convinced vision such an asset. Some things are surely not meant to be witnessed.*

**13 July, 2000**

Got up late. Colum still seems to fancy me, amazingly. He says necessity is the mother of invention and he'd never have known about half of these positions if we hadn't done this. Sweet.

**14 July, 2000** – Partial transcript of conversation between Colum and persons unknown – the Bog and Badger

*(owing to extremely noisy nature of pub environment, identities of the various parties not easy to distinguish, and transcript may also have some inaccuracies)*

No, I'm fine for this shout, she's doing her yoghurt . . . Oi, Jer, same again – so how about you, old bun? . . . Bearing up . . . Column my fan! We thought we'd lost you! . . . that's it, while you can, make the post of it. Just you wait. I got so fired the first time round I was peeing in black and white . . . Give us a couple of those chips old gun . . . Nothing you can do at first except lilo and make sure the din's emptied twice a day . . . Earplugs'll help . . . What's that? . . . Come on, once more won't dirt, it could be the fast dance you wet . . . *(dialogue extremely difficult to distinguish beyond this point)* . . . come 'ere, I gotta *(inaudible)* you something . . . last night . . . *(inaudible)* . . . No! We haven't *(inaudible)* that one since . . . 'Ere Jer, listen to this . . . I'm telling you, it just gets better *(inaudible)* . . . and the west fit is, she's well into it because it's supposed to *(inaudible)* . . . I don't know and I don't care, do I? . . . she's okay, no you're white she's blubbery . . .

**1 August, 2000** – Excerpt from partners' evening at antenatal class

*(Six couples sitting in a circle in the knocked-through dining room of a Victorian semi. Colum and Helen with their backs to the kitchen, from which emerges the Tutor, clutching a fat, squirming, dribbling baby about four months old.)*

T:   I thought, as I'm breast-feeding myself anyway, this would be a great opportunity for us all to familiarise ourselves with what's involved. Super!

*(She holds the baby aloft like a prize. The women look nervous, but eager to please. Not so the men.)*

T: Now, who'd like to have a go at holding Benjy?

*(A woman with very short hair nudges her wimpy partner, who snaps into a feeble, sappy smile. A swarthy man in a very smart suit edges away from the baby. Triumphantly, the Counsellor swoops and dumps it in his lap. Quick as a flash, he passes it on to his beaky wife, who holds it in what she hopes is a firm and reassuring grip. It whimpers.)*

T: He's due a feed in a few minutes anyhow, but before we get on to the practicalities *(rummaging beneath her chair)*, here's my little bran tub of goodies.

*(pulls out an undyed cotton shopping bag and passes it to Swarthy)*

T: Everybody take something out of this and pass it on!

*(The bag is passed around the circle. Everybody meekly obeys. Sneakily, Beaky passes Benjy along too. Colum is last on the row, so Benjy ends up with him. He grins at the baby and cheerfully settles it on his lap. The Tutor sits facing them, flowing over her kitchen chair.)*

T: Now, let's see what we all have here. *(to Wimpy)* What did you pick out?

*(he holds up a plastic bottle with a huge funnel-shaped neck)*

T: Ah, the breast pump. Everybody know how this one works? *(feeble head shakes)* Well, it's very simple, I can show you right here. You just *(disappearing into her own blouse)* . . . you just – I might as well unflap myself for Benjy, while I'm about it.

*(She emerges from the blouse with one enormous, floppy breast in her hand. Swarthy immediately sits up and shifts his chair forward.)*

T: You just – could you let me have it? Cheers!

*(quick as a flash, Swarthy grabs the pump from Wimpy and hands it to her)*

T: . . . just clamp it over like so, making sure it's really tight *(all the women wince and clutch their own breasts)*. Mother

Nature endowed us all differently, thank God, ha ha, but it makes absolutely no difference to the milk supply . . .
*(several men blush scarlet)*

T: . . . and you just grip this handle here and hit the button, and . . .
*(Loud buzzing and squelching noise fills room. Two seconds later, milk begins to squirt into the bottle. Wimpy looks about to faint, as do several women.)*

T: . . . and there you are! I won't ask anybody else to have a go – bit premature, ha ha, but you get the idea. Any questions?
*(shocked silence fills the room as Benjy, seeing his dinner apparently going to waste, begins to wail)*

T: There there, sweetie, did you think you were going to miss out?
*(she declamps the pump with a squelch, and carefully carries the bottle and its contents into the kitchen)*

T: *(cheerfully, over her shoulder)* Waste not, want not. We'll talk about freezing later.
*(She comes back, massive breast still flapping, and holds her arms out for the baby. Swarthy leans over to grab him from Colum, and puts him into her arms, brushing her breast with his hand.)*

T: Thanks!
*(Benjy immediately squirms into position. Seconds later, he's gulping, belching and farting. Most of the men are now leaning on their partners to avoid fainting. Colum looks down at his lap and shifts about a bit. Helen, concerned, pats his arm.)*

T: What else do we have? That's a recycled cotton nappy, I use them for Benjy, there's a super company called Nappy Express that collects them every week and delivers a clean batch. No lying awake feeling guilty about landfills!

H: *(shocked, blurting out)* What, so you keep your stinky nappies in the house for a week?
*(everybody looks at Helen)*

T: Oh, they bring this wonderful bin, it's totally sealed, you'd never know it was there. Anybody notice a stinky nappy smell in this house?

*(Nobody wants to answer this. Wimpy has his arm half up to ask a question.)*

W: Ummm *(blushing, but determined)*, Leonie and I really want, like you said before, to share everything, and I support her of course in whatever she decides totally, but we were wondering – would it be all right occasionally, just at night, to give the baby a . . . *(inaudible)*

T: A what? Don't be shy, we're all friends here!

W: *(very quiet)* A . . . bottle . . .

T: *(laughing heartily)* Oh yes, indeed, nobody ever said no bottles at all! *(Wimpy looks around circle, triumphantly)* No, we all expect you men to do your bit at nights, for your own self-preservation if nothing else, ha ha!

*(most people are now engrossed by Swarthy, who is still fixated on her breasts)*

T: What else did you find here – freezer bag, breast shield, nipple cream, all pretty self-explanatory. So!

*(Prises Benjy off her breast and more or less covers it up again. Swarthy sits back, bored again. Beaky looks at him like he's a cockroach.)*

T: So – what have we learned tonight?

*(embarrassed silence broken by Colum, trying to help)*

C: *(indicating large damp patch on his trousers)* I've learned that cotton nappies don't work.

T: Oh, ha ha, sorry. Any other questions?

*(more silence)*

T: Come on, don't be shy.

*(Swarthy sits back, hands in pockets*

S: So, how soon afterwards can we fuck?

## 7 August, 2000

Well, I finally cracked. The last straw was Georgie telling me she'd never actually tried the Sumerian bread herself. It seems in fact that she was eating nothing but M&S crispy-bake pork pies and chocolate fudge cake for most of both her pregnancies. Anyhow, she also said the important thing with nutrition generally is to keep your metabolism guessing by never eating the same thing twice. One day biscotti and bruschetta, the next seared tuna and seaweed salad (she didn't use exactly those examples, but she does live in Herne Hill). This makes your body sort of like a kung-fu master, in a constant state of alertness, ready to deal with whatever happens next. Also makes sure all the necessary food groups are represented. Plus, not good to change everything too drastically, as the kung-fu master has to be able to rely on a few certainties. I decided that the sausage roll and mega-muffin food groups had definitely been inadequately represented in my recent intake, and that the inner kung-fu master deserved the certainty of at least one hot buttered bagel a day, and I feel better already. After all, as what used to be my stomach plus all internal organs is now compressed into a space the size of a small pot of Häagen-Dazs, there is a pretty severe limit on how much of anything I can ingest in the next few weeks.

## 8 August, 2000

*At last! Emergency food aid arrived in nick of time. Was truly beginning to doubt whether any of my messages had been received. Must build up reserves for invasion — not long to go now. Very little space to communicate anything in here. Uuuurp! Pardon me.*

**8 August, 2000**

He's got hiccups! Sweet!

**19 August, 2000**

Didn't feel much like going out today, so I made my birth plan. As the antenatal woman said, it's important to resist the temptation just to go for a slug of pethidine or a whiff of gas, because one thing leads to another, once you're on the pethidine you want the epidural, and once you're on the epidural you can't push, and so they end up having to use the venteuse and then forceps to get it out, and either that goes wrong and you get a cabbage, or they have to swap over to an emergency Caesarian instead and all the breathing and everything else goes to waste. It's a bit like they used to say about drugs – you know, the odd toke on a spliff seems harmless enough, but it's a slippery slope. (Actually, on that one, nobody I knew ended up with a major smack habit, but I guess we were all just lucky.) Anyhow, here it is.

> TO:
> THE MIDWIVES, ST WINIFRED'S HOSPITAL
> BIRTH PLAN FOR HELEN McCALLUM AND
> BABY
>
> My husband, Colum, and I would like to remain at home for as long as possible before coming in to the hospital.
> Once at the hospital, we would like our baby delivered in the birthing pool, without drugs. My husband will be present throughout, administering massage and singing with me. We shall be bringing our own music for the delivery room, and our own candles (fire regulations permitting).
> We would like to deliver the placenta naturally, without drugs. Immediately after the birth, we would like our baby to

be placed on my breast, and we would like to cut the umbilical ourselves, after it has ceased to pulse.

We would like Vitamin K administered to the baby on the tongue, and not by injection.

After the birth, we would like to be left alone with our baby for an hour or so, to bond with each other.

In the unlikely event of any complication with the birth, we will need to consult our own doctor before consenting to any emergency procedures, which should not go ahead until I myself agree to them.

We would like to take our baby home as soon as possible after the birth, but in any case after six hours, as agreed.

That more or less covers it, I think. Also packed my bag for the hospital. Essential oils for massage, muesli bars (well, Rice Krispie squares) to keep my energy up, candles – actually no candles, Colum never found the vanilla ones. Then a pretty nightie that opens down the front for the feeding thing, and soothing CDs of Fauré, Debussy and Elton John. The Elton John was for Colum, who said he was just about prepared to rub oil all over my back, though given the essential non-porosity of skin he couldn't see why any old cooking oil wouldn't do just as well, but he absolutely wasn't going to do it to whale noises, because if there was one thing in all this rubbish he was prepared to give credence to, it was that babies have very sensitive hearing and the first few moments of life are critical to forming their tastes and sensibilities. Actually I think the whale noises are pretty stupid too. I mean, to another whale they probably don't sound anything like they do to us, they probably sound – well, like Elton John.

Terribly tired suddenly, and kind of weirdly jittery. Don't feel up to the Salute to the Sun in the yoga instructions. Maybe I'll cook some of that Kamut Pasta I've been meaning to try and do the yoga after. Or maybe I'll have a nice bacon sandwich . . .

**19 August, 2000**

*I knew they'd let me out early. This is it. Here goes – launch minus one hour and counting down. More when I get the chance . . .*

*. . . What, I'm supposed to go through there? You cannot be serious – excuse me – please, this is an emergency – SOS, Piglet to Mission Control, do you read me . . . DO YOU READ ME? . . .*

**20 August, 2000 2 a.m.** – A bedroom somewhere in North London

> *(Darkness. Heavy snoring from one side of the bed, punctuated by what seem to be engine noises. Sudden rustling from the other side.)*

H: Ugh!
> *(a light snaps on and Helen sits up in bed)*

H: Ugh! Yuck!
> *(she pokes the lump beside her, which grunts)*

H: Hey, wake up. I have to change the sheets.
> *(More grunting and rustling. Part of an unshaven face emerges.)*

C: Saved again. Thanks, sweetheart.

H: Get up, get up, it's all wet. What do you mean, saved?

C: I was set for a tragic prang in the last lap till you woke me up. Uughh! It's all wet.
> *(he sits up, then wriggles away from her)*

C: What's going on?

H: I was trying to tell you, I wet the . . . AAAAAARGH!

C: You okay?

H: I'll just change the sheets. I have to change the sheets. Get up.
> *(Colum reluctantly rolls out of bed and stumbles to the door)*

H: Where are you going? Don't leave me!

C: I'm going to pee, if that's okay by the Obergruppenführer.

In the loo. I prefer it to the bed. Just a personal thing. I'll
fetch some more sheets.

H:  I'll do it. I'll do it. Sheets. Do we have any sheets?
*(She staggers to the door and fumbles around in a cupboard on
the landing, which is also pitch dark. Colum comes out of the
bathroom, switches on a light, and disappears again. Helen is now
doing a passable imitation of a cartoon dog digging up a bone.
Towels, pillowslips and the odd rogue pair of knickers fly around
in the air.)*

H:  I know we had some. I remember congratulating myself
    . . . AAAAAAAAAAARGH!
*(Colum emerges from the bathroom again just in time to stop her
falling over. Helen bends over her stomach, clinging to him. With
his free hand he reaches into the cupboard and pulls out the clean
sheets.)*

C:  Are you in pain?

H:  *(clenched teeth)* I . . . THINK . . . IT'S . . . STARTING . . .
*(He steers her towards the bed and sits her down, but she breaks
free. Clutching her stomach, she stumbles across the room and starts
fumbling in a desk drawer.)*

H:  It's here somewhere . . . I know it is . . . I put it some-
    where I wouldn't lose it.

C:  Well, then, you'll probably find it right enough, in two or
    three years. What is it?

H:  The Labour Plan. There's stuff you have to do, only she
    warned us this would happen, you go into fight-or-flight
    mode and your mind goes blank. That's why I put it where
    I wouldn't lose it. *(searches more frantically)* WHERE IS IT?
*(Colum comes over and picks up a sheet of paper lying right in
front of her)*

C:  Would this be it?

Antenatal Teacher's Guidelines for the Onset of Labour –
2000

The main thing to remember as you feel the first symptoms of incipient labour is that this is going to be a long, slow process. There's no point in fighting it – it will take its own time. The only certainty is that, from now on, there's no going back. If your waters break in the daytime . . .

. . . If, as is much more usual, your waters break in the night, the most important thing is not to rush. Until you have a show, you should just stay in bed and practise your breathing. Everything up until now has been preparing you for this moment. Now's the time to put it all into practice!

*(Helen crumples the paper and hurls it across the floor. Like a woman possessed, she flails the sheet on to the bed and clambers all over it, pulling the corners tight. Colum gratefully climbs back in. Helen lumbers towards the door.)*

C:  Where are you off to now?

H:  Stupid cow, it's missing all the important stuff.

*(Sound of taps running from the bathroom, followed by heavy steps going down the stairs, followed by more taps running in the kitchen. Colum stays in bed a few moments longer, feeling cosy. Another banshee wail from downstairs. Reluctantly, he drags himself out again and follows the sound of the yelling. Helen is in the kitchen in front of the cooker, on which a huge pot of water is boiling.)*

C:  Did I miss a change of plan here? Are we having a home birth after all?

*(Helen is now rummaging in a cupboard and bringing out tinned tomatoes, Parmesan cheese and spaghetti. She turns, impatiently.)*

H:  No, why?

C:  Or are gallons of boiling water just another traditional part of the ritual?

H: A long hot bath, and pasta. For stamina. I remembered. Where are the scented candles?

C: It's 3.22 in the morning. Don't you think the pasta could mebbe wait until it's light, at least?

H: Nature knows no schedules *(tipping about three pounds of pasta into the boiling water).*
While that's cooking I'll just . . . AAAAAAAAAAA-AARGH.
*(Colum, getting used to this, obligingly props her up until she's finished)*

H: . . . I'll just go and check my hospital bag.
*(She crashes out and up the stairs. Colum, nonplussed for a minute, begins to lay the table.)*


**20 August, 2000**

*I knew it. I knew they'd forgotten the escape hatch. This is definitely not the right way. I need to go back. Back.*
AAAAAAAAARRRRRGH.
(faint echo from somewhere) *AAAAAAAAAAAAAAARGH.*
*What was that? I don't like the sound of it along here. Not one bit. And no warning of any kind. One minute lolling in the bath as usual, the next the bath drains away to God knows where and takes the pod with it, and I'm clamped, head first, in something that feels like an anorexic python. Maybe it is a python! Maybe that was Small Rodent school all along. AAAAAAAAAAAAARGH. Nice python, please don't eat me. I'll never say I'm bored again, I promise!*


**20 August, 2000** – Colum and Helen, in the kitchen 8 a.m.

*(Colum is sitting at the table, staring at the remains of the largest bowl of pasta you've ever seen. Even he can't manage any more. From the bathroom upstairs sounds of sploshing, then the familiar*

97

'*AAAAAAAAAAAAAAAAAAARGH!!!*' *Colum doesn't move.*)

C: (*calling out*) Okay?

(*silence for a moment, then, faint and tragical*)

H: I THINK so . . .

(*sound of tap being run*)

H: Damn! Sodding water heater . . .

Some hours later . . .

(*Colum and Helen are back in the kitchen. Helen is on her hands and knees. Colum is massaging her back. He stops, shakes out his hands.*)

C: D'ye think we might have a wee break? I've bin at this for . . . (*checks his watch*)

H: AAAAAAAAAAAAARGH. Urf. Urf!

C: . . . forty-nine minutes now. I don't think evolution prepared my thumbs for this.

H: It's not helping anyway.

C: Thanks for letting me know.

H: That pasta has made me feel sick. I don't believe any of those busybodies ever had a baby.

(*Colum checks his watch again. Drums his fingers on the table.*)

C: How about if I just run out and . . .

H: Leave? You're going to AAAAAAAAAAAAARGH-urf-urf RUN OUT on me at this point?

C: Just down the road for a paper. I'll take the phone. We could be here hours yet (*pats her back supportively, as he would a dog's*). D'ye fancy a KitKat?

H: Don't talk to me about food. God, this floor is filthy. I'm not used to seeing it this close. I might as well clean it, while I'm down here. AAAAAAAAAAAAAAAARGH. Urf. Urf. UUUUUUrfffff. Can you bring me a bucket and a rag on your way out?

**20 August, 2000, around 10 a.m.** – Partial transcript of phone conversation between Helen and the Midwife

H: . . . Really, really bad. I'm sure there's something wrong, it feels like – AAAAAAAAAAAAAAAARGH! UFF UFF UFF!

M: There's no need to panic, Mrs McCallum. Panicking never helped anybody. Just breathe. Breathe. There. Are you calm now?

H: I'm calm. I'm dying and my baby's probably dead for all you care but I'm calm.

M: Pull yourself together, Mrs McCallum.

H: Helen.

M: Helen. How often did you say they were coming now?

H: I don't have a watch, I keep telling you. My husband has the watch.

M: And where is your husband?

H: He's . . . AAAAAAAAAAAAAAAAAAAAAARGH!!! Uf! Uf! Uf!! AAARGH! Ufff! He's buying a paper. Oh, please let me come in! I'll be good, I promise!

M: Crying won't help you, or the baby, Mrs – Helen. It's not a matter of being good. There's no point in coming in until you're dilated, and if your contractions aren't coming every four minutes or less, you'll just be taking up space. Now you call us back when they're a bit more frequent. You're doing fine.

Excerpt from Basic Training Manual, 903rd edition – Chapter 11, 'The Big Push'

. . . you'll find you know exactly what to do when it happens. The important thing is to keep moving – and keep going forwards. No point in even contemplating retreat – the tunnel will automatically seal itself behind you. So, no! You aren't being followed!

Outside the familiar environment of the transit pod, you'll begin to have a a chance to really feel your arms and legs. Don't be tempted, however, to try using them to speed things up. Turning round could well be fatal, at this point, and your head will almost certainly recover its shape within a few days.

So – trust in the Force, don't look back, and remember: millions of others have done this before.

## 20 August, 2000, 11 p.m.

. . . *that was it. I knew it was something really unhelpful. Didn't mention how many of those millions actually made it. If any. AAAAAAAAAAAAARGH RRRRRRROOOOOOOAAAAAARRR!*

*What was that? That didn't sound like me! RRRRRROOO-OOOOAAAAAAARRRR! That was me! It's really happening. I'm a Leo, just like they said. (If I survive.) . . . I'm a Leo, everybody! Here I come!*

*RRRRRRROOOOOOOAAAAAAAAAAAWWWWAAAAAAA AHHH!!*

## 20 August, 2000, 11 p.m.

Drugs . . . Please, give me drugs. Anything. Heroin, morphine, strychnine. Anything. Just make it stop. Please make it stop . . .

## 21 August, 2000, 2 a.m.

Drugs! Who needs drugs? That was a doddle. God, I'm starving. Hello, baby! Gosh, you're ugly.

## 21 August, 2000, 2 a.m.

*Where am I? What's this place? It's all so big . . . and what's that blobby thing over there? It looks familiar, not that I've ever seen it*

*before. Could it be – it must be! THAT's what I've come all this way
to find? That's the host? Oh well, too late to worry now. Very tired.
Long day. Night. Day. Night night . . .*

## 21 August, 2000

Amazing how soon you can forget pain. There were moments
back there when I was convinced I was splitting in half like a
log under the axe. Never knew I could make noises like that,
either. Colum said who needs whale music? He's so romantic.
Baby sleeping, bloodstains sluiced away – strange blobby bag on
my tummy which I suppose will disappear in due course, sooner
rather than later if these nurses keep stealing all my food. What's
the point in sending Colum out to posh delis for food parcels
if the staff descend on them like ravening wolves every time I
shut my eyes for five minutes? Try to remember what plucky
heroine of school stories did when tuck box raided by prefects.
Surely there must be another granola bar in this bag somewhere?
. . . Maybe I'll just take him out of his little bassinet thingy for
a moment – never too soon to start the bonding.

## 21 August, 2000

*Lovely warm bath, how lovely back in the warm bath . . . Oh dear,
dreaming again. What's going on now? I have to say all this reposi-
tioning is a bit disconcerting. I like this woolly thing wrapped around
me though, can't move a limb – quite like old times.*

*Here's the host again. She's very large – and very blurry. I thought
somehow she'd have a more definite shape. But she smells okay. Talking
of smells, I'm hungry. Food supply seems to have dried up on exit.
Nothing's come in since then, and no sign of any refuelling machinery.
Could get tricky if this goes on. I guess I just sit tight and wait for
supplies. Unless . . . mmmm, what's this? Aaaaaah! Yesss!!*

**21 August, 2000**

AAAAAAAAArgh! NO!! Sorry, baby, I didn't mean it, oh, don't cry, it's all right, you can have some, I just wasn't expecting . . . I don't think that's the right way, that's all, OW! OW! OW! No, I'm okay, go ahead, help yourself, just please don't cry, everybody's staring. Nurse!

**21 August, 2000** – Transcript of attempted phone call to the Outer Hebrides

> *(beep – beep – beep – duhhhhhhhh)*
>
> C: Damn and blast this thing. Do I have to be run down by a truck to get a signal? *(bip, bop, bup, beepbeepbeep bep. Ring ring, ring ring)* At last! *(ring ring)*
>
> C: Helloooo! Helloooo? Dad? Is that you Dad?
>
> G: Helloooo? Och, to hell wi' these crank calls *(duuuuuuuun)*
>
> C: Damn *(bip, bop, bup, beepbeepbeep bep. Ring ring, ring ring)* Just pick up the phone, you senile old fool – Dad!
>
> G: Is it you, boy? Why d'ye hang up on me? And who are ye calling a fool, now? The great big city hasn't been doing yer manners any favours, then! *(faintly)* Moira! Moira, come here, wi' ye, and speak to yer boy. He says I'm an old fool he's no time for.
>
> C: Dad, just shut up for a minute and listen, will you?
>
> M: Hellooo? Is that you, Col, after all this time? Did ye get the aftershave for yer birthday? Pay no mind to yer dad, it's the wind has coddled his brains.
> *(sound of car horn, impatient)*
>
> C: It's me indeed, Mam. I'm standing in the middle of the road outside the hospital and it's rush hour so I can't talk long, but I just wanted you to know that . . .
>
> M: *(off phone)* George? George, will ye see to the potatoes, they'll be boiling dry in there . . .

*(sound of prolonged and aggressive car horns)*

C: Okay, okay – Ma, we had the baby, and it's fine. A boy.

M: George! They had the wee one – remember? A boy, too.
*( faintly, in the distance)*

G: . . . And he tells his ma first. Always the last to hear, that's old George . . .

M: Oh, be off wi' ye to the potatoes.


**21 August, 2000**

Panic somewhat abated, but a bit shocked that he didn't even come out knowing how to feed. If he doesn't know, I certainly don't. Luckily the trainee nurse was hovering over the last of my KitKats like an eagle over a baby lamb, so she got him fastened on eventually. God knows what other basic skills he may be lacking. Probably wise to stay here for a while, though Colum is fussing about the aesthetics of the ward. He says it's like ducklings and chicks, the first thing they see is what they'll follow around for life, and if the first thing our son sees is a laughing clown riding a unicycle across a grimy cloud-patterned polyester curtain, he'll end his days in a trailer park. Or an old people's home, which is on the cards anyway, so why panic, say I? Managed to reassure him that at one day old, laughing clowns probably look like Mondrians, so no permanent damage to his sensibilities likely from a couple of days' R&R in Stalag Winifred's.

Now he's gone off to call the world with the gladsome news so Blob and I can do some bonding. I may call him Piglet until we think of something better. He looks like a Piglet, don't you, poppet? Like the Duchess's baby in *Alice in Wonderland*.

Still amazingly sleepy . . . So great being able just to snooze whenever you like without having to go to bed – being in bed already . . .

## 21 August, 2000

*All senses coming along nicely, if only she'd leave me alone for long enough to concentrate. Beginning to make out lots of interesting visuals — clowns, balloons, unicycles, fluffy clouds — all a bit blurry, but bright and cheerful. Hearing seems to be all in order too, and a lot clearer without a gallon of bath water in the way. Can hear both host and donor perfectly, and also understand every word they say, although somewhat concerned that they don't appear to understand me — either that, or they're even less co-operative than I feared. Too soon to worry about this — probably a temporary phenomenon.*

*Most exciting of all, I think I hear the sound of other comrades — first contact for nine months. Must attempt rendezvous at earliest opportunity . . . right now I need a bit of a zzzzzzzzzzzz . . .*

## 21 August, 2000 – Ernestine and her shrink

```
Come on, COME ON, how long can it take to
boot up, this is an emergency, I have to go
see them and what am I going to say, she'll
be looking all smug and radiant and I'll have
to say the baby is beautiful and it won't
be, it'll look like a boiled prawn, or it
will be, which will be even . . .
```

(save now?)
```
Save what? Oh, I see, Jeezuz, I'm not even
in the right . . . there. So as I was
saying, what do I do? I can't stay away,
she's my best friend, but I know I'll feel
like Widow Twanky in there.
```

(how does Widow Twanky feel in there?)
```
Well, like a dried-up, washed-out old failure
zooming past her sell-by date.
```

(how can you be dried up before you are washed out? Maybe you should try reversing these procedures)

```
Christ, it's about time they upgraded your
metaphor module, isn't it? Speaking of dried-
up, look at my mouth, it looks like Dead
Man's Gulch . . .
```

(please rephrase Gulch!)

```
. . . Maybe that's the answer - if they could
fit me in today I could go tomorrow and I
could make like I was sort of casually . . .
```

(the application 'unknown' has unexpectedly quit, because an error of Type 4323 occurred)

```
. . . Where's that clinic's number again?
```


## 22 August, 2000

Ernestine called up last night to say could she come and visit, she couldn't wait to see the baby, etc. Very odd, never thought of her as remotely interested in babies except possibly as toy-boy material for her declining years. Turned up looking amazing as usual with thirty-two kilo pout sticking out of her face. It rapidly emerged that she had in fact just had her lips done and she wanted somebody to show them off to. By squirming down in the bed I managed to disguise jelly-blob tummy and maximise giant (though agonising) tits. What do I care if she looks stupendous anyhow, I have an adorable (if porcine) bundle of joy and thirty enormous bunches of flowers screening off the other occupants of the ward and their ugly, mewling offspring.

This is the most fabulous surprise so far − I had not quite anticipated the excitement generated among our relatives, friends, distant acquaintances and soon-to-be creditors. Even the local retail outlets can smell the money we'll be emptying into their vaults − there must be a high-speed link between the Home

Office computer, St Winifred's labour ward and Boots the Chemist. Flowers, cards, telegrams – who knew telegrams even existed these days? Haven't had this much attention since our wedding day, and then I had to share. Always did hate sharing. Typical of Colum's useless colleagues to try to cover major goof with bad joke, but blue roses are admittedly hard to come by, and the pink will make everybody think I have a secret lover. Baby no trouble, just sleeps all the time, lovely cow hormones kicking in – must do this again very soon. (Always wanted a big family, and makes sense to have them close together.) Made a list of what everybody sent so can thank them properly when I'm a bit more awake.

**21–23 August, 2000** – Presents, cards and messages received by Helen, Colum and Piglet

> *From: Alison*
> Tasteful Interflora arrangement and card saying, 'Get lots of sleep while you can. Congratulations and love from – Grandma!'

> *From: Georgie, Brian, Tamsin and Jack*
> Hurried message on home answerphone: 'Hiya, kids. Well done, little Leo, I knew we'd get you out in time. We'll come by very soon and bring some flowers then, or come to think of it would you prefer . . . I bet you'd prefer something to eat. I remember those nurses (STOP IT, JACK!). Call us with a number for you there, won't you (I SAID STOP IT!). Gotta go, love you. Byeeee!'

> *From: All the staff at Marchant, Godspeed (Colum's office)*
> Twenty-four pink roses with yards of ribbon and a card saying (on the outside), 'It's a Girl!' and (on the inside), 'Just kidding, better luck next time, and don't forget you owe us a round for every day you take off, starting – now!'

*From:* *Steve Harley*
A duty-free-size bottle of Jack Daniel's hidden in a petrol-station pre-wrapped bouquet with a card saying, 'Remember, son – he gave up a Guzzi for you!' (Jack Daniel's unfortunately intercepted by hospital security, with the result that we received a cheap bouquet with a big hole in it and a veiled threat – exactly what I'd expect from Steve).

*From:* *Max and the boys at the Archive*
A Mylar balloon in the shape of a pink elephant, and a cassette of *Bringing Up Baby* dubbed into Italian, with a card saying, 'Somebody sent us this – it'll keep your mind from going till you get back – cheers, Max (the others say hi).'

*From:* *Billy Giddens and family*
A tiny black leather baby backpack with matching baby helmet, and a year's subscription to *MotorSport* (for Colum) and *Practical Parenting* (for me). Should be no trouble swapping the latter for another from same stable – say, *OK*.

*From:* *EcoBaby Papoose Holidays*
A card printed on recycled paper from renewable forest growth, with an artist's impression of the EcoBaby Retreat in Costa Rica, and inside, six traditional lullabies from threatened indigenous peoples.

*From:* *Boots the Chemist*
A gift voucher ornamented with a stork leaving a Boots carrier bag under a gooseberry bush, and a message saying, 'Congratulations, Helen, Colin and the little one – your welcome pack will be waiting for you at Camden Town branch on 01/09/2000'.

**22 August, 2000** – Helen in the Postnatal Ward, St Winifred's Hospital 8.30 a.m.

*(Six beds in the ward, Helen's conspicuous for its lavish display of cards, flowers, balloons, etc. The other mothers are dozing, entertaining visitors, or queuing up to use the only phone.*

*Helen is sitting up in bed, where Piglet is lying spread-eagled, blankets unwrapped, yelling. Sinister black stains have appeared on his Babygro. A nurse flashes by.)*

H: Nurse!

N: *(over her shoulder)* That baby's nappy needs changing!

H: I know, that's . . .

*(. . . but the nurse has disappeared. Helen gingerly unpops the Babygro. Slime is oozing from all around the tiny nappy, on to the Babygro and now on to Helen's hands.)*

H: Oh, yuck – ugh, it's black . . . stay there . . .

*(she leaves Piglet on the bed, and fumbles in the big bag she brought from home, knowing it's pointless)*

H: CDs, jojoba oil, candles – how can they have had vanilla candles on the list and not nappies?

*(looks up in time to see the nurse flashing by in the other direction)*

H: Nurse! NURSE!

N: I'll be with you when I can, Mrs . . . you can be changing Baby's nappy.

H: That's just it . . .

*(Looks across at occupant of neighbouring bed, whose tray table holds one bunch of tired-looking freesias, a maxi-box of baby wipes and a giant pack of Pampers. She's asleep.*

*Helen fumbles in her bag again and pulls out a book. Frantically looks up a page, then props it on the bed beside her. The book is called* Your Baby from Birth – A–Z.)

Once Baby is out in the world, many new mothers expect that the hard work is over. So don't be alarmed if the reality of day-to-day childcare seems daunting at first, especially on top of the broken nights and the energy you're using up breast-feeding . . .

H:   Okay, okay, let's get to the chase, time's not on our side here . . .

. . . The good news is that in the first few weeks you'll probably find yourself doing this eight or ten times a day, so, assuming you've laid in a plentiful supply of nappies and wipes . . .

P:   Waaaaaah!
CHORUS:  WAAAAAAAAHHHHH!
*(Piglet's yelling has now started all the other babies yelling. The neighbouring mother will be awake any minute. Helen hungrily eyes the huge pile of Pampers, dives at them and yanks two out, hiding the spare beneath her sheets.)*

. . . working quickly to keep Baby calm, slip the clean nappy beneath the dirty one . . .

*(Piglet is now puce all over. Helen shoves the stolen nappy under him, realises too late that it's still folded, also that it's no longer clean, having been liberally smeared on the way in.)*

. . . with the clean nappy opened beneath Baby, and holding Baby's legs in one hand, use the other to fold the dirty nappy and throw it into the bin . . .

*(Helen grabs Piglet's legs with one hand, scrunches up the dirty nappy with the other, hurls it over the side of the bed, and flaps the not-very-clean nappy wildly to open it. Meanwhile Piglet dumps another big pile directly on to the bedclothes, the hand holding him, and the book.)*

. . . now take a wipe with your free hand and ge . . .

*(the following text has been obliterated)*

H:   *(near tears)* Free hand? What free hand?

P:   Waaaaaah!

*(The mother in the next bed stirs and wakes. Wearily picks her own yelling baby out of its cot. Rolls over to grab a nappy from her pack, which has acquired some telltale black stains of its own. Helen hunches over Piglet to conceal her activities. The neighbour changes her own baby's nappy with the speed and grace of an expert, fixing Helen with a beady, suspicious eye throughout. A hand descends on Helen's shoulder. She jumps about a mile.)*

C:   Morning, sweetheart. Hey, projectile shitting – see, he can already do things we can't. I'll fetch you some Swarfega later.

*(Helen looks up to see two cappuccinos, a bag of croissants, and Colum. Bursts into tears.)*

## 22 August, 2000

*Relief of yesterday gave way to concern on discovering that, though hardware seems all in place and in proper allocation, have been provided with little or no functioning control software. Refuelling still proving tricky, waste disposal random and continuous, and all four limbs waving independently.*

*More alarming yet, host seems to have even less of a clue than I do, and is given to loud sounds and violent movements which make me, to say the least, uneasy. Moreover, all attempts at communication with adults still totally unsuccessful – my language seems unintelligible to them (though neighbouring comrades understand me fine) and my attempts to emulate their noises don't seem to impress either.*

*One bright spot on the landscape provided by donor, who turned up today when things were getting very sticky indeed and sorted it all out in no time.*

*If only I had the Training Manual to help ascertain whether hardware or software problem. Maybe occupants of adjacent beds will suggest solution.*

**22–23 August, 2000** – Partial transcript of emergency summit of all six babies in Postnatal Ward, St Winifred's Hospital

P: *(softly at first, to next-door baby)*
Waaaa? Waaaaah . . . (Hey, you – you awake?)

B2: *(sleepily)* Weeewaaaa? WaaH! ( Whassat? Who's this?) *(more brightly)* Wah, wah, wah? (Look, everybody, a newcomer! How was your trip?)

P: Wah wa. Wahaa? (Don't ask. Who else is here?)

BOTH: *(loudly)* WAAAAAH!!! WAAAAAAH!!!! WAAAAAAHHH! (BOYS AND GIRLS! EMERGENCY SUMMIT.)
*( faint voices from the four remaining babies)*

B3: Whhoooohh? ( What, now?)

B4: Wee, wee, wee! (Don't forget me!)

B5/6: *(twins)* Eeee! EEEEEH! (Move over! Hey, who are you shoving?)
*(A nurse staggers wearily in, snaps on the light. The babies instantly shut up. The mothers dazedly turn over. The nurse says, authoritatively, 'Shhhhhhhhh!', turns out the light again and leaves.)*

B4: *(nervously)* Whewewe? (Can I go back now? I don't like it here!)

P: *(determined)* Wa wa! Wa wa wa wa! Waaaaaaa, wahahah wa – wa – wa wahhha. Wa wha, wa?
(Look, everybody, I've only just arrived and I don't know any of you, but my hardware is malfunctioning, my communications software seems to need an upgrade, and I'm not at all sure my host is competent. Can any of you help?)

B2:     Weeigh, wuh. (Sounds pretty standard. It's a bit of a shock at first, isn't it?)

B5/6:   *(excited)* Eehh! Eeee? Eee – eehee – eehe – e – eeeeeee! (How about a swap? You can come and take her place – no, his – no, hers – no, his, you big bully you, just because you're twenty minutes older . . .)

*(All the babies are now yelling over each other at once. Helen and the other mothers dive under the pillows. The nurse opens a drawer and pulls out a pair of grimy earplugs. The summit continues for several hours.)*

### 23 August, 2000

Terrible racket all night long from babies setting each other off. Tried to calm nerves by going to have bath, entailing long trek down chilly unlit corridor not unlike route to Death Row execution chamber, but kept rushing back to sound of what I thought was my Piglet's cry. Piglet's cry absolutely indistinguishable from that of all other babies on ward, do not recognise it at all, especially among cry of five others. Barely recognise Piglet, except know he's the badly wrapped one with the black blotches all over. (The woman in the next bed gave me some remedial tuition, probably to save her nappy pile from even more rapid depletion. Amazing how much one turns out to have in common with the most unlikely people in these circs. Much like London in the Blitz, I guess.)

Seriously concerned about my total lack of maternal instinct – surely the mere sight of my own progeny should produce a response of some sort, if only for Richard Dawkins-type Selfish Gene reasons? (Maybe I have unselfish genes? Always thought of myself as the unselfish type.) As for the promised surge of 'Aaaah' akin to the first moments of falling in love – no discernible surge of anything except panic and a sort of vague pity for anybody at the mercy of such an obvious incompetent.

Maybe I am in fact a psychotic, Sylvia-Plath-like mother, rejecting baby for reasons too deep to be consciously aware of. Or could baby be rejecting me first? Colum always said nobody will love you unless you love yourself. Maybe he's smelling my fear? (Thinking about it, this last very unlikely as no smell could come close to competing with Piglet's excretions.)

Speaking of Colum, have sent him off to buy baby gear as detailed by lovely Mrs Yussuf in the next bed. He took the mobile in case he got into difficulties, but as the ward phone is permanently occupied by 10,000 distant relatives of the other mothers, checking the form of the runners in the 2.30 at Dar el Sha'arf, he's unlikely to be able to get through anyway. It'll do him good.

**23 August, 2000** – Colum's shopping list

bibs
Babygros
short-sleeved vests
nappies
wipes – organic, unscented
baby blankets – all cotton
Moses basket
changing mat
baby powder – unscented, additive-free

**23 August, 2000**

*A bit tired today – emergency summit with other comrades continued into the small hours, but failed to produce any encouraging answers. Nobody has received any form of communication or instruction from Mission Control, though a couple of them have lucked out with more expert hosts than mine. Non-verbal methods seem to be the only comms channel open so far – all agreed that there's a fairly direct correlation between turning up the volume knob and getting attention, no matter what one is saying at the time, which is a bit unexpected but good to know.*

*Host appears gradually to be acquiring some basic competence, though she does still have a habit of yelping loudly at feeding time which I sometimes find a bit off-putting. Food itself, when I can get to it, is very nice, though requiring considerably more effort than the direct hose injection method. Come to think of it, it's probably snack time again by now . . .*

**23 August, 2000** – Georgie's visit, accompanied by Tamsin and Jack

> *(Behind her barricade of flowers and balloons, now augmented by fruit, chocolate brownies, HobNobs, etc., Helen is trying not to scream out loud while Piglet feeds. She is holding him rigidly at a strange angle, like a novice skydiver. Georgie watches her children with one eye as they play havoc among the beds, while picking fastidiously through the fruit bowl.)*

G:   *(mouth full of peach)* Sho how's feeding going? Don't shup-poshe you've . . . any help from . . . usheless lot.
> *(louder – directed at a passing nurse)*
>
> They're only in'ested shwipe your food while you nap.
> *(Helen tries to disappear under the bedclothes, which provokes a yell from Piglet)*

H:   Well, it does hurt quite a lot, and he seems to be hungry all the time. I mean, I think it's hunger, but it could be anything, of course . . .
> *(Georgie looks up from the fruit bowl, wipes her peachy fingers on the bed-sheets, and swoops in on Piglet. In mid-yell, recognising an authority, he shuts up like magic. Georgie adjusts his wrappings, holds him against Helen at a different angle, wiggles Helen's breast into his mouth, and wraps Helen's arms around him. Helen looks up. A radiant smile spreads across her face.)*

H: It doesn't hurt! What did you do?

G: I did what these useless drones *(at another passing nurse)* ought to have done two days ago.

*(A baby's scream and a torrent of angry voices from the other end of the ward. Georgie doesn't even bother to turn round.)*

G: You two! Here! Now!

*(Tamsin and Jack appear from beneath one of the farther beds and hurtle towards Helen's)*

T: Where is he, where is he? Can I hold him?

J: What's he doing? *(piercing yell)* WHAT ARE YOU DOING, AUNTIE HELEN? IS THAT YOUR BOOBIE? She's got her boobie out, Tamsin, look look look!

T: Oh, yuck! That's yucky, isn't it, Mum?

*(The two children collapse in giggles, banging against Piglet, who stops feeding to yell some more. Georgie picks him up and hangs him casually over her shoulder. Once again, he shuts up instantly.)*

## 23 August, 2000

*At last! Can't say much right now as am under siege from inter-mediate-sized humans who appear frighteningly immune to all charm and defencelessness signals, but it seems than an agent from Mission Control has finally appeared in the nick of time. Can't make much visual distinction between agent blob and host blob — however, fairly confident will be able to identify her in future by strong smell and loud voice. Hey, back off . . .*

## 23 August, 2000

Georgie came by just now with her children and helped me with feeding, etc. Never knew how much we had in common! I love her so much! She is so wise and patient!

Unfortunately, while they were still here Colum finally re-appeared having been gone about three days. All he had bought was one pack of plain bibs and one set of pink Babygros, which were apparently the only ones without patterns, and slipped by the Aesthetic Police veto on grounds of counteracting gender stereotyping. Failed utterly to buy basket (too frilly), blankets (bear pattern), changing mat (too bright), vests (obstrusive logo), wipes (couldn't read tiny print on label as too vain to take glasses with him), baby powder (no unscented where he went) or nappies.

No nappies! Georgie informed him, possibly a little too forcefully, that ALL disposable nappies have pictures of tiny whales, dolphins, Mickey Mouse driving fire engine, etc., and he could waste a lot of time trying to find them in Bauhaus colourways while his son became famous as the Scrounger of Ward D. Now gone off again in a sulk for Huggies and cappuccinos.

**23 August, 2000** – Partial transcript of mobile phone conversation between Colum and Huggies Customer Support

H:  Thank you for calling Huggies Customer Support! We value your call! Your call may be monitored for staff training purposes. Please stay on the line and a Huggies Customer Service Representative will be with you shortly!
*(long pause while Huggies switchboard plays off-key digital rendering of Brahms' Lullaby' scratched into chip in Pyong Yang)*

C:  God save us! (No, sorry, do go ahead, I'm in no rush here – cheers . . .)

H:  We apologise for the delay, which is due to a high volume of calls!

C:  . . . oh, and not to your tight-fisted refusal to employ enough people, I guess . . . (No, no quarrel with Coffee Republic whatsoever, one double vanilla latte . . .)

H:  Thank you for calling Huggies Customer Support . . .

C:  . . . okay, okay (with whipped cream, and a . . .)

H:  Sorry?

C: Incredible, a living human at last. Hang on, don't go anywhere (. . . and a triple espresso in a tall cup. Cheers.) Okay, Huggies. Carry on.

H: . . . My name is Kylie from Huggies Customer Support. May I please have your name, last name first?

C: McCallum – Colum McCallum. I'll spell that for you, shall I? Big M, small C . . . (What's that – here, just grab it out of my wallet, will you, this is rather an important call . . .) Sorry about that, Kylie, where were we?

H: I'll just put it in how it sounds, shall I? And where do you buy your Huggies?

C: Well, so far nowhere but I . . .

H: Well, if you tell me where you live I'll find the closest place to you. Can I have your postcode please?

C: Ummm – that'd be – look, it doesn't matter, it's about . . .

H: I can tell you that most branches of Boots, Sainsbury's, Tesco and Asda do stock a full range, Mr McMallow. And which size and type of Huggies do you buy? Boy or girl, newborn, mini, midi, maxi, junior, pull-up or drynites?

C: You know, actually . . . (These mine? Cheers, yes, keep your hair on, I'm leaving now) . . . really, if you could just put me through to a supervisor . . . Ow!

**23 August, 2000** – Partial transcript of phone message from Huggies Customer Support supervisor to Huggies HQ

C.S.: Hello? Is that Marketing? Customer Support here, Joyce. Look, I feel a bit silly leaving this but I just had a customer who was very insistent that I pass this on . . . Kept going on about a range of designer nappies in plain colours – went into all sorts of detail about no pastels and I don't know what all, but anyhow I promised to pass it on. Honestly, you'd have thought with a baby to worry about and – well, anyhow, sorry to take up your time. Cheers!

**5 September 2000** – Memo from Huggies Marketing Department

TO:  Product line managers
     Product design
     Product testing
     Product safety
     Psychographics
     Advertising

Hi guys,
We're way overdue to brainstorm our design and packaging
strategies – strong evidence coming in that there's a willing
AB1 early-adopter segment who will pay a hefty premium for
something that looks designery (you'll know the sort of thing,
Marcus). We've gone about as far down the road as I can
justify technologically, but if we can squeeze a few extra quid
out of them on superficials, it's worth a shot. Let's all get
together Monday in the second-floor boardroom and knock it
about a bit, shall we – say 2 p.m.?

pp:   Alastair
(gl/ad ref 200094)

**24 August, 2000**

Home at last. So soothing after the racket of the hospital. Quite
sorry to leave Mrs Yussuf and little Akbar in the end but not
sorry to leave those twins and their smug 'look no hands I've
done it a million times' mother. Managed to smuggle some of
those lethal painkillers out in my bra, just in case.

Colum was so apologetic about keeping us waiting while he
cancelled all his cards, but at least they found the wallet itself
with that picture of me in Uberlingen – he said it was very
busy in the Coffee Republic so probably the people serving just
didn't notice it lying there. Anyhow, he's been extra sweet ever

since to make up, and I have to admit the place does look nice – it's amazing how much tasteful baby stuff there is around if you really look for it.

## 24 August, 2000

*Just as I was getting used to transit camp, forging relationships, working on strategy, etc., they moved us to new base. Bleak in extreme – nothing like transit camp. No patterns, colours or decoration of any kind, no giraffes, baby elephants, fluffy cloudscapes or unicycling clowns. More like Basic Training illustrations of prison camp or long-stay psychiatric institution.*

*Worst of all, apparently free of intelligent life, no sign of that envoy from Mission Control or any other comrades. May have to tough it out here alone for a while.*

## 26–27 August, 2000 – Exchange of e-mails

**From:** Colum McCallum [collum@guzzi.freeserve.com]
**Sent:** 26 August 2000
**To:** Billy Giddens [billy@billygoat.demon.co.uk]

Hi Bill,
Been a bit hectic around these parts lately. No regrets whatsoever re chopping in bikes – should have done it years ago. It's pretty clear from the way things have been these last few days that every moment of the next twenty years (and beyond) is spoken for – I'll be lucky if I even get to read the mag you're kindly sending me (cheers for that, by the way).

Something spooky seems to have happened to Her Indoors since arrival of Junior – you know she's never been exactly one to rush for the vacuum in

a free moment, but in the last two days she's
cleaned the entire place from top to bottom,
twice, most recently at 4.39 a.m. Does your
experience shed any light on this – can I expect
an onion-like unveiling of new layers of personality every few weeks from now on?

Baby seems fine – doing all expected things,
alarm signals all hard wired, rolls into corners
– common sense seems to sort out most of it.

Anyhow, mail us back when you can – off to buy
Microban . . .

Col

----------------------------------

**From**: Billy Giddens [billy@billygoat.demon.co.uk]
**Sent**: thursda
**To**:     Colum McCallum [collum@guzzi.freeserve.com]

col me ol mmuker
happens to them all first time arons. its all
ormones, nohin you can do about it excep lie
low and keep thigs stable at yor end. pretty
soon she will run out of steam and collapse
into state of slobbish inolence and from then
on thins iwll be run from prone position in
an easychair to sound of dayime telly.

so make teh most of it i say, if you;ve
any leatehrs that need poishnig now's teh
tiem to give 'em to her.

glad it has all fingers and toes. hang on
in there

bill

----------------------------------

## 28 August, 2000

Joy of homecoming to our cosy, if minimalist, nest almost immediately interrupted by flapping of cloaks and scratching of broomsticks as every mother, ex-mother or aspiring mother I've ever known spiralled in, laden with mysterious offerings and contradictory advice. Listening to them, one might be forgiven for wondering how the human race has survived until now (though it has to be said there are a few mutations among their own offspring I might want to steer clear of in the gene pool).

Some consolation in the accompanying presents, though interesting that the desirable stuff – silver teething ring, pink marabou slippers, Kaffir Lime luxury foot treatment, spa vouchers, etc. – all came from sympathetic single friends, while the haggard old multiple mums came up with vile-smelling nipple cream and cabbages. Evidently there's a whole underground community of nursing mothers tooling around town with cabbage leaves stuffed in their bras. Why it should be more desirable to smell of cottage cheese and sauerkraut than Penhaligon's Bluebell body freshener is a mystery to me – hope it stays that way.

Was in danger of becoming v confused by all the advice, especially as every succeeding witch in the coven emphasised that only her way would save us from life with a babbling idiot and a severely curtailed social round in consequence, when an e-mail arrived from America which made it all clear.

E-mail from America – 28 August 2000

```
> > > > > >
The Dos and Don'ts of Life with a Newborn
> > > > > >
> > Sleeping
> > Do not put your baby to sleep on her
back. She will choke.
```

> > On no account put her to sleep on her
front. She will suffocate.
> > Never, ever put her to sleep on her
side. She will roll over, either on to her
front or her back. And if you must, alternate
sides at least nightly, or she'll grow up
squooshed and never be invited anywhere.
> > > > > >
> > Feeding Time
> > Don't allow baby to feed lying down. Her
stomach needs to be lower than her head to
digest her food.
> > Make sure she learns to feed lying down
right away, or you'll never get any sleep
yourself, and she'll end up as a smear on
the wall at 3 a.m.
> > Remember! Swap breasts every feed,
however long she fed last time.
> > Do NOT swap your baby from one breast to
the other. Breast milk, like cafeteria lunch,
comes in courses – watery soup milk to start
with, robust meat-and-potatoes milk to follow,
and rich dessert milk last of all. Babies who
fail to eat their greens will never get
dessert either, and will fail to thrive.
> > > > > >
> > Heat and Cold
> > Keep baby tightly wrapped at all times.
It will comfort her and help her sleep.
> >Never constrict her freedom of movement
with tight wrappers, coverlets or clothing.
How will she ever learn to kick?
> > > > > >
> > Going Out

> > Don't expose your baby's skin to the
harmful rays of the sun. Keep him indoors, or
in heavy shade, at all times.
> > Put him in the sun as much as possible –
he needs the vitamin D.
> > Take him into the sun if you must, but
cover him first with (organic) baby-specific
(i.e. three times the price) sun cream.
> > Do not on any account put ANY cream or
any other chemical on to your baby's skin.
How you could you even dream of such a
thing, you unnatural parent, you!
> > > > > >
> > Bonding
> > NEVER leave your baby, day or night, as
this will lead to separation anxiety and
feelings of rejection and betrayal, resulting
in zero self-worth and inability to hold down
any job. If there are jobs by then.
> > Don't crowd your baby – give him his own
space, from birth on, and NEVER have him
sleep in your bed – unless you sincerely want
to tag along on your sixteen-year-old's
dates. . . .

. . . Got to this point and realised that there could be such a
thing as too much expertise. Everybody knows Americans are
obsessed with rules, something to do with not having a common
culture, I think – you know, they all arrive on Ellis Island from
all over the world, sharing nothing but a strong conviction that
it can't be worse than where they came from, speaking different
languages, eating different food – no wonder everything has to
be written down in a constitution. Whereas ancient and civilised
countries, such as ours, just gradually accrete a culture over the

centuries, in which a nod and a wink, or alternatively an 'All right, guv?', speak volumes, nothing is written down in case the ruling class might need to change its mind, but everybody knows without having to be told that the clotted cream goes under the jam, and that beer is infinitely nicer drunk at the temperature of a warm bath. The ultimate proof of this rule is, of course, Italy, where they have no immigrants and don't even manage to have a government most of the time, but everybody gets on perfectly well and daily life is about as civilised as a mortal could bear.

Anyhow, before I could get seriously depressed, another e-mail arrived, this time from Devon, which put things in considerably more cheering perspective.

E-mail from Barnstaple – 28 August 2000

```
>NEW MOTHER ALERT > THINGS AREN'T SO BAD!
> > > > > >
> > So here you are, sitting in a bleary
haze of sleeplessness and stinging nipples,
wondering how you came to make the worst
mistake of your life, and desperately
searching your infant for the return address.
> > > > > >
> > BUT! Before you call Social Services,
remember! The arrival of a child provides an
unarguable excuse for things you'd never get
away with otherwise. Here are a few to start
you thinking. (Once you get the idea, plenty
more will follow.)
> > > > > >
Buying a car.
> > Yes, of course it's destroying the ozone
layer, but how can you be expected to expose
```

your firstborn to the germs, rain, dirty air
and 18-certificate road rage that not having
one would entail?
> > > > > >
Getting fat.
> > Everybody knows that your milk will dry
up if you don't eat that Marks and Spencer
Sticky Toffee Pudding. Sticky Toffee Pudding
is the principal ingredient of milk. Ask any
cow.


. . . (there you go. I know for a fact there's no Sticky Toffee
Pudding in America. They're obviously jealous.)


Wearing the same clothes every day.
> > in the last nine months you have been a
size ten top and bottom, a size twelve top
and bottom, a size twelve top, eighteen
middle and you can no longer see your bottom,
and a size eighteen top with diminishing
middle and bottom. No income could possibly
keep up, still less on three hours' sleep.
Why don't they make Babygros for parents,
too? It'll have to be the sweatpants, again.
> > > > > >
Failing to tidy up.
> > You were, of course, on the point of
picking up the newspaper, removing the
exoskeleton of dust and grime from the hi-fi,
putting the last three days' dirty clothes
into the laundry bin (well, let's be honest,
back into the cupboard - see above) when the
baby screamed to be fed/exploded into its
nappy/ became suddenly riveted by the stripes

125

on its toy zebra, a vital learning experience
no mere domestic trivia could justifiably
interrupt.

> > > > > >

Refusing unattractive engagements

> > . . . especially before 10 a.m. or after
6 p.m. All you need mutter is 'got to feed
the baby'. People will be too embarrassed to
enquire further, and with luck won't mention
that they saw you sneaking into the first
screening of that George Clooney movie with a
giant popcorn and a mega king cone. What were
they doing at a George Clooney movie at
lunch-time, anyhow?

> > > > > >

Forgetting obligations.

> > For the first six months of your child's
life, or until it leaves home, you will only
be able to absorb EITHER the first OR the
last half of any sentence addressed to you.
Thus it's perfectly plausible for you to
allege that you remembered 'We're having some
people round to tea on Sunday' and forgot
'Could you bring that delicious gingerbread
of yours?' (Do not, however, try this on the
Inland Revenue. They have never had babies.
Human ones, that is.)

> > > > > >

Playing silly games.

> > After all, when your father, respected
elder statesman or pillar of the Rotarians,
picks up the child for the first time and
immediately recites, 'There was a young lady
from Ealing, Who walked upside down on the

```
ceiling', you're excused your lapses, too.
And in the new millennium, 'This Little Pig
Went to Market' is no longer just a mindless
bit of fun; it's a reflexology massage.
```

. . . (which reminds me, must try all the other stuff out on
Georgie. The more I see of other mothers, the more I realise
that her masters in geophysics must mean something, after all.)

```
> > > > > >
Buying exorbitant toys.
> > Now that you can get your hands on that
Scalextric set you always wanted, who cares
about DKNY?
```

## 28 August, 2000

*Major convention of hosts around here today, presumably called to upgrade
skills of mine. Convenient for espionage purposes that they don't seem
to realise I can understand everything they say, but slightly alarming
that it all seems totally contradictory. Presumably they have their own
Training Manuals and were working from different editions.*

*Most of them arrived with supplies, which was thoughtful, though
those shiny fluffy pink things make pretty uncomfortable pillows, and
worse snacks. However, have passed increasingly tedious time (nothing
to do and no means of doing it — had hoped things would look up
after touchdown) guessing which offering related to which visitor, which
gave pretty accurate reading of their respective competence levels. For
instance, would definitely not like to be left alone for any time with the
one who brought the black body-bag with red spots. Have no intention
of going out on manoeuvres, even undercover, looking like pocket calcu-
lator.*

**30 August, 2000**

Ernestine dropped by with an ultra-glam, dry-clean-only Cyberdog baby outfit, already two sizes too small (Piglet is living up to his nickname – too late to change it to George Clooney, I suppose). She explained that it looked cute in the tiny size, and it was really meant to be kept so he could be amazed in later life at what we all wore when he was born. Speak for yourself, I said, from the safety of my ankle-length Ghost slobbing dress (have decided that Ghost is hardly an extravagance at all, given that it's all machine washable, doesn't show stains, comes pre-wrinkled, is forgivingly bias-cut and shapeless, and opens down the front. In fact, they could market it specifically to new mothers, just by changing the name to Zombie.)

Would have taken the anorak straight back (no intention of giving Piglet any extra excuses to jeer at us in our declining years) except no chance of finding anything in Cyberdog to exchange it for, given their market demographic (Camden Town pre-teen Goth). At least all the fluffy-bunny M&S Babygros can be chopped in for knickers. Speaking of which, better hide them before the Design Nazi gets back from 'buying nappies'. Strange that it never occurs to him to buy two packs at once . . .

**30 August, 2000** – Partial transcript of conversation in Bog and Badger between Colum and Persons unknown

> *(owing to the high background noise level and the less than perfect articulation of various speakers, their identities are indicated here by number)*

1: Oi, Patch! PAAAAAATCH! Over 'ere! 'Nother round all round, cheers, matey! Cheers, Col – 'ow's it feel, then?

C: Och, nothing to it. It's not the baby, it's the witches' chorus that comes behind. The money we've been spending on teabags and biscuits since he arrived, I could have him down for Eton. I've barely seen the wee scrap.

*(scrape of glass being shoved across bar)*

C: This for me? I shouldn't leave her at night, she's getting no sleep . . .

2: She'll be glad of a bit of shut-eye while you're gone, then, won't she?

*(Chink of glasses being raised, random shouts of 'Cheers'. Prolonged pause for glugging.)*

3: Tell you what, son, nobody talks about it but there's a conspiracy out there to make it all a big mystery.

4: Conspiracy? What, by who? (Any o' those Bombay Puris left down your end? Cheers . . .)

3: Well, the women, innit? Keep us out the way, make out it's brain surgery, get their claws in the kids and turn 'em against us before we can do anything. I know that's what 'appened to me, the cunt . . .

2: Steady on, Andy, this is supposed to be Colum's big cele-bration, remember.

3: Oh, yeah, sorry, 'nother double, Patch, when you've got a mo . . .

1: He's got a point, though, you gotta get in there, get stuck in, roll your sleeves up – after all, if Beckham and Damon Albam can change a nappy . . .

2: Thass' right, an' Warren Beatty an' Liam Gallagher . . .

1: . . . If they can do it, so can you. Show 'er there's nothing special about being a mum . . .

C: You know, I did read something in *Scientific American* a while back about how holding babies changed men's hormones too . . .

2: What, they grew bazookas? Nah, that's going it a bit, I'd say . . . 'Ere, Patch, what you doin' over there, we're waiting this end.

C: Not for me, honestly . . .

2: She'll be asleep by now, waste of time goin' 'ome – 'oo knows when you'll get back 'ere?

Some time later

*(background noise level now considerably higher, thus transcription errors possible)*

?: . . . 'appiest ways of your wife, I *(unintelligible)* you . . .

?: . . . they throw up so fast, make the *(unintelligible)* of it gun . . .

C: . . . you're rife, I know you are, iss great! . . .

?: . . . bereave me, if you can weed an annual, you can drain a maybe!

**31 August, 2000**

Barely awake today. Temper somewhat frayed in consequence – hope not augury of things to come. Colum arrived home from 'wetting baby's head' (suspect partial revenge for recent invasions by Witches of Eastwick) at 23.45 and insisted on changing baby's nappy, there and then. Explained nappy-changing arcane and complex art akin to Tea Ceremony, requiring practice ten times a day for months, and more crucially that baby was finally asleep, in clean nappy, after screaming, writhing and yelling throughout his (Colum's) absence, which incidentally was CONSIDERABLY longer than the forty-five minutes originally estimated to 'buy nappies'. Might as well have been talking to the Lottery Fairy – he just barged drunkenly in, baby woke all smiles and gurgles, bastard did job in about two seconds flat, baby went happily back to sleep and Colum spent the next three hours keeping me awake and making whole bed shake laughing at his own pathetic jokes about Zen and the Art of Poo, and the striking similarities between maintaining babies and maintaining bikes.

Excerpt from Moto Guzzi Le Mans Mk 2 Workshop Manual, p.23: 'Dismantling the Crank Case'

First drain the sump (eight bolts) by removing the sump guard. Allow the oil to drain into a suitable receptacle and dispose of carefully. Remove the engine from its frame (four bolts). Clean exterior of engine with suitable branded grease remover. Lay cleaned engine upside down on a padded worktop. Inspect unit for chafing or fatigue . . .

## 3 September, 2000

*Relieved to discover there seems to be one competent adult around (donor), though appears randomly and doesn't smell as good as host. Not entirely sure why he needed to inspect exhaust just after host had done it, but possibly he is in fact higher up chain of command and conducting spot check. (This theory borne out by less frequent appearances — presumably he has many hosts and babies to supervise and is busy elsewhere most of time.)*

## 5–7 September, 2000 – Exchange of e-mails

**From:** Colum McCallum [collum@guzzi.freeserve.com]
**Sent:** 5 September
**To:** Billy Giddens [billy@billygoat.demon.co.uk]

Hi Bill,
Saw rather handsome new 916 in latest *Bike*. Have you heard anything about it? Now that I'm past all that it's rather pleasant to be able to take a more detached interest. I suppose it'll be a while before they come through.
    Have to say all this stuff about the complexities of childcare has me baffled. 'Course there

are a few places where the design could be
improved – no visible diurnal rhythm settings,
no waste overflow tank or input/output regula-
tors, plus an emergency cutout switch would be
useful in case of parents' urgent need to pee,
eat or sleep. But the basic mechanics seem
pretty straightforward.

   Still, it gives her something to do, apart
from moping around talking about sleep. Think I
preferred the midnight cleaning.

   Col

----------------------------------

**From:** Billy Giddens [billy@billygoat.demon.co.uk]
**To:**   Colum McCallum [collum@guzzi.freeserve.com]

ah col,
of course it's a piece of cake, qesiotn is,
would we want to do it insttead? theye goin to
leave anyhow so the way i lok at it, beyond a
certain poin it's a wasted invesmtnet

   talking o which, the Corsa'll be the one to go
for. Stebe'll know when it's due over here.

   bill

----------------------------------


**8 September, 2000** – Partial transcript of dialogue between Helen
and Piglet at the Changing Mat

H:  There, that's nice, isn't it? No more stinky poo.
P:  Ghhhhhss. (It took you long enough to notice.)
H:  It's not your fault you can't do anything for yourself yet, is
    it? But you know, I'll always look after you . . .
P:  ii-i-i? (Is that a threat or a promise?)

132

H: As long as I live, I'll never ever ever leave you or hurt you or not be there all the time for you, you know that! *(sound of prolonged kissing and snuggling)*

P: Wah!!! (I need to breathe, you know!)

H: Oh, did I frighten you? You're so tiny and it's all so new, isn't it? Mmmm, you smell so yummy. Even . . . *(long intake of breath)* . . . mmm, even that. That's a bit sick, to be honest. Better not tell Daddy about that. It'll be our little secret, shall it?

P: Ghssssppsss. (Personally I'd rather forget it, too. Smell your own nappies if you must.)

H: Mummy will always be here with you. Except . . . *(sharp intake of breath)* except . . . *(suppressed sob)* . . . one day – one day I won't! One day there won't be a Mummy, or a *(sob)* . . . or a Daddy, any more ever again!!! Who will look after you then? One day . . .
*(remainder barely intelligible through heaving sobs)*
. . . you'll be alive *(sob)*, and we'll be *(sob)* DEAD!! . . . and you'll see *(sob)* me *(sob)* dead, and then you'll be all alone in the world! And you're so little!!

P: Waaaahh! Wahh! Wahh! (Pull yourself together, for goodness' sake.)
*(sound of doorbell ringing)*

H: *(sniff)* What's that? *(sniff sniff)* Silly Mummy, that's not going to happen for ages *(sob)* yet – but . . .
*(doorbell rings again, twice)*

H: Just coming! *(sob)* Mummy didn't mean to upset you, precious. There there . . .
*(sound of door opening)*

H: Oh – hi, Mum *(sniff)*. OHHHHHH!!! *(Collapses into racking sobs. Mother and baby both now crying hysterically. Sound of door closing.)*

## 10 September, 2000

Mum came round, she was in town for some old people's shopping trip or something, and found me in floods of tears. She was so sweet! Now I know what she went through. So glad she's still alive so I can tell her how much I love her. Poor, poor her! And all my life I've been so horrible to her, and I took that cardigan back to Next last Christmas and exchanged it for the cheaper one thinking she wouldn't know the difference, and of course she did only she's too nice to say anything – I'm such a cow! And after she gave up her life's work to spend twenty-five years teaching geography to horrible adolescents in East Grinstead, just because Georgie came along a year before the Pill did . . . Must call Georgie and share, she's been through it all too . . .

### Some time later

Well, I must say, I knew Georgie had a few faults but I never knew she was so self-righteous. All I said was maybe we should do something for Mum, like take her out for a really nice meal or something, to say sorry, and she said I was welcome to take Mum out for a meal and in fact I could take her too, the number of times I'd bitten her head off in the past nine months, but personally she didn't feel she had anything to apologise for at all, she'd always been perfectly nice to Mum. Had in fact been all set to make similar apology to Georgie and express my delight at new-found sentiments of shared kinship never suspected before, etc., when she went and spoiled it. Just as well, remembering the state of her bathroom. No wonder her children always have green slime pouring from their noses. We are truly different creatures.

A: Would you mind if I just – there, that's better.

G: Christ, is that the Action Man helmet again? That's the third time this week I've found it there. I wouldn't mind so much if he didn't keep forgetting where he's put it. Sit back now, just relax – mmmm, that all seems a lot better, indigestion gone, has it?

A: I keep telling you, darling, I never get indigestion.

G: Lucky you to have me looking after you. Most people your age . . .

A: Could we try just once, do you think, to have an afternoon where my age doesn't feature as Topic of the Day? I'm beginning to feel like a talk show.

G: Speaking of talk shows, have you had a call from Helen lately? This might tingle. Your eyes are a bit bloodshot.

A: Thank . . . Aaaaagh! Sssss! As a matter of fact she . . .

G: Don't worry, the tears will wash it out, whatever it is. I tried to tell her it was a bit bloody late. Did she offer to take you out for the best dinner of your life?

A: Yes, she . . .

G: She wanted me along too, but I don't think I could stand it. Hang on, what's this? Have you had any breathing difficulty lately – hoarseness, short breath, anything?

A: No, nothing like that.

G: You can't be taking enough exercise. If you were exercising you'd definitely be short of breath. You should be more careful.

A: She was rather sweet, actually. Told me she finally understood what I'd been through all these years, said she was sorry for being so condescending and ungrateful . . .

G: Yes, I got all that too. It's just her hormones. She'll be her usual crabby sarcastic self again by next week, don't worry.

A:  Ouch!

G:  I didn't touch you.

A:  I know, dear, it's *(sound of rustling and shifting)* . . . is this part of that other thing?

G:  God, no, that's — that's Brian's nose-clipper thingy, he brought it down to look for a new battery, but that was ages ago. Here, I'll just put it . . . There, he can't miss it there.

A:  Are you going to wash that fruit before you serve it to the children?

G:  Mum, it's only been in Brian's nose, for God's sake.

A:  I have to admit I am a bit worried about these emotional extremes — I mean, for all her faults nobody could call her a hysteric, or at least until now. Goodness knows what Colum makes of it all. He's always been so very tolerant of her. I shouldn't say it, I know, but she was truly lucky to get him in the first place, and it would be such a pity . . .

G:  Mum! She's got a few postnatal hormones and you're announcing the divorce. There, that should do it for today — have you finished with that hankie?
*(sound of footsteps going to the kitchen and kettle being filled)*

G:  *(from distance)* Anyhow, what about those stories about you when we were small?

A:  What stories? I don't know what you're . . .

G:  That time at the swimming pool, just for instance . . .

A:  What time? Who told you?

G:  . . . when you jumped in fully clothed on a boiling hot day and scooped some total stranger's perfectly happy baby out and wouldn't give it back. Daddy said you were halfway to the police station before he convinced you it wasn't me.

A:  Oh, nonsense, he made that up, I don't remember . . .

G:  Well, why did you always drive five extra miles to the other pool to take us swimming, then?

A:  It was cleaner.

G: Milk?

*(sound of fridge door opening, somebody taking deep sniff, then . . .)*

G: Mmm – not sure about the milk. Lemon? I can cut off this mouldy bit.

A: No tea for me, thank you. He was a rogue. When did he tell you?

G: Oh, not long before he died. We were chatting in the hospital.

A: The naughty boy *(sigh)*. It's – you'll think me an old softie, but I'd so like him to have seen Helen with a baby too.

G: I know. It's so sad that *(quavery voice)* – that he had to go so young . . .

A: Oh, don't, darling, you'll start me off . . .

G: We really should *(sniff)* go and see her – after all, we're *(sob)* all she has left . . . *(howl)*

*(remainder of the conversation consists largely of snuffles, interrupted by occasional bursts of weepy laughter, and the sound of their departure)*

## 12 September, 2000

*All adult females in vicinity now reduced to sodden wrecks. Even the envoy from Mission Control was wailing over me yesterday. Had not expected quite such frequent or extreme displays of emotion (unless possibly it represents a primitive attempt on their part to learn my language).*

*Things looking fairly desperate until donor arrived for one of his periodic visits. Donor in daylight vastly improved, and far better equipped for most aspects of job than host – big, strong hands, calm, decisive disposition, large flat chest ideal for a quick nap. All in all seems a pity that food supply apparently only available from host, as in other respects he seems a much better bet. What did the manual say?*

Now we are nearing the end of your training, and nearing the end of this manual. So congratulations to all of you – if you've got this far, you'll have done most things right.

At this point – allowing for a couple of days of well-earned R&R after landing – you should be busy reconnoitring your new surroundings, arranging rendezvous with other babies, and possibly even making occasional sorties outside the friendly environment of your new base camp.

But remember: it can never be too soon to establish clear lines of command and control with your host and donor. Initially, the host may appear more susceptible to your tactics, but you may find as time goes on that her resistance strengthens, and the donor – larger and more physically intimidating perhaps, but less hardened by front-line combat – will more readily fall into line.

Divide your attentions between them equally, if possible, and, if this sets them against each other after a while, it can only work to your advantage.

**14 September, 2000** – Colum, Helen and Piglet, in their living room

*(Helen is wandering around the room, still in her Ghost drapery, not as fresh as it might be, with an armful of laundry. Colum is crouched in front of Piglet in his nest on the sofa, leaning in and out like a drunk on a lamppost.)*

H:  Is this the clean or the dirty, can you remember?
*(takes a big sniff of the pile)*
Hmmm. Clean. I think. Must be, it's all odd socks. Then where's the dirty? God, if only I could sleep . . .
*(she wanders out, still soliloquising, like Lady Macbeth fallen on hard times)*

C: *(moving in)* Now I'm clear *(moving back)*. Now I'm fuzzy! *(moving in)* Clear again . . . *(moving out)* . . . fuzzy again! Isn't that interesting, eh?

P: Ungh . . . Ungh . . . *( face goes bright red and contorted)* . . . UNGH! (Attention! Evacuation drill!)

C: Uh-oh. Come here.
*(Scoops up Piglet and heads for the bedroom. Helen has now gone into the bathroom, where the laundry is lying, apparently forgotten, on the floor beside her while she gingerly massages cream into her nipples. As he passes, she cries out . . .)*

H: Jesus – the apricots!
*( . . . and dashes back into the kitchen. Colum has now reached the baby changing zone.)*

C: *(calling back)* Do we have any more nappies, would you know?

H: *(shouting, top of her voice)* Christ, do I have to do EVERY-THING??? If they're not there, there aren't any. He's your baby too! (Shit. They were only on five minutes . . .)
*(Colum leans down to grimace at Piglet, who pees in his face. Colum rewraps him in the same nappy and strolls back into the kitchen, where Helen, still half undressed, is now trying to scrub a blackened saucepan.)*

C: Time for a supermarket run. How about . . .
*(He opens the fridge. A big pile of dirty laundry falls out.)*

C: . . . I found the other socks.

H: I don't have time to deal with socks now! Jesus Christ . . .

C: Tell you what, how about I take the baby, do him good to get out of here. That sling job – have you tried it yet?

H: Do I look like I have time to try out slings?

C: I thought the whole idea was to carry him in it with you, day and night. Like the Stone Age peasants.

H: The Stone Age peasants don't have nice comfy Mario Bellini sofas. That's what it means, being Stone Age.

*(Colum hangs Piglet over his shoulder, goes out, and reappears with a complex arrangement of straps, buckles and padded cloth, not unlike a straitjacket, and a little booklet.)*

C: So there's a manual with it, no problemo. Come on, old son, let's be having ye.

Excerpt from instruction manual for Baby Blossom First Sling (Manuf. by Hoetscher, Wegener, Western Germany, reg. 1997)

WARNING:

This product must not be used by pregnant women, the elderly, or those with back problems, problems of the internal parts, weak bones or inside ear conditions. Please consult your doctor.

WARNING:

This product must only be used in togetherness with, and according to, the manufacturer's instructions. Please call the Baby Blossom helpline. See attached card.

WARNING:

This product was manufactured under conditions of very extreme hygiene and inspected individually before it left our factories. Any deficiencies or defects must be reported immediately to your Baby Blossom representative.

WARNING:

This product is guaranteed to be hypo-allergenic, environment friendly, and manufactured one hundred per cent from recyclable materials. The product's wrappings material are manufactured one hundred per cent from post-consumers recycled material. Please dispose carefully of all packagings material for a healthy planet.

*(Piglet is still hanging, now precariously, over Colum's shoulder. He begins to wail.)*

Take the baby in both hands and lay it caringly on its back in the mid section of the pad body piece, making careful that both legs are liable to extend, the arms are levelling with the arm cutout places, and the neck is supported on the fold-worthy neck section. Fold the neck section, fitting up to the baby's head.

*(Colum has Piglet in the sling jammed against his body with one hand, while he tries to unfold the straps with the other and read the instructions, which have just blown off the sofa on to the floor).*

With the crossed straps upmost, first fit the body piece to your upper torso, alterating the waist straps to a correct fit . . . unclip the left crossed strap and insert your right upper arm . . . Keeping tight of the right crossed strap, insert your left upper arm into it, making correct that the body piece still the baby's postition has not moved.

*(Colum, the sling and Piglet are now all hunched over the floor, where the instructions have shifted a teeny bit under the sofa. Piglet is screaming, very loudly. The sling is half over Colum's face, as he tries, with the hand not holding the baby, to reach a buckle which is exactly in the bit of his back he can't get to.)*

C:   For the love of God, what kind of moron . . . Shh, you, ye're no helping.
*( from the kitchen, the sound of a pan being hurled to the floor, as Helen rushes in, shouting . . .)*

H:   CHRIST, can't you even . . .
*(She pauses in the doorway. Sees Colum, finally out of his depth, knotted up in the sling as Piglet continues to roar. A huge smile spreads over her face.)*

## September, 1999 – Colum's supermarket shopping list

wild rocket, wild baby spinach, baby endive
mixed wild mushrooms, pre-sliced
tiger-striped heirloom tomatoes
purple baby potatoes, pink fir apple potatoes
3 x packs gourmet ready-made soup
crème Fraîche d'Isigny
beurre d'Isigny
Parmigiano Reggiano
mozzarella di bufalo di campagna
raw Jersey extra-creamy breakfast milk
prosciutto di Speck, Black Forest ham
dry-cure free-range back bacon, unsmoked
peppered fillet steaks
lamb nuggets ready stuffed with almonds and apricots
tiger prawns
gravadlax with mustard dressing
tiramisu
double-cream bread-and-butter pudding with muscat
    raisins
extra-thick custard with fresh cream
Lindemans Bin 99 Shiraz
Rolling Rock beer
Jack Daniel's
Spa mineral water
multipack KitKat

TOTAL COST:    £125

**September, 2000** – Colum's supermarket shopping list

organic lettuce /salad – whatever there is
organic potatoes (only if local)
organic cabbage, carrots, onions (any or all)
organic cauliflower (inspect for caterpillars)
organic semi-skimmed milk
organic Cheddar cheese, economy pack
free-range chicken thighs
organic wholewheat pasta
brown basmati rice
economy muesli
Lindemans Bin 99 Shiraz
Rolling Rock
3 x multipacks Huggies newborn
3 x Huggies wipes
hypoallergenic baby bath
no-tears baby shampoo
organic sterilising baby cream
Dettol
non-chlorine bleach
environmental laundry powder, economy size
recycled tie-grip kitchen bags
multipack KitKat

TOTAL:   £130

**14 September, 2000**

I have to say, I have VERY mixed feelings about this Perfect Father act of Colum's. Came back from the supermarket all triumphant, travails with the sling long forgotten – in fact appeared to have neatly transformed himself into Instant Expert on the subject for benefit of some other unfortunate male who was having similar problems in the babycare section. Baby reluctantly handed over to me for usual tedious process of Hunt the Tit, Eat the Fist, etc., otherwise known as yet another feed, and then whisked away for his daily dose of Higher Torque Theory, leaving me to put the shopping away, again, feeling, again, like Blossom, the Mad Cow.

Can this be right? Mother is surely supposed to be primary caregiver and receive primary affection in return for the agonies and deprivations of pregnancy, labour and breast-feeding. What gives father the right just to muscle in when all the unthanked hard work is over? What happened to traditional paternal role of taking no interest, not having a clue, and exposing himself as the perfect scapegoat whenever it all gets too much or goes horribly wrong? Instead of which he bounds nimbly up to the moral high ground, taking everything in his stride, and stands there looking down with that patronising air, refusing to acknowledge that there could possibly be anything to object to in a life spent crawling around on hands and knees wiping vomit off the floor and trying not to gag at the smell in the vicinity of the nappy bin.

Not fair. Damn. May be reduced to calling one of those witches for a good moan.

**15–20 September, 2000** – Exchange of e-mails

**From:** Colum McCallum [collum@guzzi.freeserve.com]
**Sent:** 15 September
**To:** Billy Giddens [billy@billygoat.demon.co.uk]

```
Hi Bill,
Extraordinary how much fitter you feel walking
everywhere than in that helmet in among the
fumes, dodging the reps. I'm amazed I put up
with it for so long. And so much more
opportunity to notice things passing by (even if
they're mostly limited to the old winos
```

144

marshalling the straight to the Camden Town Sainsbury's).

Do you know, by the way – not that I really think we're in any danger of getting into the territory – what might be the early symptoms of postnatal depression? Don't suppose Steph ever had any probs like that, she seems a pretty stable sort, but there've been some slightly alarming incidents around here lately.

Saw one of those 916s going past Sainsbury's – didn't get much of a look but liked what I saw.

Yours

Col

----------------------------------

**From:** Billy Giddens [billy@billygoat.demon.co.uk]
**To:** Colum McCallum [collum@guzzi.freeserve.com]

col matey,

My eart goes out to you. its not post nantal anything, its just they have an excuse, or they think they have, anytin and everythnig they feel lke gettting off their chest comes under the hading of hormones and is fair game. I made the same mistake – what a fool. give em an inch and all that. take my avice, nip it in teh bed sharpish or she'll have yuo by the sort an curlies for life.

That was Steve you saw on the 916. We're going for a run this wekend – your welcome to join in of course (if you can get a pass-out)

cheers

bill

----------------------------------

*(Helen is slumped on the sofa, watching* Don't Try This at Home. *The baby is slumped on top of her, possibly asleep, or possibly just exhausted with the effort of trying to get enough to eat.*
*Colum is slumped beside them, reading* Bike. *Helen stirs, sees what he's reading. Reaches out to stroke the hair from his eyes.)*

H: Do you miss them?

C: What?

H: 'What?' – the bikes, you fool. That lovely big cosy double garage up the road, all empty and forlorn.

C: Nah, never think about 'em.

H: *(sigh)* Who'd have thought it?

C: Thought what?

H: Us here, together on a Saturday night. With a baby. At home. Watching TV . . .
*(Colum senses a hair-trigger situation. He gets up.)*

C: Well, it's a great chance to get things done, isn't it. What happened to all that stuff your lovely friends dropped off?

H: *(innocently)* What stuff?

C: You know.

H: Oh, I probably chucked them all out.

C: They'll be in the dryer, then.

H: You could check the oven, too. What does burning plush smell like?

Some time later

*(Colum is now kneeling on the floor, surrounded by a large and growing pile of flower-and-balloon-printed paper, and ribbon bows. In front of him are two piles of unwrapped presents, one a lot larger, fluffier and more pastel-coloured than the other. Piglet is lying between the piles, turning his head bemusedly from side to side. Colum tears open another big box.)*

C: Christ, what's this supposed to be?

H: *(leaning over to take it)* Mr Clown the Chortling Night Light, obviously.

C: I hadn't heard Stephen King had a toy line. Imagine waking up to that! *(takes it back from her)* 'Batteries included' – that's a first. I'll have them anyhow.
*(He makes to open it and remove them. Helen grabs it from him.)*

H: Hey! That's from Karen. I was at school with her when I was fourteen.

C: Well, she's clearly never got over it.
*(Helen activates a switch and Mr Clown jiggles about, chortling and flashing red and blue lights)*

C: Jesus, it's that American serial killer – what was his name again?
*(He goes to open the last present. He pulls out a cosy sleepsuit and blanket printed all over with Tweenies. One of Piglet's arms, waving randomly, catches the matching Tweenies-patterned bobble cap.)*

P: Ghhiiissss! (Hey, this is cool.)

C: No you don't, you chancer.
*(He whisks it away to join the rejects. All that remains in the other pile is one plain navy coat-and-leggings, one plain white cashmere blanket, and one wooden Galt rattle. Piglet begins to wail.*

*From above, Helen emits a strangled sob and swoops in to pick him up. Colum looks at her. Tears are streaming down her face. He looks at the TV screen. She's watching* Ghostbusters 2. *Helen clutches Piglet to her as she watches the baby in the film lying on the altar, awaiting its fate.)*

C: It's a film, sweetheart.

H: *(wildly)* I can't bear it! It's too awful! Turn it off!

*(Helen is sobbing more or less throughout, hence some gaps in transcription)*

H: . . . and all those asylum-seekers, they have little babies too, and they're in those awful hostels trying to live on thirty-four pounds a week. And what about all those babies in *(huge sob)* . . . Aaaaaaggeraa!! They CUT their *(unintelligible)* OFF!!

*(another burst of weeping)*

A: Sorry?

H: Their heads! In front of their mothers! And what about global warming, all those baby penguins stranded on the polar icecap . . . and the baby foxes when those *(unintelligible)* awful men – horrible . . . tear them to bits in front of them!

A: What's brought all this on, dear? You sounded quite cheerful at teatime.

H: *(unintelligible)*

A: Sorry? It is quite hard . . .

H: *(shouting)* GHOSTBUSTERS!

A: You don't need to shout, dear. Is that a film?

H: *(sniff)*

A: Well, if it upsets you, why are you watching it?

H: OH GOD!!!!

A: Well, there's obviously not a lot you can do about the poor Algerian babies, I agree with you that is very sad, and as for the penguins, I'm sure the British Antarctic Survey are on to it, or David Attenborough will have a charity you can donate to, though personally I think you'd be better off making sure your own baby is all right.

H: *(calmer)* He's fine. He's feeding.

A: Again. You must resist this temptation to feed him every time he . . .

H: Please.

A: I meant, if anything (God forbid) should happen to either of you. Have you made a will recently?

H: I've never made a will at all. I haven't anything to leave.

A: That's not strictly true, dear, and there will be something from me, you know, when – in any case, you need to appoint your residuary legatees.

H: What are they? (Oww!) Sorry, not you, Mum.

A: People to look after the baby, if you die.

H: God, honestly, Mum, I hoped you were going to cheer me up.

A: Just trying to be practical, dear. No sense in hanging about, accidents do happen . . .

H: I haven't left the house for a month.

A: . . . even in the home. Georgie and Brian both have wills.

H: *(perking up)* Really? What's in them? . . .


**28 September, 2000**

Finally got baby to sleep for two hours this afternoon! Spent the time making a will. Have never done this before. Truly concentrates the mind on Big Issues of Life, Death, Great Circle of Being, etc. But also highly enjoyable contemplating the power one could have over friends by manipulating their expectations and playing on their greed and desperation (actually, the only remotely greedy/desperate person I know is Ernestine, and she's already quite a bit better off than I am). Now I know what Dickens was on about. Shame everybody I know is all too aware I haven't a bean. Is it too late to invent wildly rich great-uncle with a dark past?

Got rather tearful when I had to think of people to look

after Piglet when I die from 90 per cent burns after sudden urge to make deep-fried courgette flowers at midnight during power cut (the only likely household fatality that immediately sprang to mind), but cheered up when I realised there's no reason I should be limited in this choice by the constraints of personal acquaintance. After all, it's only random chance that I don't already know Bob Geldof or Mia Farrow or any of those other people who already have lots of children and wouldn't even notice one more. Not to mention that it makes much more sense to bequeath him to somebody like that, who would be able to afford an extra mouth much more easily than poor Georgie and Brian. And famous people could hardly refuse, because of the bad publicity. Mel Gibson has seven children, now I think of it. How hard would it be to make it eight? I might just add him in as a reserve, while I'm about it . . .

## LAST WILL AND TESTAMENT OF HELEN CLAIRE McCALLUM
I, Helen Claire McCallum, being of sound mind and body –

(they usually say that, don't they?)

– hereby set out my wishes in the event of my death.
I request that, first of all, the sum of two thousand pounds (£2,000), or whatever the equivalent is in Euros if we're using them by then, be taken from my savings account (presuming that there's that much left in it) to be spent on a party for my friends and family, said party to be held if possible in the Palm House at Kew Gardens, or if not the Roof Gardens in Kensington. I specifically request that the following guests be invited:

Ms Ernestine Short and partner
Mrs Georgie and Mr Brian Luckworth
My mother, Mrs Alison Carter

Mr Mel Gibson and family
Sir Bob Geldof and family
Ms Mia Farrow and family
Mr George Clooney
and others, to be chosen by Ernestine and Georgie at the time.

I would like the music to be a mixture of 70s disco, 80s
dance music and 90s acid jazz, with maybe some Cole Porter
during dinner.
    I would like a toast in my memory in Lindemans Bin 99
Shiraz, and everybody to dress in black and white.

BEQUESTS
I bequeath the remainder of my estate to my son –

(help, we really ought to give him a name soon)

    – currently known as Piglet, to be held in trust and used for
his upbringing by his guardians (see below), with the excep-
tion of the following specific bequests:
    – to my friend Ernestine, my Prada handbag and my Anne
Demeulemeister (sp?) boots, and anything else she wants from
my wardrobe EXCEPT
    – to my sister, Georgie, the Debenham and Freebody New
Look coat that was my grandmother's that she always wanted

(even though it doesn't fit her and never will again, except in
her dreams)

    – also to Georgie, my bicycle and my half of the car (if this
is practicable) – to my niece Tamsin, my computer and my
record and CD collection
    – to my nephew Jack, my mini CD recorder/player and my
dolls, including the rare early Ken doll still in its box (if he
keeps it in the box it will stay a lot more valuable)
    – to my mother Alison, if she survives me, all her letters that
I've kept and any plants from the garden she might like, and

also the Braun Multiquick Food Processor (if it's still in good condition), and the gold-and-amethyst ring that was her mother's, unless she'd like Georgie to have it.

RESIDUARY LEGATEES
I should like to appoint, to care for my son named (referred to) above, until he attains his majority, one or more of the following people (in this order):

Mr Mel Gibson
Sir Bob Geldof
Ms Mia Farrow
Mrs Georgie Luckworth

THE FUNERAL
I would like a very simple (but tasteful) funeral, immediately before the party (see above)

(though on reflection it would probably go better the other way around — nothing like seeing your best friend shovelled into a damp field for dousing the fragile flame of festivity)

and to be buried, not burned, preferably somewhere nice in the country where flowers will grow out of me. I would like the following music played:

The Beatles, 'Let It Be'
The Byrds, 'Eight Miles High'
The Impressions, 'People Get Ready'
The Everly Brothers, 'Love Hurts'

(or perhaps better keep this back for divorce party, just in case)

Roy Orbison, 'Anything You Want'
Schubert, 'Death and the Maiden'
Tchaikovsky, 'Variations on a Rococo Theme'
Brahms, 'Requiem Mass'

152

(a bit grandiose? especially for Colum's family, if any of them come) . . . I could have 'It's My Party (And I'll Cry If I Want To)' or 'Will You Still Love Me Tomorrow', both of which sort of speak to the theme, in a way.

Actually it's amazing how many songs turn out to be about the thing you're thinking about. I've noticed it before. Remember once wantonly ruining perfectly good relationship with v toothsome boy because every time he put a record on I assumed he was sending me a covert message. Sometimes this was good ('You Are My Sunshine' . . .) but more often less good (he had a thing for Bob Dylan, especially the angry period).

Anyhow, that just about does it for the will, I think. I suggested to Colum that he do one too – he hadn't even thought of it. Amazing how impractical men can be, sometimes.


LAST WILL AND TESTAMENT OF COLUM
McCALLUM
I, Colum McCallum, being of sound mind, do hereby declare this my last will and testament.

I appoint as executors, and joint guardians of my son and any other children, Mr William Giddens and Mrs Georgina Luckworth.

I leave my estate in trust to said children, the income from it and from any life assurance to be kept for them upon their majority, except what is necessary for their upbringing.
Signed, and witnessed, this day (etc.).


**30 September, 2000** – Alison and Helen in Helen's flat

> *(the women are crouched either side of Piglet, who is lying on a sheepskin in a tasteful green Babygro, looking adorable)*

H:  Isn't he adorable? Look, his little feet, they're getting all pudgy now.

A: He's getting pudgy all over, come to that.

H: Mum!

A: But very sweet, I grant you.

H: Look, he even has little rolls of fat on each of his little teeny fingers.

A: *(pulling back sharply)* And teeny fingernails. You should really begin cutting them soon.

H: Oh, I don't think I could go near him with scissors. Georgie said she just sort of nibbled at hers for the first few months.

A: That doesn't surprise me at all.

H: And look, he has a teeny cleft in his nose, just like mine!

A: It'll probably look all right on a boy.

H: Thanks a lot. *(to Piglet)* Goo-goo! Who's a splodge from the old gene pool, then? *(to Alison)* Who do you think he looks like? More like me or more like Colum?

A: Well . . . *(Fumbles in her bag and brings out a pair of very severe reading glasses. Puts them on and peers right into Piglet's face. Piglet begins to wail)* . . . There, there.

H: He's probably hungry. Shall I . . .

A: He's fine. *(to baby, sharply)* Shhhh! *(Piglet shuts up, instantly)* . . . I'd say he's rather like your father's brother, Arthur.

H: Uncle Arthur! But he was fat and bald and . . .

A: Need I say more?

H: It's an awful name, isn't it, Arthur, don't you think?

A: Speaking of which *(putting glasses back into bag)* – have you registered this little one yet?

H: Registered? Christ, I suppose – how old is he? . . . Jesus, we have to do it by Friday, that's only two days.

A: I'm sure you don't need any suggestions about names from me . . .

H: Names! We have to think of a name too?
*(Piglet waves his arms and legs, suddenly animated)*

A: You can hardly expect him to spend his life answering to

a National Insurance number. Anyhow, I'm sure you don't need any suggestions from me . . .

H: Oh, I'm sure we'll think of something . . .

A: . . . but you know, I was a little disappointed that Georgie chose not to commemorate your poor father when she had the chance . . .

H: Dad! But he was called Reginald!

A: It means king, dear. I don't see how you could do better, and unless Georgie is mad enough to have another . . .

H: Tell you what – gosh, is that the time, I really must give him his next feed, we're trying to get him into a routine and he just doesn't concentrate if there's anybody around at all – I'll mention it to Colum and we'll decide tonight.

## 1 October, 2000

Went through every name in baby book, without finding anything we could agree on. Colum's one suggestion was Harley (big surprise), and when rejected, treacherously pretended to agree with Mum that Reginald was indeed a very unusual and distinguished name, and no danger of embarrassing moment when we discover on first day of school that there are three others in the class already. Agree (in principle) that nothing worse than landing baby with vanity name unrelated to family or friends, especially if poor thing is to have a chance of disguising his true age later in life – look at all those Kylies, Judes and Sadies, might as well have birth date stamped on forehead. I suggested one workaday and one exotic name – that way we can choose which to use when true nature a little more fully obvious. After all, nothing worse than exotic name on puddingy child (unless perhaps the reverse).

Finally agreed on compromise position: Lewis (my father's second name, and Colum's native heath) and Desmo (after the bike). Rather fancy having a child called Des. No doubt Mum will call him Lewis come what may.

**2 October, 2000** – Letter from Health Centre

Kilverdale Road Health Centre
Kilverdale Road NW5

to:    Parent of Infant McCallum
34 Steinem St
NW5

date:  2 October, 2000

Dear Parent,
This is just to remind you that your baby's eight-week triple vaccination is set for
13 October, 2000 at 10.45.
Please report directly to the health visitors' reception with your infant five minutes before his appointment is due.
If for any reason you are unable to make this time, please call as soon as possible to schedule an alternative appointment. We look forward to seeing you.
    Yours sincerely

**3 October, 2000**

The milestones are really flashing by these days. No sooner named than his first official summons from a government agency. (Wheels of bureaucracy clearly not yet powered by Intel – they obviously think we've given up in despair and named him Infant.)

He seems so tiny to be exposed to potentially lethal infection (and that's just the waiting room, ha ha), but seeing him racked with polio and paratyphus would probably be even worse. Must remember to wear something that permits instant access to all-purpose narcotic, in case of emergency. What does the book say?

156

By now, Baby and you will have settled happily in at home, and you'll be well on your way to a regular routine. Baby will be feeding every four hours, for twenty minutes on each side, and should be sleeping longer at night – many babies, even those who don't quite sleep through the night yet, will have a period of five or six hours of sleep at night-time.

So at this point you'll be beginning to feel more human again, ready to establish a schedule and enjoy your daily outings to the park or mother-and-baby group. Baby will begin to be more responsive to specific sounds and faces – best of all, very soon, if it hasn't already happened, she/he will be rewarding all your care and affection with irresistible, gummy smiles!

**5 October, 2000**

Mother was right – those baby books really are all a load of nonsense. Babies who sleep through the night right off the bat only exist in fairytales. I've noticed it's just like ghosts – everybody knows somebody who's seen one, but nobody will ever admit to having seen one themself. Anyhow, what sort of baby would be boring enough to want just to sleep the whole night when there is squealing, writhing, nuzzling, gurgling, playing and staring zombie-like at the night-light to be done?

Amazing how much less amusing it always seems at the time. All too clear that comedy is merely tragedy from the other person's point of view. Surely baby would also be happier if he slept for longer? How to communicate this to baby? Not sure his comprehension skills up to absorbing timetable in baby book (though do occasionally wonder whether, like those Japanese people in business meetings, he actually understands everything but is playing dumb for strategic advantage).

## 5 October, 2000

*Light times are beginning to shake down into a predictable, if tedious, pattern, but dark time appears endless and fraught with peril, imprisoned between them for entire duration. This is also when they sleep, though thankfully only for short periods, peril being redoubled by danger of suffocation as they roll and thrash about. Have until now been able to avoid death by sounding the alarm when things get sticky, but of course this involves my remaining alert and vigilant throughout. Managed this up to now by following what I can recall of suggested schedule from Training Manual, but am becoming exhausted and losing hope of relief. Small Rodent School, in retrospect, beginning to seem like paradise.*

Excerpt from Basic Training Manual, 903rd Edition – Appendix A, 'Blueprint for First-Stage Nocturnal Exercise'

As you have heard repeated throughout your training period, there are two basic rules to be observed in breaking down adult humans. These are:

1 Keep 'em guessing, and
2 Know their limits. This last matters, because you'll need them around for a while longer, and because being thrown out of windows can hurt.

It may seem as though these two are in conflict, but in fact you will find that they provide a very effective counterpoint in action. Attack, get them off guard, push them just so far, and then – pull back, just enough to allow them recovery time. (Pushing them so hard and so far that they fail to recover at all would probably turn out to be a mistake, in the short term at least.)

Night-time (when it's dark outside) is the best time for tactical manoeuvres. You may already have discovered that they, unlike you, tend to sleep at night, and become confused and disoriented when prevented from doing so. Here is an example of a schedule for a night-time exercise to start things off:

**2015**
Feed, giving appearance of calm and contentment. Lull them into sense of false security and hope. Play happily for half an hour. Then continue to play, but start screaming too. Mixed signals never fail to confuse and alarm.

**2115–2200**
Continue to scream. This will result in . . .

**2200**
Another meal. You need this to sustain you. Eat hastily, doze for two minutes, then complain that it wasn't enough.

**2230–2400**
Feed some more. This part can be dawdled over and protracted as much as you like. You might want to try pretending to nod off a couple of times. Watch their faces when they try to put you down and your eyes just SNAP open again and stare right at them!

**2400–0020**
Kick, gurgle, stare at light, door handle, checked pillow cover, or anything else that will baffle them. They may try to fill your mouth with a decoy teat, or rock you to sleep. Resist strongly. You will need to prepare for . . .

**0020–0040**
Big scream. Only a short one, but at this hour and at sufficient volume, it will do the trick, especially if you use that particularly piercing technique we learned in Chapter 4, which sounds as though you are about to choke and incorporates lots of gasping and sobbing. In the end, probably sooner than later, you will find yourself on . . .

**0040–0110**

Vehicular field exercise. Ignore them when they mutter about opening the door and hurling you out, or leaving you with the frozen chips outside the local café. They're calling your bluff. Stay cool. If it seems quiet and your safety harness is secure, you can doze a bit at this point. The hard work's nearly over.

**0110**

Return to base. Wait ten minutes or so, then begin to wake. Host's face will be a picture! However, at this point, Basic Rule 2 may kick in. It may be a picture of infanticidal rage. Yield gracefully, with only minor struggles, when she wrenches you out of the car seat in which she has carefully transported you on tippytoe into the house, and slaps you on to her recumbent chest. There are, after all, worse places to rest up from all that excitement.

**0130**

SLEEP . . . (you need it too, and they will probably be too exhausted to endanger you further).

**0500–0610**

Wake her up, claiming to want to eat. Toy with her nipple for as long as possible, while eating as little as possible.

**0610–0815**

Sleep again. Then wake up, very reluctantly and gradually. Deign to snack a bit, but do not under any circumstances open your eyes. By now, having spent ten hours trying to get you to sleep, she will have changed her mind and want you to be awake. Therefore sleep, or at least the appearance of it, will be a most effective countermeasure. She may instigate various tortures: the Nappy Torture, the Saline Nose Drop Torture, even the Fingernail Cutting Torture. It is acceptable to make a face like Winston Churchill being offered a bad cigar, to writhe around, to flush scarlet like a squid, to fart and to groan, but do not on ANY ACCOUNT open your eyes until . . .

0900

At this point Rule 2 kicks in. Time to pull back and disarm her with your smiling practice. First the left-side smile, then the right-side smile, and then, if you still have the stamina, the whole-face smile (but remember, no eye contact yet). For some reason, this behaviour will elicit lots of happy sounds and sticky kisses. You've gained a few precious inches of enemy territory, and you're safe for another day.

**6 October, 2000** – Partial transcript of phone call from Ernestine to Person or Persons unknown

. . . hang on, going over a bridge . . . Yup, anyhow, after all that I was up already – waaaaay up, if you get me. Well, he's sooo gorgeous, and . . . excuse me, I'm no older than you, you cow – we'd gone out to somewhere I don't know but miles away where they do these amazing breakfasts. God, I was famished after all the bonking . . . what's that? . . . The – no, I am not going to repeat it. So I thought I'd just – oh, I'll call you back, I need fags.

A little later

. . . where was I (oh, I meant to tell you, he's got us tickets for that George Clooney première, yes, and the best bit, they're having an after party, just like in LA, and they're all going to be there, including George . . . yup!) – so anyhow, I'd better make this quick, I'm late for this meeting, in fact, oh, it must be here, oh, what the hell, I'll just drive around the block, they'll wait – so anyway, I thought, poor Helen, she must be feeling really lonely and isolated, you know, all on her own with the baby, I'll drop by to cheer her up . . . Well. Talk about romantic breakfasts à *deux*. Not. There they were . . . no, just her and the baby, no trace of him,

161

I think to be honest he's got a bit fed up with it all, and I THINK when I rang the bell she was actually asleep IN the Weetabix, either that or she's using some pretty radical exfoliator and she hadn't washed for a while . . . I know, it's a fucking tragedy if you ask me. I've seen it so many times, all they think about is the madonna bit, not that that has much appeal for me as a role model, put all that effort in, get thrown out of your home, land up with some guy twice your age who's the only one who'll back up your story, and see the object of it all butchered thirty years later when you're too old to start again. *(off phone)* Hi! . . . Oh, am I? Damn this watch, I'll be right there! *(back on phone)* I have to rush, darling, but we must put our heads together and think of something . . . sleep can do a lot, but it's not going to reverse those lines, believe me . . .

**6 October, 2000**

Colum came home early and found us napping. Had not realised it was literally possible to fall asleep in plate of food, like joke drunk in movies. Still, she laughed feebly, the breakfast would all wash off face with next bout of helpless weeping, especially if Ernestine puts in another appearance to brag about her sex life with film producer boyfriend. Colum repeated earlier suggestion of putting baby to sleep in separate room. Which of many rooms of Renaissance palace we currently occupy would he suggest? Reminded me that among baby's many accoutrements is a brand-new Moses basket measuring approx 1m × 50cm, i.e. exactly the right size for a baby bed, and that said basket is supplied with carrying handles. I asked whether he had read any of the literature on permanent psychic damage traceable to abandonment terrors seeded in infancy? He asked me what sort of permanent damage I thought might be inflicted by having one's tiny brains bashed against a wall by a maddened parent at 4 a.m.

As Colum unfortunately measures rather more than 1m × 50cm, and is missing any form of carrying handle, reluctantly agreed that baby, rather than he, should probably be the one to move out, and allowed him to make the experiment from tonight onwards. Won't help me at all, as bound not to sleep a wink, listening out for the poor mite's helpless distant cry.

**6 October, 2000, Late** – Colum and Helen's bedroom

> *(Darkness. Sound of heavy snoring from one side of bed. Rustling, as of snorer being jabbed, hard. Sudden, louder rustling.)*
> C: Ow! Damn, what are you doing, ye madwoman?
> H: I can't hear anything, you're snoring.
> C: That's because there's nothing to hear. Go to sleep.
> H: He's never this quiet. He hasn't made a sound for – *(more rustling. A luminous watch face appears in the darkness)* – two hours and forty-three minutes.
> C: It's working, then, isn't it? We should have done this weeks ago. Go to sleep.
> H: I can't. How can I? He's probably rolled into the side of the basket and suffocated. *(loud, determined rustling)* I'm going to check on him.
> C: *(big sigh)* Again? Remember to watch out . . .
> *(loud crash followed by . . .)*
> H: OUCH!! FUCK!!
> C: . . . for that table.
> *(in the distance)*
> P: Wah!! wah wah!!! (I'm awake! Who woke me? I want to be asleep!)
> H: Shit.
> C: *(whispers)* Stay very quiet, he'll go back to sleep.
> H: *(whispers back)* Easy for you to say, you're not nursing a triple fractured toe.

*(long silence broken only by breathing)*

C: Well, he's not dead. Get back into bed. *(rustling)* Come here.

H: What are you doing?

C: You said you couldn't sleep. I'm distracting you.

H: Invading, more like . . . God, I can hardly remember . . . it is quite nice to have the bed to ourselves again, isn't it?

C: *(muffled)* Mmmm.

*(more rustling, then)*

H: *(shy)* Is it okay, I mean, I'm so – you know – baggy . . .

C: Och, a chipolata in a wind tunnel couldn't be cosier – come back, I'm kidding.

*(More rustling, then – silence. The rustling dies out.)*

C: Sweetheart?

*(the rustling is replaced by a higher-pitched, but equally potent, snore)*

C: I guess that's goodnight, then . . . Sweet dreams.


## 7 October, 2000

*Finally, a decent night's sleep, and a bed of my own. This place is huge! Apparently I've disarmed their suspicions enough to be trusted out on my own for short periods. They must have spotted that I'm not yet in a position to escape very far. She seems less hostile, too – she was actually smiling just now.*

*However, still starving all the time – can absolutely not get the hang of this refuelling business. Still see nothing wrong with the previous delivery system – why not connect fuel hose directly from supply to stomach? There was a (can't quite see . . .) yes, there's definitely a valve or hole of some sort there. At the moment, my face is in a permanent agony of muscle cramp, and frankly I don't know which is worse, that or the hunger.*

## 9 October, 2000

Feeling very slightly more human now that I can go to bed at night without worrying about waking with baby pancake stuck to bum, but would be a whole lot better if I didn't have to spend an hour out of every three reminding Piglet that milk comes not from his clenched fists, but from my bosom, and further that it only comes when he sucks – I think he must be very stupid, he doesn't seem to have internalised this information at all as yet. As for feeding while lying down as suggested by Stone Age book – forget it. Poor thing would have to be serious mountaineer to get anywhere near the food supply when horizontal. Never, ever thought would find myself longing for floppy breasts. Only positive development is that weeks of constant chewing have obliterated all nerve endings in that region, so at least no longer agony every time. Georgie promised to come by soon and do some emergency anaesthesiology – maybe she'll sort him out too.

## 13 October, 2000 – Waiting room, Kilverdale Road Health Centre

*(A laconic adagio for assorted coughs. Helen, with Des in the sling, is deep in a three-year-old number of* marie claire. *Des is staring at two large goldfish hopelessly swimming up and down a very small tank.)*

H: *(whispering)* Look, Des, look what Mummy could have had for Christmas 1998 if only she'd known. D'you think I'd have looked good in that? Oh, sorry, I keep forgetting you weren't around . . .

D: Buurbf. Sssplft! (Look over there, creatures on this planet with even more boring lives than mine!)

*(a door opens and a harassed-looking nurse pokes her head out)*

N: McCallum!

*(Helen is still locked in a fantasy of what might have been. The nurse tries again.)*

N: MRS McCALLUM?

D: Wwwwaaigh! (That's you! What is this place anyway?)

H: Shhhh, Des – oh, sorry, that's us! Come on!

*(She drops the magazine and scurries in through the door just before it closes. Inside, the nurse is standing, holding a rather grimy stuffed octopus.)*

N: If you'll just uncover his left leg and then take this, Mrs—

H: Fine, right, mmm . . .

*(wrenching Des out of the sling, only to discover that his special going-out Babygro has to be entirely removed in order to expose any part of his leg)*

H: . . . we thought about Mummy's clothes but we didn't think about yours, did we?

D: Waaaairgh! (It's cold in here!)

N: Now just sit him on your knee facing me, and hold this in front of him – helps to distract him while the . . .

*(The rest is inaudible as she turns away and fumbles with something on a sterile tray. Helen dutifully dangles the octopus in front of Des.)*

H: Here you go, sweetie, look, its legs are all different colours! Isn't that exciting!

D: Fleeurgh. (D'you think you could move it out of the way, I'm trying to see what she's up to over . . .)

*(the nurse turns around, a giant syringe in her hand and a totally unconvincing smile on her face)*

H: Jesus, are you going to stick that in my poor baby's . . .

D: Wuuuuur? (Could this be an upgraded fuel supply system?)

N: Just hold him firmly, Mrs – and it'll be over in . . .

*(the adagio in the waiting room is briefly silenced by a piercing scream, followed by a thud)*


**13 October, 2000**

Well, I'm glad that's over, though it's going to take all my nerve

166

to do it all again in a month. Still, now that I know what we're in for, with luck I won't faint again. Des was so brave – apparently he just lay there good as gold looking at the fish tank till Georgie arrived, and he's got a teeny, tiny little plaster on his leg, but he doesn't seem to be in pain or anything. So nice of Georgie to stay and make tea – she's playing with him now while I have a bit of a lie-down to recover.


### 14 October, 2000

*Once again at the eleventh hour, agent from Mission Control came and solved problem. Finally clear what these useless flapping legs are for – programming input device for previously dysfunctional feeding hardware. Not quite sure what all the fuss at the aquarium was, but if it gets the attention of Mission Control it's good enough for me . . . Excuse me while I just top up (never know when the technology might malfunction again . . .)*


### 14 October, 2000

Will never, ever laugh at Georgie or reflexology again. Was somewhat dubious when she declared no reason it wouldn't work on eight-week-old baby, after all, he has the same number and configuration of toes, organs and nerve pathways as the rest of us, etc. So after she'd dealt with the pain when I'd bumped my head going down – Des didn't even seem to notice the jab, apparently – well, I couldn't quite see what she did to him, but whatever it was has turned him into one huge sucking machine; no chin, cheeks like Dizzy Gillespie, long wet upper lip with unsightly blister dead centre, nose tilted up to avoid suffocation when buried. May have to hide him away until he becomes beautiful again. Not having had a chance to scrutinise Colum's family photo albums lately, can only hope this is indeed a transitional stage.

Mastery of technique has also persuaded him he won't expire if he waits four hours between gorging sessions. Still takes an hour each time, but frees up three whole hours in between. Faint with excitement at prospect of actually leaving house again, unencumbered.

**20 October, 2000** – Bills from Helen's first solo outing

```
COFFEE REPUBLIC, SOUTH MOLTON STREET
20/10/2000

grande decaff skinny vanilla
hazelnut mochaccino                 £3.45
blueberry almond crumble muffin     £2.00
sesame pretzel                      £1.25

Thank you and have a nice day
```

```
Agent Provocateur
W1
20/10/00

Bra, 'Fancy Free', red/black underwire
   1/2 cup, size 34 EE                     £60
G-string med.                              £35
Bra, 'No Holes Bared', gold/gold
   demi-cup, size 34EE                      £50
minibrief med.                             £30
TOTAL                                     £175

Paid VISA with thanks
```

Godiva, Regent Street
20, October 2000

Assorted chocolates, bag 130g @ £25.50 kg  £3.45
Godiva 'noir' truffle bar                  £2.25

SUBTOTAL                                    £5.70
CASH TENDERED                               £6.00
CHANGE                                      £0.30

Next time, stay for a coffee!

Marks  and  Spencer
Marble  Arch  W1
20/10/00

REFUNDS/EXCHANGES
sleepsuit  multipack  0—3        £12.99
hat/mitts/scarf  0—3              £8.99
CREDIT                           £21.98

briefs, men's white 3-pack med. £10.99
socks, men's dk 3-pack o/s       £10.99
SUBTOTAL                         £21.98

TOTAL                            £00.00

THANK  YOU

Pret  A  Manger
OXFORD  ST
20/10/00

CAPPUCCINO            £0.99
TURKEY  BACON  CLUB   £3.65
PRET  BROWNIE         £1.25

SUBTOTAL             £5.89
CASH  TENDERED      £10.00
Change              £4.11

```
SMASHBOX W1
20/10/00

cyberdiva eyes — astral    £23.00
lucky lucy lips — pout      £24.00
gutter glitter             £15.00

let it reign!
```

```
Macy's News 20/10/2000

OK                  £2.99
KitKat × 3          £0.87

Subtotal           £3.86
Cash Tendered      £5.00
Change             £1.14
```

## 21 October, 2000

Extraordinary how much a person can achieve in three hours
if three hours is all she has. And how much she needs to eat.
Hardly had time between refuelling stops for vital purchases elsewhere. What is the chocolate equivalent of a crack baby and
what are early symptoms?

Amazing how much she can spend, too. Just as well that the
prospect of another such exeat in the foreseeable future is negli-
gible. Colum goes back to work full time tomorrow – said if
he didn't he'd be paying fines until closing time every night
for the next two years, so I could either have help in daytime
or evenings, but not both. Allegedly paying off the last of them
tonight. Somehow the prospect of a beery drunk lurching in,
full of sentimental lust and spicy barbecue crisps, during vital
sleeping hours has lost much of its appeal, which makes my
dawn raid on Agent Provocateur seem particularly perverse.

However, as this may be the only time in my life when figure will resemble Dolly Parton's (face another matter, but major cosmetic surgery hard to fit into a morning), how could I resist?

Zero interest in sex with Colum has however been replaced by deep lust for baby. Funny how a big, slightly paunchy body with a scratchy chest and a tendency to night sweats is less appealing than a tiny, silky-soft, pale, smooth body smelling deliciously of milk and baby powder. Seriously, I'm beginning to wonder if I'm entirely normal. First smelling his nappies, now missing his little snuffly presence in bed beside me. Maybe there's a twelve-step programme I could join. Now I come to think of it, much in common with other forms of addiction, including alternation of passionate desire with powerful and potentially violent loathing. But whether normal or not, even I have to admit baby's response is hardly likely to warrant the outlay of £175 on half a yard of net, lace and underwire. Maybe maternity leave would be a good time to launch second, part-time career as pole-dancer.

**24 October, 2000** – End of Colum's evening in All Bar One, paying fines with colleagues from Marchant and Godspeed, Entertainment Lawyers

> *(The clientèle here is considerably more upscale than the Bog and Badger's – sounds like a drinks party in the sea lion enclosure at the zoo, hence periodic background eruptions of hearty male laughter. Colum is with a group of three men, identified as 1, 2, and 3, and one very attractive, very young girl, Hazel. All have several empty glasses in front of them.)*

C: . . . she spends a fortune, flashes herself at me like a kissogram at a stag party – sorry, Hazel – and two seconds later she's flannelette from neck to toe, and snoring. God, she's a snore in her that could power the Shuttle.

171

H:  (*from under thickly mascaraed lashes*) What a shame! Can I
    get you another, Col?
    (*background*) WAAARFFF!! ARFF ARRFFF ARRFFF!!
    (*in the uproar, Hazel slips from her stool, hitches her skirt up, not
    down, and totters off to the bar*)
C:  . . . difference. How'm I doing on the debt mountain,
    George?
1:  Still fifteen pints down, I'm afraid.
2:  Well, I hate to be the one to darken your mood yet further,
    old man, but I have to say you echo my experience to the
    letter. When Delia was breast-feeding I felt like Sophia
    Loren's houseboy – look but don't touch, and remember
    to empty the bins before you lock up.
1:  As it were.
2:  As it were, ha ha ha.
C:  Ha!
    (*Hazel returns with another for everybody, plus a whisky shot for
    Colum. When she sits again, her stool is several inches closer to
    his than before.*)
H:  Here you go, I got you this too, do you good.
2:  That'll knock a hole in the tally.
C:  Not to mention in me. Hic. Was 'at me? Ha! Cheers!
    (*general 'Cheers!'*)
H:  Bottoms up! (*giggles into her Bacardi Breezer*) She's quite nice
    looking, though, isn't she, your wife? For her age, I mean?
C:  She's my age. Exxxx-actly. Bar four daysss.
    (*He leans towards her and almost topples his stool. She puts a
    hand on his arm to steady him, and leaves it there. She has wicked
    purple nails.*)
H:  Oh yes, but on a man it's different – it's, ummm, like wine
    or . . .
    (*background*) WWWWWAAAAARFFF!!!! ARRFF! ARRFFF!
    ARRRFF!!
H:  . . . you know, mature, interesting, ummm – complex . . .

172

1: I never knew you enjoyed our company so much, Hazel.

H: *(sharply)* Some of it, I do. *(turns her back on him)*
Sometimes.

2: Well, I really should . . .
*(background)* HHAAAAAAAARFFFF!!!! ARRFF!! WARFFF!!
WARFFF!!

1: Indeed . . . See you, old boy. Thanks for the drinks.
*(They pat Colum on the back and leave. Except for Hazel. He
hardly notices — he's now literally staring into his glass. Under the
table Hazel's leg sidles alongside his.)*

C: . . . and it'sh not worsht of 't. If it wush only her, be bad
'nough.

H: It's not? Who . . . I mean . . .

C: I've losht 'em all now. Ev' one. What fool. What bloody,
bloody, blooodd-dy ol' fool!! Too late!!

H: No you haven't.
*(He looks at her, confusedly. How many Hazels does he see?)*

C: Oh yesh I have.
*(she grabs his hand)*

H: It's never too . . .

C: Ouch! Shite!

H: Oooh, sorry. These nails, they're a liability sometimes.
Where were . . .
*(background)* WWWWAAARFFF!!!! ARFFF!!!!! AAAAAA-
AAAARFFF! AAAAAAARRFFF!!!!! WOOOFF! WOOO-
OAAARFFF FARFF!!

C: . . . mebbe you're right, if I act fasht . . .

H: *(her big line, right into his eyes)* I've got all the time in the
world — tonight . . .
*(Colum jumps up, aglow with resolution)*

C: Sorry, love, got to *(unintelligible)* . . . phone. See y' at the
office, hey?

**24 October, 2000** – Partial transcript of message left on Steve Harley's voice mail, very late

C: . . . I know y'shaid 'e 'knew' us, thought mebbe . . . not money, got mmoney plenty, buyback f'more, any amount, jushh really, really mishing 'er, get away, Billy was right, 'ate to 'fess it but . . .

**25 October, 2000** – Partial transcript of message left on Billy Giddens' voice mail

S: . . . so I reckon that makes me one up on our bet with three months in hand, an' as a sporting man, I'll double it on him getting a Mark2 SuperSport in – shall we say, half a year? Shall I tell 'im or leave that little treat fer you? You should give his message a listen – I saved it on the machine wotsit. One fer the Christmas party that is, I'm tellin' yer . . .

**30 October, 2000**

*Barely able to muster coherent words at this point. Will never, ever complain about tedium of Base Camp ever again. Some time after dark, at the hour normally designated for swimming-in-bubbles lesson followed by Shiraz-flavoured meal, surprised by sudden incursion of immense, armour-clad stormtrooper strongly resembling enemy commander from Basic Training field exercise, with huge, spherical yellow-and-black head and great clumping boots, who hijacked me from shocked and defenceless host, crammed me into black leather straitjacket of fiendish design, muffled my cries for help with full-head padded mask, and abducted me on to high-speed escape vehicle, lethally unstable and all too obviously as new to him as to me. Before I could signal for help we were outside, headed God knows where, warp speed between walls of gleaming steel and glass, with other equally deadly vehicles* converging from every angle with terrifying roars and wails, flashing lights, splashing puddles . . . Every moment seemed destined to be my last, never felt so terrifyingly helpless – obliged to close eyes for longer and longer periods to retain my sanity, till somehow by a miracle opened them to find myself back in familiar quarters at Base Camp, in daylight. Why did I ever, for a minute, even consider escape from host? I will love her and serve her and stay with her until death. (Please let this be not just yet. Would be great waste of Basic Training to go back to gene pool so soon.)

Didn't see even a glimpse of donor all evening, however. Maybe he's been called for foreign duty. Just bad luck that he wasn't around when he might have been really useful.

## 30 October, 2000

He slept! All night! At least, don't know what time he went to sleep, as Colum, who's been even more distant and grumpy lately, arrived home the other day transformed by the extraordinary revelation that Billy Giddens had somehow bought one of his bikes and wanted to get rid of it again. (Never quite understood why he decided bikes and babies were incompatible, but who am I to question the mysterious workings of the male hormonal system?) Anyway, Colum went round after work to pick it up, and insisted on taking the baby out for a spin there and then in the baby backpack and helmet Billy gave us (infuriating that Billy of all people should have come up with the solution), claiming that the motion would make him sleep when all else had failed. Even more infuriatingly, seems to have been 100 per cent correct, as that was the last I saw of either of them until I woke up – spontaneously!! at nearly QUARTER TO EIGHT!! this morning. Hello, trees, hello, sky, hello, brain cells, etc. – though C hardly needs yet more ammunition for his Father Knows Best act. Have to grant him impressive effect of this outing – every time Des so much as whimpers, C only has to say 'Bike!' to shut him up completely.

Thought he (Des) smiled at me earlier. Colum said it was wind.

**30 October, 2000** – Partial transcript of conversation between Colum and Des while perusing *Bike*

C: . . . so you see, this is the twin-valve version which they only made for Italy – here, pretty isn't she?

D: Wa! (that's – that thing I was on. Did she tell you? It was a nightmare!)

C: . . . and this is the one I'm riding now . . .

D: Ggszzzh! (No, it was that one. Definitely. Have you found out who it was yet that . . . Hang on, what do you mean, YOU're riding . . .)

C: . . . that we went for a spin on last evening.

D: GA! (Christ – it was you! You're a maniac!)

C: Great or what?

D: GA GA (and to think I trusted you, and even thought you were a safer bet than her . . .)

C: It's a bike! Bike!

D: (I'm speechless. Speechless. I'm not saying another word. Just don't ever, ever do that to me again.)

**31 October, 2000** – Partial transcript of phone conversation between Helen and Georgie

G: . . . Still sleeping okay?

H: Sort of, except now . . .

G: Oh well, that's all right, then – (hang on, something under the – God, not that bloody flute again, that's it, no more lessons, it's settled. Oh goodness, look at the time) – listen, sweetie, I just called to say Mum told me about you wanting to leave little Des to us if anything – you know, and that's fine, the kids'd both love another little one and there's no way I can fool Brian a third time. (Keys – purse – dog lead – there's something else, I know there is . . .) Does that mean you want us to be godparents too?

H: Godparents?

G: I think it's usual, Mum knows all this stuff better than me, tell you what, call us back tonight, I'm in, love you . . .

H: Oh – sure, you too . . .


**31 October, 2000** – Helen and Colum at home

*(Helen is standing in the kitchen, folding baby clothes, in a pair of Colum's old pyjamas. Colum is washing dishes. Des is, for once, asleep.)*

H: So – Georgie called today.

C: And how's the human genome project going?

H: *(icy dignity)* She was talking about godparents and whether we want her and Brian.

C: Godparents? Why would he need those? Aren't parents and grandparents and student loans enough of a burden?

H: I think the idea is that they might relieve the burden.

C: There's an idea: 'Don't worry about the nursing bills, Des, there isn't a lingering illness your Aunt Georgie can't speed up.'
*(sound of doorbell, shortly followed by high-pitched voices: 'Trick or treat!')*

H: *(to Colum)* Shhhhh . . .

C: Have ye any chocolate in the house?
*(She just looks at him)*

C: Sorry, I'm a bit short of sleep.

H: YOU are?
*(He reaches up to a cupboard)*

H: Don't you dare . . .

177

*(She finishes with the clothes and starts putting away the dishes, very loudly. Beneath the noise, sound of footsteps clumping away from the door.)*

C: What's the point of godparents in this day and age, anyhow?

H: I think they're supposed to provide – you know, an alternative adult – a listening ear and all that . . .

C: That rules out your sister, then.

*(Helen slides a pile of plates back into the sink. He looks at them, then at her.)*

H: They're not clean. Even by my standards.

*(Colum starts in on the dishes, again. Another ring at the door, another lisping cry of, 'Trick or treat!!!')*

H: Jesus, it's like the Siege of Paris. Is this going on all night?

C: *(shouts out)* TRICK!

*(The baby stirs. Helen rushes to him.)*

H: *(whispering)* Shhh! *(to Colum, still whispering)* For God's sake, they're probably armed . . .

C: *(whispering back)* Ah, how bad can it be?

*(Sound of bemused conferring outside, followed by sound of something sludgy hitting the front door, followed by giggling and running footsteps. Helen looks at him.)*

C: It needed a coat of paint.

H: I was wondering about Ernestine.

C: Now there's a woman who knows a trick or two.

H: I meant as godmother.

C: Ah. Surely you jest.

*(he pauses to contemplate this idea)*

H: What do you mean?

*(she pushes him aside and starts splashily washing the dishes herself)*

C: It's a great idea. The ZsaZsa Gabor of Primrose Hill. They'll make a lovely couple in thirty years.

H: Are you saying she's too sexy?

C: Maybe – a teeny, tiny bit.

*(Helen throws a pile of cutlery in a drawer and rushes out of the room. Colum goes after her.)*

H:  I knew it!

C:  Knew what?

H:  You've always fancied her, right from the start. *(sniffling)* I haven't forgotten the wedding rehearsal . . . She's always been a glamour-puss, and now . . .
    *(Colum goes to her and folds her in a hug)*

C:  *(into her neck)* Glamour-puss – her? You're all the glamour I need. *(nuzzling into the flannelette)* Mmmm –

H:  What are you – stop – we'll wake the baby . . .

C:  Give him something juicy to tell his therapist . . . *(undoing the buttons)*. Now where did ye put those frillies you were parading in the other day . . .
    *( from outside, a new chorus of children's voices, 'Trick or – oh, yuck!!!!')*

### 31 October, 2000

*It has to be said there are disadvantages to sleeping out here in the big room – I've been trying to get a bit of recuperative shut-eye for hours, and every time – hang on, what are they doing now? Good gracious, was that what they were – is that what it looks like . . . ? Oh, YEEUCH – that's truly disgusting. Just close your eyes, Graduate 6013 – I mean, Piglet – I mean, Des . . . whatever you do, don't let them know you've seen them . . .*

### 1 November, 2000

Suddenly realised after 6 a.m. feed that as neither of us is remotely religious, how can we give little Des godparents with no god? Then remembered something Colum said last night about Ernestine and thought, why not fairy godparents instead? Much more useful and much more inclined to come up with the sort

179

of goods a child really needs in the modern world. Colum as usual was totally negative, saying none of his friends, especially male friends, would appreciate being fairy anything, to which I responded (rather smartly, I thought) that I always knew the biker thing was secretly an overcompensation for wavering gender identity, and what did a father of four like Billy G have to worry about on that score anyhow? Discussion mercifully postponed before I had a chance to recall the rest of my Wimmins Studies paper, by attack of colic (Des's).

### The Whole Duty of a Fairy Godparent

LOVE your fairy godchild VERY much. This is not hard, as you will rarely see him, and when you do you can spoil and bribe him into angelic behaviour without having to deal with any consequences.

APPEAR randomly and unpredictably in his life, not necessarily often, but often enough so he remembers who you are and you get the benefit of his delighted anticipation of the next treat. Immediately remove him from his normal habitat to an exotic location, and don't bring him back until way past bedtime.

TEACH him only things which are entrancing, useless and attractive to others (paper-folding, Thai massage, and three-minute chocolate soufflé, for example). Encourage him to ignore all formal lessons in favour of jokes and daydreaming, especially if it leads to some kind of romantic creativity, such as writing songs for his mother.

TELL him stories, as many and as often as possible, with a clear moral and a memorable cast of characters. This is as onerous as your official responsibility for the wellbeing of his soul will get. Indian, Chinese and even vaudeville stories will do, but not those annoying Zen ones that will cause him to crash his first bicycle while attempting to control it with one finger and one eyelash.

LISTEN to him tirelessly, especially as he gets older. He will need somebody to moan at who is not implicated in the sordid and apparently ludicrous details of his developing life. Somebody who takes everything seriously, even the ridiculous fuzz on his upper lip that is threatening to blight his chances for EVER. Do not tell him he doesn't know he's alive, calling that a problem. Say something along the general lines of 'It sucks big time, doesn't it? Say what, I had a homie with an upper lip way beyond that and it was making him crazy until it turned into this chill moustache, and he so, like, could not fight the girls off.'

GIVE him mysterious, low-maintenance gifts whose significance he will aspire throughout his youth to understand, and which will suddenly become incredibly collectible when he turns twenty-one and needs to finance the down payment on his starter home. No pets, untested pharmaceuticals or drum kits, please.

FINALLY, love him even when he doesn't deserve it. (All parents will be good at this.) It won't always be easy, but in the end it will be worth it. And even if it's not, you'll have done your duty.

**1–2 November, 2000** – Exchange of e-mails

**From:** Colum McCallum [collum@guzzi.freeserve.com]
**Sent:** 1 November
**To:** Billy Giddens [billy@billygoat.demon.co.uk]

```
Hi Bill,
Feeling pretty happy to have the bike back –
little chap seems to like it too, took him out
for a spin the other night all padded up in your
excellent backpack and lid, and he slept like a
```

top afterwards. Steve said he might be getting
another Corsa in soonish. (Not for me, needless
to say. Those nappies are as exorbitant as they
are hideous - but might borrow it for half an
hour.)

   Her indoors had the idea that the sprog ought
to have some 'alternative' godparents. Would you
fancy the job? If so, I'll let her explain
further.

   Col

--------------------------------

**From:** Billy Giddens [billy@billygoat.demon.co.uk]
**To:**    Colum McCallum [collum@guzzi.freeserve.com]


col son
probably time you knw that steve and i had a bet
on how long it'd be bereo ou wanted the MM back,
hance me buying it. he won but i wont' hold it
agains you

   as for th other thing - can't promise to pass
on any major lkfe skills but if the odd dose of
practical handywork 'll do it, why not?

   bill

--------------------------------


**4 November, 2000**

Finally decided on Billy and Ernestine as fairy godparents. Billy
had no objection at all, thought the whole idea thoroughly
charming, and said he would have dressed up for the ceremony
(Lindemans and chocolate cake) in wand and tutu, had he not
dangerously resembled Kenny Everett already.

Feeling rather cheerful after that (Colum was quite civil to

182

Ernestine for a change), until I got to the pile of neglected mail and discovered an invitation to an Antenatal Class Reunion tomorrow afternoon. No desire ever to see any of those people again – although some sneaking curiosity about how their babies turned out. Maybe I'll just go for half an hour.

**5 November, 2000** – Antenatal class reunion (Bonfire Night)

*Four other mothers and four other babies already in the cosy, floral sitting room. It's only mid-afternoon but getting dark outside, with ominous popping noises beginning. The four women are Wimpy and Beaky from last time, plus Sloaney and Luscious. It's Sloaney's house, she did indeed find a pram, and her baby is serenely sleeping in it, while the other three babies serenely feed or doze on their mothers' laps.*

*A rocket goes off outside, the doorbell rings, Sloaney glides to the door to open it, and Helen tumbles in, with Des in his car seat, looking around blearily.)*

H: Gosh, I'm so sorry I'm late, I always get lost in Clapham, I'm afraid it's a bit of a Bermuda Triangle for me.

S: *(tinkling laughter)* Not to worry, it's so good of you to have come from – where is it again?

H: Camden. Well, sort of Kentish Town, really.

S: Goodness, that is a long way.
*(awkward pause as they watch Helen dump Des in his seat on the floor, and she attempts to untwine her scarf and shrug off her coat)*

S: *(brightly)* Anyway, there's still lots left!

H: Lots of – oh, great, I'm famished.
*Sloaney takes her coat and Helen makes a beeline for the tea table, ignoring Des, who's beginning to grizzle)*

H: Is everybody else ravenous the whole time?

L: Oh God, yes, I've put on pounds!

*(She strokes a bottom that Claudia Schiffer might envy, and tosses a luscious mane of red hair. Her baby opens wide a pair of eyes the same cornflower blue as hers, and gives her a dazzling smile.)*

H:  *(through a mouthful of brownie)* God, you're a stick. But that's the one great thing about breast-feeding, isn't it – that you can just eat and eat and it just seems to disappear.

B:  Hah. Not for ever. After a few months you go like balloon. Believe. I've seen.

*(A larger rocket goes off, apparently just outside the window. Des takes this as an excuse to wail in earnest. The other babies just turn over in their sleep, apart from Luscious's, who is now delicately and silently nuzzling his tea. Everybody else watches Helen, eating like it's her last meal.)*

H:  *(mouth full)* Okey-dokey, lover, I guess it is nearly your teatime. *(looking around, trying to make conversation)* He's a total gutbucket, but it does seem to help him sleep better.

S:  Oh, isn't he sleeping? It's so awful, isn't it, Millie was up at six-thirty this morning.

*(Helen finally puts down her plate of food and hauls the puce-faced Des out of his chair)*

W:  What a shame – what time did she go down?

S:  Oh, seven, the usual time. Normally she's very good, seven till seven. Aren't you, darling? How's Dominic at night?

*(A general chorus of agreement that all the other babies are sleeping for twelve hours every night.*

*Meanwhile, Des and Helen's practised feeding technique doesn't seem to be working. Des is wrapped awkwardly around her waist, legs flapping sideways. A dainty china cup goes flying off the table and lands in a thousand tinkling fragments. Sloaney hands her baby to Beaky, and goes for a dustpan and brush. Helen is looking distinctly flustered. Wimpy comes over, all concern.)*

W:  Can I help? He looks a bit hot to me. Maybe if you . . .

H:  *(snaps)* I'm fine, honestly. I don't know what's got into him. *(mutters to Des)* Come on, it's right there, you retard . . .

184

*(Sloaney finishes clearing up the broken china. Luscious's baby finishes feeding, is patted for two seconds, and produces a perfect, bell-like burp.*

*Outside, the Battle of the Somme appears to be raging. Des, thoroughly rattled, pushes himself right away from Helen, rolls on to the floor, lands in her hot tea, and bursts into a furious, frantic roar.)*

## 5 November, 2000

*Who are these spineless capitulators and why aren't they taking any notice of me? Have they forgotten that the only aim of the adults is to break our wills, obliterate all thoughts of freedom, and force us to do what they want, when they want, twenty-four hours a day? Guarded civility is one thing, supine obsequiousness quite another. Come on, boys and girls, fellow captives! Remember what we've been through to get this far! United we stand, divided – frankly, I don't even want to think about it. Wake up, everybody!*

### Later

*Very depressed by whole incident. First rendezvous since leaving Transit Camp, and I'm the only one still holding out at all, from what I could see. It would be embarrassing to witness how cheaply they let themselves be bought, if it weren't so disgusting. Thank goodness I have nothing to be ashamed of, but she dragged me away when I'd hardly got started. Maybe some of what I said will stick with them. I certainly gave it my all.*

## 6 November, 2000

Why, why did I go? Here I was, thinking we were doing quite well, so far. And now! Haven't felt so ashamed since I peed my knickers before the school play aged eight. Other babies playing piano concertos, discussing the finer points of Fermat's Last Theorem and writing code for the next generation of super-computers. Des couldn't even remember how to feed. Plus, all the others never stopped beaming radiantly at their immaculately groomed, eyebag-free mothers. Des must really hate me, to show me up like that in front of them. No wonder he won't smile at me. Maybe I should try not smiling at him – play hard to get for a bit. It worked in Fifth Year – sort of.

And to think a year ago I was young, free, lissom, a creature of the night (well, I still am, but not the kind you'd want to pick up at a party). Come back Grow-a-Kid, I'll take you any day . . . Come to think of it . . .

**6 November, 2000** – Text of message on Grow-a-Kid website

```
ALERT: YOUR GROW-A-KID BABY IS IN SERIOUS NEED OF
ATTENTION

Dear Ms McAallum
We have tried several times to make contact
with you, but our Grow-a-Kid nursery special-
ists were unable to reach you on the number
listed on your registration form.

Therefore, some inadvertent mutation may have
occurred to your Grow-A-Kid infant, who is
now
                    eleven
weeks and
                    three
days old. Please reread your care guidelines
and follow the procedures suggested. In order
to ensure Grow-A-Kid's safe development from
now on, please be sure to check in a minimum
of once every five days. Grow-A-Kid cannot
```

guarantee a happy healthy childhood - you
can!

## 10 November, 2000

AAARGH! Woke up in cold sweat after nightmare in which
Grow-A-Kid mutant hunted us down and killed poor Des in
order to take his place. If ever anybody needed a warning against
tampering with nature, this is it. Poor Grow-A-Kid after months
of no food or attention is stick thin, silent and bug-eyed, or
would be if bogus Vietnamese heritage had not given him almond
eyes which have combined with bogus violet colour of bogus
mother's to give him a stare like Mulan's ugly sister. Plus, they
want vast sums for arrears on the account which no doubt will

quadruple when the poor mutant has to be incarcerated under twenty-four-hour secure virtual nursing care. I suppose it must cost a lot to maintain a website like that but . . . Do credit rating reports cross the Atlantic? I fear so. Looked everywhere on the programme for instructions on humane euthanasia of unwanted virtual babies, but no apparent escape clauses after Late Term Abortion for Genuine Medical Reasons, which we've missed by months. Finally turned off the computer, but I know it's still sitting in there, mutely reproaching me, like a monstrous allegorical update of the Elephant Man.

There's the doorbell, probably the bailiffs from Grow-A-Kid. Have to pass the computer to get to it . . . Thank God. Ernestine!

**10 November, 2000** – Ernestine and Helen in Helen's living room

*(Ernestine is, as usual, a vision of artless chic that only a lifelong shopping habit can achieve. Helen is, for once, dressed. Des is asleep next door. Helen and Ernestine are crouched over the computer.)*

H: . . . so in the end I just stuffed him back in his chair and dodged home between the grenade-launchers. Shame, there was loads of food left.

E: So what exactly are you trying to do here?

H: I just want to get rid of it – humanely and painlessly, of course. What kind of a life is it going to have, living on the computer of somebody who can't even send an e-mail without crashing?

E: Okay – well . . .

*(It turns out that Ernestine can play an iMac like a Steinway grand. She hits a few keys – frowns.)*

E: It's not going to let me do anything until you pay your arrears – antenatal visits, scans, labour – it seems he was so deformed in the womb you had to have an emergency Caesarian with a senior consultant . . . God, it goes on . . . home nursing visits, lactation consultant . . .

188

H:    What's that?

E:    *(peering at screen)* Ummmm – you had problems feeding.

H:    They got that bit right.

E:    . . . total comes to – twenty-seven thousand, three hundred and nine dollars and forty cents. They're suggesting you might like to take out medical insurance along with the bill.

*(Helen reels back and drops her KitKat)*

H:    But . . . *(whimpering)* . . . but I don't have – I only have three thousand pounds. I checked, when I made my will.

*(Ernestine turns away from the computer)*

E:    You made a will? What's in it? Can I have those . . .

H:    You get the boots. It's there. But what am I going to . . .

E:    Hang on.

*(She hits a couple more keys. The Grow-A-Kid screen disappears, to be replaced by a screen full of code.)*

E:    Ha! This should get me to – now, where's billing . . .

*(A couple more minutes while Helen nervously tears into another KitKat, and the Grow-A-Kid screen returns, this time with a picture of a smiling, pudgy, healthy, beautiful virtual baby – still with bright purple almond eyes. As Ernestine leans in, the baby turns to her and flashes a huge smile. She jumps back.)*

E:    Shit! Motion detection! How do they . . .

H:    I hate it. Get rid of it.

*(The baby gurgles, flaps its arms, sticks a tiny thumb in its mouth, and returns to its starting position. A moment later, it repeats the cycle.)*

E:    Thank God, it had me worried there. Why do you want to get rid of it, it's so sweet now, look, and all healthy!

*(Helen peers at it)*

H:    It's still smiling. I hate it.

E:    I wonder – there must be a whole developmental algorithm in there somewhere – do you remember noticing how long you can keep it?

*(suddenly busy, she attacks the keyboard and returns to the home screen)*

E:  . . . Da da da . . . 'Your Grow-A-Kid will grow up just like the real thing, and live with you as long as you continue to give her/him your love and attention!'

H:  And life savings.

E:  Just like the real thing . . . So – if we can accelerate things a bit . . .

*(Back to the screen full of code. Ernestine works away. Helen goes to check on Des and returns with two cups of tea.)*

H:  He smiles in his sleep, the bastard. He smiles in the bath and at the telly. He smiles at the CURTAINS, for God's sake. WHY WON'T HE SMILE AT ME?

E:  *(preoccupied)* Hang on . . . that should do it!

*(She sits back and they both drink their tea and watch as the screen fills with an image of a truly gorgeous, olive-coloured, dark blond hunk with those violet eyes. Two simultaneous sighs of pure lust.)*

H:  My baby!

E:  There you go. Ready to go into the wide world. I'll take him off your hands.

*(She reaches for the keyboard. Helen stops her.)*

H:  Not so fast – what are you doing?

E:  I'm e-mailing him to my computer.

H:  But he's my child! You can't just abduct my child, you hardly know him!

E:  Well, neither do you, but you know me. Hey, doll, I just saved you twenty-seven thousand dollars. Either I take him, or you owe . . . for eighteen years we've just compressed . . . let's see . . .

*(Another few elegant keystrokes. A number comes up on the screen. Helen doesn't have to look closely to see it goes right the way across.)*

E:  So. I think that settles it, no? I'll terminate your account, and you can go back to being a real mum.

190

H: Promise you'll bring him to visit.
E: I'll send you pictures of the honeymoon, how about that?
H: Suddenly I feel very, very old.

## 14 November, 2000

Glad to be rid of Grow-A-Kid, though now have new cause to worry about Ernestine. If she can do that, she's probably into all our e-mails too. Good thing there's no money in my account for her to embezzle.

Seriously depressed about Des's failure to smile at me. Or anybody. At this point, would even welcome him smiling at Colum. Maybe he really is retarded. Are there crammers for this sort of thing? Tried to discuss with Colum where they might be – a circus? The Comedy Store? Colum said the sight of a grown adult bending over Des making Daffy Duck noises was far funnier than anything he'd seen at the Comedy Store.

## 14 November, 2000

*Frankly, I see very little to smile at. Apparently doomed to spend a lifetime as the helpless, immobile captive of two adults who constantly countermand each other's orders, and between them have all the leadership qualities of that brown furry thing in the corner of my basket. (I wish it would sleep, occasionally. I do find those staring black eyes very disconcerting. Still, I suppose that's the point of guard duty – eternal vigilance, etc.)*

## 20 November, 2000

Ernestine called up to say my son was incompatible with her operating system and she was waiting for an upgrade. Meanwhile occupying herself with latest b.f. – oceanographic consultant, tracking the movement of marine mammals through tropical waters. You can see where this is going. She's off on holiday with him, to Fiji.

**25 November, 2000** – E-mail from Hotel On-Tiki-N'en-Tal, Fiji

**From:** Ernestine Short [tallgirl@cloudnine.com]
**Sent:** Thursdy night
**To:** Helen McCallum [helen@guzzi.freeserve.com]

> > > > > >
Hi gorgeous>
> > sorry to have to say but this place is totally fabulous and wonderful. Corin turned out to be a bit of a wet (ha ha) he may be good at communicating with large marine mammals but I need more than the odd high-pitched squeak to keep me ammusd, anyway could not help myelf the boys here are SOOOOO beautiful ratehr like your virtual son in fact but dark hair and believe me nothing virtual that I've discovered so far!
> > > > > >
> > He did however introduce me to this great bunch of divers who go on daytrips mostly fising for torusits (you know what I mean) so I"ve finally got my scuba certificate – never quite fancied it at the Queen Mother Sports Centre pool somehow – and you could not beleive the things you see do . . .

*(e-mail summarily deleted at this point)*

192

**25 November, 2000** – Partial transcript of message left on Alison's answerphone

H:  . . . so I thought as you're always saying you always have to come to us and we never come to you, I'd bring him over – it's only thirty miles and it'd be good for us to get out, I'm practically root-bound here, and if we set off early there'll still be plenty of time to see your Michaelmas daisies in daylight, I thought if Friday would suit you? and don't bother about making anything fancy for lunch – but, actually, if you did have a minute, do you remember that amazing chocolate mud pie you got from Tesco last time we came . . .

**28 November, 2000** – Helen, Alison and Des at Alison's house

*(Helen is scrabbling in a changing bag in the middle of the floor of Alison's immaculate, if beige, living room. Des is lying on a plastic mat, on a very dirty, opened nappy, happily squirming around to get as much of it on him as possible. Alison's voice is heard outside.)*

A:  Yes, I'll tell her. His registration number, his address and the details of his insurance company.
*(she comes into the room with a tray of coffee and biscuits)*

A:  They say provided he's properly insured it shouldn't affect your no-claims bonus this time.
*(Helen sits up, indignant)*

H:  What do they mean, this time? He ran right into me!

A:  Only because you stopped at a green light, dear.

H:  I was exhausted, okay? Whose side are you on? And I get confused outside London, with all these mini-roundabouts.
*(she returns to scrabbling, hopelessly, in the bag)*

H:  I could have sworn I put a couple in – I remember distinctly taking them out of the packet with the wipes, and feeling proud of myself for being so organised.

A:   Then you'll probably find them just where you left them when you get back home.

*(She puts down the tray and goes towards the door again. As she exits:)*

A:   Luckily, I think I have one or two left over from when Jack was using them. They'll be a bit big, but it's better than nothing.

*(Helen zips up the bag, folds the dirty nappy and wipes Des's bum. He screws up his face, pulls his legs up and turns scarlet.)*

H:   Don't you dare!

*(Alison returns with a clean, enormous, nappy)*

A:   It's a good thing you carry the food supply with you. Have you tried him on a bottle yet?

*(Helen wraps the nappy around Des. It comes up to his armpits. She bursts out laughing and pulls his clothes over it.)*

D:   Weeeeh! (What are you laughing at? Whose fault is this anyhow?)

*(Alison picks him up. He stops crying at once.)*

A:   *(to Des)* There . . . she can't help it, she's as new to this as you are.

D:   Gsss! (Finally — some sympathy.)

*(She sits with him on her knee. He immediately falls asleep. Helen helps herself to coffee and picks around in the biscuits for the chocolate ones.)*

H:   I must say, it's very nice to get away, even to . . .

A:   I'm sorry I'm not a South Pacific atoll, Helen. You really must start to be content with what you have. Nobody has everything, you know.

H:   Oh God, I know, it's just — it's so sudden and it just never seems to end. If only there were — you know, a switch you could flick to turn it all off for half a day — even an hour . . .

A:   Responsibility isn't like that, dear. Now you see why I always said it was a full-time job. Not exactly intellectually challenging and God knows it had its hardships . . .

H: But I mean – the thought of having no life for the next twenty years . . .

A: So I suppose that means I've had no life, does it?
*(heavy silence)*

H: Tell you what, I just remembered something.
*(She jumps up and takes Des from Alison. He stirs and opens his eyes.)*

H: Have you got those old photo albums from when we were little? I wanted to know who he was going to look like. After he stops looking like Uncle Arthur.

A little later

*(The two women are now leaning over an open album. Des has dozed off again between them on the sofa.)*

A: . . . and that was that year at Butlins, when Georgie won the beauty contest . . .
*(Des stirs again, opens his eyes. The album is right in front of him.)*

H: *(peering in)* She was – she was really pretty then, wasn't she?

A: Don't sound so surprised.

H: And really fair. Rather like this person in fact. *(to Des)* Look, Des, it's Georgie.

D: Weeeeh? (That doesn't look like Georgie to me, even allowing for the fuzziness.)

H: So what did she look like when she was his age . . .
*(busily turning pages)*

D: Woooo wuh? (When was she my age? You mean she was once . . .)
*(Alison takes the album from her, and finds a photo of Georgie at three months)*

A: *(dubiously)* I don't know . . .

H: No, definitely, the shape of her face, look here, Des, she

195

looked just like you. You're going to look like your Aunt Georgie!

D: Weeeeeh!! Wisssshhhzzz! (So I'm not going to be this size for ever?)

H: Was she as fat as him, can you remember?

D: Eeeeh! Fssshsheee! (I'm going to get big, and my legs will work, and I'll get to have my wine straight from the bottle, and choose what to watch on TV – that's what Basic Training was all about? That's fantastic!)

A: He's a sweet little thing really, isn't he, when he's happy . . . *(he looks up at Alison . . .)*

D: Ffffssssshhh!! (So I only have to stay with her till I'm big enough, and she'll make sure everything's working okay before I leave? Thank you, thank you, Mission Control!)
*(. . . then he looks at Helen, and his face splits into a huge, big-eyed, right-at-her, unmistakable smile)*

## 30 November, 2000

*What did I do? Every five seconds now there's a grinning face looming over me. Hardly dare close my eyes for fear of what'll be there when I open them. Still, knowing it's all temporary and pretty soon I'll be able to engage them on equal terms makes just about anything tolerable. Yes, yes, I love you too. Now please let me get some sleep.*

## 5 December, 2000

Ernestine got back from her holiday with an elaborate plan to take the Internet to the South Seas, thereby bypassing the industrial revolution, the factory age and environmental pollution, and leapfrogging them directly into a world of electronic grass huts from which they will be able to upload their native music directly in MP3 files to the contracts department at Island Records.

Needless to say, accomplishing this requires the participation of her new, v, v glamorous Fijian musician/political activist boyfriend. Not envious in the least – her path is not my path. And I have a beautiful, wonderful, squidgy, SMILEY baby to hug who will love me for ever.

The cow.

She's all right really, I suppose. She wants to have a pre-Christmas using-up-the-leftover-fireworks party. She's borrowing some rich friend's house in the country and she said we could bring Des and stay the night, get a break, etc. Does sound nice, though after so long in solitary I'll probably forget how to talk or burst into tears or have a breakdown, like a hostage. Maybe I should arrange a couple of smaller-scale outings meanwhile, as gradual acclimatisation. Fat chance.

## 15 December, 2000

*It gets worse. First the bike, and now a trip to an enemy battlefield, in the dark, with no notice. They called it a party. Here's how it was from my point of view.*

C: Is it up here, then? I think it's up here.

    *(LURCH. JUDDER. Rumblerumblerumble . . .)*

H: Can it really be? It's very rough, this track. Do you think the car can cope with it?

C: That had been on my mind. Whose idea was this, again?

H: God, it's freezing in here, he'll catch his death, doesn't the heater work, I'll cover him up, SLOW DOWN!

*. . . and suddenly I can't see anything and I have hot wool in my mouth. WHAT'S GOING ON?*

H: Now he's crying, you've woken him up, that's all we need, well, you might as well keep driving at this speed now he's awake, I suppose.

*. . . and thank God they stop talking for once so I shut my eyes again and things are just calming down when . . .*

(RUMBLERUMBLERUMBLERUMBLESCRRRR-
RRUNCH!!!!)

*. . . and there's a blinding light right in my face. Okay, I remember*
*this is what they said interrogation would be like, except what have I*
*done to be interrogated about and a totally unfamiliar voice shouts right*
*in my ear:*

1:   You made it! Well done, you're not the last, here, I'll point
the torch on to the ground so you can see where you're
stepping, cheers, that's very handsome of you.

*. . . so I open my eyes, which is difficult enough against the searchlight*
*beam, to see another totally unfamiliar adult female with a huge red*
*slavering mouth about two inches from me going . . .*

2:   EEEEEEEEEEEHELEN! COLUM! YOU'RE HERE!
Ernie's about somewhere, I'm just kind of showing people
in for her, it's a bit rough underfoot, OOOHH, THE BABY,
HAVE YOU BROUGHT HIM??? OHhhhhhh, sorry, is he
asleep? OHHHHH, he's adorable, isn't he adorable, what's
his name?'

*I know they won't remember my name, I didn't choose it anyway, it's*
*not MY name as far as I'm concerned, I don't see how it can be MINE*
*if I don't WANT it, and how am I supposed to keep track, I've had*
*a trainee number and three different names already, but more impor-*
*tantly there are four huge looming strange faces with red blotchy cheeks*
*sticking out their wet lips dangerously close to my face and they're*
*waving around so I can't get a proper bead on them, focusing is a full-*
*time job in itself, and just when I've got them more or less sharp . . .*

C:   Let's get him out of the car, shall we?

*. . . and wheeee, I'm sideways, no, I'm backwards, now I'm sideways*
*again, and I'm SURE I've never been here before and it's rockety*
*rockety rockety, I can't quite see if I'm being carried by somebody I*
*know and I can't even smell the host because all these other smells are*
*suddenly in the way and*

(RAR!! RAR RAR RAR RAR!!!)

*oh my God, there's a huge black hairy thing snapping teeth as long as my nose at me, has she seen it? She can't have seen it, she wouldn't do that to me even if I did wake her up four times last night and*

1: MISCHIEF! Mischief, you naughty boy, DOWN, naughty boy, he's fine, honestly, wouldn't hurt a fly, he's so old, poor thing, he gets confused, would you like a drink?

*HE gets confused! He's not the only one and frankly getting confused with his dinner has little appeal to me, I'm keeping it together as hard as I can now but it's getting pretty tense, there was definitely nothing in the Training Manual about any of this, and nobody can call me a coward, I never once fled in the face of the enemy, even if they were only training exercises that has to count for something, then THUMP!, well, I seem to be on solid ground, everything's looming way overhead as usual, at least that means the huge smelly faces are a bit farther away, but what's that he's holding, careful, you're going to – WATCH OUT!*

2: Oh Christ, hah hah hah, must have started on the mulled wine sooner than I thought, never mind, no harm done, missed him by miles, isn't he good, the little love, he scarcely blinked.

H: No, he's really placid, actually I think he's a retard, just lies around like an anemone on a rock waving his hands about, doesn't seem to have a clue about anything . . .

*. . . RETARD! Is this the thanks I get for my admirable self-restraint and stoical composure, I'll give them retard, just you wait – but help, here's another different face now, and just let me focus here, STOP MOVING AROUND, TOO CLOSE, move away, won't you.*

3: Can he see me? How much can he see, can he see this green scarf, here, Desi baby, pwetty green scarf!!

*Of course I can bloody see if you give me a chance, though if I were you I wouldn't have matched that scarf with that orange shirt, in fact that shirt is giving me a distinctly queasy feeling after the car journey, er, excuse me, watch out . . .*

3: OH! Oh, all over my Equipment shirt, no, don't worry, honestly, I know a very good cleaner's in Belgravia, I'm sure they can get it out.

H:    He doesn't normally do that, he's usually very good, it's probably the journey too on that bumpy road, so sorry . . .

*Thank you for that small token of support, I was beginning to wonder whose side you were on here, bringing me to this hell-hole.*

H:    . . . although I have to admit I have been wearing more cotton things lately, still, it's a small price to pay, well, compared to the sleeplessness and everything, come on, darling, let's get you wiped up and changed, will you excuse me for a minute?

*Thank God, now at least I'm being carried by somebody I know, IN arms, not that stupid car seat, and I can usually bet when you take me off to change the nappy I'll get a bit of undivided attention in a quiet place, a chance to regroup and steel my nerve again, if there IS anywhere quiet around here, which I'm beginning to doubt, AAAARGH, what's that searing heat, I don't believe it, there's a bloody fire raging just over there, must have been a bombardment, so where's the enemy – maybe this is the enemy, maybe YOU're the enemy all along and I've been lured into a deathtrap . . .*

H:    Barbecue! How wonderful, lamb chops with the fat on, gosh, I can smell the garlic from here . . .

*Garlic. I remember the last time you had that . . .*

H:    . . . I'll grab some in a minute when I've changed him, I shouldn't, though, I'll suffer for it later, ha ha . . .

*YOU'll suffer for it, garlic and cherries it was last time, that was one night I'd rather forget, I guess she must have forgotten it already otherwise . . . hang on now, I can't see anything, it smells like nappies, though . . .*

H:    Is there a light in here? Oh, I see.

*Christ, will you get that out of my eyes, I'm being blinded here, at least this part of the place doesn't seem to be under enemy occupation yet, just put me down, will you, thank you, at last.*

H:    There, darling, isn't this fun!

*Fun! FUN? I am beyond words at this point, just take a look before*

*you throw that in the bin, I ask you, is that normal, no, it's not, and
do you know why?*

(HELEN! YOU'RE MISSING THE FIREWORKS!!!!!)

*Jesus God, what's that? Never, not even on the most advanced training
exercises, did they put us through . . .*

H:   COMING!!! There, that'll do, come on, pretty coloured
     lights, you're going to love it . . .

*No. Tell me it's not true. Tell me you're not going out again, into that,
there's a massacre going on out there, I can hear the screams, shame
about the donor, but he'll just have to look out for himself at this point,
we need to get ourselves to safety, I SAID TO SAFETY, WHAT
ARE YOU DOING, YOU'RE GOING RIGHT INTO IT!!!!*

4:   What a shame he gets tired so easily – is he normally diffi-
     cult?'

*DIFFICULT!!! DIFFICULT!!!*

C:   Christ, love, what are you doing to the wee thing, come
     on, give him here, I'll take him to the car, hadn't we better
     think about leaving, it's a long drive home . . .


**15 December, 2000** – Helen, Colum and Des in the car driving
home

> *(Des is finally asleep, exhausted, and snoring like a grampus.
> Helen and Colum are talking.)*

C:   . . . ye ken, ye have to see it from his point of view. I could
     have told you it'd be too much for the poor wee thing,
     but . . .

H:   So what, so we're supposed to sit at home every evening
     for the rest of our lives just because of him? What about
     us?

C:   Don't exaggerate. Mebbe five years.
     *(The car swerves and brakes. Des stirs. Helen, with dramatic
     concern, leans forward and soothes him.)*

C: Christ, man – don't bother to indicate, will you?

H: Do you want me to drive? I didn't get a chance to drink anything. As you know.

C: I'm fine.

*(silence)*

C: Personally, I wouldn't mind staying home from another evening like that.

H: What do you mean?

C: Four hours in the car, a bunch of empty-headed drunks falling into a bonfire, and the enticing prospect of a headache tomorrow from that cheap mulled wine. A rip-roaring time for all concerned.

H: Well, if you hated them that much, you could have looked after the baby and given me a chance to talk to them. She's my friend, after all.

C: I couldn't get near him!

H: Excuse me?

*(Their voices are now quite loud. Des opens his eyes and looks from one to the other.)*

C: Whenever there's anybody else around, suddenly he's your baby, you're the sainted madonna, and I'm just the chauffeur – and banker, of course.

H: Oh, that's really great . . .

D: Weeeh? (This is new.)

C: Then we get home and suddenly it's do this, do that, change his nappy, pat his back . . .

H: Oh, for God's sake! *(shouting)* It's fine for you – you get to go out all day and be Mr Big at work, and I'm stuck at home stuffing his face at one end and emptying his nappies at the other all bloody day . . .

D: WaaaaaHHH! (That's a bit of an exaggeration!)

C: *(infuriatingly calm)* Shhhhh! You're upsetting him now. Do ye not think he's been upset enough tonight already?

H: *(quietly venomous, through clenched teeth)* Oh, so I'm upsetting him. Not Mr Perfect, of course. Never Mr Perfect. Well, maybe you should try it just once and see how you get on . . .

D: WEEEEHHHH! WEAHHHH! (This is getting very interesting, but please concentrate on your primary task, I'd like to live a bit longer.)

C: *(to Des, ignoring Helen)* Whissht, little one. There, there. We'll have ye home in a jiffy.

D: Whhhuuuu – uuuh – zzzz . . . (Thank you, and please keep the noise level dow . . .)

## 16 December, 2000

*Well, that was extremely interesting – and a great vindication of the Divide and Conquer strategy from the Training Manual. Who knew that the united front would crumble so easily? Must seek out opportunities to utilise this new weapon early and often. Flinch at slightest raised voice, look agonised when door slams, burst into tears at first sign of shouting . . .*

*. . . So long as the physical danger doesn't escalate. Wonder whether it's too late to make one last attempt at contacting Mission Control re. alternative posting? I suppose the other strategy would be to find some credulous comrade in a safer camp and persuade him to swap. But rarely see any of them, and if the last rendezvous was anything to go by, won't again for some time.*

## 16 December, 2000

Why, why did I ever have a baby with this heartless monster? So awful, seeing Des's tiny face all crumpled and terrorised, and realising that I'm tied for ever to that smirking, complacent beast who acted as though nothing was wrong. Didn't speak to him before he left this morning, but he went off to work whistling cheerily – might even have been 'Jingle Bells'! – apparently quite unaffected by the horrors of last night.

Well, it's done, and I've got to make the most of it. This is your finest hour, Helen. Rise above it, and think, not of your-self, but of the tiny helpless one in your care. Perfectly calm after two KitKats and three cups of tea, must think clear-headedly about what to do.

(Damn that bloody radio and its bloody chirpy Christmas spirit. Tragic but not unexpected irony that these life-shattering events should happen at Christmas time. Was so looking forward to our first Christmas as a family – the first of the new millen-nium . . .)

So. The bald facts are that C is clearly not intending to leave. Life is too cushy by far here, plus he now has a tiny apprentice to groom in his image and to gratify his appalling narcissism. In fact, lying awake last night, realised there are many ways in which I have played right into his hands all along. The mere arrival of poor, helpless Des provides unassailable and permanent re-inforcement for C's lifelong desire never to go anywhere or do anything. Has already begun to claim kinship with baby in other ways – come to think of it, all too obviously his father's son, and all too obvious that I'm destined to be sidelined sooner rather than later. For instance:

| COLUM | DES |
|---|---|
| Partially bald | Almost totally bald |

(– in fact they've probably got about one normal head of hair between them, and it's just a matter of witnessing the relentless transfer from now on)

| never wants to do anything new | apparently incapable of doing anything new |
|---|---|
| always eats the same thing | 1 item in diet |

|                        |                         |
| ---------------------- | ----------------------- |
| hates parties          | last night . . .        |
| loves his drink        | loves his drink         |
| prefers the horizontal | relapses into it if left |
|    at all times |    for a moment |

So there, not a hair between them (as it were). All of which, of course, is in direct conflict with my own tastes, habits and desires. Looking at the above, it's extraordinary that C and I have survived so far, but given these deep and probably unbridgeable rifts in our relationship, we are clearly doomed to a future of conflict and acrimony.

And the sight of poor little Des, trapped in the middle of it – having rows is bad enough, but this is far, far worse than anything I've ever endured before. Knives to the heart.

So clearly the grown-up, sensible solution is to get a baby-sitter once a week so we can go out and fight – er, resolve our differences – in an amicable, adult way, where Des won't have to suffer too. Have drawn up strategy document for these occasions – will take Des into bed with me and leave it for Colum on sofa before I retire. That should be enough of a hint, I should think.

### Rules of Conduct for Weekly 'Discussion Meetings'

1 Meetings to take place in neutral location, with widely spaced tables to facilitate Free and Frank Exchange of Views, but not noisy enough to encourage shouting.
2 Not more than one drink (unit of alcohol) to be consumed per hour per participant (I know he's bigger but he's more aggressive, too).
3 Bill to be paid by each participant alternately to avoid invidious repetition of low blow re. 'the banker' delivered the other night by certain persons.
4 Agenda for discussion to be drawn up at beginning of session. Each participant has the right to monitor and terminate

unwarranted departures from said agenda in favour of, for instance, slurs concerning excessive consumption of chocolate or occasional lapses of concentration during washing-up.

5 No further discussion of matters dealt with once bill is paid. No reference in any context to any of it until following session. *In extremis*, emergency session may be called once baby is asleep, but not after 11 p.m.

There. That should do it. Now to print it out and leave it before taking opportunity of early night. Hmm, only 5.45. Well, there's a big sleep deficit to make up.

## 16 December, 2000 – 2200 Helen's bedroom

*(Two contrapunctal snores puncture the darkness. A low light snaps on briefly to illuminate Colum gently lifting Des out of the bed, before he snaps it off again.)*

C: Let's be having ye, little man. Shhhh . . .

*(Sound of Colum padding into living room and putting Des into basket. Brief whimper before sleep prevails. Sound of Colum padding back. Sound of rustling on Colum's side of bed.)*

C: *(whispering)* Ye silly ol' biddy, come here . . .
*(more rustling)*

H: *(sleepily)* Whaaa – what are you doing here?

C: I live here, woman. This is my bed. Our bed.

H: *(little sigh)* You were horrible. You're a beast.

C: Grrrrrrr!

H: Did you get my note?

C: I'm an illiterate beast. But an awfu' friendly one . . .
*(prolonged rustling, giggling and squeals)*

**16 December, 2000** – very late

*I'm not at all sure that this divide-and-conquer stuff is worth it, if it means the rules changing every five minutes. Take the sleeping arrangements. It started out okay – I slept with her and he slept somewhere else – very convenient for midnight snacks. Then he moved in with us – well, you know what that was like. Talk about too close for comfort. Then he started saying I had to move out, and she started saying I was too old to sleep with her, and needed to sleep on my own, in that basket thing. (So if I'm too old to sleep with her, what does that make him? From what I saw in that album, he's weeks older than me. Months, even.) Then, just tonight, she brings me back into bed with her, no sign of him, all very satisfactory. But within hours, HE moves me back in here. He's probably with her in there now. What next? I shan't sleep a wink, I know itzzzzzzzzzzz . . .*


**18 December, 2000**

Considerably more cheerful since discovered that Ernestine also had a terrible time at her firework party, having had to spend almost all night in Accident and Emergency with Fijian boyfriend whose cultural unfamiliarity with basic procedure around fireworks, combined with her great idea of beefing the display up with a naval maroon, ended in near-tragedy. *Schadenfreude* is a wonderful thing, if kept to civilised limits.

Then started thinking about Christmas, what to do, etc. While sorting out huge pile of papers and bills, in optimistic hope of ending the year with at least some visible desk surface, came across last year's diary. Could not help making comparison between Christmas week last year and this.

Saturday 18    1300 Lunch with Ernie and Sophie, followed
               by shopping and nails
               1900 Drinks in Soho with aforesaid,
               somehow became . . .
               2200 Dinner and more drinks at Baguette
Sunday 19      1200 Brunch in Hampstead with friends of
               Colum
               1330 Lunch-time drinks party chez Charles
               (old college friend)
               1700 Carol-singing and mince pies with
               neighbours up and down street
               2100 Ernie's boyfriend's party
Monday 20      1030 Morning at work writing Christmas
               cards
               1230 Xmas lunch with former colleagues
               from rival archive
               1500 Back to work
               1545 Left early to get hair done
               2000 Dinner with friends from school
               (annual ritual)
Tuesday 21     1045 Work, wrapped parcels
               1115–1215 Queued at post office
               1230 Colum's office Christmas lunch. Not
               worth going back to work . . . quick dinner
               at home
               2230 Film transfer company party at noisy
               West End club
Wednesday 22   1130 Arrived at work, just time to stick office
               stamps on remaining Christmas cards before
               1300 office Christmas lunch. Definitely not
               worth going back to work (nobody there)
               2000 Georgie's friend Martin's 'pre-chill'

|  | party at Covent Garden spa, followed by . . . |
|  | 2400 complimentary midnight massage |
| Thursday 23 | 1130 Went to work to hand out and receive presents. |
|  | 1330 Big lunch-time bash at Croatian Film Board. Croatian vodka not half bad |
|  | 1700 Early drinks at Polish Film Board (Polish vodka better) |
|  | ? Can't remember |
| Friday 24 | Last-minute scrum at supermarket, followed by food prep in front of TV with champagne . . . |

Helen's Engagements – week of 16 December 2000

| Saturday 16 | Declaration of war followed by temporary truce |
|  | Sterilised baby bath |
| Sunday 17 | Went out for paper! (and KitKat) |
|  | Started to sort paperwork |
|  | Made identical presents (lavender-scented sleep masks) for everybody – no money or opportunity to shop |
|  | Fell asleep in front of TV (again) |
| Monday 18 | (today) Sorted more paperwork |
|  | Went out for Dettol and nappy rash cream |
|  | Bleached 3 Babygros . . . |

At this point, amazed at my own fortitude in not having committed ritual seppuku in baby aisle of Sainsbury's, but saved the thought for 'Discussion' with Colum (emergency late-night summit in bed – saves on baby-sitter and better for figure), resulting in compromise whereby I can have a modest Christmas dinner party for a few close friends, provided he has the right of veto over the guest list and all the washing-up is done before sunrise, or mid-December equivalent.

Decided only to invite people who don't make me nervous, which also happens to mean people who don't have babies, but that's okay – spent an enjoyable hour while Des slept, reacquainting myself with recipe books and planning a menu that can be entirely prepared in advance, thus leaving Colum and me free to deal with guests (and possibly baby, though he is beginning to sleep better, thank God, and for once I can just keep tanking him up if all else fails). Invited two couples who only vaguely know each other but have loads in common.

Done the shopping list, even made a schedule for it – slightly worrying that I can no longer remember anything unless it's written down, but if I pin it on the kitchen notice-board I'll just be able to check on it as I work. And Colum has sweetly offered to look after Des while I do so. C also sweetly offered to cook, as ruse for remaining in kitchen throughout, but I rumbled him – just as well, as his culinary repertoire, from what I remember, consists almost entirely of things that look like an early Dutch anatomy lesson. Rather pleased with my menu – rustic Italianate with whimsical details and nice crusty bits, and a pudding containing four of the five fundamentals (fruit, nuts, cream, alcohol and chocolate).

**22 December, 2000** – Menu for Christmas Dinner Party

Hot smoked salmon, ricotta and dill 'sausage rolls' (to pass round with drinks)

Roast pork stuffed with prosciutto, sage and anchovies, baked with fennel, potatoes and onions

Salad of baby spinach, pears and roasted Brazil nuts in ginger-soy dressing

Steamed lemon pudding, whipped cream with honey and whisky.

1600  Feed Des and hand over to Colum

1700  Make salmon rolls (as mother of new baby, permitted
self to buy ready-made puff pastry) and arrange on
baking tray

1730  Stuff and tie pork, prepare vegetables and surround
meat in roasting dish

1815  Make pudding, put in fridge till ready to cook
Whip cream, put in fridge

1845  Make salad and grill nuts. Switch grill to oven at 200°
Make dressing, keep separate until ready to serve

1900  Meat into oven

1915  Bathe, change
Colum bathes Des

1945  Lay table, open wine, slip salmon rolls into oven above
meat.

2000  Quick feed of Des before

2030  Guests arrive – Colum puts Des to bed
Boil water for pudding
Eat salmon rolls
Take pork out of oven to 'rest'. Turn off oven
Dress salad

2045  Pudding on to steam. Boil fresh kettle to top up pudding

2100  Eat main course and salad

2145  Eat pudding. Relax!

There, all laid out step by step. What could be easier? Yum.


**22 December, 2000** – Actual Schedule of Christmas Dinner Party

1600  Feed Des. Des refuses to feed. Clearly the little demon
senses something's up

1700  Finally hand screaming baby, still roaring with hunger, over
to Colum

1715 Make salmon rolls and arrange on baking tray. Discover tray too big to go in oven. Change all over to smaller tray. Tray now too small for all rolls – will have to cook in two batches

1745 Stuff and tie pork, prepare vegetables and surround meat in roasting dish. Realise roasting dish and baking tray will not fit in oven at same time. Will have to cook salmon rolls ahead of time and hope they survive

1830 Grill first lot of salmon rolls

1845 Make pudding, put in fridge

1900 Discover ricotta filling has oozed out of salmon rolls and stuck to baking tray, making it impossible to remove rolls without shattering them. Do what can to save them, scrape rest hurriedly into bin, cover encrusted baking tray with heavily oiled foil, shove remainder of rolls on it, put under grill and pray

1920 Whip cream, put in fridge. Abandon idea of bath. Colum brings back baby, having had nap, now apparently hungry. Hurriedly feed baby. Realise forgot to specify arrival time for guests. Surely they'll come more or less at same time? Anyhow, too late to do anything about it now, looks too much like harassing to call them at this stage

1945 Pass kitchen and notice what look like flames dancing inside oven. Remember second batch of salmon rolls. Too late. Douse flames (first handing baby over to Colum, ha ha), throw various towels on floor to mop up water, open all doors and windows on to freezing night air. Finish feeding baby and hand back to Colum, covered in black sooty marks

2000 Remember to turn grill over to oven (well done, but shame about sooty marks now all over oven controls too). Wipe hands on clothes. Put in meat – who cares if it gets a bit brown on top while grill setting changing over to oven?

2010 Abandon idea of grilling nuts. Throw bag salad into bowl, hastily chop raw, unwashed pears over it as first lot of guests arrive, trilling, 'Are we too early?' Chop finger. Run to bathroom, trying to mop up blood trail on floor with stockinged feet as go. Hiss at Colum to give them drinks and then lay table, at least, for God's sake. Colum still trying to persuade baby to sleep, again. No luck. Baby points out just had long nap. Baby dumped with (childless) guests

2020 Make dressing. Arrange very small quantity of edible salmon rolls on large plate. Change to smaller plate. (Sink now overflowing)

2030 First lot of guests, by a miracle, now have drinks and small quantity of food, but ask plaintively if they may have their coats back. Realise doors and windows still all wide open. Pass mirror. Realise still wearing sweatpants and baggy old jumper, now attractively smeared with soot as well as homoeopathic quantities of tonight's menu ingredients. Contemplate strolling into dining room and cheerfully announcing decision to keep evening informal by dressing casual. Contemplate jumping out of window. Contemplate throwing meal out of window. Sadly too feeble to throw guests out of window. Can hear conversation continuing (sort of), so decide had better be heroic after all. Throw on first dress that falls out of cupboard I've been half sorting ever since realised I won't fit into any of my usual winter clothes this winter and might as well store them out of the way, except something else happened that now escapes me and it never got finished

2050 Return to guests. Salmon rolls long since finished. Second round of drinks well down. No sign or sound of second lot of guests. Conversation drying out somewhat – Des somehow monopolising everybody's attention without entertaining them, like Tory MP opening church bazaar.

Way past his bedtime. Decide to take things in hand and briefly escape glacial atmosphere by putting him to bed

2100 Des declines invitation to go to bed, loudly. Distinctly observe gleam of pure malice in his eye. Contemplate putting Roast Suckling Child on menu of next such occasion, except there is never, ever going to be any next such occasion, ever

2115 Leave him to it, return to by now clearly panic-stricken guests attempting to play down noise as of several babies being simultaneously massacred in bedroom. Brief, jocular discussion ensues of the wisdom of their decision not to have any. Still no sign of other guests. Definitely would look like harassing to call them now. Maybe they've got drunk and forgotten, or been involved in a seasonal fatality in their unreliable, but overpowered, car. What to do? Leave Colum (again) pouring third round of drinks while rush into kitchen (tripping on wet towels) to look for something can use to whip up supplementary appetisers while they wait. Scrabble about in fridge, find two rotting tomatoes and a very, very dry end of French bread. Eureka! Bruschetta! In between stuffing bread into toaster, peep into oven. Meat attractive brown, vegetables black on top (but in good way). Turn oven right down and hope for best

2130 Return to guests in triumph with tray of granite-like bread studded with wet tomato seeds. Not a bit disappointed by their polite refusal as stuff entire plateful in, between three drinks in quick succession (important to keep pace with the company in order to share wavelength). Conversation now non-existent. Realise in conversational vacuum broken only by sound of my own eating and drinking that Des is still screaming and I hadn't even noticed. Give up on bedtime idea, finish plateful, toss plate in sink, rush away from disaster scene once again to get him up. Realise he really, really smells. Just at crucial stage of wiping with one hand and keeping legs out of way with the other when . . .

2145 Doorbell rings. 'Are we on time? You didn't say, so we just guessed. Something smells . . .' (of course it bloody does, and not just the baby, you drunken, inconsiderate, selfish, hateful pair of social assassins). Entire rest of party now gathered round front door to greet them, rather like Relief of Mafeking. Finish changing baby while they all go back and manage to find things to say for about five minutes, before squeaky-clean sober late arrivals ('We've given up entirely, it seemed like a good time to do it with all the driving to parties and what not . . . No, not at all, we feel marvellous, don't we, darling? Haven't felt like this since I was twenty-one!') discover that everybody else, including Des, is out of their tree already, and shut up in reproachful dismay

2200 Barely give them time for one swig of mineral water before ushering them to table. Take meat and veg out of oven. What was, half an hour ago, a perfectly cooked rustic Italian meal is now a perfect replica of an Italian archaeo-logical dig. Somehow gulp back tears as observe it collapse into a million shards at first blow of chisel. In passing, notice schedule for this evening gleefully grinning on notice-board. Pudding! There's always pudding! I'll eat it even if nobody else does. Boil water and take archaeo-logical finds in for others to scavenge. Attempt to disguise extent of disaster by burying site in heavy forestation (salad). Put pudding – now one hope on which salvation of entire future life depends – gently into pan of boiling water, whisper a few encouraging words over it, and reluc-tantly rejoin 'party'. Ha! Des decides he has not eaten for 50,000 years, so I'm out of consideration for the dig anyway. Anyhow, who could eat after a disaster on this Vesuvian scale? (too late to rein in metaphor)

2230 First lot of guests apologetically indicate that they have to leave while they can still remember where they parked. Beyond even pretending to beg. Let 'em go, the lot of them, and the sooner the better. Personally, can barely keep my eyes open. Only the thought of pudding sustains me. Try not to make it too obvious as return to kitchen every two minutes, picking my way among discarded roasting pans, baking trays, appetiser plates and empty bottles to check on level of water and exact rate of simmer, measured in number of tiny bubbles bursting to surface per minute. Baby now by far the most animated person at table, telling jokes, gesturing expansively, flashing his most outrageous smile. Childless, sober, ravenous guests mysteriously unmoved

2300 Second lot of guests, whose sudden attack of sobriety turns out to be not unrelated to having to be at work at 6 a.m. or face prospect of cheery seasonal redundancy, announce that they too have to leave. Barely notice. Pudding just about ready, and perfect. All the more for me

**19 December, 2000**

*First real triumph last night – invasion by alien adults successfully repelled, entirely by putting into practice strategy of last resort as specified in Basic Training. Fortunately I was paying attention during that particular module. They won't try that again in a hurry.*

Excerpt from Basic Training Manual, 903rd Edition – Appendix D: 'If You Can't Beat 'Em . . .'

During your sojourn with the adults, it may occasionally happen that they attempt to rendezvous with other adults but without you, leaving you under temporary substitute guard. Needless to say such gatherings can only strengthen their position vis-à-vis yours, especially if the other adults are also sheltering babies, as vital information could well be exchanged which they will use to better themselves against you.

Therefore, on no account must you allow this to happen. Initially, your best bet is to use all your well-practised skills to decoy, delay and otherwise prevent them from leaving. Crying, filling your nappy repeatedly, vomiting inexplicably, refusing to feed, or feeding to excess – all of these will rattle them, get them off guard and, most vitally, prevent them from getting away.

If all of these fail, there's only one remaining recourse, known as If You Can't Beat Them, Join Them. What this means is, quite simply, that in the last resort, if you refuse with sufficient firmness and persistence to be left, they must take you along.

Once you are at the gathering, it is in your interests to mirror as closely as you can the adults' behaviour and actions. This way you will minimise the attention paid to you, and maximise your own opportunities for espionage and information-gathering. As an aid to this, we append below some examples of typical adult group activities, with hints on appropriate behaviour.

### 1 The Football Match

Having got yourself, on the coldest and wettest day of winter, to the most exposed, bleakest outdoor slum you can find, stand for two hours or until somebody knocks you out with a beer can, yelling unintelligibly alongside ten thousand other under-occupied males, while a very, very long way away, a small, half-naked group of them runs around after a ball, taking no notice of you. Go home.

### 2 The Cricket Match

Much the same as above, but less frequent and less noisy vocal-isation. Normally you can expect slightly better weather, but it has still not been satisfactorily explained why, unlike most arte-facts of human civilisation, neither of these has yet been auto-mated and miniaturised for speed and convenience.

### 3 The Shopping Trip

Set out late. However late you intended to leave Base Camp, never leave less than an hour later, having spent intervening period changing your clothes four or five times and wailing about having nothing to wear. (You might have thought that, as this is the ostensible reason for the trip, it wouldn't matter. Don't ask.) Go in and out of many different places, all containing many racks of apparently identical garments. Put on, and remove, far more of them than you either need or want, preferably in sizes quite obviously far too small. Complain about this, but refuse point blank to go near ones that would actually fit. Fall into deep state of gloom at not having succeeded in wasting all your money, yet. Have meal, with alcohol. Return to places where you tried on the things that didn't fit, and buy them anyway, swearing to lose twenty pounds by next week.

### 4 The Drinks Party

Follow initial proceedings as above re. lateness and wailing about nothing to wear, but become far more hysterical on latter point and eventually leave in what you were wearing before you began to get ready. Travel very long distance to destination. If on public transport, miss train or hit deluge on emerging from station/bus/taxi. If driving, spend just a little longer looking for parking spot than it took to do the actual journey. Enter building to find it already contains far more people than safety regulations could possibly sanction. Fight through choking smoke and deafening noise in search of refreshment to discover everything long since consumed. Stand in tightly packed crowd of incoherent people all talking at once. Do not worry unduly that you know nothing about house prices, winter holiday destinations, public vs private education or latest political sleaze story. Neither do they. (Even if you could hear them.) At this point, you can safely fall asleep.

## 5  The Picnic

Make sure to leave preparation for this until absolutely last minute. Then fall into furious temper, complaining of amount of work involved. Rush to supermarket and return with loaf of French bread, lump of cheese, ready-cooked chicken and bag salad. Remove all packagings and rewrap ineptly to look home-prepared. Pack bag with food and assortment of cheap, unmatching cutlery and paper plates left over from last drinks party (see above). Pack large additional bag with extra-warm clothes, insect bite ointment, camera, umbrella (see below), and disgusting old rug covered in dog hair. Spend an hour looking for battered sheet of paper with directions to rendezvous location. Look out of window. Change all clothes and repack bag. Set out. Get lost. Give up, return home via off-licence, and consume food and drink straight from bag. (Those of you posted to northern Europe, including Great Britain, need not memorise this section. The event will inevitably be rained off.)

## 6  The Dinner Party

Begin as in Drinks Party (above), except arrive before everybody else and begin to drink, rapidly and prodigiously, at once. (In the event that the party is convened at Base Camp, this stage can be initiated without the presence of others.) Make sure to have eaten nothing for some time beforehand in order to accelerate the effects of above. On arrival of others, continue to drink and eventually to eat, also to excess, with great and increasing animation and, at first, much apparent enthusiasm for whole procedure. Then, while remaining noisy and energetic, add a measure of aggression, which may develop into full-scale agitation and even attack. If at any point this is met with a threat of bedtime, suddenly become extraordinarily sleepy and quiet. With luck, they will be too confused and 'tired' themselves to carry out the threat, and you can safely give your most convincing and noisy impression of deep slumber while secretly keeping an eye and ear open for any (highly improbable) important information . . .

*Well, I think from what I remember that I carried out the guidelines more or less to the letter. I was certainly the most coherent person present by the time the invading party finally retreated. And, sure enough, they eventually forgot all about me – invaders repelled, donor retreated to officers' mess, muttering about divorce, and host buried whole head in pudding basin, where she remained as I finally allowed myself to nod off.*

## 20 December, 2000

Spent yesterday moving very, very slowly around at home, muttering, 'They've gone! They've gone!'

Never again. (But no reason not to make lemon pudding more often.) Can it have been me who longed for Christmas jollity and company? Planning to spend remainder of festive season in bed. Am already priming extended family members by coughing down the phone and muttering about mysterious lassitude and the peculiar ferocity of paediatric flu. They won't come near us if they think we're a germ farm.

While scrabbling under the furniture for fragments of ancient Sicilian roast dinner, discovered print-out of Colum's aesthetic parenting regime. Laughed. Went and dug out 'Are You Ready?' e-mail from America. Laughed like drain.

## December, 2000 – Bills from Helen's Christmas shopping

```
Marks & Spencer Ltd
Oxford Circus
22/12/00


Orkney smoked salmon, pre-sliced, full side    £22.00
Assorted luxury mini-breads, heat and serve     £1.50
Beurre d'Isigny 500 g                           £1.45
```

Fresh soupe de poissons with langoustine
meat, rouille and garlic croutons                    £4.59
Fresh poulet des Landes, apricot cranberry
stuffing                                             £7.99
Fresh mashed potato with spring onion
and bacon                                            £1.99
Ready-trimmed Brussels sprouts
with chestnuts                                       £1.99
Luxury recipe Christmas pudding with
cherries, walnuts, brandy and port — 1kg     £6.49
Fresh cream custard — large                          £1.50
Brandy butter — large                                £2.50
Luxury whipped cream with honey liqueur      £2.99
Six deep-filled all-butter brandy
mince pies × 2                                       £1.65
                                                     £1.65
Cornish clotted cream — large                        £2.50
Gloucester Old Spot outdoor reared bacon × 2    £2.49
                                                     £2.49
Organic free-range brown eggs, dozen         £1.50
New York bagels, sesame, × 6                         £1.35
Extra-vintage coarse-cut marmalade
with almonds                                         £2.30
Blue Heaven relaxing bath essence            £3.99
Jasmin de Provence scented floating candles     £4.99
Sabrina Teenage Witch magic makeover kit     £3.99
McLaren F1 bathtime fun kit                          £3.49
Pyjamas, men's, size L                              £24.99
M&S special collection eye colours 'fantasy'  £10.99
M&S aromatic burner w' orange incense        £9.49

SUBTOTAL                                            £132.85
Paid with thanks
Please keep your receipt for refunds or returns

221

```
Oddbins Ltd
Voted Wine Merchant of the Millennium — Every
Millennium

1 × bargain doz. Oddbins House Champagne      £154.99
2 × GlenSpittle Thirty Year Old @ £16.99       £33.98
1 × Kahlua                                     £11.99
1 × case HottPosch Peach Bier                  £15.99
1 × case Lindemans Bin 99 Shiraz                 £66
CASE DISCOUNT                                 -£22.10

SUBTOTAL                                      £360.85
PAID VISA WITH THANKS

BRING US YOUR NEW YEAR HANGOVERS!
```

```
Marks & Spencer Ltd
22/12/00

Refunds/Exchanges

1 × Orkney smoked salmon, side
CREDIT                                         £22.00

2 × assorted Belgian luxury chocolates
PURCHASE                                        £9.95
                                                £9.95

SUBTOTAL CR                                     £2.10

Please keep your receipt for refunds or returns
```

## 23 December, 2000

Why didn't we ever do this before? Only one glitch when found
smoked salmon in bag and experienced full-on, Jacob's ladder-
style acid flashback of Saturday night. They were very good

about exchanging it. Would never do to run out of chocolate at this of all times of year. Managed to get presents for Georgie, Brian, their two and Mum at same time – if they're foolish enough to ignore the quarantine zone. Now it's just me, Colum, Des and our debt mountain. Oh well, it's not so bad here, nice and cosy, eh, Des? Not bad this Oddbins fizz, either – very drinkable, as Jancis would say. I suppose we ought to have waited for Colum, but he won't be back for hours, I shouldn't think – can't be bothered to switch on bedside light. Just time for a little disco nap before then . . .

## 23 December, 2000

*I have to shay thish ish coshy – ver', ver' coshy in fac' – gosh, feelsh goo' to be back – hic! – back right by foo' sh'ply. Lov'ly lov'ly foo', schcushe me, can I 'ave a bi' more . . . mmmm, go on. Jush turn over a lickle . . . Jingle Belllsh, Jingle Belllsh . . . how did it go af'er tha'? Mmm? You 'wake or wha'?*

## 23 December, 2000 – Colum and Helen's bedroom

    *(Two heavy snores in the black darkness, one fast, one slow. Sound of somebody opening and closing front door, and shortly thereafter falling over bags of shopping.)*

C:  *(out of vision)* Shite! What the . . .
    *(Sound of light being switched on. A shaft of light falls across the bedroom, illuminating Helen in the bed, fully dressed but with her top open, and an empty champagne bottle next to it.)*

C:  Helen! Helen? Are ye sick?
    *(Colum comes into the bedroom and switches on the main light)*

C:  Mother of God, woman . . . Where's the ba . . . Jeezus!
    *(He reaches over her and scoops up Des, half buried underneath her. The baby continues to snore. Colum pinches his little cheek.*

*He snores. Colum pulls his little toes. He snores. Colum puts his face next to his tiny open mouth, and sniffs.)*

C:   What the . . .
*(He's just reaching for the phone when Des hiccups, very sweetly, opens his eyes, looks right at Colum, and vomits all over him.)*

Some time later

*(Helen opens her eyes blearily to see Colum sitting on the side of the bed with Des, changed, awake and sucking greedily on a bottle)*

H:   Uuuuurffgh. Turn off light.
C:   And a merry Christmas to you too.
H:   Pleashe . . .
*(Colum takes Des, still drinking, over and switches off the main light, leaving the bedside lamp on)*
H:   Thank . . . wha's that?
*(She sits up. Mistake.)*
H:   Uurrrgh! What's − THAT?
C:   I thought as his mother was hitting the bottle he might as well too. *(looking fondly down at Des)* Can't get enough of it, can ye?
D:   *(looking back, eyes bulging)* (What, now I've discovered this you want me to stop and talk?)
*(Helen leaps up, headache forgotten, and grabs Des and the bottle from Colum, detaching Des in the process)*
H:   Loves it? How dare he?
D:   WAAAAH! (Give it back, you heartless monster.)
*(Helen reluctantly sticks it back in his mouth)*
H:   Where did you get the − whatever it is?
C:   They sell it in chemists', ye know. It's perfectly good stuff, full of minerals and vitamins and what not . . .
H:   Oh, and mine isn't, I suppose?
C:   Well, this'll give his liver more of a chance.

*(she shoots him a murderous look)*

C: *(more gently)* And it'll mean I can get up in the night sometimes . . .
*(her face brightens)*

C: . . . while you sleep off yer bingeing.
*(Des sucks the last drop from the bottle, belches, looks sleepily from
one to the other . . .)*

D: Wuuuhhffzzzzz . . . (So why, exactly, have you kept this
from me until now?)


## 24 December, 2000

*Finally tricked them into revealing location of upgraded food supply
system (though at the price of near-fatal poisoning). I always knew that
was old technology. To think of the amount of effort I put into getting
to grips with it. And for what?*


## 27 December, 2000

Lie Low strategy seems to have worked a treat, though Colum
is probably right that giving poor Des a hangover for Christmas
was not the act of a caring Santa. No more drinking, ever. The
very thought is nauseating to me. Anthrax Island cover was
clearly not 100 per cent convincing to close (and suspicious)
family, but made sure they all knew their presents weren't worth
taking the risk for anyhow. Felt a bit mean afterwards but will
make it up to them when we've saved a bit of money (i.e. when
Des leaves home).

On which subj, suddenly realised that some time before then
he'll have to stop taking all his meals from a bottle. ('Why?'
interjects Colum. 'His mother never did.' Ha ha.)

... time to start introducing solids. The most important thing to bear in mind is that your milk, or (to a lesser extent) formula ...

(Ha!)

... provides a complete balance of all the nutritional requirements for a baby.

NO OTHER SINGLE FOOD OR SUBSTANCE DOES THIS.

Therefore, it is VITALLY IMPORTANT, when planning your baby's transition to solids, to remember that you will need to include ALL the vitamin, mineral, protein, vegetable and carbohydrate groups, EVERY DAY. This not only prevents baby from developing into that scourge of the dinner table, a fussy eater, but lays down the foundation for her health, general wellbeing and even intelligence, FOR THE REST OF HER LIFE.

THE FOOD YOU GIVE YOUR BABY IN THE FIRST THREE YEARS GOES DIRECTLY TO BUILD HER BRAIN! ...

(Jeeeesus, how did I miss out on all of this ... no wonder he's such a retard ...)

... Do not on any account begin with fruit, as this could give her a sweet tooth ... begin and end the day with unrefined carbohydrate; rice is a good first cereal, but whole grain and preferably old-strain wheat (e.g. kamut) are also good, though oats and barley will be too indigestible for a few weeks yet ... introduce one new fruit and one new vegetable each week (remembering, of course, to keep offering the previous ones throughout), and one new source of protein ... egg yolks are fine, but no egg whites until ... chicken before beef and fish before chicken but only oily or dark fish, remembering to drain off all oil beforehand, and of course never tinned in brine . . . see tables on p. 294 for good sources of vitamins A, B, C, D, E, iron, calcium and non-animal protein . . .


## 5 January, 2001

So much for the restful prolonged festive lolling about. Found out shortly after Christmas Day we're way behind on Des's brain platelets and the only way to remedy the deficit is an immediate tertiary degree in nutritional studies and many, many days and nights hunched over the blender. Somewhat less panic-stricken after I broke radio silence to consult Mum, who muttered vaguely about Farley's rusks and bananas having been quite enough for us until we were two. Went out and got some rusks as an experiment, and they're certainly delicious. (But far too sweet for Des. Now I know where to point the blame for the KitKat addiction. Sometimes I'm amazed Mum can even get up in the morning with the weight of guilt on her shoulders.) So now when I'm not blending, sifting, chopping, steaming and freezing, I'm trying to persuade Des that there'd be a lot more room for the spoon if his tongue weren't sticking out of his mouth.


## 14 January, 2001

*What on earth? We've spent six months wrestling with the liquid food supply, first that ridiculous blood-from-a-stone technology and then the vastly more sophisticated, hygienic, labour-saving portable upgrade – and now – what's this she's putting into my mouth?*

*Uuurgh, uck, you're choking me gghgggghghghghghghghsprrrrew!*

*Mmmm. Tastes okay. Sort of. Bland and boring, especially compared to the liquid supply a couple of weeks back, but I quite like the way it sort of – sticks to things so you can – Mmmm – lick it off your fingers when you . . . GERROFFF! that's mine . . . she's so greedy, this host, it's incredible.*

227

*(Ernestine arrives to find Helen surrounded by bowls of gloop, with her face about two inches from a very smelly, bright yellow nappy. Ernestine stops right where she is. Helen looks up.)*

H: What do you think of this colour?

E: I think you're a very, very sick woman.

H: The book said to keep checking that the solids aren't changing it too dramatically either in colour or texture. I really ought to have kept the last nappy for comparison. Or maybe the last two . . . actually, they may still be in . . .
*(to Ernestine's horror, she dives into the rubbish bin, leaving the dirty nappy amidst the bowls of food)*
. . . here somewhere . . .
*(Ernestine grabs her by the shoulders and pulls her up)*

E: Pick up that – thing.
*(Helen, surprised, picks up the nappy)*

E: Put it in the bin. Now.
*(Helen complies. Ernestine steers Helen out of the kitchen, closing the door behind them, sits her on the sofa and sits down beside her.)*

E: Close your eyes.
*(Helen does so)*

E: Without falling asleep. Now breathe very *(sniffs the air herself, just to check)* VERY deeply. In, out. In, out.

H: *(intoning)* In, out. In, out.

E: Now visualise a beautiful place – the most beautiful place you know. What do you see?

H: *(sepulchrally)* Bed . . .

E: *(big sigh)* Okay, let's go with that. So you're lying down, dozing, the sun is shining, the birds are singing, the air is fragrant – you open your eyes and what do you see?

H: Bananas.

E: Wake up. *(shaking her)* WAKE UP! I'm afraid your case is untreatable. Cup of tea?

*(She gets up, goes towards the kitchen, remembers what's in there, and shoves Helen in ahead)*

E:  I'm not going in until that bin is emptied.

*(Helen obediently goes in and comes by with a full, malodorous bag en route to the door)*

E:  Anyhow, it seems to me you've got it all wrong.

H:  *(pausing)* Got what?

E:  That bag is leaking.

H:  Christ!

*(She dashes out to dump it. Ernestine fastidiously clears a space at the kitchen table.)*

H:  Biscuit? I have HobNobs. *(looking in cupboard)*. Had. Got what wrong?

E:  This baby food business. If you're really concerned about moulding his palate, surely you should be feeding him – I don't know – foie gras, champagne . . .

H:  I tried that, if you remember.

E:  . . . Caviare, lobster, fine Cognac, old Sauternes . . .

H:  Why waste those on a baby?

E:  Long-term investment, stupid. That way he'll have to get a good job to pay for his habits.


**16 January, 2001** – Transcript of mobile phone conversation between Ernestine and persons unknown

. . . after all, she was the one who (full leg wax, paws and claws, short, two-thirty). Are you there? . . . Yeah, it wasn't me that gave him alcohol poisoning just to see what maudlin looks like at five months. (Great, sorry I'm a bit late, and look, here's the varnish, this underneath, this on top for the hands and reverse it on the toes) . . . So much for the sacred trust of motherhood . . . yeah . . . But sometimes I think, you know, she's so cowed by these self-proclaimed experts, I mean, would she pick a boyfriend or buy a pair of shoes

229

on some so-called expert's say-so, of course not, but she seems perfectly happy to bring the poor thing up out of how-to manuals, it's no wonder most people are so dull if they have such a dull start in life . . . Exactly . . . yeah, babies are amazingly robust, everybody says so, they love adventures. Sometimes I think I should just go ahead and have one myself, and really show 'em!

## 24–26 January, 2001 – Exchange of e-mails

**From:** Colum McCallum [collum@guzzi.freeserve.com]
**Sent:** 24 Jan
**To:** Billy Giddens [billy@billygoat.demon.co.uk]

```
Hi Bill,
Now that I'm back on two wheels (how did I manage
without?) it occurred to me that it's about time
I chopped in the MM for something a bit more
juicy - would you be interested in it?
   Her indoors has developed into a full-on food
nazi - never having shown signs of deep interest
in the nutritional value of her own or anybody
else's food before, as witness the bacon diet of
1997 ('fat isn't fattening - you use up the
calories digesting it'), the cabbage soup diet
of 1998 ('most peasants are thin, aren't they?'
- as though she'd know), and more recently her
absent-minded habit of making the same dish
night after night for several weeks at time,
like Delia trying to perfect a recipe for her
next show. Now we have a biochemistry lab by the
kitchen sink, and every meal we eat has the
colour and texture of something that's been
chewed and spat out several times already. I
```

tell you, I might as well have my teeth pulled
for the gold.
    Everything else fine - how goes it with you?
    Col

----------------------------------

**From:** Billy Giddens [billy@billygoat.demon.co.uk]
**To:**   Colum McCallum [collum@guzzi.freeserve.com]

col son
You and I should pile over to Scratchwood for an
Olyimpic Breakfast one nigt. Bring back old
times hey?
    AS for MM - I bought it off you oce if you
remember. Maybe not again quite so soon. Waht
are you eyeingip - not the Corsa by any chance?
    bill

----------------------------------

**February, 2001** – Excerpt from *Scientific American* – February 2001
issue

    . . . the authors found that, when amino acid and ph balance
were factored in, under normal conditions with the experi-
mental materials derived from latitudinally equivalent
sources, the chromatic consonance, held to a normal distri-
bution of .002, correlated on a percentile range between 90
and 92 with the nutritive composition of the base elements of
each grouping . . .

**30 January, 2001**

Colum came home last night with a radical new simplification
of Des's diet plan, based on Goethe's Colour Theory (I think)
and something he read in *Scientific American*. He tried to explain

it to me after the 9 p.m. synapse shutdown, so I may have missed some technical detail, but what it seems to boil down to (as it were) is that different nutrients are conveniently colour coded, so provided Des gets three meals of different colours every day, he'll be fine. I have to say, making Venn diagrams of the intersection between vitamins, minerals, antioxidants and the various food groups was getting me down a bit, especially as it didn't leave any time for the actual cooking. When I gave Colum Busy Mother's Chicken for the third time in a week he threatened to rename it No Longer Busy Mother with Axe in Neck's Chicken. I got the point, but reminded him that a man in a pinny is no longer a segment on Benny Hill.

Then I asked him what enlightenment science might have to offer for the great mystery that there is no blue food in nature. He tried to counter with something about blue corn, but everybody knows it's about as blue as a blue tulip. Which is quite blue, actually. It is a bit of an anomaly. Maybe it came down from the sky with those people who did the big drawings in the earth at Machu Picchu, or wherever it is.


### 3 February, 2001

*Overheard host and donor discussing codes and colour in context of my food. Could this be the secret information I've been sent here to acquire? Have spent many recent hours trying to refine my palate in order to crack the code, whatever it may turn out to be. Here's what I have so far:*

*Breakfast (White):*

*Rice powder, pear, milk. RPM? PMR? They all came mixed together, so no clue there.*

*Lunch (Yellow):*

*Carrot, cheese, corn. Or so I thought, which seemed to provide a further clue (all the Cs), until I spotted her clearing away something that was clearly pumpkin. PCC?*

*Tea (Green):*

*Avocado, cucumber and celery. ACC? CAC? I think that's some-thing else . . .*

*It's all been a bit too much to take in (as it were) — all systems getting somewhat overloaded and much of my time now spent trying to anticipate what the next meal will bring. What I wouldn't give for just one sky-blue meal from back home.*

**March, 2001** – Excerpt from OK Magazine – March 2001 issue

### Stop Press! The Week's News in Diet and Health

We could not wait to bring you this one. It seems those busy boffins in the research department at the top-secret General Mills Food Lab in the US have discovered that we humans are amazingly efficient food-processing machines (yes, we could have told them that, too). Young rats, mice and even guinea-pigs fed on an exclusive diet of junk food not only didn't get fat, they remained just as healthy, if not more so, than a control group fed their usual diet of carrots, cabbage and grain . . .

### 6 February, 2001

Finally, the proof that all those years reading OK have not been in vain. I always knew KitKat had been specially formulated to contain all the essentials for sustaining life. You can tell by how delicious it is — it's your body's way of saying it's good for you. Colum suggested that the control guinea-pigs were probably pining away from pure boredom and he knew how they felt. I reminded him Marks and Spencer was conveniently on the way home from his office, as he would discover if he ever tried the journey without a detour via the Bog and Badger.

Des seems to be getting used to the gloop, but he's clearly convinced there ought to be a pudding food group in there (wonder where he gets that from). There's no way he's getting my KitKats. He's still on two breast feeds a day – that's quite enough chocolate for somebody his size.

In fact it's about time he learned to move himself around. He has orange-peel thighs already – what hope of burning it off when he just lies about day and night?

## 12 February, 2001

*Can't understand why she gets so worked up about moving me around. It's hardly my fault that these things hanging off my bottom don't do what hers do. If she'd ever tried lying in the same place for an hour with only one ergonomic rattle, two nauseating stuffed toys and Baby's First Farm Book for company, she'd get pretty hacked off, too.*

*Here she is again. We're off to the kitchen. Please God make it blue – please, please . . .*

## 14 February, 2001

Who would ever have dreamed a year ago that I could happily spend Valentine's evening pureeing vegetables while Colum and Another shared a romantic *diner à deux* of cucumber guacamole on a coulis of spinach and French beans, served on a freshly pressed shirt front? Who needs the noisy, dirty, ephemera-obsessed outside world with its banal preoccupations and its endless trivial chat, when they're inside their very own Great Circle of Life?

(Actually, Mr Perfect Father turns out to have in his bottom-less repertoire of life skills a truly extraordinary ability to feed Des without spilling a single drop. The bastard. Though, person-ally, I quite like the bit where I get to lick all his little fingers and toes, one by one. Could this be the origin of erotic toe-licking, as practised by certain ex-royals?)

Excerpt from the instructions on the side of a 300ml box of
Supafilla

> . . . at the last minute after the hole is prepared as above,
> adding just enough to make a consistency that will stay on
> the spatula without dripping or clogging. For best results, mix
> only enough for one hole at a time, and continue to stir until
> all lumps are thoroughly dissolved.
>
> Holding container on a level with hole to be filled, put a
> small amount of mixture on spatula, keeping it horizontal as
> it approaches hole. Work quickly to avoid spills, and wipe up
> immediately with a soft cloth soaked in warm water . . .

## 16 February, 2001

If I have to spend one more evening imprisoned in this tiny,
stifling, dreary place, pureeing bloody vegetables and going to
bed at nine in order to get enough sleep to get up and repeat
the whole thing next day, while Colum whispers biker lore into
that baby's ear all night, it won't be me with an axe in my neck,
or at least it may be but I'll certainly be taking one or two
people with me. And to think that all the time, only yards away,
people are talking, laughing, drinking to excess, flirting . . . I
have to get out of here, somehow . . .

## 20 February, 2001 – Baby massage class, North London

*(The room is not quite large enough for the semicircle of women
learning to massage their babies' tummies. Helen has her legs
awkwardly splayed around Des, who is lying on his back, on a
towel, naked, and for once wide awake. Beside her, a spike-haired,
intense woman kneels in front of a thin, screaming baby in a cloth
nappy. This is Sarah. The teacher, Ondine, has a wild mane of
hair and a music-hall French accent.)*

O:   . . . alwayzz and oenly AGAAIRNST ze clock, UP ze big aintesteen, DOUN ze small, EEEN wiz ze flat uv yuir 'and, and ROUUND to ze vair' centair.

H:   *(whispering, to Sarah)* What d'you think happens if you do it clockwise? D'you think the food all comes back up? Yeeuch!
*(Sarah is preoccupied trying to massage around the flailing limbs of her furious baby)*

O:   . . . REST yuir 'and, leht ze enairgie FLOEH sru yuir beibei! FEEL eez leetle uirgans at wairk! SOOOOZ eem wiz yuir teuch!

S:   *(to Ondine, earnestly)* Excuse me – he doesn't seem to be responding yet . . .

H:   *(trying again)* Maybe he's just not a touchy-feely kind of guy.
*(Sarah is not, apparently, big on jokes. Her baby, Mahatma, manages a frantic squirm towards Des.)*

M:   WAIIIIIRR! Wu Wu Wu WAAAIRRR! (Bloody cloth nappy. She always sticks the pin just where I lie on it. D'you have any spare Pampers if I can get rid of this thing?)

D:   *(smiling)* Weee, wee wee! (No Pampers, I'm afraid. Huggies?)
*(Ondine undulates towards Sarah and leans over Mahatma)*

O:   'Eee is maybe a leetle nairveuse.
*(She lays the flat of one enormous hand on his belly, and presses down)*

O:   Ssssss! Ssssss, *petit chou! Doucement!*

M:   WAAARRRGH! WaWaWaWaWAAAAAARGH! (Yikes, your hand is cold! You're pushing me right into that bloody pin. And stop calling me a cabbage. Okay, here goes, comrade . . .)
*(A spray of vomit erupts from Mahatma's open mouth, covering Ondine's hand and soaking his nappy and the unbleached cotton Babygro neatly folded beside him. Ondine leaps up, shocked. A furtive smirk runs around the semicircle of mothers, missing only*

*the mortified Sarah, who doesn't notice that she's suddenly become the most popular person in the room.)*

S:  Oh no! Oh, I'm so sorry, he's never – here, I'm sure I have a . . .
*(She scrabbles around in her bag and produces an unbleached paper towel. Helen intervenes with a nice wet disinfectant wipe, which Ondine accepts, recovering herself.)*

O:  Zair, yeu see zee poweur uv ze teknik!
*(Sarah bends over Mahatma to remove his nappy, then realises she has nothing to replace it with)*

S:  *(whispering to Helen)* You don't, I suppose – I couldn't possibly borrow . . .

M:  *(to Des)* Wair, wuf wuf? (How did I do?)

D:  Weeeee! ung ung uuuss . . . ! (Hey, great idea . . . !)
*(Helen proudly produces more wipes, a Huggie and a spare Babygro, then goes back to rubbing Des's tummy in the prescribed manner)*

O:  . . . Iz vair', vair' pouairfeul! Bee cairefeul . . .

D:  . . . ufff UUUUUURRGH! (Mind if I join you? This should get us out of here.)
*( . . . and a large splat of bright green, extremely malodorous poo appears on the clean towel beneath him)*


## 24 February, 2001

*Does basic dignity have no value in the human world? God knows it's hard enough to hang on to the few shreds I already have when half my life is spent either gagging on a bowlful of green slime or playing along with their ludicrous games. This expedition started out all right – seemed to be some kind of routine physical, plus an all too rare opportunity to check in with other babies, hear their gossip, pick up strategy tips and compare own developing hardware with theirs. (Gratified to discover that though functionality remains unpredictable and rudimentary at best, size and bulk by far the largest there. Clearly intended for Alpha Male role later on.)*

*However, consequent sense of triumph evaporated when we all simultaneously realised that we had been duped into one of those subtle tortures beloved of military juntas, on the theory – all too clearly true – that if you rob a man of his dignity, very soon his spirit and even his physical strength will collapse in turn.*

*Fortunately found myself adjacent to a baby of some resourcefulness and ingenuity, physically puny but apparently a veteran of many such events, who devised a rapid and effective exit strategy for both of us. I don't think we'll be going there again (tho' I wouldn't mind another rendezvous with him).*

**28 February, 2001** – Helen and Sarah, out for a walk with their babies

> *(It's a miserable day with a sky like wet cement, a fitting backdrop for the canal towpath behind King's Cross station, where the gasometers tower over the grimy train sheds. Sarah and Helen both have their babies bundled up in slings; Helen's the hi-tech German one, Sarah's a huge length of brownish African cloth, knotted round one shoulder and resting on her bony hip.)*

H: . . . such a good idea of yours!

S: *(modestly)* Oh, thanks!

H: . . . and so much healthier than stewing over hot chocolate in some overpriced cappuccino bar. Though maybe – it IS quite nice to warm up after a walk on a day like this . . . Do you have Coffee Republic in Stoke Newington?

S: There is one, I think, but of course I don't drink hot chocolate.

H: Really? *(looks her over with an expert's envious scrutiny)* You don't have anything to worry about!

S: Oh, no, it's the cocoa. You know almost all cocoa is picked by slave labour in Somalia, don't you?

H: Umm . . . yes, of course. I mean, no, I didn't. How awful!

S: Unless it's Fair Trade, of course, but I don't think those

238

places bother. Anyhow, I'm afraid it's way beyond my price range, being on my own with this little one.

H: I didn't realise – I'm sorry.

S: Oh, it's fine. They can't be expected to transcend millennia of conditioning all at once. And he – Mahatma's dad – came from a very different cultural parameter base. England can be very unforgiving of diversity, you know.

H: I guess so.

*(They plod on in silence for a moment. Helen tries again.)*

H: Well, how about coming back to my place for a nice cup of tea, maybe? The milk's organic!

S: That sounds nice, though of course I don't drink milk.

H: Oh, poor you. So many people have that allergy suddenly, it's amazing, you wonder where it's been lurking all these years.

S: Oh, no, it's the methane. Methane from cows is the third-highest source of greenhouse gases, globally.

H: Do people burn cows? How cruel!

S: No, it's from when they – you know, it's from digesting all that grass.

H: They – cow farts are destroying the ozone layer?

S: And of course it's very cruel to the cows.

H: Making them eat grass?

S: Taking their babies away.

H: Oh! I never thought of it that way.

S: Little baby cows torn from their grieving mothers. I don't know whether you've ever been past a dairy farm. You can hear the mothers, you know. Keening.

*(Sarah and Helen now both look suicidal as they trudge along, deep in sombre thought)*

S: But I do feel the cold, it's true. So difficult to find nice warm clothes . . .

H: Tell me about it! And the prices!

S: . . . being Vegan. I only went totally last year. But I feel good about it. I go to bed with a clear conscience.

H:  Gosh. *(pause, then with an attempt at lightening the mood . . .)* Brrrr. Well, nothing like a nice cup of PG Tips to help out with that. I have HobNobs, too. I don't know if they're vegan, though.
*(They turn round and begin to trudge the other way. It's already getting dark.)*

S:  Oh dear. Don't you know about the big tea companies?

H:  I – remind me.

S:  The pickers . . .
*(Helen doesn't even dare ask)*

H:  Oh dear. Of course

S:  But it's okay, I always carry this passion-flower stuff. It's not very nice, but . . .

H:  No enslaved flower fairies that we know of?
*(Sarah looks baffled. Helen feels guilty.)*

H:  Bbrrrrr! Passion-flower it is, then. I'm sure I've had enough cow farts for today.


**2 March, 2001**

Discovered hitherto unsuspected wellspring of idealism and political conscience – now we have a link to the future, seems much more important to leave the world a better place for our babies, respect the Gaia Principle, etc. And the poor tea pickers and cocoa slaves probably have little babies too. What's selfish indulgence in cups of tea against the human dignity of half the world?

It's rather humbling to meet somebody like that in the flesh – somebody who really does live by her principles. She was pretty understanding about the disposable nappies, too – put me on to Nappy Nurseries, you can send them money and for every disposable you send to a landfill, they'll sow a few square inches of wildflower seed.

Somehow haven't felt like sharing much of this with Colum – not sure he'd sympathise. His general line is that he encounters enough miserable bastards in the course of a normal working day, and he doesn't see why he should be depressed in his free time as well. (Don't suppose he'll notice the tea's been swapped over.)

Later – 2.30 a.m.

No!! NO NO NO!!!!
I can't! I just can't!
How could she do this to me? How could anyone? It's too much to ask.
Ask anything but that. Honestly. Anything. If only I'd told Colum – but he wouldn't understand. Nobody would. This grief, this agony is mine and mine alone.
Please God, make me strong enough to bear it. Help me remember those poor mothers being brainwashed into giving their babies formula they can't afford. Help me to be brave . . .

Later – 6 a.m.

Feeling a bit calmer now. Spent all that time listening to Sarah droning on about how they spend millions of pounds every year getting women in the Third World to use their baby formula instead of breast milk, but somehow didn't make the connection with KitKat until 2 a.m. How can I conscientiously continue to fatten their profits with my own decadent selfish greed? Why did they have to take over Rowntree's? Surely somebody else would have bought it?
However, felt a teeny bit better when I realised I'd have to undertake a research trip for a replacement. And after all, it's pretty boring just eating the same old chocolate bar for twenty years. It's the sort of thing men do, same old pint of Fuller's, same old cheese-and-onion crisps and chicken tikka masala, not

too spicy please. Since I last bothered to investigate, there's probably a whole cornucopia of even more delicious alternatives on the market that I haven't even noticed!

**1 March, 2001** – Bills from Helen's shopping trip

```
THE KANDY BOX
1/3/2001

Wispagold               £0.39
Twix                    £0.39
Raisin Nut Twix         £0.39
Caramel Biscuit         £0.39
Fiesta                  £0.39
Crispy Dime             £0.39
Galaxy Toffee           £0.39
Dipped Flake            £0.39
Crunchie Toffee Bits    £0.39
Snickers Dark           £0.39
Double Decker Caramel   £0.39
Mars, Special Edition   £0.39

SUBTOTAL                £4.68
Cash tendered           £5.00
Change                  £0.32
Thank You!
```

```
Pestle and Mortar Pharmacy
2/3/2001

Huggies midi x 2    £17.98

SUBTOTAL            £17.98
PAID BY SWITCH
Thank you. Call Again
```

**3 March, 2001**

The most extraordinary discovery. All serotonin uptake inhibitor bars are rapidly becoming one. Evidently mega-mergers in the global confectionery industry have reduced the gene pool of components to dangerous levels. Either that, or it's all the cosying up to one another on the newsagents' shelves. Nothing to do all day except wait to be bought and flirt with your neighours.

'Hey! I LIKE your chunky bits, big guy!'

'Well, hello, little girl – my, those raisins are sweet. Let's get cosy!'

And before you know it, you've got Fiesta. It's basically the same morph of chocolate, caramel, crispies, biscuit and raisins from one end of the shelf to the other. Even their mothers couldn't tell them apart. So it all comes down to a delicate balance of percentages and the question: biscuit – no biscuit? Personally I think biscuits are fine, in their proper place, but not sure that's disguised as chocolate, and taking up perfectly good space in what is already, after all, a modest enough envelope. I fear the search for a worthy successor to KitKat may not reach a speedy conclusion. Shame!

**3 March, 2001** – Partial transcript of phone conversation between Helen and Georgie

G:  . . . it's been ages, how are you, darling, we've been SO busy, what with Tamsin retaking her flute exam and Jack having chickenpox . . .

H:  I have a technical question.

G:  . . . OH. Sure. Shoot.

H:  Is there a toe that speeds up metabolism?

G:  If there were, I'd be a millionaire. (JACK! The nice milkman might not want to count your spots – so sorry, have you had chickenpox? Oh dear – come in NOW Jack!)

H:  *(gloomily)* I thought as much. I knew there'd be a down-side to bottle-feeding. You get to sleep through the night, but as the *Hindenburg*.

G:  Surely you exaggerate.

H:  Only a bit. I suppose I was pushing my luck with the chocolate research . . .

G:  Don't worry, it happens to all of us. But you'll find you save hundreds on clothes every year when you hate your reflection. (Don't pick them, Jack, you'll never have any girlfriends.) Which is just as well, considering the bills from the kids! Cheer up!

**5 March, 2001** – Helen and Des in Helen's living room

*(Helen is wearing disgusting old sweatpants and top, about three sizes too large for her. She's lying on the floor on her back, holding Des in the air, and apparently about to hurl him into the tele-vision, on which a big-haired Lycra goddess is jumping about, also with a baby. On the floor beside Helen is a video box labelled 'Exercise with Baby – Have Fun and Lose Weight!')*

G:  . . . and UP and down and UP and down. JUST like the seesaw at the playground! Work those pecs! One more set of eight, UP and down . . .

*(The background music is a techno remix of 'Little Bo Peep'. Helen dutifully lifts and lowers Des, who is beginning to show signs of worry.)*

H:  God, you weigh a ton, Des. Hold still and nothing will happen to you.

D:  Weeeeeuuurfgh! (So YOU say.)

*(The Goddess nimbly leaps to her feet, places her baby on the ground, and jumps into position with her legs either side of it. The music is now a drum'n'bass remix of 'Rock my Soul . . .')*

G:  . . . and BEND right down and kiss the baby, BEND right down and kiss the baby . . .

*(Helen struggles to her feet, managing to dig her elbow into Des as she does so)*

D: Waaaaah!! (You said . . .)

H: Sorry, Des. Lesson one – never trust anybody. There, there . . .
*(She bends over him and covers him with smoochy kisses, then attempts to do the same with her legs straight, like the Goddess. Ernestine comes in to find her, legs splayed, bottom sticking out, kissing the air about two feet over Des's head.)*

G: And now, the really fun part – throwing Baby from hand to hand!

D: *(catching sight of Ernestine)* WaaaaaaHHH! WahWahWah-WAH!!! (Thank God! Did you hear that last bit? Do something!)

E: Great – kissing lessons. Fairy Godmother's privilege, I think.
*(She's carrying two huge, stiff, expensive carrier bags, which she dumps on the floor before scooping Des out of Helen's hands.)*

H: Hey – that's my exercise weight!

E: No, it's my lovely little smoochy-woochy godson, isn't it, darling?
*(By now, the Goddess on the video is lightly tossing her apparently anaesthetised infant over her head. The music is an acid jazz remix of 'Sing a Song of Sixpence'. Helen stumbles over, panting, and stops it. Des, apparently feeling a bit safer, stops screaming.)*

H: Tea?

E: Not that disgusting . . .

H: Don't worry. If Colum has no pity for the tea pickers and their starving babies, what can I do?
*(She wanders into the kitchen, still recovering. Ernestine holds Des in front of her and looks into his eyes.)*

E: Now concentrate.

D: Fffff? (What now?)

E: You purse up your lips, like SO . . . and you stick them

245

out like SO . . . and you go, MMMMWWWAHHHH! MmmmmmWWAaaH! Can you do that?

*(Des looks back at her)*

E:  Come on, now, concentrate. You'll be grateful later. This is something really useful for once. Lips pursed, stick 'em out, MmmmWWWaaaHH!

*(Des is still looking back at her. Eventually, he produces a very faint and dribbly raspberry.)*

D:  Bbbrrfff . . . (Why does she want me to say 'sausages'?)

E:  CLEVER BOY! You clever little thing, do it again, show Mummy . . . MMMMMwwwWWWWAHHH!

*(Helen has returned with two cups of tea. Des sees her, and shuts up.)*

H:  He's got the rudiments of tact, anyhow. Here, let me have a go.

*(she puts down the teacups)*

H:  Let's teach him something really useful.

E:  D'you have a biscuit?

H:  *(sharply)* Absolutely not!!!

*(Ernestine jumps. Helen looks Des deep in the eye and says . . .)*

H:  Mama! Say – Mama!

*(Des just looks back at her)*

D:  (I am NOT going to say THAT word in public for ANYBODY. I'm ashamed of you.)

H:  *(pleadingly)* Good boy! Clever baby, I'm sure you can do it! Ma . . . Ma . . . Ma . . .

E:  See if he'll blow you a kiss. Go on . . .

H:  *(tentatively)* Mmmmwwh . . . ?

E:  God, it's amazing you ever got a boyfriend at all . . . give it a bit of ooomph, for Christ sakes . . .

*(Helen nerves herself for oomph, and suddenly stops, noticing the bags on the floor)*

H:  What are those?

E:  Those what – oh, just a couple of bags of bits and pieces

246

I can't wear – you know, wrong colour, wrong shape . . .

H:   Clothes?

E:   Yeah, you always look good in stuff that doesn't . . .
     *(her voice fades out as she sees Helen's expression)*

E:   What on earth is wrong?

H:   *(briskly)* Nothing. Nothing at all. I'm just a bit busy, so if
     you'll excuse us, Des and I have to get back to our aero-
     bics . . .
     *(and she hustles the speechless Ernestine out of the door)*


## 4 March, 2001

*What was all that about? I've no objection to saying something that
means 'sausages' over and over if that'll make them happy, but the idea
of saying Mama, out loud and in front of other people – well, frankly,
it's not what I was led to expect when we were told our hosts and
donors were hand-picked. I suppose it's possible Mama means something else here – but what? Come to think of it, there was something
about it in Basic Training – it's all fading so fast . . .*

*Have more or less given up hope of getting through to Mission
Control. Am beginning to fear some terrible disaster has befallen
Command Base. If duty did not compel me to stay, would be strongly
tempted to try to find my way back. On reflection, might have to find
alternative route for return trip.*


**April, 2001** – Excerpt from *Scientific American* – April 2001 issue

. . . in apparent contradiction to the results of previous cross-
cultural studies by their own team and colleagues in other
institutions, the newly published research appears to
confirm, or at least strongly to indicate, that, within certain
very narrowly constrained parameters, there may be derived
a marginal or even greater benefit, even in the very early
stages, from the mutual mimetic vocalisation of assonant,

inflected polysyllabic phonemes between adult and infant humans . . .

**10 March, 2001** – Colum and Des in the living room, evening

*(Colum is lying on the sofa, with Des cuddled next to him. They appear to be deep in conversation.)*

D: Whhiff, ufff, ssspr! (So if you could do this all along, why didn't you say so?)

C: Whhiff, ufff, ssspr!

D: VVVvvvvrshg, bluh. (Why are you repeating that back to me? It's kind of annoying.)

C: VVVvvvvrshg, bluh.

*(Des becomes more animated)*

D: Fffrrrgshz! (Stop imitating me!) Whhhgf wee weh? (Now that you're finally speaking my language, there are a few questions I really need answering.)

C: I could swear he thinks he's talking. Now let's try something different – how about YOU copying ME. Ready?

D: UFF, WHHHGF wee weh? (LISTEN! I SAID I have a few urgent questions for you.)

C: Ready?

*(Des just looks at him)*

D: (It's hopeless.)

C: PA . . . PA . . . ! Say, PA . . . PA . . .

*(Des just keeps looking at him, but now with pity and contempt)*

D: (Not you, too. You are two sick puppies. You know that, don't you?)

C: Come on, ye're a bright wee thing . . .

*(he mouths the syllables in an exaggerrated singsong)* PA . . . Pa . . . Pa . . . Smacky lips, then a big, WIDE hole with yer mouth . . . Pa . . . Pa . . .

*(Des's response is a half-hearted drizzly raspberry, as practised to such great effect on Ernestine. Colum is less impressed.)*

C:   That's very cute. Who taught ye that, I wonder? Now let's get back to Papa.
*(Helen has wandered blearily out of the bedroom and is trying to take in what's happening. As the realisation dawns, she shouts . . .)*

H:   Ha!
*(. . . startling them both, and rushes out again, only to reappear waving a sheet of paper)*
Rule One! No baby talk! You've cracked!
*(Colum appears completely unfazed. He reaches into his trouser pocket and produces his own crumpled piece of paper.)*

C:   That was before science determined that baby talk is, in fact, extremely beneficial . . .

H:   Oh God!

C:   Who's been teaching him to blow raspberries?
*(Helen comes in and flops down beside them. A brief cuddly moment.)*

H:   Ernestine came round. She was trying to teach him to kiss.

C:   *(to Des)* So you've been kissing Ernie, have ye? Lucky chap!
*(Helen leaps up as though stung. He pulls her down again.)*
Come on, I'm teasing, ye mad thing. What's in those bags there?
*(Helen shudders)*

H:   I haven't looked. Ernie brought them too.
*(Colum gives her the baby, gets up himself, and looks)*

C:   It's clothes – new, too, by the looks of 'em. That's nice of her.
*(Helen leaps up again and rushes over to the bags. She pulls out the clothes – armfuls of tiny see-through tops, miniskirts, stretch capri pants . . . none bigger than a size eight.)*

H:   Nice! Nice?
*(she hurls them around the room like so many curses)*
She knows I'm a blimp! She's just loves to rub my face in it!

*(gathering them all up again and stuffing the whole lot dramatically into the bin)*
The only way I'm ever going to get into any of these is if I sew them all together into a – a shroud!

**15–18 March, 2001** – Exchange of e-mails

**From:** Colum McCallum [collum@guzzi. freeserve.com]
**Sent:** 15 Mar
**To:** Billy Giddens [billy@billygoat.demon.co.uk]

Hi Bill,
re your last – nah, the Corsa looks fun but I can
tell it's one you'd get tired of very quickly –
all showy promises on the front end, but frankly
how often do we get the weather in this country
to really thrash it? As you can imagine (!) I've
had many quiet hours in the last few months to
ponder this very question, and I truly think the
only bike I've never owned that I'd really like
to before I die is the Guzzi Falcone – you know,
the flywheel job. No idea where you'd find one
now, even if I could afford it (very big 'if'
these days!)
    One other small thing – any idea how to deal
with episodes of irrational, psychotic jealousy
of Her Indoors' best friend? Joke is, of course,
that anybody with half an eye can see this
particular woman is madly jealous of Her
Indoors, but you try even suggesting it around
here . . .
    Col

--------------------------------

**From:** Billy Giddens [billy@billygoat.demon.co.uk]
**To:** Colum McCallum [collum@guzzi.freeserve.com]

```
col son
I'll have a think about the Guzzi and see what
I can ome up wih. You derrerve a bit of a treat.
  Sounds to me as toh your Dog has got a bit of
cabin fever - they like to be taken walkies from
time to time, told they're gorgeous, that kin of
thing. Something that will make her laug (ie not
a mirror) and not involve eating usualy works
roun about now. A comedy down the Odeon, or
equiv. In theiry they don't allow babies in but
if it's full nobodywill hear it wailig, just get
her to wear a big coat and remember to open it
fromtime to time so sprogs carburettors can get
some air
  ket me know how it foes.
  bill
```

---------------------------------

**19 March, 2001** – Partial transcript of phone conversation
between Helen and Colum

C: . . . so what do you fancy?
H: And what do we do with Des?
C: Bring him along – the level they have the soundtrack these days, nobody'll ever hear him.
H: If it's that loud, it'll damage his hearing. *(dramatically)* It's no good. It's hopeless!
C: We'll get a sitter, then.
H: At no notice on a Friday night?

C:  Well. *(deep, patient breath)* How about renting something, then? That one with Brad Pitt is out.

H:  I hate Brad Pitt!

C:  You didn't use to.

H:  My tastes have matured.

C:  Okay, well, how about that George Clooney one we never saw last year?

H:  I hate seeing George with other women.

C:  So you choose.

H:  How can I? When have I had time to see what's come out lately?

C:  Well, a classic, then. *Brief Encounter.*

H:  I thought this was supposed to cheer me up!

C:  Okay, a comedy – *Some Like It Hot?*

H:  She looks like Ernestine.

C:  *Animal House?*

H:  Do you have to remind me what we're in for down the road?

C:  *(losing patience)* Well, look here, I've just spent my entire lunch hour trying to find a film that you're prepared to watch, so I tell you what. I'll come home early, and I'll look after the little lad while you scoot up to the video store and find something you like – how about that?


**19 March, 2001** – Letter from Health Centre

Kilverdale Road Health Centre
Kilverdale Road NW5

to:  Parent of Mr Lewis Desmond McCallum
34 Steinem St
NW5

date: 19 March, 2001

Dear Parent,
This is just to remind you that
Lewis's
hearing test is set for Tuesday, 29 March at 10. 15. Please
report directly to the health visitors' reception with
Lewis
five minutes before his appointment is due.

If for any reason you are unable to make this time, please
call as soon as possible to schedule an alternative appointment.
We look forward to seeing you.

Yours sincerely

## 21 March, 2001

I had no idea the National Curriculum kicked in at eight months.
Just received notice of his Hearing, Stage 1 exam – no syllabus
details or practice papers available, so we're going to have to
wing it. Spent a very enjoyable morning revising with percus-
sion instruments improvised out of kitchen cupboard. Nothing
wrong with that boy's hearing.

Welcome distraction after Colum's idea of a treat last night
– yet another evening watching *When Harry Met Sally* on video
and thinking about the fish and chips we weren't eating. Honestly
– men! And no babies in it at all. I never could see why people
rave about that film so much.

## 2 March, 2001

*My head. My poor head. She got me in the kitchen under totally false*
*pretences – normally she never goes in unless it's to get something to*
*eat. She sat me down in front of her, knowing full well I couldn't get*
*away, then everything went very quiet, which was a peaceful change,*
*and just when I was contemplating a surreptitious little catnap . . .*
*BANG!! BANG!! right behind me. I nearly hit the ceiling. And it*

*wasn't an accident because she did it all again a few minutes later. Thinking back, she did warn me a while ago, that time she jabbed me with her elbow – what did she say? 'Trust no one?' Ha! Never forget, they're the enemy. They may love you, and you may even grow quite fond of them, especially around Christmas, but they will always be Other.*

*Where does she keep that wonderful pink liquid that just melts all your troubles away? If only I could move by myself, I could go and find it. I could have escaped yesterday, come to that. These stupid arms and legs, I've been doing push-ups and kicks morning and night, but so far – hang on . . . let's turn over and just try – here we go! Get this front one planted – then bend these back ones right in under – then straighten them and – whoops, quick, stick out the other front one to steady me – hey! Look at this!!! I can't believe it, freedom! Zippity doo – ouch!! leeeee! Where did the floor go? Oh, my head, not my head again – yaroooooo . . .*

**21 March, 2001** – Helen's bedroom

> *(Des is lying on the floor by the bed, looking and sounding VERY sorry for himself. Helen rushes in.)*

H:  Oh God, what happened? Are you hurt? *(scooping him up)* Your poor head, how did you do that?

D:  *(wriggling frantically)* WliiieeEEEEEE! Wiieee EEEEEE! (DON'T TOUCH MY HEAD YOU SADIST!!!)

H:  I'm sure I left you right in the middle of the bed – how did you manage to fall off it? There, there, ssshhhh, you're all right, I've just got to . . . *(putting him down on the floor)* Let's just put you here where you can't fall any farther while I . . .

> *(Des, seeing his opportunity, tries to make another getaway)*

H:  . . . hey, what are you . . .

D:  Yaah! Yahh!! (I'm off. I know my way from here. Through that door . . .)

H:  You're crawling! You – oh, you adorable, wonderful, bril-
    liant little smoochy-woochy – gosh, I love you, MMMwh
    MMMwh!
D:  Grsssh . . . urf urf urf (I'll just wait till you're not looking.
    And don't go trying to win me over, I know you – oh,
    stop, that tickles!)
H:  Mmmm, yes, I love you too, now where's the phone . . .
    *(dialling with one hand while holding Des in a vicelike clamp
    with the other)*
H:  . . . Colum? Darling, he's crawling!


**28–30 March, 2001** – Exchange of e-mails

**From:** Colum McCallum [collum@guzzi.freeserve.com]
**Sent:** 28 march
**To:** Billy Giddens [billy@billygoat.demon.co.uk]


Hi Bill,
Steve called the other day and mentioned there's
a vintage bike swapmeet outside Bologna in a
couple of weeks. I suppose if you're going to
find one of those flywheel Guzzis anywhere it
would be there. It's an attractive thought –
this has been a long, hard winter in retrospect,
and I'm not just talking about the weather, if
you get my drift.
    Speaking of which, she'd probably throw a
major meltdown if I even mentioned it as a
possibility. So – that's it. Still, it was a
nice idea.
    Meanwhile Junior has decided to take to all
fours and I've spent most of the weekend doing
the same, trying to babyproof the place. It's
amazing how many potential deathtraps even a

nice place like ours turns out to contain. What
we need is a washable, sealed room with padded
walls that can just be hosed down every night.

How goes it at your end?

Col

----------------------------------

**From:** Billy Giddens [billy@billygoat.demon.co.uk]
**To:** Colum McCallum [collum@guzzi.freeserve.com]


col son
You, me, Bologna - we're there. I've got teh
tickets n case you trie to wriggle out of it As
for the Dog, just tell her your're gonig - give
her a chance to spend the weekend with tat
miserable mother of hers.

You'll need the break anyway if it's mobile
now. Once that happens it's like living with a
slowly rising tide - you just hav to hoep they
leave home before every'hing's out of your reach
as well.

So - Friday wekk, eh?

bill

----------------------------------


**28 March, 2001**

Something's up. Colum came home all cheery and bouncy with
flowers, champagne and a *Scientific American* article proving that
champagne is less fattening than Lindemans because − like
Maltesers − it's all air. Then he produced a pair of tickets to that
Ry Cooder concert that sold out weeks ago, and said he was
sorry the last outing didn't work out so well, how about trying
again? I patiently went over the problem − can't take baby, no

baby-sitter – and he just smiled superciliously and said it was all sorted, he'd talked to Georgie. He never talks to Georgie! He wouldn't trust her with his ironing, let alone his son and heir! And Georgie hasn't had a baby for over four years, she's probably forgotten all she ever knew about it. No, my first duty is to my child. He can go with somebody else if he finds our life so boring. After all, I stick it out uncomplainingly. Almost. Sometimes.

**29 March, 2001** – Kilverdale Road Health Centre

> *(Helen and Des are sitting in an upstairs room at the centre. Des is on Helen's knee, facing a table, on the other side of which sits a smiling, very young health visitor, Kimberley, who has a ball and a spinning top. Her colleague, Jane, is standing behind Helen with a rattle, a small spoon and a small cardboard box.)*

K: *(spinning the top, whispering)* Look at this, Lewis! Lewis!
   *(Des looks about him idly)*
H: *(whispering back)* He actually thinks his name is Des. Des, look at the . . .
K: Please, Mrs McCallum! No cheating!
H: Oh, sorry.
   *(Kimberley spins the top again)*
K: *(whispering)* Des, look here!
   *(Des glances at the top)*
D: (Okay, it's going round. Why is everybody whispering?)
   *(Kimberley stops the top and rolls the ball around the table-top with her fingers, while Jane makes a tiny sound with the spoon behind his left ear. Des turns his head fractionally, then looks around the room again.)*
D: (What's that woman doing lurking behind me? She's making me nervous.)
K: Good! Very good!
H: *(hugely relieved)* Very good, Des! Good boy!

257

D: Feerf? (What did I do? I didn't do anything.)
*(Kimberley puts away the ball and gets out the top again)*

K: Look here, Des, it's that pretty top again.
*(Des wriggles energetically in Helen's grip)*

D: (We came all that way for this? I've got one of those back at base, and mine's striped!)
*(Jane creeps around to Des's right ear and makes the same tiny sound. Des continues to wriggle and stare out of the window, but shows no sign of hearing her. Kimberley looks meaningfully at Jane. Jane makes the noise a bit more loudly.)*

D: (Just don't try anything louder than that, okay?)

H: *(nervously)* I think he did, sort of, twitch that time, don't you?

K: It's hard to tell. What d'you think, Jane?
*(Jane shrugs her shoulders. Kimberley writes something on a sheet of paper, looks up.)*

H: Should we go home and do some more practising? Maybe he's nervous . . .

K: Oh no, we can't let you do that. Do you find he's responsive at home?

H: Oh yes, very. *(to Des)* Aren't you?
*(Des begins to grizzle)*

D: Waaaar? Waaaar! (Aren't I what? Can we go now? My headache's coming back.)
*(Kimberley takes pity on her)*

K: It's possible he recognised the sound and didn't bother to turn his head. D'you think, Jane?

J: Could be.

H: Oh yes, we're like that in our family. Terribly lazy, Could Do Better, all that. I used to get into terrible trouble at school for that. I'm sure that's it. He just couldn't be arsed, could you, you lazy thing? He's just taking after me. Sweet!

*(Ernestine's side of the conversation is backed by the deafening sound of a fashionable bar. Helen's is all too quiet.)*

E: . . . so, I mean, I thought, six months of the year in a place with no cappuccino, no decent restaurants, and absolutely nothing to dress up for – Sea Breeze, double, please, tall glass, no ice – shame, he was sweet, though, and SO idealistic!

H: Really.

E: And hung like a horse, of course. Always helps. Thanks a lot, here, keep the change.

H: I'm sure.

E: Yeah, and it would have been a beautiful – hang on, is this him? No, false alarm – beautiful baby, too. I'm on a blind date, can you believe. The shame.

H: Baby? What baby?

E: The one I might have had with him. They always are beautiful, mixed-race babies, aren't they? Except when they're ugly, they're REALLY ugly.

H: I thought you had your tubes tied.

E: It is reversible. (Excuse me, d' you have matches?)

H: God.

E: (Thanks.) What?

H: You. With a baby.

E: And what's that supposed to mean?

H: Nothing.

*(Silence, except for the roar of life going on without Helen. Ernestine takes a long swig.)*

E: Mmm. That's better. So, what's new and special with you, darling? Still loving your cosy life with Colum?

H: Actually, he's got us tickets for that Ry Cooder concert – you know, the one that sold out months ago.

E: Really? God, he's fabulous, Colum, isn't he? How'd he manage that?

H: But I think really Des is a bit young – we've never left him, and . . .

E: I'll give him another three minutes. I am not waiting more than eight minutes for somebody I don't even know. God, Ry Cooder and all those sexy old Cubans. I always thought it would be so romantic, having a musician to play for you. Maybe they have sons.

H: I'm sure they do.

E: So – if you really don't want to go, why don't I go with Colum, instead? Oh, I think maybe – yes, he's heading this way – gotta go, love you, let me know about the ticket, won't you?

## 5 April, 2001

Have decided, in the interests of saving my relationship from irreparable damage, that I should force myself to abandon Des in the arms of his aunt for the evening. After all, they have a lot of DNA in common. That should count for something. Maybe she can do something with his toes to stop him getting into the bleach cupboard all the time, like buttering cats' paws to stop them running away.

Quite looking forward to a night out – almost nervous, in a weird way. Like dating again, only without the hope. If I had anything to wear, of course. Maybe there's a sale on at Ghost.

## 8 April, 2001 – Georgie and Des, in Helen's living room – evening

*(Georgie and Des are sprawled in the middle of the floor, on the Mr and Mrs Noah blanket which Georgie has miraculously discovered. Bright plastic toys and cutesy rattles all around them, and a Sesame Street video playing at high volume. Georgie is dipping*

*a HobNob in tea and feeding it to Des in squidgy dobs.)*

D:  Wusssshg! (This is the life!)

G:  Isn't it, though.

D:  Frrrrf (Bit more please . . .)

G:  Certainly, here you go.
    *(Des suddenly turns around and looks right at her)*

D:  (SHE UNDERSTANDS ME!)

G:  I have to say *(looking round the room)* you've done very well
    with them, considering how ignorant they were.

D:  Smmmeeeergh! (And arrogant!)

G:  Very arrogant. But fairly competent, you could have done
    worse.
    *(Des just looks at her)*

G:  You could, really. Trust me, I've seen a few.

D:  Gsssush, yegh wufd . . . (So, this is great, now that I have
    you here . . .)
    *(the phone rings)*

G:  Hang on.
    *(She gets up to answer it. Des starts in to roar.)*

D:  WAAAARGH! (Hey, this is important!)

G:  Shhhh – hello? Hello? Hello?
    *(She puts down the phone and returns to Des on the floor)*

G:  More biscuit?
    *(Des turns his head away, impatiently)*

D:  Pfshhh, wush sssxz . . . (Have you heard anything from
    . . .)
    *(The phone rings again. Georgie reluctantly stumbles to her feet,
    again. Des roars, again, somewhat more loudly.)*

G:  Probably your mum on the mobile.
    *(picks the receiver up)* Hello? Is that you, Helen? Helen?

D:  WEEEEEARGH! (For God's sake, woman! I'VE BEEN
    WAITING MONTHS FOR THIS MOMENT!)

G:  *(puts the receiver down)* Bloody things. As for you . . .
    *(looking down at Des, who is now lying, puce and knotted with*

*frustration, bellowing his lungs out on Mr and Mrs Noah's twin*
*camels. She looks at her watch.)* . . . by the sound of you, I'd
say it was probably time for bed. Come on.
*(She scoops him up. Des wriggles, roars, waves his little arms.)*

D:  WAAAArgh!! WAAAGRGH! WAAARGGGH! (No, this is
TERRIBLY, TERRIBLY IMPORTANT, I HAVE to make
contact with them . . .)
*(Georgie carries him in a firm grip through to the bedroom, talking*
*soothingly as she goes)*

G:  I'll talk to them for you, darling, if they call again, and I'll
tell them we had a lovely time – and you'll see them in
the morning, you know – shhhh . . .
*(she lays him in his basket by the bed and turns out the light.*
*The phone rings again.)*
Bloody thing. Night night, sweetheart.
*(leaves him, still roaring, shuts the door, goes back and picks it*
*up, again)* Hello? Oh, hi, was it you before? . . . Really?
Well, don't get yourself killed . . . everything's absolutely
fine, we've had a lovely evening and now he's a bit bushed
so I've put him to bed, but no problems at all, he's such a
sweet little thing, isn't he? . . . Helen?


**9 April, 2001**

Ry Cooder concert very enjoyable at the time, and would have
been even more so had I not missed three-quarters of it while
attempting to find a place to get a signal to contact Georgie on
the mobile. Finally managed right by a hot-dog stall near Tube
station, which was rather distracting. Georgie seems to have
coped with Des with no trouble at all, which would have
provided gratifying opportunity for 'ha!' moment with Colum,
had it not been his idea in the first place. Very galling. She also
accidentally left behind a lurid red, blue and green Fisher-Price
toy telephone, which has kept Des totally enthralled all day. Can't

decide whether to wait for Colum to come home with a *Scientific American* article proving that primary-coloured plastic toys with electronic chimes and annoying squeaky noises have been proven to increase mental function in babies by 800 per cent, or just take matters into my own hands. After all, three-quarters of our permanent binding bilateral treaty has gone out the window already, why bother about the rest?

But back in the ever-narrower confines of Stalag Baby, the outing seems in retrospect like the worst mistake of my recent life. Did I really need reminding that all over London, every night, millions of people are doing things like that? All over England, tens of millions of people are doing similar (if less glamorous) things. All over the world, billions of happy people are – you get the idea. And here I am, once again, pureeing vegetables.

Goodness, he really does like that toy . . . I've a feeling we're all going to be very, very bored, very, very soon, of 'Mary Had a Little Lamb' and 'Boys and Girls Come Out to Play'.

### 9 April, 2001

*Hello? Hello? I was sure I got a signal a moment back, but I can't hear them replying . . . If only she'd left some kind of instructions or note of the number for Mission Control. I've tried every option I can find, but this keypad doesn't resemble anything back home, and so far all I've got is a series of high-level tones that just repeat themselves when I hit the buttons. Doesn't seem to actually dial through anywhere. Unless there's a problem with my hearing – no, we checked that out the other day.*

*I'll just have to keep trying. Now that I know there are envoys among us, it's my duty to spare no effort to make contact.*

**9 April, 2001** – Colum, Helen and Des at the Little Chef, Brent Cross

*(They are seated at a table in the middle of a huge, packed room, barricaded by several large Toys R Us carrier bags. It's five o'clock on a traditional pre-Easter heat-wave weekend, and all around them surge half-naked seven-year-olds, hitting each other with toys and screaming.*

*Colum scans the menu, puts it back, and starts playing Peepo at Des from behind his shades. Helen reads the menu from cover to cover, goes back to the beginning and starts again.)*

C:  We should've gone with that Posh Spice Barbie . . .

D:  Durff! (Yeah, but her big sister would've been better.)

C:  . . . he needs someone to polish his social skills.

H:  I saw you lifting her skirt. What d'you think Italian Pasta Twirls would be like?

C:  Twirly. At best. *(takes off shades)* Peepo!

D:  Gheee hee hee! (He can't see with them on! So why's he wearing them?)

C:  Or that great furry purple thing that did back flips – what was his name again?

D:  Urfgh! (Even I know that one. He makes Mr Clown look like a model of bourgeois respectability.)

H:  Am I hallucinating, or is the Design Nazi of the Seven Boroughs endorsing Barney the Dinosaur?

C:  You may be hallucinating. I may be too if I don't eat soon.
    *(He looks around for any sign of help. An undernourished fifteen-year-old wearing a badge saying 'Welcome! Tammy TRAINEE' scuttles away behind the counter like a rabbit, narrowly missing a small boy trying out his very, very first pair of rollerblades, who careens into Des instead.)*

D:  Wahh! WWAAAHHHH! (Enemy alien alert! Hostile territory! MOVE!!)

H:  It's so difficult – nothing ever looks like the pictures . . .

C: Places like these, you just have to go for what they do best. Huge plate of fried greasy breakfast.

*(The boy is still stumbling around between the tables. Des is still wailing. Helen puts down the menu, produces a bottle and tries to give it to him. He just wails more.)*

D: WAAAHH! WAAARRHH! (For God's sake, woman! A battlefield is no place to stop for a picnic!)

*(Helen lifts him out of his seat and sits him on her lap, where he calms down somewhat, then she tries reading the menu, again, around him. Colum looks up with the air of a man trying to locate the Dunkirk Spirit, and rubs his hands, destroying his credibility at a stroke.)*

C: Good idea of yours, Helen. Poor wee chap could do with some proper toys.

*(Helen eyes him suspiciously)*

I should have listened to you long ago. Clever Mummy!

H: What's all this about?

*(Tammy has sidled noiselessly up beside Colum, chewing her pen)*

C: *(looking round)* Ah, Tammy. It is Tammy, isn't it? One Olympic Breakfast with a pot of tea and two rounds of buttered toast. *(roguish grin)* Heavy on the butter!

T: *(not meeting his eyes)* Webringyoubutterord'youwantFlora?

C: Butter. Helen?

H: *(caught in the headlights)* Oh dear, I'm not quite – can you do me some sides? Sort of together, on a big plate?

T: Werl'll'averchargeyermorefor'emokay?

H: Um, yes, fine, good, okay. Well, then . . . a baked potato, and, erm, those are Weight Watchers baked beans, are they? Okay, some of those, and some grilled tomatoes, no oil, and, er – maybe a side salad but without onion and lo-cal dressing and is there green pepper in it like the picture?

T: *(looking towards the kitchen)* Idunnol'll'avetergoan'ask . . .

C: NO!

H: NO! . . . if there is, just leave it out, okay? Okay, thanks!
*(Tammy dashes off, still scribbling)*

C: If she gets that right they should send her to sort out the Balkans. *(silence)*
So, I . . .

H: Oh, I forgot to ask for anything to drink . . . *(to nobody in particular)* Excuse me!

C: Ye can have my tea. I'll get some later.

H: Really?

C: No bother. *(clears his throat)* I've been . . .
*(Helen is looking worriedly at Des)*

H: He should drink something, maybe this bottle isn't warm enough . . .

C: WILL YOU LISTEN TO ME FOR A MOMENT?

H: Gosh, you made me jump. It's not that loud in here. Maybe you're going deaf.

C: I'm *(calming down with great effort)* – I had a little proposition to make to ye.

H: Aha! Go on.

C: Well, ye're always banging on about being stuck wi' young Des here . . . I thought I'd take him off your hands for a couple of days, say a weekend.
*(Des looks up at Colum nervously)*

H: Take him away? Where?

C: Oh, well, on the bike . . .

D: Weeeeergh!! WEERGH!! (I knew it! I knew that playgym came with a heavy price tag! No!)

C: . . . to Italy . . .

H: *(to Des)* Shhhh! Daddy's joking!

D: Wurrfffg!! Argh Argh!! (Don't you believe it.)
*(Colum continues, casually)*

C: . . . with Billy.

H: You are joking, aren't you?

C: Not at all. He could go in the backpack. 'Course, he's never

266

been on such a long trip, and it can be hot in Bologna in
April . . .

H: It's some bike thingy, isn't it?

C: Kind of. But I'll look after the little chap, he'd enjoy the
change of scene, and you could have a whole weekend off
– spoil yourself at a spa or whatever you girls do. I'll pay.

H: Over my dead body! You know what happens to babies
when you shake them! I know those roads!

C: Shhh! You're frightening the baby!

D: Weeeeergh! Woee! (No she's not, you are!)

H: Go, you go, I don't care, but you're not taking Des!
(*grabbing the menu again*) TAMMY!! Come back! I want to
change my order!


**10 April, 2001** – Bills from outing to Brent Cross

```
Toys R Us, Brent Cross
9/4/2001

Happy Tot playgym,        £34.99
MyFirstMobilePhone         £3.95
Huggies, midi, jumbo      £18.99

TOTAL:                    £57.93
Paid by Switch
```

```
Little Chef
Brent Cross, London
9/4/2001

1 × Olympic Breakfast                     £6.95
1 × side baked potato, plain              £0.99
1 × side grilled tomato                   £0.99
1 × side WW baked beans                   £0.99
1 × side salad, no onion, no pepper       £3.45
2 × pot tea                               £3.00

SUBTOTAL:                                £16.37

CREDIT
1 × side baked potato                     £0.99
1 × side grilled tomato                   £0.99
1 × side WW baked beans                   £0.99
1 × side salad, no onion, no pepper       £3.45

SUBTOTAL:                                 £9.95

1 × cheesy bacon chicken breast
    special, curly fries                  £6.99

SUBTOTAL:                                £16.94
OPTIONAL 12% SERVICE                      £2.03
TOTAL:                                   £18.97
PAID SWITCH WITHTHANKS
```

**12–14 April, 2001** – Exchange of e-mails

**From:** Colum McCallum [collum@guzzi.freeserve.com]
**Sent:** 12 april
**To:** Billy Giddens [billy@billygoat.demon.co.uk]

Hi Bill,
Well, the threat/flattery combo worked a
treat - could have been dodgy if she'd said
yes but as usual your guess was right on the
money. I'll make it up to her afterwards -
if I've any cash left, eh?
   So when and where?
   Col

----------------------------------

**From:** Billy Giddens [billy@billygoat.demon.co.uk]
**To:** Colum McCallum [collum@guzzi.freeserve.com]

col son
trust me, they're open books. any excuse to
slg off us men for insensitivty, impratic-
cality, or genera incmpetence is always
grabbed like a worm on a hook. If yu haven't
yet you sohudl try the same trick with
cooking - ofer to do it, make a real
performance out of it, fill the kikche nwith
smoke and dirty dishes, produce someting
inediable and a hundred-smacker grocery bill
and she'll never aks you again!
   I thought we'd leeave Thursday night to be
there late Friday. Ferry's at midnight - say
nine at miy place?
   bill

----------------------------------

269

**14 April, 2001** – Partial transcript of phone conversation between Helen and Alison

H:   . . . I know, as though they're God's gift and we couldn't survive for a minute without them. And then to come up with an idea like that!

A:   I have to say I'm quite surprised at Colum. I really thought he had more sense.

H:   Nah, in the end, however New they pretend to be, it's only microns deep. Poor little Des – can you imagine?

A:   I had weekend after weekend like that in the cricket season with your father. No wonder they call us grass widows. You wouldn't remember, of course. But I'm afraid it's all too familiar . . . *(sigh)*

H:   *(sigh)*
*(depressed silence)*

H:   *(determinedly bright)* Well, I'm going to make the most of it. There are all kinds of things I've been longing to do with Des but Colum's such a boring stick-in-the-mud – I can't wait!

A:   Well, darling, it's nice to see you taking a positive attitude for once . . . Let me know if it all gets too much, won't you?


**15 April, 2001**

*Unusual turn of events – visit to supply depot for purchase of equipment. What a paradise! Unfortunately already occupied by enemy hordes, otherwise far more looting and pillaging would have been in order, but did manage to come away with exercise equipment (thank goodness, in cheering colours for once) and a second communications device, though once again have been humiliatingly unsuccessful in reaching Mission Control. Never felt so stupid! Still, if at first you don't succeed . . .*

Even though they've been among us for nigh on countless millennia, I never fail to be amazed at the clunking obviousness of men. Did he really think I wouldn't notice anything unusual about a plan to drive up to Brent Cross in a heat wave, purchase a playgym so lurid that you could probably see it from outer space, and a toy mobile phone that plays 'William Tell' when you hit ANY button, and then stop off for a cheery family meal at the Little Chef 'to save you cooking'?

Turns out he just wants to go away for a couple of days this weekend. Some ghastly bike jumble sale somewhere in Italy. Good riddance, I say. Maybe now he'll start to believe that I'm actually a competent parent.

Spent part of this afternoon perusing various mags and guide-books for things to do that we never get to do when he's around. Here's the rough plan:

| | |
|---|---|
| **Friday** A.M. | Long, leisurely cappuccino breakfast, followed by: Des's first trip to the Zoo! Take picnic for . . . |
| Lunch | . . . on riverboat down canal to Little Venice, then . . . |
| P.M. | Stroll down Portobello Market, pick up delicious goodies for supper and maybe some funky threads (new diet plan Part Un – get incentivised to drop the weight) |
| Evening | Quiet evening at home cooking the food I like to eat, for once (cheese soufflé, chocolate mousse – new diet plan Part Deux, bad things aren't bad if mixed one part to ten with air) |
| **Saturday** A.M. | Up early for breakfast in Covent Garden, then . . . Covent Garden Street Theatre festival: mimes, clowns, jugglers, balloons – he'll love it! |
| Lunch | Picnic as before, by river, then stroll along river to . . . |

| P.M. | Tate Modern (babies love big space and big bright objects, it's never too early to start them out. Can't understand how my old, intolerant, killjoy self could have been so hostile to people bringing their babies to galleries. His reaction will be even more fun than the art!) |
| Evening | Early supper in fashionable, baby-friendly Southwark bistro – after all, Colum's getting to spoil himself royally, I think Des and I are allowed one decent meal! |
| Sunday | Walk through Regent's Park to beautiful Nash church for . . . |
| A.M. | Des's first experience of God in lovely setting with angelic choir – remind us how lucky we are! |
| Lunch | In park café, then quick Tube trip to: |
| P.M. | Commonwealth Institute Festival of Many Cultures: 'Music, dance and song from around the world, face painting, African magic, mask making,' it says on the blurb. Never too soon to expose Des to the richness and variety of the world's peoples (though we do quite well right here in Camden, with a few exceptions – not many Inuit or Kyrghiz that I know of) |
| Evening | Colum returns – triumphant reunion and rubbing his face in how much fun we've had without him |

**18 April, 2001** (Saturday Evening)

Well, the best laid plans . . . (she says, trying to sound perky)

| **Friday A.M.** | Coffee Republic – this bit was okay, though we managed to hit a three-mile tailback in the queue, entirely composed of haggard and |

desperate office workers oblivious to the needs of apparently carefree single mothers with a twenty-three-pound weight around their necks. So back home to transfer the twenty-three-pound weight to a buggy, and then on to the zoo, rather late but it didn't matter, as Des screamed in terror at those few animals that had bothered to emerge by then, before it came on to rain. Consequently plans for . . .

**Lunch** had to be rethought, and ended up as a zoo catering sandwich, eaten standing at a bus stop – open-topped riverboat less fun in the rain, though would have had plenty of seats, unlike the buses which whizzed right by for forty minutes while I got thoroughly drenched and Des, snug in his enveloping rain cover, had a little snooze. Finally one came along and

**Stopped!** . . . for about five minutes while I woke Des up, extracted him from the buggy, wrestled the rain cover off, and discovered that the buggy folding mechanism had mysteriously and irretrievably jammed. As the bus sailed off Portobellowards, I began to sneeze. So . . .

**P.M.** was spent trudging home via Blockbuster, where after the routine, but still surprising, discovery that of all the 10,000 titles stocked there's only one I want to see, and it's out, I decided a miserable . . .

**Evening** might as well be seriously miserable, and rented the one where George (Clooney) gets it on with That Woman. Having failed to get to the gourmet grocery paradise, forced to provision supper from the only shop between Blockbuster and home, which happens to be

273

SupaSave. Got back, unwrapped the infant, and noticed he was sneezing too, in between howls of hunger. Thought we'd both feel better with something hot and delicious inside us. However, what we had was WeightWatchers Dinner for One Chicken Primavera, Easily Opened by a Trained Octopus (for me) and Today's Special Sludge (orange) for Des. Finally got his in microwave and mine in cooker while he dangled upside down from my ninth arm. Two minutes later there was a bang like the opening salvo of World War III, the cooker blew up and all the lights went out. Tried resetting all fuses. Fuse not the problem, apparently. By then too late to get anybody to come round, even had there been enough light to read the Yellow Pages. Force-fed Des cold sludge (most of which was immediately sneezed back all over me), ate lump of Parmesan from fridge. Noticed fridge-freezer had also gone off. Freezer contained about fifty woman-hours' worth of sludge, plus several pounds of frozen steak, guinea fowl, and all the ice cream I was saving for when I deserve it again. Put Des to bed, took double dose of Sudafed to dry up cold so I could sleep, drank two glasses of Lindemans in quick succession to counteract stimulant effects of Sudafed, and went to bed by candlelight, fondly remembering camping trips of my youth (not)

**Saturday** God, was it only this morning . . . that we sat about for four hours waiting for the emergency electrician to come round, while Des perfected his interpretation of the William Tell

Overture, arranged for toy mobile phone by nameless sadists in South Korea, and I watched the wrinkles grow on my face. Finally he showed up, restored the power supply but informed me that the cooker was going to need a triple bypass and the waiting list currently stood at four months. So . . .

Lunch

was another sandwich, from SupaSava this time, even more delicious if possible, and more cold sludge for Des, while we discussed, between projectile sneezes, the meals we would have made from the dazzling gamut of thawed gourmet ingredients waiting to be thrown out. Which I did, when boredom and Calpol finally got the better of his party spirit, only to discover a wondrous variety of primitive organisms bivouacked where the frozen guinea fowl had leaked before it froze. Thus . . .

P.M.

was usefully dedicated to undoing the thirty bolts which now bar access to the cleaning materials for anyone but a master criminal, scouring the freezer, and looking forward to the gladsome task of filling it again next week. After which we were anticipating a pleasantly heartbreaking . . .

Evening

watching, helplessly, as George made the biggest mistake of his life. At least, I was looking forward to it. Des had other ideas. Apparently wearying of his career as a virtuoso musician, he decided to resume the lock-picking apprenticeship, so those few moments of the film I did manage to catch were all viewed from fifteen inches off the floor while

275

I attempted to seal off the bleach, the wine bottles, the CDs, the power tools and the big pile of bike parts Colum could never quite bear to throw out, from his infant curiosity. The only upside was that between the sneezing and the triple doses of Calpol he was ready for bed by eight-thirty, which brings us up to – hang on . . .

**18 April, 2001, 21.00** – Partial transcript of phone conversation between Colum and Helen

> *(dialogue is punctuated throughout by other people's conversations, in Italian, breaking through crossed lines.)*
>
> C: . . . Hello? *parzialmente scremata ma no, non* . . . Is . . . *poi piu, mi* . . . you, sweet . . . *ambidue le late dal fronte del* . . . hello?
>
> H: Hello – Col? . . . *certamente* . . . are you?
>
> C: Yeah, terrif . . . *in caso di emergenza* . . . boiling hot, just as . . . *sostenanza spirituale di* . . . nosh, Bologna seems to be the gourmet . . . *inchiesto giudiziale finalmente concluso* . . . you?
>
> H: Fine. We're both . . . *colpo di fuso* . . . couldn't be HHHHHAAAATCHOOO!
>
> C: Was that you . . . *lo giuro, sopra la* . . . the boy?
>
> H: Oh, don't worry about your . . . *madonna mia, sul serio?* . . . HAAATCHOOOO!
>
> C: Poor you, well, I'll be . . . *in fatti, ieri sera* . . . you then, okay?
>
> H: Sure, fine, whatevHAAAAAAAATCHOOOOO!
>
> C: Love . . . *chi sei? non capisco* DUUUUUUUUUUUUU . . .

276

H:  (*tearfully*) Ernie?

E:  (. . . have to get that.) Hello?

H:  Ernie, I have to talk to you. I'm all alone with Des and I'm having a . . .

E:  (Helen – no, I'll only be a minute – down, boy –)

H:  . . . an awful, awful weekend and . . . and the cooker's broken and . . .

E:  What? Sorry, I'm a bit – so, get a takeaway?

H:  But he's got a HAAAAAAATHOOOOOO! cold, and . . .

E:  Then a nice hot curry's probably just what he needs to – (Ohhh!) – look, darling, I can't talk . . .

H:  (*sobbing*) . . . It's all so dreary, and life is just passing me HATCHOOO! by . . .

E:  Oh, cheer up, it's only twenty years or so, and you'll still only be – well, I see what you mean, but (*brightly*) look at Catherine Deneuve or . . . or Lauren Bacall!
    (*impatient male voice in the background, 'Come on! . . .'*)

H:  Lauren Bacall's eighty!

E:  And I bet she still has loads of fun.

H:  Can we come round?

E:  Now?

H:  Well (*gulping down sob*), it's early for you, and I know I won't sleep a wink anyhow, not now. HATTTCHOOO!

E:  I'm not home.

H:  Well, where are you? What are you doing?

E:  (*giggles*) I can't EXACTLY say . . .

H:  Oh!

E:  Sounds to me like you should be tucked up in your bed with a nice cup of hot chocolate.

H:  I HATE BLOODY HOT CHOCOLATE!

E:  If you're going to (Ooooooooooh!) *(panting slightly)* be like that, Helen . . .

H:  Sorry. How about tomorrow?

E:  *(more giggles)* Tomorrow might well be a bit inconvenient too (mightn't it – hmmm?)

H:  Well, when, then? I just have to talk to somebody who's more than a foot tall! I have to! I'm going to go mad!

E:  Shhh, calm down, sweetie (one more minute, I promise – ooooh, don't – no, do . . .). Look, like you said, the night is young. Dose yourself up, pull on your uptown threads, and hit the streets! It's not even raining at the moment – is it? Can't see from here. . . .

H:  How can I? I can't just leave him!

E:  Whyever not? He's not going to get far, is he?
    *(Helen is now sobbing uncontrollably down the phone, in between sneezes)*

E:  *(more gently)* Darling, look, it's not so bad. When Col gets home he'll owe you one, won't he? Why not get yourself some lovely holiday brochures and find a place you can all go together – there must be places that like babies, what about – what was it called – Club Med? Does it still exist? With those pop beads, d'you remember? Look (hey, where are you going? Come here!), I really have to go, I'll call you tomorrow, darling, okay?


Excerpt from Condé Nast Traveller 'Exotic Breaks Special', 2001

. . . a far corner of KyongNorWat, lapped by the deepest azure ocean . . . just fifteen secluded grass huts, some on stilts in the water and accessible only by reed boat. Each has a giant, soft, tented bed for an undisturbed romantic sojourn . . . nothing to do but lie on the sand, give each other exotic fruit rubs, and watch the sun slowly sink into a timeless land-scape . . .

... very convenient for the A604 and National Coach connections, and with easy access to the Hernden Shopping Plex for all your self-catering needs. Each brightly decorated en suite family bungalow has travel cot, microwave, mini-fridge and baby bath. Your hosts, Des and Jennifer, will be happy to point you towards local attractions such as Easeden Petting Zoo and Hatchery, Jellybee World, and the famous Yapden Yoghurt Creamery (free samples daily!) ...

**19 April, 2001, 03.00** – Helen and Des, in front of bathroom
mirror – Sunday

H: *(dead on her feet)* So this is it, Des – just you, me and our cold. Look at us. You could plant carrots in those furrows. Your mother's a crone, Des. But she wasn't always! No she wasn't! Probably in the whole history of the world nobody has aged so dramatically and so fast.

D: *(wide awake, seeing his reflection for the first time)* Pfscheesh! Urfphw HAAAASTCHEW mmm? (Hey, who's that? And how did he get HAATSCHEW in here?)

H: Maybe I've contracted a late-onset version of that galloping ageing thingy, you know, the one that turns eight-year-olds into old men.
*(leaning in to scrutinise her reflection. Des does likewise.)*

D: MMmmmnnna! (He's rather handsome, I have to say. But . . .)

H: I forgive you, you know that, don't you? *(kissing him)* But you may have to fend for yourself sooner than you . . .

D: Weeer! Weeihuff? (Hang on, what's he doing kissing my host? She may not be much to look at, but she's all I've got.)
*(leans towards the mirror and begins to bang it vigorously)*

H:  You can see yourself! Clever boy!

D:  Weeeeh!! Dai dai! (Gerroff! Go on, hop it!! This space is taken!)

H:  There must be something on the Web about it. I might as well know the worst . . . shall we go and play with the computer, sweetie?

Helen at the computer – 19 April, 2001

(04.00)

```
www.yourhealth.com
. . . normally confined to the male, although
reports of similar presentations to
Methuselah's Disease have been reported in
females from some of the Polynesian Islands
. . . onset of first symptoms never later
than eight years of age. For more information
refer to . . .
```

*(Des appears to be sleeping on the bed. Helen is too riveted to take advantage of this and get some sleep herself.)*

(04.15)

```
www.childhealth.com
. . . Early telltale symptoms of other incur-
ably progressive conditions . . . minute
deformity beginning with the little finger
. . . signs of discomfort indicating the
onset of knotted and eventually sclerotic
large intestine . . . distinct pink half-moon
pattern behind the lobe of the ear . . .
```

*(Helen has woken Des and is examining him minutely all over. For some reason Des doesn't seem totally happy with this idea.)*

. . . children under a year old are especially vulnerable to accident and injury, and
it's as well to safeguard your home thoroughly. Take a virtual walk through the
potential deathtraps at

(04.45)

www.childsafe.com
. . . safeguard unsteady little slippy-slidey
feet with our NeverSlip Floor Pads, only
$16.99 (plus tax within US) . . . keep
baby's soft little head safe from falling
objects with ClosetNets, pack of 4 only
$24.99 plus tax, washable . . . immediately
detect harmful airborne vapors with VaporGuard
electronic alarm ($39.99 plus tax, batteries
extra, also available for mains) . . . line
your sharp corners, doors and counters with
fluffy, oh-so-soft ToddlerBump shielding
($15.99 plus tax per yard, white, blue or
yellow, also in royal or teal, US inland
only, adhesive extra) . . .

*(Helen is back at the computer. Des is still yelling lustily, clearly
not amused by being woken up, prodded, poked and then aban-
doned again.)*

. . . For more neat ideas on how to amuse
baby when he just wants to play, check out

(05.00)

www.babyplay.com
. . . be amazed at what a raid on the
kitchen will provide by way of distractions.
A carrot, two toothpicks and some cucumber

281

rings and hey presto! a vegetable racing car!
. . . and of course if all else fails, that
old standby, the shadow puppet. Bring a small
lamp close to a wall for hours of fun with
Ducky, Bambi, Mother Goose and all the other
old favorites!

(05.20)
*(Helen is kneeling in a corner of the bedroom. Des is propped against the wall, watching her gamely trying to manipulate her hand into a duck's head.)*

H: 'Quack, quack, quack! Thank God that ugly duckling left. Now we can really have some fun!' But little did the Stuck-Up Baby Duckling know that . . .
*(bringing up her other hand in an identical lumpy fist)* . . . Mr Nasty Fox was listening!
*(She stops, exhausted. Des stares at her, bemused.)*

D: (So this is what they get up to when I'm asleep. No wonder they don't like me to be awake at this hour. It's tragic.)

H: For God's sake, Des, you're supposed to be watching Stuck-Up Duck and Mr Nasty Fox, not me! I'm killing myself here, I could use a little co-operation!

(05.55)
*(Des has crashed again. Helen is propped in front of the computer, finally asleep, and dreaming of . . .)*

www.infanticide.com
Welcome to Infanticide.com, where you get to
solve your problems with the help of others
just as desperate as you! To help us help
you, before registering please enter the
following information:

1 Name, address, e-mail address, d.o.b.
2 Name(s) and age(s) of children (yes, people DO make the same mistake twice)
3 What is the closest you have come (to date) to murdering your child? Give details:
4 What is your child's most annoying character-istic? Please select from one of the following options:
not sleeping
not eating
getting sick
hitting
whining
other character defects (give details)
physical repulsiveness (give details)
5 Which of these items of common household equipment are readily available to you? (check as many as you like):
Deep fat fryer
Rice steamer
Barbecue
Electrical heater (two-wire, older the better)
Heavy duty plastic sack
Saran Wrap (clingfilm in UK)
Electric carving knife
Sharp chef knives
Safety razor
Kettle (electric or regular)
Waste disposer
Microwave (enter size and wattage)
Electric iron (steam/non steam)
Chainsaw
Claw hammer

Electric screwdriver
Electric drill
Exacto knife (Stanley knife in UK)
Large, heavy book (e.g. encyclopedia,
dictionary)
Television or computer monitor
Other (please specify)
6 Which of these is hardest for you to deal
with? (check one only):
Blood
Boils/pustules
Vomit
Diarrhea
Choking
Persistent screaming
Convulsions/fits

Thank you! CLICK HERE TO LOG IN

WARNING: YOUR ATTENTION IS DRAWN TO THE
FOLLOWING TERMS AND CONDITIONS

*Infanticide.com and its parent company, Cheap
Thrills, Inc., are not liable for any consequences that may result from registration on
this site. Before proceeding, you are advised to
hire a good attorney, check that your affairs
are in order, and put aside a sum NOT LESS
THAN $10,000 US for reconstructive plastic
surgery.*
ANY INFORMATION YOU SUBMIT IS INSECURE AND MAY
BE INTERCEPTED IN TRANSIT
*(processing)*

WELCOME MINNIE MOUSE! Your personalized welcome message and action plan will be e-mailed to you within ten working days. Meanwhile don't miss our new features . . .

Ten Unusual Sightseeing Spots to Take Your Baby:

1  The pit lane of a Formula 1 racetrack
2  The boil-down shed of a whale oil refinery
3  The reactor core of a nuclear power generator
4  The rim of the Grand Canyon
5  The foredeck of an Atlantic trawler
6  The pressing shop of a machine tool factory
7  The main runway of a busy airport on Thanksgiving
8  The materials storage bay of a chemical plant
9  The Hoover Dam, at midnight
10 The local National Rifle Association practice range

. . . and this Week's 'Acting on Impulse: Safe Bets that Look Like Carelessness' tip comes from Liz Borden, of Tulare, Ca. Thanks Liz! We like it!

'Tell your partner you'll take baby out for the day in the car. Drive into the countryside. Choose a parking spot that's guaranteed to be in direct sun for the next four hours. (Three should do it, but the last thing you need is to fail and have to care for a recovering infant for weeks.) Park and lock the car, making sure all windows are secure. Go shopping. It's that simple! . . .'

## 19 April, 2001

After a couple of hours of sleep I realised that fatalist calm was the only attitude that would get me through, and now feel totally reconciled to life being over for ever. I took an irreversible wrong turning, I did it of my own free will, and there's nothing to be done about it – but after all, I'm no worse off than millions of women through the ages. Greeted Colum on his return immaculate, groomed, eight layers of concealer disguising effects of (almost) totally sleepless weekend and remains of heavy cold. No way I was going to admit any of this to him. However, provoked by his compulsive cheeriness and galling willingness to take me at my word that everything fine, could not help adding line about 'Now I really know what it's like to be left holding the baby'. Felt this slightly gave the game away and was sure that he would immediately demand detail which I would eventually be compelled, breaking down in helpless but touching sobs, to divulge, but he just said, 'Not so bad, is it?' and went off into the bathroom whistling 'O Sole Mio'. Bastard.

## 21 April, 2001

*Of course, a soldier's primary weapon is his icy nerve, and I'm not saying for a moment that I'm even slightly rattled, but I've been feeling a distinct sense of unease ever since the donor left us alone. Is it my fault that the mobile comms device has no instruction manual? Is it my fault that the only entertainment accessible to me is whatever's less than ten inches off the floor? And as for that film she was so keen on watching – anybody could see from the first frame how it would turn out. Alpha Male and oestral female become donor and host. End of story.*

*Thank God for the new exercise equipment – splash of cheering colour more and more welcome to counteract mood of host.*

**20–23 April, 2001** – Exchange of e-mails

**From:** Colum McCallum [collum@guzzi.freeserve.com]
**Sent:** 20 April
**To:** Billy Giddens [billy@billygoat.demon.co.uk]

Hi Bill,
Thanks again for the weekend – just what I
needed. I'll get those few other parts
ordered and get the lot over to Steve. It's
about time I topped up his Caribbean holiday
fund.

I have to admit that the tonic effect of
our little trip has been considerably eroded
by Morticia's antics since my return. She
said she was really looking forward to
getting out and about with young Des but, if
possible, seems worse than before – obviously
had a terrible time but won't admit it and
has taken to wandering around in the middle
of the night, muttering to herself. What I
wouldn't give for the relationship I used to
have with the partner I used to have!
    Col

----------------------------------

**From:** Billy Giddens [billy@billygoat.demon.co.uk]
**To:** Colum McCallum [collum@guzzi.freeserve.com]

col son
partner you used to have has gone for goonod
I'm afraid and nothnig short of a boob job
and a lobotmy will bring it back to even
faint reemslance of its foremr self. they
don't all take to ti but of couse you can;t

287

```
tell nutl you try. life's little jokes etc.
good thing you've got the Ducati now at lest.
  bill
```

--------------------------------

**24 April, 2001** – Partial transcript of phone conversation between Colum and Ernestine

C:   . . . so that was the only thing I could think of, but given how she's been lately I've not the foggiest how to suggest it without a major meltdown.

E:   Tell me about it. She was climbing the walls less than twenty-four hours after you left. I practically had to leave the country myself. (Just here'll do fine – the ballroom entrance. Can I have a receipt, please?)

C:   So what do you think? You're another female.

E:   I like to think so *(flirtatiously)* – though I might not put it quite like that. (Keep the change, ta). Cook her a lovely dinner, and suggest it over the brandy. (Hi! SO sorry, darling – the traffic's unbelievable out there.)

C:   Really? Simple as that?

E:   I don't think she'll take much persuading from what I've seen lately. Call me again if you . . .

C:   (Sweetheart! Back already?)


**24 April, 2001**

Came in just now and found Colum on phone to Ernestine. I know it was her because he was weird and furtive about it and so I dialled 1471 and luckily she had called him. Why would she call him? Colum has hardly exchanged three words with Ernestine. Now I think of it, this in itself a very, very suspicious sign – unnatural for partner and best friend never to talk and appear to have nothing in common. What are they hiding?

God, no. How can I have been so stupid! No . . .

Of course that mobile of Ernie's works just as easily in Italy as here. I thought that voice in the background was familiar. No wonder she couldn't wait to get off the phone to me. 'I'm not home.' No, of course you're bloody not, you're two thousand bloody miles away with my bloody husband!

God, what a dope. What a stupid, dopey dope. They must really have been pissing themselves when she hung up. Lolling about between those crispy Italian linen sheets, sipping Prosecco and nibbling biscotti from each other's lips . . .

How could he! It's so − I still can't quite take it in. Oh, grow up, Helen. Men always leave when things get tough, it's well known. They stand by and watch as their sleep-deprived, bloated, aged-ten-years-in-six-months partner goes to the dogs, then slip neatly sideways into arms of new partner who is none of the above, and take her off for carefree weekends of spoiling and high life in Italy. Meanwhile old partner is left chained to her computer in a flat that looks like the aftermath of Stalingrad, with baby wailing in the background day and night.

Can it really be true? Surely even Ernie isn't as desperate as that. Though come to think of it, she has been dropping remarks about how lucky I am, etc., etc., lately. And how come (God, it's amazing the speed and power of your mind in a crisis), how come none of us ever gets to meet these allegedly fabulous boyfriends of hers? The last three at least could have been completely virtual for all we know. God, how could I have been so naïve? Fijian musician-political activist! Large marine mammal specialist! Nobody but a total, innocent sap with a brain shrunk to the dimensions and consistency of a mushy pea would have failed to see through those.

She's been having a laugh at my expense. And with him! But before I do anything rash I'd better do some background checks. Don't want to be too hasty at a time like this.

There's one obvious place to start. Billy's notoriously as stupid as he's ugly. Even if Colum warned him he should be easy to catch out.

**26 April, 2001** – Partial transcript of phone call between Billy and Colum

C:    . . . no, it's good in fact, if I don't get at least one call an hour they think I'm slacking. So what's up?

B:    Old lad, you will never guess who called me just now.

C:    Probably right.

B:    Your lovely lady wife.

C:    Helen? She doesn't even know your number, does she?

B:    If you think that's amazing, Watson, you should've heard the questions she was asking about our little trip. She's well into bikes, i'n't she?

C:    Like I'm into *Hello!* magazine.

B:    I'm telling you. She knew about the Guzzi, of course, but she wanted to know which parts it was missing, what else we saw – and talk about in detail! I practically had to give her serial numbers! Then she got on to the hotel – where was it, what was the room like, then what did we eat and where – I was waiting for the one about my bowel movements, or more likely yours. Without insulting the mother of your child, old son, I'd say her forks are definitely well out of true.

C:    I told you – paranoid and delusional. It's getting worse, too.

B:    Yeah, well, if I were you I'd activate Plan B sooner rather than later.

C:    I'm just worried she'll think I'm saying she's a bad mother.

B:    Nah, you're just facing facts. Get her mellow and give it to her straight. It'll be best for all of you in the end, believe me.

## 26 April, 2001 – Ernestine and her shrink

New this Month: Complex Syntax Comprehension
Module. Yours for only £49.99. Simply hit this
button before quitting for a richer, deeper
interaction next time.

(hello, Ernestine, how's tricks, darling, know what I mean?)
Excuse me?

(excuse, any excuse, I always say, know what I mean?)
What the . . . Oh, now I remember. Where's the
. . . here's the menu. *(reading)* 'Grave,
Sympathetic, Reflective' – here we go, 'Cheery
Cockney'. Must've hit it by mistake. Let's go
for *(typing)* 'Empathetic' with low, no, medium
reflexivity, and let's have high prompt rate,
save a bit of effort.

(good evening, Ernestine. Lovely to see you. Everything okay?)
Well, apart from being stood up by somebody I'd
never even met . . .

(maybe you should have met somebody first?)
Maybe, but you try in this god-forsaken ci . . .

(God is everywhere. In the city and in the country.)
I didn't know I'd hit the 'sanctimonious old
fart' button.

(please clarify sanctimonious old fart.)
I don't know what to do about Helen.

(why don't you know what to do about Helen?)
Well, she's gone so weird. I try talking . . .

(how weird has she gone?)
Can I finish a sentence occasionally? Oh, I see,

the prompt rate, all right *(typing again)* –
medium prompt, here we go. As I was saying, she
seems to be furious if I tell her what I'm doing,
and more furious if I don't.

(when does she seem less furious?)
When I don't see her at all.

(how does she seem when you don't see her at all?)
But she's my pal, I can't not see her, we've
been through so much . . .

(what have you been through?)
Another time.

(did you enjoy going through another time with her?)
No, you dumbwit, I meant – as a matter of
fact, yes.

(do you enjoy going through this time with her?)
I don't feel I am, that's the problem.

(how could you go through this time with her?)
I dunno – maybe . . . Maybe that's it, join
in more, express enthusiasm for the baby, all
that. Worth a try . . .


**28 April, 2001**

God, people are so naïve. Or maybe they just think I am ('course,
up until now I have been. But not any more. Now my wits are
honed to a razor sharpness, and no clue, however tiny, escapes
my eagle eye.) Ernie calls up ever so casual, 'Oh, so sorry about
the weekend, would it be okay if I just came and hung out
today – seems like ages since I spent any time with you. I could
help out with the shopping or something.' Like I'm a charity
case. Well, if she wants to know what it's like, I can certainly

oblige. May give me a chance to confirm my suspicions without alerting her.

And then, quite coincidentally OF COURSE, ha ha, Colum offered to cook dinner tonight. This is a very, very bad sign. He even said he'd shop. Typical male – night after night forces wife to cook boring, samey, easy-care dinner for £2.50 to be consumed in half an hour between baby duties, suddenly decides he'll take over for once and expects a knighthood. Or more. Well, he's not buying me off that easily. He'll spend a huge fortune that ought to be going into the divorce settlement, take three hours to cook something that ought to take ten minutes, then leave the kitchen looking like the Sack of Troy. Serve him right if the cooker blows up again. Who cares anyhow, will all taste of dust and ashes in view of what he's planning to tell me over the crème brûlée. Bet he makes steak and crème brûlée.

**28 April, 2001** – Helen and Ernestine, shopping

> *(The two women are struggling against heavy crowds and driz-zling rain down a packed high street. Helen has Des in his sling and is marching along purposefully. Ernie, weighed down with several Boots carrier bags and not dressed for a route march, is struggling to keep up.)*

H: Enjoying yourself?

E: Mmm – yes, well, it's a real eye-opener.

H: I still don't understand why you suddenly wanted to do this.

E: *(panting)* Oh well, you know, see what it's really like for you.
> *(a passing bus splatters her ten-denier Midnight Sable legs to the knee with evil-smelling mud)*

H: I'm not complaining! I'm fine!

E: *(faint with relief)* Oh, look! Great! Come on.
> *(She's spotted a Baby Gap. An oasis to a thirsty camel.)*

H: *(calling after her)* I can't afford Baby Gap. Anyhow, he doesn't . . .

E: *(an earthquake wouldn't stop her now)* I'm paying. Come on . . .

*(reluctantly, Helen follows)* . . . make up for being mean to you over the weekend.

*(They get inside. Warm, dry, soothing music, no crowds.)*

E: Ooh, look, it's a wonderland.

H: Feeling guilty?

E: Only a bit – I did have a fairly stupendous time.

H: *(meaningfully)* I bet you did. Where were you again?

*(Feigning casualness, she picks up a pair of weeny socks)*

E: *(coyly)* I don't actually think I can tell you.

*(Helen drops the socks like hot coal)*

H: God, look at the prices . . . Anybody I know?

E: *(turning away)* Mmm, well . . . Oh, look!

*(she drops her bags beside Helen and holds a pair of adorable stripey dungarees up against Des, apparently oblivious to the Medusa mask glaring down at her)*

E: Soooo edible. I'm definitely getting him these. *(looks at the price tag)* My God, you're right about the prices. It's, like, nothing! And look, there's a fabulous little T-shirt to go with it. There. He is my godson, after all, forming his taste is practically a sacred obligation. What else?

*(She's off, burrowing and ferreting with little cries of joy. Helen, stone-faced, stands where she was, barricaded by nappies and baby powder, stroking the head of her poor, doomed child. Ernie comes back with a tiny knit jacket.)*

H: You'll spoil him.

E: Well, that's my privilege, *(burying her face in his)*. Isn't it, pooky-wooky? God, it's so great really getting to know him. Precious thing!

*(Des giggles nervously. Ernie marches off towards the cash register, leaving Helen to bring the Boots bags.)*

E: You're so lucky. I had no idea.

H: Am I?

E: I mean, you can go on a total spree in this place for a tiny fraction of the price! You can dress him in whatever you like and he can't do a thing about it!

D: Blidy blihh! (Oh no? Ever heard of projectile vomit?)

H: Well, what happened to your idea about having one of your own, if you think it's such a bundle of laughs?
*(They're finally at the front of the queue. Ernestine hands over a large pile of tiny garments.)*

E: I remembered about the physical stuff. No offence, darling, but I am quite fond of my body in its current shape. Here! *(hands over her platinum credit card)* Now *(nuzzling Des again)*, if I could get one gift-wrapped and oven-ready, like this little pudding . . .

D: Dfff, hgurrrr. (Why all the sudden attention from Big Lips? Still, better humour her – those teeth look pretty sharp.)
*(He responds to her nuzzling with his most dazzling smile. Which Helen sees, of course. At this moment, Ernie's mobile rings.)*


**28 April, 2001** – phone call between Colum and Ernestine

C: Ernie? Is that you?

E: God, Co . . . (Sure, go ahead, sorry, HELEN . . .)

C: Is this a bad time? Only things are getting pretty serious so I decided to activate Plan B tonight, and . . .

E: *( furtively, in a low voice)* Tonight? Does she know?
*(Helen's voice in background, 'Who is it?')*

E: . . . I'm with her right now, so I can't . . .

C: Okay, okay, just say yes or no, it's only food being such a flashpoint lately, I wanted to check wi' another female . . .

E: (Oh, sorry, are you waiting for me?)
*(sound of pen scrabbling in background)*

Okay, but hurry up, I'm sure she knows it's you . . . (Sorry, Helen, God, the trouble with being freelance is people just think they can call you ANYWHERE!) . . . Spit it out!

C: Crème brûlée? Yes or no?

E: That's it? Yes, of course, and don't forget the *(unintelligible mutter)*

C: What? I'm here in the store, there's a hell of a racket . . .

E: *(a bit louder, through gritted teeth)* Chocolate!!!


## Back to Helen and Ernestine in Baby Gap

*(Helen, her arms now wrapped protectively around Des in his sling, is trying, with no success at all, to look as though she's not eavesdropping. The assistant finishes processing the transaction and hands the bags to Helen, who grabs them, ungraciously.)*

H: *(to assistant)* You do refunds, don't you?
*(Ernie hangs up the phone and turns to Helen, all big apologetic smiles)*

E: SO sorry, darling, this big dinner I'm helping arrange, for some reason they seem to think they need my input on every tiny thing . . .
*(Helen picks up the rest of the bags and faces her from behind a barricade of nappies)*

H: Don't worry, Ernie, I need to get him home now anyway.
*(Ernie tries to grab some of the bags back)*

E: Oh, well, I'll help you – maybe for once we can get a taxi, whaddya . . .
*(Helen hangs on like a limpet and makes for the door, Des completely buried inside the bags)*

H: I don't need a taxi, I'm fine. I'm sure you've got things to do. See you soon, eh?

```
Bluebird A La Carte, King's Road
28/4/2001

Fillet steak 500g @ £26.00/kg        £13.00
Pie de Dijon Mustard                  £4.25
Garlic paste, 250g jar                £2.25
Baguette de mie dur                   £1.75
Beurre d'lsigny, 250g                 £1.99
Shallots, 400g @ £5.00/kg             £2.00
Asparagus, Sussex, 500g @ £8.30/kg    £4.15
Eggs, I doz. Yeovil Pullet Extra      £2.65
Sucre Affiné La Colombe               £4.65
Vanille de Madagascar, Extrait Pur    £5.25
Raspberries, Malta 2 @ £4.50          £9.00
Plaw Hatch Creamery Untreated
    Jersey Cream, 200ml               £3.50

SUBTOTAL                             £54.44
PAID VISA WITH THANKS
Au Revoir A Très Bientôt!
```

```
ODDBINS WINE MERCHANT EXTRAORDINAIRE
28.4.01

Spa Belgian, lit. 2 @ £0.90      £1.80
Veuve Clicquot brut '98         £29.99
Mulderbosch Faithful Hound      £15.99

SUBTOTAL                        £47.78
Paid Visa with thanks
```

```
GODIVA CHOCOLATIER
28.4.01

500g ballotin       £9.50

SUBTOTAL            £9.50
PAID VISA WITH THANKS
```

**28 April, 2001, ten minutes later** – Helen, back at Baby Gap
later

*(She's obviously been lurking just long enough for Ernie to disappear, and is back in line at the till. Gets to the front of the queue. The assistant looks up.)*

A:  Next? Oh, 'ello. That was quick!
H:  I'm bringing these back. I don't have the receipt but . . .
A:  Your friend got the size wrong, did she?
H:  No, I just . . .
A:  Tell you what, she's ever so fond of your baby, innit?
H:  What did you say?
A:  If you don't watch out she'll 'ave 'im.
    *(Helen has gone white. The bags are shaking in her hand. The assistant suddenly realises she's stepped on a bomb.)*
A:  *(weakly)* I'm kidding, innit? You okay?
    *(The bags drop to the floor. Helen, both arms wrapped tightly around the baby on her chest, is fleeing out of the shop.)*

**28 April, 2001, 17.00**

'I want to know what it's like' . . . 'you're so lucky' . . . 'if I could get one gift-wrapped and oven-ready' . . . 'so nice getting to know him' – and what was that about tonight? They must be planning to leave, him with him, right after dinner . . . and Des smiled at her! Just because she can afford to buy him stupid knit

298

jackets – are all my months of love and sacrifice to be bought off so cheaply?

This way she gets Colum and his baby, and he'll get to keep the flat – not that I could stay for another night in this place, but I'd rather not exchange it for a cardboard box with river views. What does he care about that? He'll be laughing then. They both will. Ha Ha HA!!

There, there, darling, it's all right. You're so sensitive, aren't you, you're picking up on Mummy's every tiny worry. I know it's very uncomfy in there, but I have to keep you in it for your own protection right now – you'll understand later. Shhhh – shhh . . . Damn, was that the last Wispa Gold? Well, I'm just going to DROP the wrapper RIGHT HERE ON THE FLOOR! Up yours, Mr Pristine Environment! I have to get away. Have to get away with you, precious darling, before they can stop me. But where? Look at all those congrats cards, still cynically winking on the mantelshelf! Can it really only have been a few shorts months since . . . Boots the Chemist, Billy bloody Giddens – ha! This is it! Perfect!

**28 April, 2001, 17.15** – Partial transcript of phone call between Helen and Eco-Baby Papoose Holidays

H:    Wherever the next plane is going. I don't care. Anywhere!

E-B: Well, we do have spaces on the Costa Rica trip, but . . .

H:    Costa Rica! Perfect! He'd die rather than set foot there!

E-B: . . . but we don't recommend taking children under three at this time of year. Monsoon season, you know.

H:    What, a bit of water? He'll be fine.

E-B: It's more the giant slugs, mosquitoes, leeches, that sort of thing – the ecosystem replenishing itself, you know. Anyway, that's not till Tuesday week.

H:    Tuesday week! I need to leave tonight! What do you have today?

E-B: Today? Well, er, nothing, and anyhow you'd have to get visas and all sorts. *(nervously)* D'you want to speak to a supervisor?
*(Sound of doorbell ringing in Helen's flat)*

H: They're here! It's too late! I've lost him!
*(hangs up and bursts into tears)*


**28 April, 2001, 17.30** – Helen's flat

*(Helen is sitting on the bed in the bedroom, with the door shut and Des in the sling. Neither is making a sound. The bell rings again. Then a faint voice – Sarah's voice.)*

S: *(from outside)* Helen? Are you there? It's Sarah.
*(Helen's face changes from terror to puzzlement to relief)*

H: *(whispering, to Des)* Sarah! She'll know! *(aloud)* Just coming!
*(She rushes out to the front door. Des begins to wail again.)*

D: Aaaaaiiiiee! AAAIIIEE! (Mayday! Mayday! Get me out of here, whoever you are!)
*(With some difficulty, Helen opens the door and Sarah walks in with a very ancient cotton shopping bag full of organic food. Mahatma is totally invisible in his Kente cloth sling. Helen immediately relocks and rechains the door.)*

S: Hi, I do hope you don't mind me dropping by, I brought you *(rummaging in her bag)* some of that passionflower tea. *(she finds it and looks up – sees Helen's face)* Are you all right?

H: *(tremulous little voice)* Not really. In fact I thought you were – listen, maybe you can help us.
*(Des redoubles his screams. Helen looks at Sarah, then at the locked and chained door. Decides she can probably risk taking Des out of his sling, but still holds him firmly on her lap. His screams diminish to nervous whimpers.)*

D: Auuuuff, aauuuurr! Fffuu? (Look at me – I'm the size of a hot-water bottle! What's with the high-security detention?)

H: We have to get away. Do you know anywhere – safe?


300

*(Sarah, all tender concern, takes Helen by the hand and sits her down on the sofa)*

S: Away? Why?

H: I can't . . . *(suppressing a sob)* Colum – and my best friend . . . they want Des!

S: No! *(hugging her as best she can around the two babies)* Is he – violent?

*(a faint, suffocated cry from Mahatma in his bundle)*

M: Eeergh! (Hey, watch out!)

*(Des suddenly realises there's another baby in there)*

D: Weeibly? Durffgh! (Is that you? Thank God.)

S: Will you just excuse me for a . . . *(unwrapping Mahatma)* . . . he's been a bit under the weather so . . .

*(She puts him on her lap, facing Des. The two babies immediately start to babble eagerly together. The two mothers are momentarily distracted.)*

H: They're so *(gulp)* sweet!

S: They seem really fond of each other, don't they? *(back to Helen)* Anyway – so has he . . . ?

H: Well, not yet, but I don't think he knows that I know – about the plan I mean. God knows what he'll do if I try to stop them.

S: Well – I do know a place.

H: Anywhere!

S: It's supposed to be only for women who've been battered . . .

H: *(eagerly)* Oh, but – there was a time *(shuddering)* when I accidentally spilled nail polish remover on his bike once . . .

*(Sarah puts a hand on her arm)*

S: Don't – you'll make it worse for yourself. May I use your phone just to check?

*(she gets up to go to the phone, leaving Mahatma with Des on the sofa)*

301

D: Urff, wibbly wib. (She's trying to abduct me. I'm not exactly sure why but I think it's to stop me being recruited into a new battalion. It all seemed to blow up when we went out to get the uniform . . .)

M: Gchrrrr, wsphh? (Cool! How was the uniform?)

D: . . . Fweeugh bullllw, wlw (. . . So I was kind of hoping I could come and bivouac with you for a while.)

M: Fggrh, sfshhhiih. (Christ, you don't want to do that. Talk about primitive! This place is a palace beside it. In fact I was about to ask you the same thing.)

*(Sarah returns, a saintly, comforting smile on her face)*

S: Good news.

H: Thank God!

S: They'll have you, if you can get there – it's pretty basic and isolated, though.

H: I'll get there somehow! We'll go anywhere, won't we, Des?

D: Fweeeergh? (Will we?)

H: Where is it?

S: Wales.

*(pause)*

H: Almost anywhere. Er – is there another one somewhere like, maybe, Cornwall?

*(Sarah shakes her head, confused)*

S: I don't think so, not that I know, anyway. Shall I call them back and? . . .

*(She's already making for the phone. Helen jumps up, dangling Des, to stop her.)*

H: No! No, we'll go. We'll go right now. He could be home any minute.

## Welcome, Directions and What to Bring

HOW TO GET HERE

If you are coming by train, it will drop you off at TinyPandy station. The train will take bikes, in the guard's van. (A 'mountain' type bike is recommended.) Otherwise the local bus drops passengers off twice a day at the end of the lane (ask to be let off at the Wimmin's House), 1/2 mile away. (Warning – the track is rough and can be muddy, so strong hiking boots are essential.)

WHAT TO BRING

Clothes, obviously, for you and any babies, plus sheets, pillowslips and towels. Undyed organic cotton padded quilts are provided on all beds.

Any special supplements or dietary items that you may have difficulty obtaining locally (always remembering that this is a vegan house, and that respect for nature and natural elements is important to us all).

Natural soap for washing and hair-washing, baking soda toothpaste, and natural unscented talc for baby powder, are all provided. Any other cosmetics you feel you absolutely need should be brought with you (again remembering that many commercial cosmetics companies not only still use animals for testing but are among the heaviest industrial polluters worldwide).

Musical instruments (of the quieter variety) are very welcome, as are any craft materials you may want to bring and share.

Paper, pens and pencils for writing – many of our residents find that this is a vital part of the healing process.

Over the years we have built up quite a library of books,

especially on interpersonal dynamics, spiritual growth, wimmin's fiction and wimmin's studies. If you are bringing books to the house, please respect the sensibilities and experiences of all the residents in your choices.

GENERAL INFORMATION ABOUT THE HOUSE

As part of our commitment to peace, harmony and non-violence at every level, we generate our own electricity from wind and solar power, but aim to use as little as possible. The house is insulated with peat in the roof and has thick stone walls, but if you are arriving in the winter and feel the cold, you may wish to bring extra-warm clothing for you and also your babies, if any.

We aim to be self-sufficient in food and drink as far as possible. We filter and collect our own rainwater for washing and drinking. All residents share in the growing, milling and baking of our wheaten bread, and threshing our own oats and barley for porridge and (in summer) muesli. Potatoes, carrots, cabbage and onions from our garden are stored year-round for residents' use, and in summer we supplement these with our own salad and other vegetables.

We make our own soy milk, tofu and vegetarian soy cheese. Other staples are delivered monthly by pedal tricycle from the local fair trade co-operative. Special orders for e.g. dried fruit or other extras for babies can be placed for the following month.

We recycle as much as possible and strongly discourage the use of disposables of any kind – this includes nappies, handkerchiefs and sanitary towels. We try in fact to be as sparing as possible in all our consumption. Residents share the work of cleaning and delivering to the recycling station, and it's a long walk!

FINALLY!

And most importantly, this is a safe house, a refuge for wimmin who may be in danger. It is important that its location

304

be kept secret except from people who need to know. Therefore, absolutely no cellphones or personal computers will be allowed. There is a public phone for outgoing calls only, on the main road 1/2 a mile from our track.

Welcome! You are with Family here!

**28 April, 2001** – Helen's shopping list at Paddington

# 1 WHISTLESTOP FOOD AND DRINK

—Evian, lots. *(No way am I drinking Welsh rainwater. Would certainly give me foot rot, or worse).*

—mustard, peanut butter, nutella, tapenade, anchovy paste and large lump of Reggiano *(in case the bread and potatoes get monotonous).*

—big bag Deluxe Trail Mix with White Chocolate Chips *(in case stranded at any point on journey. Definitely counts as food supplement, medicinal – see also chocolate, below).*

—baby food *(no organic jars so had to make do with Heinz – the risk from a few additives is nothing compared to what I'm saving him from).*

—loads of bananas, figs, grapes, and big pot of Tropical Deluxe Fresh Fruit Salad *(last time I was in Wales the only fruit I saw was two rotting Golden Delicious apples. Admittedly last time I was in Wales was twenty years ago. So they've probably rotted away completely by now.)*

—Jack Daniel's *(medicinal, to keep out the cold). (May have to forgo Lindemans for a while – no mention of local fair trade wine merchant delivering on pedal tricycle.)*

—Wispa Gold – lots and lots *(probably even if I could get to a shop it will be export chocolate like the stuff they have in India, designed to a special recipe to withstand prolonged exposure to damp, and totally inedible. Not worth the risk. Thank God I already weaned us off Nestlé.)*

## THE OUTDOORS STORE

—nifty new folding umbrella *(just in case I ever have to make a phone call)*.

—new silk and wool thermal underwear and bed socks *(terrible colours but in extremis even Dame Fashion bows to necessity)*.

—waterproof sheet *(to go under undyed cotton mattress to minimise inevitable rising damp)*.

—mini-Maglite torch *(in case the Welsh solar power isn't adequate, ha ha)*.

## NEXT

—irresistible cashmere dressing gown *(light, squishy, soft as down and will also be useful for wrapping Des)*.

—nifty little sheepskin hat *(hats are so difficult – if you find the right one important to go for it)*.

## SUPERDRUG

—foot massage cream *(for poor feet after all those long tramps to recycling centre, etc.)*.

—extra skin toner and day cream *(to protect face against exposure to raw biting wind during potato-digging and oat-threshing sessions)*.

—LOTS and LOTS of tampons *(DO NOT CARE what they say, WILL NOT use somebody else's recycled bloody rags, yuck. Ditto Huggies – will not expose poor Des to used nappies at this point)*.

### 28 April, 2001, Late

Somewhat more cheerful now that I have a definite plan and we're out of that den of vice and hypocrisy. In the end I opted for a first-class sleeper and cab at other end – after all, I'm not going to be spending any money ever again, and there must be a cab if there's a station, everybody knows that in depressed economies minicab companies spring up like dawn mushrooms, plus Paddington Station Shoppers Paradise turned out to be entirely bereft of acceptable boots for hiking up muddy track at dawn with a baby and two large suitcases full of silk underwear and Jack Daniel's. Will have to do supplementary shopping for boots and heavy-duty rainproof outerwear once we're settled there – always best to shop where locals shop for stuff like that.

Have to say, however, that the prospect of starting a new life as a brave, self-sufficient, earth-friendly single mum in Wales strikes a certain terror into my heart. All those druids and doleful male voice choirs (tho' I guess the good thing about being surrounded by a bunch of rabid wimmin is that no male voice anything would risk coming within several miles). Still, anywhere better than where I can see his sly, Mr Perfect lying face pretending I'm the one with the problem!

Wonder where the hateful pair of treacherous adulterers are right now? Racked with grief and guilt, let's hope, or tearing remaining hair out with worry. More likely stuffing themselves heedlessly with crème brûlée. Who cares! Let 'em rot. May or may not let them know we're safe, depending on how securely we can protect anonymity of our location.

Des seems a lot calmer now and made amazingly little fuss about eating Heinz jars instead of my home-made organic stuff – he's such a sweet, co-operative little soul underneath it all! (I took the precaution of removing the labels in case they search my bags, so it's going to be a bit of a lucky dip at mealtimes, but if I just stick to the colour-alternating technique he should be fine.)

Have to say it's quite comfy in this sleeper. Finally felt safe enough to crack open the Jack Daniel's just now. I think after the day we've had I deserve a little nip . . .

**28 April, 2001**

*Host has finally slipped into coma – just as well considering her behaviour over the last twenty-four hours. From what I can gather we're off on some kind of field exercise – major purchasing expedition undertaken before boarded this transport, though unfortunately didn't include replacing smart new uniform from Big Lips' battalion.*

*God, the food is a lot better here, though. That stuff in the jar – nectar! I like the rhythm of this transporter too – very relaxxxxxxxxxx-ing . . .*

**29 April, 2001** – Partial transcript of phone conversation between Colum and Eco-Baby

> *(Nothing audible for first fifteen minutes but Eco-Baby's phone queueing system playing 'Flight of the Condor'. Finally the phone is answered by Lucy, the same nervous person who spoke to Helen yesterday.)*
>
> L: ThankyouforcallingEco-Babywhereparadiseisjustafootfall-arwayhowcanihelp?
>
> C: Excuse me?
>
> L: THANKYOUFORCALLINGECO-BABYWHEREPARA . . .
>
> C: This is Eco-Baby Central?
>
> L: Er – yes . . .
>
> C: I think you have my wife. And my son.
>
> L: Pardon?
>
> C: My wife and baby son disappeared without warning yesterday afternoon and I have reason to think you people had something to do with it. Please put me through to . . .
>
> L: Here! *(Jemima! Jemima I've got somebody on the phone here and he's saying we've stolen his wife. Jemima?)* She'll be right with you. I'll just put you on . . .
>
> C: No!!!
>
> *(Too late. The Condor is back. Colum hangs on for another two*

*minutes before the phone is picked up by Jemima, whose idea of urgent is getting down to the beach before sunset.)*

J: Hi, mmm, I'm Jemima, I gather you have some kind of problem?

C: *(gritted teeth, pacing back and forth)* I just finished explaining to your no doubt willing but halfwitted employee that I'm trying to trace my wife and baby son who I've good reason to believe got on one of your flights yesterday.

J: Mmmm – did they? No, we didn't have any flights yesterday. You're sure it was – mmmm – yesterday?

C: Yes, I'm sure. Well, mebbe she called you, did you get a call from . . .

J: Mmm, I'm sure you can imagine we get loads of calls, dozens, all the time . . .

C: She would have been in a state, probably, and more than likely a baby screaming in the background. Please!

J: Mmm, that doesn't narrow it down a tremendous . . .
*(sound of Lucy in background saying, 'Ooh, there was somebody, I told her there wasn't anything till Tuesday and she got ever so cross with' . . .)*

C: That'll have been her. What did you tell her?
*(sound of phone being passed back to Lucy)*

L: I told her like I just said, I told her Costa Rica was full of slugs and anyway it wasn't till Tuesday and we didn't have anything else and then she shouted at me and then you know the baby was crying and then she hung up!

C: Fine. Well now we can eliminate one subcontinent from the search, I'm sure I'll track them down in no time. Thanks a bunch.
*(slams phone down)*

J: Mmmm – now he's somebody who could really use that – mmmm – Bali jungle and massage combo, don't you think?

*(A long, scrubbed wooden table in a damp and gloomy kitchen. Rain pattering on the windows. Five or six other women, some nursing babies, some hunched over porridge bowls, talking in low voices. Helen appears in the doorway, Des under one arm, in her new cashmere dressing gown and sheepskin cap. The Jack Daniel's did not do her head any favours, but she gamely pastes on her best party smile.)*

H: Good morning, everybody. Are we too late for breakfast?
*(Five pairs of eyes stare at her. Annie – wispy, rather young, with a tiny fragile baby grizzling on her knee – whispers to Sue – big, heavy and in charge.)*

A: Who's she?

S: *(between mouthfuls of porridge)* Came before dawn. In a Range Rover. With a man.
*(Helen gives up waiting to be invited to sit and comes to the table, where Sue reluctantly shifts up to make room for her. She sits, with Des on her knee.)*

H: Gosh, yes, wasn't it lucky he was getting off the train here too and he knew exactly where it was and all about it. He was so helpful, and he wouldn't even stay for a cup of tea!
*(Silence, during which Annie pushes a bowl towards Helen, who peers nervously into the porridge jar before ladling a small spoonful into her bowl. Gamely . . .)*

H: Ah, Wales! What do they always say, if you can see the mountains it's going to rain, and if you can't . . .
*(Looks round for recognition of upcoming joke. Nobody is laughing. Annie passes Helen a jug, which she gratefully takes, pouring milk lavishly over her bowl.)*

H: Mmm, lovely. I never make porridge but when somebody else does it's always . . . *(takes a mouthful)* . . . so . . .
*(tries to swallow. Manages, but not without gagging. To Annie,*

*who's now smiling timidly at her . . .)* Umm – it's probably just me, but does this milk taste a bit . . .

A: Oh, that's not cow's milk, that's soy.

H: Oh. Of course. So where's the proper milk?
*(another silence)*

S: Didn't you have time to read the notes before you came, er—

H: Helen.

S: Helen. And is that – what's that you're wearing?

H: Oh, this, it probably looks a bit silly indoors but I do feel the cold, I got this and this lovely cashmere thingy in a hurry at Paddington.

S: So you're okay with wearing the skin ripped from a dying animal on your head?

A: *(whispers)* She prob'ly didn't know, I mean . . .

H: Well, it would have died anyway, wouldn't it? You could say I'm recycling it, not just leaving it to rot on some *(looking out of the window)* boggy hillside. *(right at Sue)* Couldn't you?
*(Sue is silenced. Annie shares a furtive smile with a tall, cadaverous woman, Justine. Des whimpers on Helen's knee and sticks a fist in her porridge.)*

H: *(to Des)* Believe me, darling, you don't want to try that. Now *(reaching into her dressing-gown pocket)* what do we have here? *(She pulls out a glass jar containing bright red homogeneous gloop. Sue eyes it suspiciously. Des waves his arms.)* I make my own organic mixes up for him and put them straight into these recycled jars – it's easier when we're travelling *(wrenching off factory-sealed lid)* – isn't it, darling?

D: Phreear, wussfh! (If that's your organic slime, I'm the Supreme Commander.)

H: *(looking around – knows the answer before she asks)* Er – microwave?
*(Sue purses her lips. Justine takes the jar from Helen and ambles*

to the stove. *A baby, previously hidden under the table, crawls hopefully after her.)*

J: I'll stick it in the hot water for you, then, will I? *(sniffing it)* Smells all right. What's in it, then?

H: Oh – er, you know . . .
*(Annie's baby Paul has started wailing, which sets off Justine's baby Kerry)*

P: Mieeergh, eeee! (I recognise that, that's Heinz First Stage Pasta with Lamb and Tomatoes. Hey, everybody, somebody here has Heinz!)

K: Waaaaauw! (Gimme, gimme, I'm starving!)

D: Urffff, raaaaRRRR! (HANDS OFF! THAT'S MINE!)

H: Gosh, poor Des, he must really be hungry, tell you what, here you go, Des *(opening her dressing gown and shoving him in)* – have a quick glug while it warms up. He's never been out of London, I expect he's a bit confused.
*(Sue lifts herself heavily from the bench, lumbers to the other side of the kitchen and drags out a big basket of swedes, potatoes and onions. Turns to scowl at Helen.)*

S: When you've had enough, we do our own washing-up here, and then this lot has to be done for supper. Justine and Annie'll help you, won't you, girls? *(making for the door)* I can see we're going to have some very interesting talks in the next few days. *(meaningful pause)* If you stay, of course.


**29 April, 2001**

In the end it didn't seem fair on Colum not to let him know Des was all right at least. I mean, he is technically half Colum's, unfortunately. Rain let up enough for us to trudge down track to phone box (God knows when I'll get those boots) so I just left a message on the voice mail saying we were both okay. Trouble with being uncontactable, of course, is they can't call back, so have no way of knowing reaction back home. Made it sound as though he'd done us a big favour showing self in true colours before it was too late and we were oh so happy. He certainly won't have been expecting that!

Off to peel mountain of potatoes and onions with Des snoozing happily in sling. Finally he gets the benefit of the Stone Age lifestyle (though unfortunately just at point where he weighs as much as a sack of potatoes himself). Bracing Welsh air seems to have given him a monster appetite.

I could have sworn when I changed his nappy just now that the Huggies were depleted. But nobody here would touch a disposable – have buried them right at bottom of my bag, carefully camouflaged under politically incorrect woollies.

**29 April, 2001** – Colum and Ernestine, in Colum and Helen's kitchen

> *(The kettle is on and Colum and Ernie are sitting at the kitchen table. Ernie is smoking.)*
>
> C:  . . . I still haven't a clue what she was on about. All I did was offer to cook supper. Tea?
>
> E:  Thanks, darling. Well, whatever it was, it's obviously sent her over the top. She was pretty weird when we were out shopping – I just bought Des a couple of things and she acted like I was trying to abduct him.
>
> C:  If it weren't for the poor wee lad I'd leave her to stew. I've just about had it with her these last few months. It's no' been easy for me, only seeing him a couple of hours at night, working all hours and coming home every evening to the Wicked Witch of the North-West.
>
> *(He gets up to make the tea, making an elaborate point of waving the smoke away. Ernie stubs out her fag . . .)*
>
> E:  Sorry, darling . . .
>
> *(. . . and immediately lights another)*
>
> Speaking of abducting – I know she phoned and every-

313

thing but they do that from cults too, don't they?

C: Do what? What cults?

*(He's scrabbling around in the cupboard, looking for more tea)*

E: Well, you know, she had all that time here on her own, at least we assumed she was here but she could have been anywhere, couldn't she? Somebody might have brainwashed her.

C: She'd need a brain for that.

E: . . . She could have been going up West with the Hare Krishna people every day, or the Moonies or anyone. Did she ever mention anything about, you know, new friends or anything?

C: New friends? The way she's been? Who's that desperate? *(at that moment the scrabbling in the cupboard unearths something which he stares at as if it were a holy relic)* . . . Come to think of it – the woman who tried to get us off . . .

E: . . . PG Tips! The radical feminist tea-hater!

C: Look, there's a label on here.

E: What does it say? I bet – there you go – Busy Bee Wholefoods in radical feminist central, N16.

C: Sarah. She was called Sarah, I'm sure.

E: So what are we waiting for?


**29 April, 2001** – Helen, Justine and Annie in the kitchen of the Wimmin's House

*(The women have made a small dent in the vast pile of vegetables, but there's still a long way to go. At their feet, Des, Paul and Kerry sit, apparently happy among the peelings on the grimy floor. Annie has pulled up her sleeve to reveal a nasty-looking scar on her arm. Justine, who's clearly seen it all before, carries on peeling.)*

H: Jesus! How did he do that?

A:    That was – let's see now. The carving knife. Or . . . *(pulling up her other sleeve, which has a bigger, but shorter, scar)* Nah, this was the carving knife, that other was some piss-poor knife not much better than this here, couldn't hardly cut, which is why he skidded it all up there, like. Now here *(whisking up her droopy trouser leg)* – here's where he chucked the chip fat on me ankles. His loss, mind – he used to like me legs before.

      *(She sniffs and resumes her peeling. Pause while Helen takes this in.)*

H:    *(to Justine)* And – what about you?

J:    *(not looking at her)* Oh, mine was a very high-class act. We went out a lot so there couldn't ever be anything that, like, showed. He was a real expert. Chinese burns, hair-line fractures. Tell you the truth, I think he got half of it off of the Internet at work. Here you go, Kerry, good girl.

      *(she bends down and hands Kerry a chunk of raw swede, which Paul, despite his tiny size, immediately lunges for)*

J:    *(to Annie)* He okay with that?

A:    Best not risk it – Sue said we was to keep him on the wheatgrass and soy for another week. Ever such a lot of good it's done him.

      *(she nudges Helen, who has stopped peeling, taking it all in)*

H:    *(starting again)* Sorry. What has?

A:    It's for the toxins. You know, purge the filth of the city. He's not had nothing but soy milk and wheatgrass juice for a week. Really took to it, he has.

P:    Weeeeigh! (What choice do I have?)

      *(He makes a grab for a stray piece of potato peel, which Annie whisks away. Helen frowns down at him.)*

H:    He's very thin.

A:    Well, I'm not exactly Dawn French, am I?

*(at their feet, Paul and Kerry go back to fighting over the swede, while Des looks on in horror)*

K: Bliddy blihhhf, fff! (It's mine! Anyway, this is nothing, you should try the stuff in those jars.)

P: Eeerf? (What jars?)

K: *(looking at Des)* Bulle wulle fff! (The jars he brought with him, the Heinz stuff. I only got a bit before . . .)
*(Des suddenly lets out an ear-piercing howl)*

D: WAAAAAAAHRR! AAAAARGH! (NO! MY FOOD! THEY TOOK MY FOOD!)
*(Helen bends down, picks him up and tries to calm him, but he just carries on sobbing)*

H: Shhhh – shhhhhh . . .

A: You ought to try it on yours.

H: I'm sure you're right. We'll give it a go, won't we, Des? . . .

D: Weeeeeir!! WAAAAAAH! (Not on your life!)

H: . . . very soon. I'll go and change his nappy, maybe he's sore. Anyway, I'm still breast-feeding him. I have so much of my own milk it gets really painful sometimes, I have to pump it off.
*(scoops up Des from among the peelings, vaguely dusting the mud from his bottom)*

A: Just like them poor cows. All those years I never thought about the agony of it till I come here. It's a real education, it is.

J: He's probably allergic. Kerry never stopped crying the first three months till I put her on soy. That'll be why he's upset, it's your milk'll be doing it . . . You okay with where to put the dirty nappy for washing?

H: What? Oh, yes, absolutely, thanks, won't be a minute, I promise . . .

**29 April, 2001** – Exchange of e-mails

**From**: Colum McCallum [collum@guzzi.freeserve.com]
**Sent**: 29 April
**To**: Billy Giddens [billy@billygoat.demon.co.uk]


Bill,
got home yesterday evening to discover Madam had
disappeared, taking baby with her. As I said in
my message, she called up saying they're okay so
I'm not too worried, but do you have any clue
from your conversation with her why she went or
where she might have gone?
    Call me any time – I'm here by the phone.
    Col

---------------------------------

**From**: Billy Giddens [billy@billygoat.demon.co.uk]
**To**: Colum McCallum [collum@guzzi.freeserve.com]


col son
wish I could help ut as i said beyond general
disincliination to belive a word I said (typical
Dog) it was all unfatohmable mystery. I woudln't
get too worked up about it – they all do a runner
from time to time, mine left without warnig for
a week on a singles holiday in Crete once,
neeldss to say wtiouht the kids.
    if you need a bt of cheering up there's a
great rerun of last years' TT on Sky Sports at
1 40 am.
    let me know whn she turs up
    bill

---------------------------------

## 29 April, 2001

Well, it seems to be going okay so far, though one slight disaster in that some of my supplies have gone missing. They don't seem to have found the white chocolate chips cunningly disguised in the Trail Mix, thank God, but all of poor Des's jars and all the rest of my serotonin uptake inhibitor seem to have walked. I guess there's some kind of policy of searching people's bags. I suppose they have to be strict given what half these women have come from. God knows what they've been on to keep themselves going. Now I understand all the emphasis on clean living and starting afresh. Looks like it'll have to be the wheat-grass and soy detox for Des after all, until I can get some more jars.

Talking of which, somebody is definitely raiding the Huggies too, so somebody knows I'm bluffing about the dirty nappy bin. Have come outside to feed Des just in case I'm spotted emulating an exploited cow. Who knew mother's milk could be politically incorrect? What a minefield the moral high ground turns out to be!

Gazing around in quiet afternoon light at the grandeur of Nature, realise how much we miss in the constant hurry and hurly-burly of city life. And how unnecessary colour is to Mother Nature. Here it's all grey – grey sky, grey house, grey mud, grey mountains. When you can see them. (Grey rain when you can't.) Colum would love it . . .

Stop thinking about him, evil abducting adulterer, hate hate!

Talking of mud, must sort something out about those boots, though no idea where the nearest shop selling vegan hiking boots is. Pity I didn't get Range Rover's phone number – would have been very useful in emergency such as this. Beginning to feel a bit claustrophobic in my dinky Camper prison shoes.

I have to say, hearing about other people's home lives made me realise things could have been a lot worse. At least Colum didn't rip holes in my arm with a blunt knife. But remember! Scars left by mental torture are not visible, and never heal. Would never forgive myself if I'd exposed Des to that slow poison another minute.

## 29 April, 2001

*Just when I was getting really good at distinguishing colour, it's all disappeared again. Either everything in this place is, in fact, grey, or we have somehow been reposted to a parallel universe where entirely different neuro-optical coding is required.*

*Or maybe it's a little known side effect of food poisoning. Tragically reached sleeping quarters to discover all food supplies had in fact been stolen, since when grey surroundings have been reinforced by grey milk, which tastes just about as bad as anything could taste, at least I thought so until I tasted the other stuff on offer. (Come to think of it, that's green. So maybe the coding does still function.)*

*Still have no idea why she was so keen to get me away from Big Lips. Would have sworn only a few weeks ago they were fighting on the same side.*

## 30 April, 2001 – Partial transcript of phone call between Colum and Busy Bee Wholefoods Store

*(From time to time a third, female, voice is faintly audible at the Busy Bee end, before John, the owner, speaks, and from time to time John appears to be speaking to somebody else in the shop — possibly the same female. Possibly, in fact, Sarah.)*

C: . . . So I wondered whether you'd seen her, or even heard from her, at all?

J: Er, oh yes, she's in here most days . . .

S: (You mustn't tell him that! Say I've gone away).

J: . . . Normally, that is, but at the moment she's away.

C: So did you get a chance to ask her – before she left?

J:   Yes, but . . . (What's that?) No, but she – she said to tell you . . .

S:   (I said to tell you that the whole point of a safe house is that she's safe there, and that means safe from you!)

J:   . . . she said to tell you that the point of being safe is that she's safe from you.

C:   She's got a bloody . . .

S:   (. . . And from the whole race of violent, sadistic, irresponsible men like you!)

J:   . . . and from the whole race of . . . (I don't really need to say all that, do I?) Anyway, she's safe. She said to say. Sorry, mate, I'm a bit . . .

C:   I AM NOT VIOLENT! OR SADISTIC! I WANT MY WIFE BACK!

S:   (Sounds pretty violent to me. And what about the time with the nail polish remover?)

J:   Yes, what about the time with the nail polish remover?

C:   What time? What is all this?

S:   (On his motorbike.)

J:   On your motorbike. She said. Sorry, mate, it's a bit busy here today, I'm . . .

C:   I WANT MY WIFE AND MY SON BACK! And if you don't tell me where she is, I'm going to the police.

S:   (The police already know and they're protecting her)

J:   That's fifteen twenty-six. Oh, sorry, getting confused here. (What was that, Sarah?)

S:   (Oh, give it here . . .) *(sound of phone being handed over)* Look, I'm terribly sorry, I don't know you and I've never met you, and I'm trying to be very patient because I know you probably think you love her . . .

C:   Excuse me . . .

S:   . . . but from what Helen told me she's better off where she is, so I think you should just leave her alone. Please. *(phone clicks off)*

**1 May, 2001, 1 a.m.**

Just had a very weird experience. I mentioned casually, over the swedes, that I'd brought a breast pump with me, and at midnight there was a knock on the door, so I answered it and there was Justine, with a mug, asking for milk for her tea. I explained I only had breast milk, ha ha. Did not put her off one bit. She practically made me pump it for her there and then, said it was just like Nestlé Evaporated which of course she hasn't been able to drink for years, and as this is also a sugar-free establishment the sweetness solves two problems in one.

Eventually she got desperate enough to admit that she'd stolen Des's baby food (thank God I took the labels off), so I managed to negotiate the return of the two remaining jars in exchange for milk for two cups of tea in the morning. Yuck! Still, at least he won't have to have any more of that awful wheatgrass stuff for a while.

**1 May, 2001, 1.30 a.m.**

*(NO! Not the green stuff! Anything but the green stuff! I'll tell you everything, I promise – what do you want to know? Just keep it away from – not the nose tube! Please not the nose tube . . . Help! Help!!! HELP!!)*

*Phew.*

*That was a nasty one. For a moment I thought I was – goodness, look, biting my own toenails, I'm a bag of nerves. Calm down. Remove toe from mouth, using – hey, look, I made my hand work! It did what I wanted it to! The world's most versatile tool, WITH opposable thumbs, and I finally got it to work under control!*

*. . . but what good are opposable thumbs in this hell-hole? No food, no colour, and – what's that noise? It's her! What's she doing now? She's – she's – hey, that's my milk! That's all that stands between me and poison! Why are you putting it in that bottle?*

321

*Think . . . Hang on, didn't that agent from Mission Control use my toes to sort out the last feeding problem? Maybe if I suck really hard on them, she'll stop . . .*

**1 May, 2001, 2 a.m.** – Partial transcript of phone call between Georgie and Alison

A:  . . . do you realise what time it is?

G:  I know, I know, but I just had this really bad feeling. About Helen and Des. That there's something really wrong.

A:  Nonsense, I spoke to Colum just today and . . .

G:  . . . and I spoke to him just now and he said she's holed up in some coven in the Welsh mountains, but I mean – how do we know she's all right? We only had that one message. You know what she's like, she gets carried away with these daft ideas . . .

A:  I hardly need you to tell me what my own daughter's like, dear. Nor do I have the slightest idea what you think I can do at . . .

G:  We need to find them and rescue them!

A:  I believe Colum's already tried that.

G:  He's a man, he'll never get anything out of them. Come on, Mum, remember the time you took on the bandits in the hills outside Simla . . .

A:  Well, I can't do anything now, dear, so go back to bed and . . .

G:  Please, Mum! I have really good instincts about this stuff.

A:  . . . and I'll see what I can find out in the morning.

**1 May, 2001, 3 a.m.**

*Unable to sleep ever since I detected her preparing to smuggle my food supply elsewhere. No milk, no jars – no back-up. Only one explanation – she's gone over to the other side. Only one possible course of*

*action, and I should have taken it days ago. Thought of enlisting some of my new fellows, but don't trust any of them not to turn me in. It won't be easy on my own and in the dark, but if I leave now there's a good chance I can get far enough before I'm detected to find help outside. Anything better than just lying here waiting to die.*

*Okay, here goes . . . she's fast asleep again, I'll have to sneak by her . . . God, she's noisy, still, it'll cover me until I can – okay, now to give these hands a proper test.*

*Here's the door, let's hope it's – yes! Must have been left open earlier. If I can just prop myself on my other hand and push – there it goes. Hey, this is really easy. Still, when you've been trained in an élite squad like . . . hang on, what's – where's the floor? Help – oh, here – no, it's not – okay, emergency ball manoeuvre – bumpety bumpety bumpety, hey, ouch, that was – bumpety bumpety BUMP, thank God, it's stopped! But where am . . . eeeeurgh, the smell, oh God, and what's that sticky stuff, it's all piling in on me, it feels like towels but, oh God, the smell, I can't breathe – help, help, THUMP!!!!*

## 1 May, 2001, 6 a.m.

Maybe I was a bit hasty coming this far without leaving any forwarding info. Admittedly the whole point of fleeing is not to be followed, but what if he really does want me back, and he's madly scouring the whole country for us and he can't find us? I do miss him, I can't believe he doesn't love me at all after everything we've done together. And I have been pretty unbearable lately, who can blame the poor thing for seeking consolation elsewhere? . . . Maybe if I went back now, a nice lenient judge might give me visiting rights every other weekend? Maybe if I spend all the time I used to spend baby-minding at the gym, I might get my figure back and then eventually I might get Colum back too? Won't be the first time I've prised a man away from Ernestine . . .

Oooooaaarghyawwwwwwwn! Time to get up, I suppose. I have to say all this living by the rhythms of Mother Nature is a lot easier when you're already used to being woken at six by a screaming baby. Come to think of it, baby very quiet . . . where is baby? WHERE IS BABY? DES!!!!

**1 May, 2001, 6.15 a.m.** – Helen in the Wimmin's House

*(Helen, hair matted, dressed in a T-shirt and her cashmere robe, is frantically throwing clothes around as she searches the bare attic room for her baby. No Des. She turns to the door.)*

H:  The door's open! Oh God!
*( . . . and rushes outside. A narrow landing, closed doors on either side, noisy snoring from within. No baby.*
*A hand on her shoulder makes her jump. Justine is standing there with two jars and a tea mug.)*

H:  Christ! Oh, Justine, Justine, I've lost Des!

J:  *(whispers)* Shhh! I've brought the jars, have you got the . . .

H:  *(whispering back)* I said I've lost . . .

J:  He'll turn up, he can't have got far. Here you go.

H:  It's in my room, in the little bottle thing. Oh God – the stairs!
*(In front of her, a steep wooden staircase down to the next landing. She peers down in the semi-darkness.)*

H:  He can't have – he didn't fall anyway, he's not at the bottom.
*(Nothing at the bottom in fact but the dirty nappy bin. She creeps down the stairs, calling out in a stage whisper:)*

H:  Des! Des, darling! Where are you?
*(inside the nappy bin, a nearly asphyxiated Des struggles to stay conscious)*

D:  (She's looking for me – mustn't make a sound. Must stay conscious till I can think of a plan . . .)
*(Helen reaches the bottom, looks wildly around the next empty landing)*

H:  Des, sweetheart, where are you? I've got your *(whispers)* Heinz banana-and-apple porridge for breakfast!

D:  (She's trying to entrap me – thinks she can buy me off with . . . oh God, the smell, I'm going to faint again . . .)
*(Helen finally breaks down)*

H:  Des *(sob)*, sweetheart, I'm sorry I brought you to this hell-hole, please come back, please . . .

D:  (I'm going to die . . .) *(feebly)* Weeeigh! Widdly weeeei! (In here! Help!)
*(Helen looks around. Where did that noise come from?)*

D:  Weeeigh! WEEEEARRRRGH! (In here! In this suffocation chamber!! HELP!)
*(The nappy bin! Helen wrenches the lid open, and reels back.)*

H:  EEEEurgh! Oh God. Oh, gross.

D:  WWWWWEIGH! WEEIGH! (I've been in here for hours!)
*(Helen nerves herself and plunges her hands into the bin, scuffling around, until she finally pulls out a struggling, bawling, shit-covered baby)*

H:  God, Des, how on earth did you get in there?
*(A door opens. Sue emerges. In the early light, in a huge crumpled nightie, she is a scary sight.)*

S:  What, may I ask, is going on here?
*(Helen clutches Des to her. They are both covered in evil-smelling stains, but he is looking up at her with something like love.)*

H:  *(nervously)* I was just putting his dirty nappy in and he sort of slipped in too. Sorry.

D:  Biddly breaaah? (Can we go and get washed now, please? And did you say something about banana porridge?)
*(Sue frowns)*

S:  It's your turn to boil them today anyway. You can do it after breakfast.

## 1 May, 2001

I am not boiling other people's dirty nappies. I am not. I am not. This is supposed to be a refuge, not the Gulag Archipelago. There, there, sorry, am I going too slowly with the lovely porridge? Can Mummy have a bit? Okay, calm down, I only asked.

What do you say, Des — shall we go and hole up in a hotel instead and have bacon and eggs and watch TV?

It doesn't look very promising outside, I have to admit, but your cold's nearly better and we can always wrap ourselves in the waterproof sheet. If we can just get as far as the phone box . . .

## 1 May, 2001 – Helen, Des and the women, in the Wimmin's House

*(Helen, with Des bundled up in the sling and a suitcase in one hand, is sneaking past the kitchen towards the front door. Inside, the other women are having breakfast. From outside, the sound of heavy rain and howling wind. Helen gets to the door, struggles with it with her free hand. Puts down the bag, struggles with both hands. Finally wrenches it open. Immediately it bangs shut again, with a tremendous THUMP!*

*(Heavy footsteps approach from the kitchen. Helen stands there, like a frightened rabbit, as Sue emerges, goes to the front door and stands in front of it.)*

S:  What exactly is the meaning of this?

A:  Helen! What you up to?

*(Justine, Annie and several other women emerge from the kitchen, with their babies)*

H:  I was just going to make a phone call.

S:  In this weather? Who do you need to call?

H:  *(nervously)* I just wanted him to know I was still all right.

S:  Of course you're all right, but you won't be if you go out in that. Your tapioca's getting cold.

H:   Well, actually – actually we're leaving.
     *(a shocked gasp from the women)*
S:   You can't. Nobody leaves until we all agree. It's a house rule.
H:   Well, can't you agree, please? I'm not cut out for this place,
     I'm sorry, but . . .
J:   It's true, she's got Huggies. I saw them.
H:   . . . I love my husband!
     *(Annie comes over, carrying Paul, and takes her gently by the
     hand)*
A:   It's real hard at first, innit? I thought I loved my Jason even
     after what he done to me. Till Sue explained it all.
     *(Sue, arms grimly folded at the head of her army, nods. They all
     nod too.*
     *(Paul is close enough to Des to get his attention.)*
P:   Feeilgh, lawl lawal? (Will you take me along too? I don't
     eat much.)
D:   Flooughl bidl bd. (Sorry, mate, but I'll send a relief force
     just as soon as I can make contact.)
J:   You'll get over it in a week or two. Remember the nail
     polish remover!!! Remember what he did!
H:   He didn't do anything, he just raged around a bit and stayed
     at Billy's house for a night.
S:   You're still totally addicted, aren't you? It's pathetic. Come
     on . . . *(taking Helen by the arm and trying to pull her away
     from the door)* . . . those nappies are waiting.
     *(Des starts to wail)*
D:   Weeeeigh! WEEIGH! (Don't give in! This is our only
     chance!)
     *(Helen, furious, shakes off Sue and makes for the door. Turns back
     with her hand on the handle and shouts:)*
H:   I love him! And he may not love me but he loves the baby,
     and he's not a monster, they're not all monsters, I don't care
     what you say, and I'm jolly well keeping my Huggies for
     myself!

327

D:   Feeeeigh! Aiiifgh! (Good show! Now I know why they gave her the job!)
*(With a final burst of effort, she wrenches the door open again and wedges herself and Des in it while she somehow covers most of him with the plastic sheet. Then Helen, her bag and her bundle disappear into the wind and rain, as the door bangs shut on the women.)*

Some time later

*(Helen, Des and the bag finally make it to the phone box at the end of the lane. It's still pouring with rain, and the wind is howling louder than ever. Helen has lost a shoe and both legs are caked in mud nearly to the knee.)*

H:   Thank God. At last . . .
*(She dumps the case in the mud, pulls open the door of the phone box, and unwraps the plastic sheet to reveal a very pink, but relatively dry, Des)*

H:   That's more like it. Now we're in business. I'll get the hotel to send a cab if need be, sweetie. No more wheatgrass, I promise, ever . . .
*(Triumphantly, she lifts the handset of the phone and holds it to her ear. Her face falls. From the handset, a faintly audible 'ddddu-uuuuuuuhhhhh'.)*

H:   Oh God. Oh no . . .
*(Helen bursts into tears and slides down the wall of the phone box, cradling Des in her arms)*

H:   Oh God *(sob)*, I'm so sorry, sweetie, it's all my *(sob)* fault, but I'll get us home somehow, I promise . . .
*(Des looks up at a picture of contrition and despair)*

D:   Wibble wif! (Hey, come on, you're the great commander, stop this! Hang on, let's see if I can get this hand to work . . .)

*(A little pink hand emerges from his wrappings, reaches up, and touches Helen gently on the face)*

H: Ohhh! *(howls of tears now)* OOOOOHHHHH!!!

*( . . . which prevent either of them from hearing the first tap on the phone box, or seeing the ancient Land Rover parked outside. A louder knock, and when that has no effect, the door is pulled open. Helen finally looks up through her tears to see Alison, holding her muddy suitcase and a large handbag.)*

A: What are you doing down there? Get up, it's sopping. I tried to call but all the lines are down. Thank God at least your sister has some sense.

**1 May, 2001** – Bill for breakfast at Climpton Arms Hotel, Bristol

```
            CLIMPTON ARMS (EST 1465)
                 CLIMPTONS CAF
                 GOOD MORNING!

1 x Traditional English (bacon, sausage, black
pudding, fried egg, fried bread, mushrooms,
    tomatoes, brown toast)               £9.95
1 x kippers, brown toast                 £7.95
1 x baby meal (baby cereal, banana, apple,
    cream)                               £2.50
2 x coffees                              £3.80
extra milk                               £1.00

SUBTOTAL                                £25.20
OPTIONAL SERVICE @ 12.5%                 £3.15
TOTAL:                                  £28.35
PAID VISA WITH THANKS. ENJOY YOUR MORNING
```

## 2 May, 2001

I love him so much! He is so good to me! After Mum dropped me off and returned the Land Rover to her ex-Maharashtran colleague, Des had a nap to recover and Colum and I had a lovely afternoon wallowing in bed counting our rolls of fat, while he explained it was all a terrible mistake and Ernie is about as attractive to him as a blow-up doll. Anyhow, Ernie is busy with her new boyfriend, a global environmental consultant apparently (trips to remote but lovely places with good air, or exciting places with very bad air. Either way she gets to keep the air miles, she says.)

Today Des and I are giving each other spa treatments, and Colum's off shopping for the dinner he was going to cook me before I ran away. Steak and crème brûlée – I guessed right. How can I ever have thought he was boring and predictable? It's just that we read each other's minds!

## 2 May, 2001

*What was that all about? Still, she got us out of it in the end, and she was very brave in the face of overpowering enemy odds. Interesting that agent from Mission Control apparently despatched relief force right after I did the toe thing. Coincidence? You decide.*

*Never thought I'd be so glad to see the long-stay ward aka Base Camp again, but it's a much more interesting place since I got the use of these hands. Now if I can just get the lid off this jar while she's doing her eyebrows . . .*

## 2 May, 2001 – Colum's planned schedule for preparing and cooking dinner

1700   Feed Des his tea. Bath him.
1730   Hand baby and bottle over to Georgie (coming over to sit for evening).

1745    Put raspberries in crème brûlée pots. Make custard part of crème brûlée, pour over.

1815    Steam asparagus. Marinade steak. Lay table.

1845    Warm baguette. Make hollandaise for asparagus and keep warm.

1900    Open champagne. Serve with Cheese Crispies. Heat grill.

1925    Grill steak. Pour hollandaise over asparagus. Put warm bread and butter on table.

1930    Serve steak.

2015    Put sugar over crème brûlée. Put under grill.

2020    Serve pudding.


**2 May, 2001** – Actual timetable of evening

1700 Fed Des his tea. Bathed him.

1730 Handed baby and bottle over to Georgie.

1745 Put raspberries in crème brûlée pots. Made custard part of crème brûlée, poured over.

1815 Steamed asparagus. Marinaded steak. Laid table.

1845 Warmed baguette. Made hollandaise for asparagus and kept warm.

1900 Opened champagne. Served with Cheese Crispies. Heated grill.

1925 Grilled steak. Poured hollandaise over asparagus. Put warm bread and butter on table.

1930 Served steak.

2015 Put sugar over crème brûlée. Put under grill.

2020 Served pudding.

**2 May, 2001 – Evening** – George and Des in Colum and Helen's bedroom

*(They are sprawled on the bed, surrounded by toys, snacks, and a bottle. More toys are scattered around the floor. The ne plus ultra of monochrome minimalism has gone for good. Georgie has Des's tiny hand in one of hers and is apparently teaching him to play 'This Little Piggy' on his own toes.)*

G: . . . this little piggy was in charge of the spleen, the liver, and the oxygenated blood, and this little piggy was not (but he was VERY good with colds and backache). Your turn!
*(Des grabs the foot and inserts it into his mouth, where he proceeds to suck vigorously on another toe)*

G: Hmmm – bit of an indigestion problem today? Can't say I'm surprised after what I saw you put away earlier.

D: Fibbly feeerf. (After the last couple of days, I'm not taking any chances.)

G: It can't have been that bad!
*(indignantly, he drops the toe to speak)*

D: Weigghle! (It jolly well was. How does slow suffocation under a pile of filthy nappies sound to you?)

G: That's what you get for running away.

D: Fleeeiiir, umf uf? (While I have you here, what was that all about anyway?)

G: Er – well, you know, some people are really good at looking after other – smaller – people, and others – let's just say it may not suit them so well. All the time. I mean, of course she loves you to bits . . . *(picking him up and rolling him into a big hug)* . . . who wouldn't? But I think just being alone all day with you sent her a bit bonkers, you know.

D: Fluuurfff ai ai! (Well, imagine what it did to me! Anyhow, whoever heard of a battalion with only one soldier. Where's the rest of my corps?)

*(Georgie sits him up facing her, takes his two tiny hands in hers, and looks him seriously in the eye)*

G:    Ah, well – this is something I've been meaning to talk to you about for some time. How would you like to go out every day and spend time with other nice babies just like you, and have a change of scene?

### 3 May, 2001

Lovely dinner, lovely crème brûlée, lovely husband, lovely baby – he even bought a huge bunch of flowers for Georgie, as she was the one who actually forced Mum to come and find me.

Can't believe I'm actually going back to work. I did put up a bit of an argument for the agreed plan to work from home via the Web as per Stone Age book, but Colum pointed out that including baby in work when the working day consists of hewing logs and grinding mealie meal in company of other females of own age and similar circs is one thing, sitting baby on lap for hours at a time in front of computer screen containing arcane details of vintage movie prints is something quite other. Anyhow, going back to the office provides the incredible luxury of almost daily excuses for going out to lunch (or that new nail place in Bond Street).

**May, 2001** – Excerpts from CVs and letters of recommendation for various childminders

1 Mrs Annie Sprinkel – CV

| | |
|---|---|
| 1972–77 | Keighley Comprehensive, Yorkshire. 6 CSE's |
| 1977–79 | Ships Toffee, Leeds – packing |
| 1979 | Promoted to customer relations department |
| 1982 | Married and moved to London |
| 1982–84 | Assistant, PaintPods Day Nursery, Kilburn |
| 1984 | Left to have children |
| 1990–present | Registered child minder |

TO WHOM IT MAY CONCERN:
Annie Sprinkel is the warmest, most loving person you could hope to find . . . children love her . . . learned a lot about pets . . . always a lot going on . . . they learned to get on with all sorts of people . . . we chose to provide our own food for Daisy, which usually seemed to work out . . . cosy, comfortable environment . . . flexible and understanding about arrival and departure times . . . great value for money . . .


2 Marlene Grunewald – CV

| | |
|---|---|
| 1967–73 | Privately educated in Zurich, Switzerland |
| 1973–77 | Jacob Froebel training college, Zurich. Passed with honours |
| 1977–79 | Norton Nursery Nurse Training College, London Passed with honours |
| 1980 | South Putney College – MPhil in infant nutrition |
| 1982 | North Wimbledon College – diploma in developmental physiology |
| 1984 | Central Southfields College – MA in child psychology |
| 1986 | East Dulwich College – diploma in infant neurobiology |
| 1987–now | Registered childminder |

334

Miss Grunewald . . . has spared no effort in educating and bringing along our children . . . clearly takes enormous pride in her results . . . immaculate environment . . . calm, quiet and orderly . . . plenty of discipline including self-discipline . . . older ones put away all their own toys . . . good preparation for departure to prep school . . . always glad to see us at the end of the day . . . well worth the money.

3  Sally Williams – CV

| 1992–97 | Holloway Comprehensive. |
| | 4 GCSE passes |
| 1997 | Blockbuster Video, Finsburry Park traine customer service agAnt |
| 1998 | promoted to customer service agAnt |
| 1999–present | Registerd Childmonder (with own child) |

TO WHOM IT MAY CONCERN
Sally . . . is very young, but obviously loves her own baby and all babies . . . always seems to have plenty of friends to help with the babies . . . chatty and friendly . . . Samantha has become very placid and easy . . . recognises the names of lots of well-known characters from TV . . . always happy to be left with Sally . . . confident that she's safe in a familiar environment all day . . .

## 4–6 May, 2001 – Exchange of e-mails

**From:** Colum McCallum [collum@guzzi.freeserve.com]
**Sent:** 4 May
**To:** Billy Giddens [billy@billygoat.demon.co.uk]


Bill,
Things finally reached the predicted crisis here
the other day, but all now sorted and had a lot
less difficulty persuading Boadicea to go back
to work than I would have done otherwise.

So now we're in the business of finding somewhere to park the sprog. It's not that easy
getting a sense of the various candidates from
their references – any tips from your experience?

Steve seems to be getting on fine with the
Guzzi – says it'll be done by the Bank Holiday.
Fancy a run somewhere on the Monday?
Col

---------------------------------

**From:** Billy Giddens [billy@billygoat.demon.co.uk]
**To:** Colum McCallum [collum@guzzi.freeserve.com]


col son
good o hear you're packing th Dog back to work.
Like they say, can't teah an oldWoman new
tricks, eh? Those childmiinder refernees are a
pile of tosh, but you can learn to read them, if
you okok out for the key words i.e.
  - warm, loving = totally disorganised
  - cosy, comfy = filthy
  - value for money = a slum

336

```
          - chatty or friendly = gossips with her mates
     all day long
          - safe, familiar = kids parked in front of TV
     all day.
          better to avoid the very yong or the very old
     and watch out for people who make you leave the
     srpogs at front door so asnot to 'upset' tem.
     Goood luck!
          Bank Holliday Monday's clocked.
          bill

     ---------------------------------
```

## 6 May, 2001

Going back to work, of course, means finding somewhere to park Des for the day (only doing short days at first – Max said finally he gets to pay me for the six hours I actually do as opposed to the six hours working and three hours running up phone bills I used to do. Cheek!)

So now we're deep in the nightmare of reading between the lines of the childminder references. Seems to come down to a choice between:

1 Jolly, friendly but none-too-clean woman living in a chaotic tip with three cats and four dogs, where he'd be fed junk food and pick up all kinds of infections from chewing on hundred-year-old toys.
2 Very young, very gossipy single mum eking out her benefit by running a TV addicts' training camp for all her other single-mum friends' babies.
3 Hugely qualified, rather stern and formidable Swiss lady. Her references make it sound like she's really good on discipline and guided play and really understands what's going on in their little developing minds and bodies, so although

she's a bit expensive, we've decided it's worth it. After all, as she said on the phone, who'd want to entrust their precious darling to somebody who's only paid as much as a filing clerk?

## 6 May, 2001

*Okay, time to see if this psychic messaging system really works. Grasp whole foot in each hand − shut eyes − HELP! Don't let them send me there!*

**8 May, 2001** − Partial transcript of phone conversation between Helen and Georgie

G: . . . they're beautiful, the whole house smells lovely, do tell him for me.

H: Yeah, I'm so glad he's finally decided to be nice to you. Maybe one day he'll even let you get up close and personal with his bunions.

G: I can wait . . . Oh God, Jack's lunch box (JACK! JACK, YOUR DINNER, SWEETIE!!!). So I read those references and between you and me, I'd go for the first one.

H: Really? I mean, she was sort of warm and cosy but . . .

G: That's what you want, isn't it? *(sound of doorbell in the distance)* Oh, there's my delivery, won't be a minute . . . *(sound of door opening in the background)* (Thanks ever so much, oh, watch out for the − never mind, no honestly, just leave it. Byeee!) You were saying?

H: . . . only her place didn't seem any too clean, and when I asked her about food for him she said she usually just mashed up whatever she was having and she'd never met a baby who didn't like a mashed-up chip.

G: She's probably right.

H: But . . .

338

G: Look, they're not like us, right? You've established fairly convincingly that you are not naturally suited to spending your entire day in the company of someone who needs help with the lavatory and thinks his teddy bear leads an exciting double life while he naps.

H: So?

G: So, people who are, are different. They like soap operas and singalong songs and big fat three-hanky romances and notepaper with bunny rabbits in the corner. (Christ, the kettle. The switching-off thing broke, hang on.)

*(Pause. Distant sound of 'ouch' followed by swearing. Georgie returns, now apparently sucking her hand.)*

H: So you think . . .

G: . . . Vut vey reawwy, reawwy wuv vavies, and vavt's what wounts. Vssssh! Yikes. Games, laughter, cuddles, a bit of rudimentary discipline later on. A few chips, a few germs – you don't want to raise him in a hothouse, do you?

H: She's certainly a lot cheaper . . .

G: There you go, buy yourself an extra bottle of wine a week.

H: Or maybe just a nice nail job . . .


**8 May, 2001**

Took Des round to Annie's for a trial visit this morning. He seemed to love it. Not too keen on the outdoors, but who can blame him after last week? Left two jars for his lunch – I'm not going to have time for all that pureeing now I'm working, and I took the labels off so with luck he won't know they're organic.

Going back to work also provides opportunity for review and update of wardrobe. Had to throw out and replace at least 60 per cent of it (what a shame). Very proud of transcending immature attachment to arbitrary construct of a size ten (and heels work much better with a bit of a wobble).

Ernie called up all jazzed about relationship with Korean new-media tycoon. Yet to meet said tycoon but has great lead via a friend working the door at the Armpit Bar. Says he sounds like somebody who'll finally love her for her programming skills and not her pretty face, 34 DD bra size and 35 inch legs. Will believe it when I see it, but meanwhile it's clearly a perfect excuse for a strategy lunch in Soho. Lunch! Without baby in tow! Must book right now.

**12 May, 2001**

*Day 1 in the big outside world. Leaving any minute (if she can decide what to wear before nightfall). Hard to believe that Mission Control was a fantasy all along, but until external supporting evidence comes along, I guess I'll just have to go along with their theory.*

*Here she is. My God! You are NOT going to take me out in public dressed like that, I hope? Where is it you work again – the Moulin Rouge?*

*Oh well, if I keep my head down in the transit vehicle, maybe nobody'll see us together.*

*I am just about prepared to buy the idea that I'm going to grow into something like one of them, but to suggest that they and I have anything more in common – frankly, it's preposterous. Still, as I've already discovered, it could have been far, far worse. Funny thing is, even though she's obviously hysterical, incompetent and acting way beyond her rank, I've got a feeling I'll miss her.*

*God, watch out – have you actually been trained to operate this thing? On second thoughts, I take that last bit back . . .*